# RESPECTABLE GIRL

# RESPECTABLE GIRL

## FLEUR BEALE

**SIMON AND SCHUSTER**

**SIMON AND SCHUSTER**

First published in Great Britain in 2006 by Simon & Schuster UK Ltd
A Viacom company.

1 3 5 7 9 10 8 6 4 2

Simon & Schuster UK Ltd
Africa House
64–78 Kingsway
London WC2B 6AH

A CIP catalogue record for this book is available from the British Library.

ISBN: 1 416 91099 9
EAN: 9781416910992

Typeset by Rowland Phototypesetting Ltd, Bury St Edmunds, Suffolk
Printed and bound in Great Britain by Cox & Wyman Ltd, Reading, Berkshire

# 1

## Chapter One

It is strange how one word can change things.

I had not known that my world was fragile until Aunt Frances caused it to break by uttering that single word. But that word, that single word, *spoiled* — cracked open the landscape of my mind and there is no return from that.

On the day of the Word, the weather was glorious — sea, sky and mountain all shone blue under a brilliant summer sun. I was working in the vegetable garden but I was also keeping an eye on the progress of a three-master sailing in from the north. It was the *Camberwell* and she was from Sydney via Auckland, coming to our little town of New Plymouth with a cargo of goods and passengers. Dr Feilding's new bride was on board. I craned my neck to see if he was on the beach waiting for her.

I watched the surf-boat leave the beach to row out to the ship to bring the passengers ashore. I screwed up my eyes. Yes, that was Dr Feilding in the boat, I was sure of it. How romantic! I ran around the house to the front garden to tell Rawinia, my stepmother. But the garden was empty. Instead she came from the house, calling to me.

'Hana?' She used the Maori form of my name – a habit she persisted in despite Papa's objections.

I took a breath to tell her the news, but then I saw the tickets she held in her hand and my words died.

She held them out. 'You left these on the shelf and your father will be home soon for his luncheon.' She spoke in Maori, the language she, I and my brothers used when Papa was absent.

I took the tickets and held them close to my chest. 'Oh! I forgot to hide them! But where? I cannot think of a place secret enough.' Papa, if his eye lighted upon them, might well slip them into his pocket and sell them again. Of course, he would promise to buy more but he would likely forget to do so. I was still waiting for him to replace my cloak which he had sold to old Heta when we lacked money for him to buy drink.

Rawinia jerked her head in the direction of Aunt Frances's house. 'Let Mrs Woodley take care of them.'

And so it was that I changed my patched and darned house dress for my blue cotton walking dress, tied my hat of straw on my head, and walked all unknowing and carefree to meet that word that was to crack one of the few certainties in the fifteen years and ten months of my life thus far.

To be perfectly truthful I didn't walk, I ran. I tend to indulge in unladylike behaviour on occasions when neither Rawinia nor Aunt Frances can see me; the fault no doubt, of having played all of my childhood with Jamie my twin and Arama our halfbrother. But it was a truly glorious day

2

and our little raggle-taggle town, as Aunt Frances called it, felt safe and happy. I stopped for a moment to consider it. Try as I might, I could not see it through my aunt's eyes. I loved the wooden houses with their vivid, rioting gardens. Most houses had enough land for a vegetable garden, an orchard and paddocks for a cow or two, as we did. Sometimes I wondered if I would be more in tune with her views if I were her true niece rather than a god-daughter and unconnected by blood.

I did, however, see her point about the bad roads. I lifted my skirt well clear of my ankles and leaped across yet another chasm in Lemon Street where the rain had carried away the soil. Yes, the roads were bad, but we had nowhere much we could travel to by road because the bush – tall, deep and impenetrable – kept us confined to a narrow strip of land on the coast.

People complained about the land problem.

I shook my head. I would not think of such things on such a day. I ran on down our street and turned right into Liardet Street. Mrs Herbert was in her front garden, snipping back the rose that grew up the verandah post. I knew that Aunt Frances only acknowledged her with a polite smile, but I always passed the time of day with her. I liked her.

'Good morning, Mrs Herbert!' I called.

'And a lovely morning it is, dearie,' she called back over her shoulder.

I stopped to chat. 'How are you today, ma'am?'

She manoeuvred her bulk around to face me and

beamed. 'I'm well, Hannah love. Very well. It's grand to think that my babe will be born free and proud in this country. With all my heart I thank the good Lord we had the courage to cross the oceans in that wicked wee boat.'

'When do you think the baby will come?' I asked. The words were out before I recollected how scandalised Aunt Frances would be at the question.

But Mrs Herbert smiled and rubbed the huge mound of her stomach. 'I'm hoping it'll be this month and that's the truth of the matter.'

She would surely split in two if it didn't arrive soon. 'Will you announce it in the paper? *On the 17th February 1859, the wife of J. Herbert delivered of a son.*' I plucked tomorrow's date out of the air.

She looked much struck by the idea. 'We might at that.'

I leaned over the gate and spoke softly for her ears only. 'Be careful or you'll be birthing the child in the middle of the roses!'

She shrieked with laughter and I went on my way with it ringing in my ears, while in my mind I heard Aunt Frances's voice deploring my colonial manners. As for talk of birthing a baby, I hoped she would never discover that I had spoken of such things.

When I was nine and her daughter Judith ten, we asked Aunt Frances where babies came from, for Judith didn't believe my version of the great mystery. 'Their mothers find them under gooseberry bushes,' Aunt Frances said, her face a rich pink.

4

'I told you so!' said Judith.

I was not satisfied. 'Rawinia says gooseberry bushes were brought here by the Pakeha,' I saw her frown at my use of the Maori word, but I refused to be diverted, 'by the *white people*. And if that is so, then where did the Maori find their babies?'

Aunt Frances went pinker. 'I do not know! Things are different with the natives.'

I love Aunt Frances. She was Mama's friend and although we are not blood kin, she is very dear to me and she holds the memories of my mama so she is doubly precious. I do try not to vex her and so I would not let her see today that I had been running.

I slowed my steps, watching the holes in the road as it dipped down to cross the little footbridge over the Huatoki Stream, but I did not linger to watch the water in case Papa took it into his head to arrive early for his luncheon, met me on the bridge as he walked up from the town and remembered the tickets. I hastened up the slope and turned into Brougham Street, smoothed my skirt and prepared to arrive in a ladylike manner.

The Woodley's house in Brougham Street is one of the biggest houses in the town, with four bedrooms, a dining room, a drawing room and a study for Mr Woodley. I could not imagine living in such a mansion, and I did not envy Aunt Frances and Judith the cleaning of it. I knocked on the door as Aunt Frances liked me to do, and waited. I sniffed in the scent of the roses climbing the posts beside me, and turned to look out at the sea where the Sugar

Loaves pointed their sharp summits into the summer sky. The surf-boat had reached the three-master.

The front door opened and Judith pulled me into the coolness of the hallway. 'Did you get them? Will your papa let you go?'

I took the tickets from the pocket of my dress. 'Jamie went to the hotel to talk to Papa last night and asked for permission while he was in a convivial mood.'

Aunt Frances came to greet me, then led the way to the kitchen where we sat down at the table. 'It was kind of Jamie to bestir himself on your behalf, especially when we know he would rather mend a plough than grace a ballroom.'

I giggled. 'I was surprised too. But do you know what I think?'

Judith clapped her hands. 'He's in love!'

'Judith!' Aunt Frances exclaimed, but there was no hiding the interest in her eyes.

I began shelling the peas piled on the table. Judith went back to the ironing. 'I believe he is sweet on Lavender Shapton,' I said. 'His eyes didn't stray from her for the entire length of the church service.'

Aunt Frances grew solemn and the worried look she so often wore in relation to me and Jamie came to her face.

'Lavender Shapton is a very good sort of girl, I have no doubt,' she said. 'But she is not the girl your dear mama would have wanted for her son.'

Judith, out of sight of her mother, rolled her eyes. I stifled a giggle.

6

Aunt Frances shook her head. 'That is the one problem with this new country,' she said. 'I do not regret for a moment that we packed up and came here, but I do worry about finding suitable partners for you and Jamie as well as for my own children.' She cast Judith a worried look.

'Oh Mama!'

'I do not intend to marry,' I said.

'Then you will not be wanting to go to the ball,' Aunt Frances said, favouring me with her sweetest smile.

I laughed. 'If I do not go, then how will I learn the ways of society? Perhaps I will fall all unknowing to a compliment if I do not learn to recognise one.' How I relished the cut and thrust of an argument. Papa encouraged it in all his children even though I was a girl.

Aunt Frances frowned. 'It is unbecoming to expect to receive compliments, Hannah.'

I chuckled. 'But Aunt Frances, how often have you told me that I am the image of Mama?'

Judith crowed with mirth and Aunt Frances allowed her face to relax into a smile. As I'd hoped, she went off into a reminiscence. It was one she had told me a thousand times but I hung upon every word. I kept my hands busy with the peas or she would likely break off and say there was work to be done and no time for idle chat.

'I remember so well,' she began, 'how beautiful your mama looked on the night of her coming-out ball. Her hair, so smooth and dark, with a ringlet tumbling onto one shoulder . . .'

At this point I did allow myself to wonder just how like Mama I really was, for my hair never behaved with such decorum. It straggled and dribbled around my face, even when I dragged it back in a plait.

Aunt Frances was well back in the past. 'Lovely Angelina,' she sighed. 'Her eyes so blue and her cheeks most becomingly flushed. There wasn't a young man for miles around who didn't fall under her spell as she stood with her mama and papa to greet her guests.'

Judith and I sighed. We pictured the dress, white silk embroidered with pearls, its low neck showing off Mama's creamy shoulders.

It was then that Aunt Frances uttered the fateful word.

'She was so beautiful. Who can wonder at it that she was spoiled?'

*Spoiled?*

For a heartbeat of silence nothing happened, except that a dark stain lay sudden and shocking upon the perfect portrait of my mother. I gasped for air and my hands crashed down among the peas. 'Spoiled? *Spoiled?*'

I heard one of Judith's irons thump onto the table. I saw Aunt Frances's head jerk upwards. She stared at me, her mouth agape.

I jumped up, sending peas and pods flying across the table and onto the floor. 'How dare you say such a thing of Mama?' I shouted. 'That is a cruel falsehood!'

My words tumbled like the peas, scattering through the room. 'Mama was *not* spoiled!' I faced her accuser, my hands knotted into fists and my breath coming in heaving gasps as if I'd run to the very top of the mountain. 'She was not *spoiled*!'

Aunt Frances dropped her head into her hands and I thought I heard her moan but my heart did not yield. Judith, by the stove, stared with bulging eyes, her body as motionless as the chimney.

At last Aunt Frances straightened her back. 'Dearest Hannah, you know how I loved her. Beautiful, charming Angelina. She was as beloved to me as a sister.' The familiar story poured from her lips. 'The day she arrived here was my very own miracle. I had no idea she was coming. I went down to the beach to welcome the new arrivals and I near fainted from joy when through the surf they carried not a stranger, but my dearest friend in all the world.' She glanced at me but I would not be comforted. She reached out a hand to me. 'You cannot know how it was, dearest Hannah! I missed her so much and thought never to see her again. It was the answer to all my prayers when they dropped her, her baggage and your papa onto the black sand.'

I believed her but I couldn't forgive her. Mama was not spoiled.

'And that's another thing.' I jabbed a finger on the table with each word I uttered. 'How is it that you always put my papa last, after the baggage? You don't approve of him. He's too colonial for you, isn't he?'

'Hannah!' Aunt Frances was appalled and I heard Judith gasp. Truth to tell, I was horrified myself. It was one thing to lose my temper with Jamie, Papa, Arama or Rawinia

9

but quite another to do so with Aunt Frances. She, who had taught me to behave as Mama would have wanted. She, who insisted to Papa that I have piano and dancing lessons the way a lady should.

My temper faded and I hung my head. 'I am sorry, Aunt Frances. Truly sorry.' Then I quite ruined the apology by saying, 'But you should not say such things about Mama.'

Aunt Frances gathered up the pods left on the table. 'It is a good thing for a daughter to love her mother. But you must behave at all times in a manner that would have made her proud. And that is all we will say about this matter.' She gestured at the floor. 'Pick those up, if you please.'

I let it rest for I was lucky to escape with so slight a scolding. I scrabbled around on the floor for the peas.

Mama was not spoiled.

I did not stay long. I put the tickets on the table before I left. 'Will you keep them for us?' I asked.

'Of course, dear child.'

I did not need to explain why it was better for Jamie and me to leave our tickets with Aunt Frances. My papa could charm the birds from the sky and the fish from the sea but he was also somewhat inclined to change his mind, especially when he'd been at the hotel for an evening. Jamie and I had differing opinions about why he spent so much time in the hotel. I believed it was because he still mourned Mama. Jamie disagreed. He always said, 'Nonsense, that's just how Papa is. And he has Rawinia now.'

But Jamie was wrong. I knew it in my heart.

I bade Judith and Aunt Frances farewell. If Aunt Frances noticed the slight constraint in my bearing she made no comment.

I walked in a decorous manner until I was out of sight. Then I ran across the footbridge. I picked up my skirts and ran up the other side, leaping over the runnels and holes. Just before I reached Liardet Street, a couple of drunken soldiers from the barracks on Marsland Hill accosted me, lurching towards me to block my path. 'Now, where would a pretty colleen like you be goin' in shuch a hurry?' asked the taller of the two.

I didn't slacken my pace. I ducked to avoid his groping hands, gave him a sharp push so that he cannoned into his companion, and kept running.

My mama had not been spoiled.

I scrambled down a bank that was a shortcut to our cottage. In three years and two months I would be nineteen, the age Mama had been when she lost her life giving birth to Jamie and me.

No matter what Aunt Frances said about marriage, and she said plenty, I had no mind to marry. It was a dangerous business for a girl who could not believe in gooseberry bushes.

I passed the Herberts' house, but Mrs Herbert wasn't in sight. I hoped her baby would arrive safely. She made me laugh and her husband worked hard and talked little. The longest speech I'd heard him make went something like: *Aye, Hannah, very soon now I'll be farming my own land, see if I'm not.*

I prayed that Mrs Herbert would be alive to see it, with a string of bouncing children at her feet.

I was almost home when a blinding revelation poured into my head. Aunt Frances had been jealous of Mama.

Poor Aunt Frances.

# 2

## Chapter Two

Papa pushed his chair out from the luncheon table. 'A meal fit for a king, Rawinia, queen of my heart,' he said, smiling at her, and then at me for he knew part of the effort had been mine. 'I am indeed a lucky man.' He nodded at Jamie and Arama. 'Lads, take heed. When you choose a wife, choose one who can cook. Choose one who will keep your home comfortable and your fire warm.' He took one of Rawinia's hands. 'Choose an angel like the dove of my heart.'

As usual, Rawinia laughed and replied, 'Take heed, Hana! When you choose a husband, choose one whose words have the wisdom of the ancestors. Choose one whose hands show that he will work for you and your children.' She turned my father's hand over to show the smooth skin unmarked by toil.

I propped my elbows on the table, my chin on my hands. I had never considered Papa's funning with Rawinia before in relation to my mother. Could Jamie be right? Was it true that Papa no longer mourned Mama?

I asked, 'Papa, was Mama the love of your heart too?'

I should have known better than to try to get real

information from him about Mama. He went off into his usual patter.

'Your mama, my very dear Hannah, was beautiful and charming. She captured my heart. Mine!' He thumped his chest, rolled his eyes and pulled his face into a comical expression. 'I, who had reached the grand age of thirty unscathed, fell to one glance from your dear mama. I was her captive, her slave, her bondsman.'

He rose to his feet. 'And you, my daughter, are her living image.' He leaned over to clap Jamie and Arama on their shoulders. 'Boys! We must indulge in some target practice for I declare we will soon be needing to defend your sister from all manner of adventurers.'

We laughed, but as usual, Papa had evaded giving me real information. I tried a different approach. 'Who does Jamie look like?' It was not something either of us had thought about, for Jamie didn't enter into my desire to learn more of our mama and our ancestry.

Jamie laughed at my question. 'I'm a changeling.'

The four of us studied his face, topped with the untidy blond hair that bore no resemblance to either my dark hair or Papa's sandy straggles. Jamie's eyes were the brown of newly turned earth whereas mine were blue and Papa's a faded blue-grey. Papa kept his chin covered by a neat beard but I suspected it did not have the determination of Jamie's chin.

'Who does he look like?' I repeated.

Papa stroked his beard and shook his head. 'Alas, my children, I cannot answer your question. All I can tell you

Jamie, is that you don't favour anyone in my family. As to your dear mama's family, I cannot tell you for I never met them.'

I beat my fist on the table. 'It is so unsatisfactory. I want to know!' I turned to Rawinia and Arama. 'You know your whakapapa ...' I glanced at Papa, and changed quickly to English, 'your ancestry. Yet we know nothing of ours. Nothing at all!' I stared at Papa in frustration for not only did he declare he knew nothing of Mama's family, but he would tell us nothing of his either. All we knew was that they considered him a disgrace and had their bank send him money every three months so long as he stayed away from them on the other side of the world. Quarter day, when the money arrived, was always a day for celebration in our house.

Papa sidled towards the door. 'You are beautiful. You have a good brain and a good family. That is enough for any young lady. Be thankful that you were born here and not into the confines of the English aristocracy, or into the poverty of the lower classes.'

The door shut behind him and Jamie laughed. 'Give it up, Hana! He will never tell you more. He may not *know* any more.'

But he did, I was sure of it.

Jamie and Arama too rose from the table. 'What are you doing this afternoon?' I asked. 'Where are you going?'

Jamie patted my head. 'Nowhere a girl would wish to go.'

'How do you know that if you won't tell me?' I pleaded.

I reached up, took his hand and turned to look into his face.

He grinned at me and said, 'A brother knows these things.'

I dropped his hand. He was becoming altogether too much like Papa in his responses to my questions.

Arama grinned at me. 'We're going fishing.'

'There will be rain before nightfall; be home before the rivers rise,' Rawinia said. She took Arama by the shoulders and shook him. 'You hear me, Arama?'

'I hear you, Rawinia.'

I smiled to myself. Arama appeared compliant but always, he walked his own path. Even Papa had given up telling him to call Rawinia *mother*. 'I hear you, Papa,' he would say – but he always called her *Rawinia*. It was the custom of her people.

He told her now, 'I bind your words into my heart.'

It would be better to bind them into his memory, but I said nothing as I waved them goodbye except to sigh for the days when I too went with them on their expeditions.

'It is the way of the world,' Rawinia said, hearing my sigh. 'And we have work to do before the storm comes.'

The day was hot. The blue sky pressed down on the green world with not a wisp of cloud to be seen. We spent the afternoon in the garden picking any fruit and vegetables that were ripe. Behind us on the skyline the flanks of the mountain glowed the deep blue that heralded bad weather. The air had the clarity that comes before a storm too. I could smell the cows in the paddock, rose petals from the garden, the warmth of ripe apples – all sharp and clear.

I gathered a basket of peas and thought of Aunt Frances and my mama. Aunt Frances was wrong and I would not think of it further.

Instead, I chatted about Mrs Herbert. 'May I go and help her when the baby comes?' I asked. 'Just for a few days. She has no family here.'

Rawinia shook her head and frowned. 'Mrs Woodley won't like it. That Mrs Herbert is nothing but a slave and Mrs Woodley is a rangatira. She knows what's best for you.'

Sometimes – and always to my discomfort – Rawinia and Aunt Frances had exactly the same ideas even though they expressed them differently. Aunt Frances would simply say of Mrs Herbert that she wasn't our sort of person. She would never call herself an aristocrat, but I think if I told her Rawinia said she was a rangatira she would smile and look pleased.

I did so hope that Mrs Herbert would not die in childbirth as Mama had died.

Clouds gathered as the afternoon wore on. Rawinia kept looking at the sky. 'I hope they come home before the rain begins,' she muttered at least a dozen times.

'They will,' I said. 'They'll get hungry.'

'It's the rivers I worry about,' Rawinia sighed. 'Those boys, they think the spirits of the ancestors will save them from all harm.' She shook her head and said tartly, 'But the ancestors need the help of a little common sense from the person they are protecting.'

Now I worried too for I knew exactly what she meant. A river swollen with rain ran swift and gave no clemency to the foolhardy traveller who tried to cross it. Jamie and Arama were more foolhardy than most.

We had carried in the last of the apples when the rain started. Rawinia said nothing more but I saw her lips move and I knew she was reciting the karakia of her ancestors asking their protection for Arama and for Jamie too.

The light was all but gone from the day when they returned, laughing, soaked and carrying three kahawai on a string of flax. I spied them through the window and called to Rawinia, 'They're home!'

Her shoulders relaxed but she said nothing. The pots, however, received quite a beating.

The rain became a storm after we had retired for the night. It broke over the town and mostly, I suspected, over our house. I huddled under my blankets, more to hide from the lightning and the crashing thunder that followed, than to shelter from the water dripping onto my bed. Jamie poked his head around the door of my room. 'Scaredy cat! Here!'

He threw an opened umbrella to me. I seized the handle and held it fast. Could lightning penetrate an umbrella? I trusted not and felt a little safer. The drips from the leak over my bed hit the umbrella and slid down onto the floor.

The thunder ceased sometime before the morning and I slept, but when I woke in the daylight the rain still fell, smashing down on the land. I got out of bed, jumping to miss the puddles on my floor, and went to the window.

Outside, the garden bent and bowed under the onslaught of the rain. It would be an inside day for me and Rawinia; we would make pickles and preserves of the crops we had gathered yesterday. So much for my plans to visit Mrs Herbert. I sighed and watched Jamie and Arama run through the garden, dodging the mud, and out into the paddock where our two cows waited to be milked. I turned from the window, dressed quickly and hurried down the passage to the kitchen to help Rawinia prepare breakfast.

The rain fretted my nerves. I would burst if I had to stay in the house all day. 'Rawinia, this afternoon may I go and visit Mrs Herbert? I'll work hard this morning, I promise!'

Of course she grumbled, but not about me leaving her with most of the work. 'Mrs Woodley won't like it, Hana girl, I'm telling you.'

I hoped she wouldn't say anything to Jamie, but she didn't even give him the chance to shuck off his raincoat before she started telling him.

He listened, then handed Rawinia the pail of milk and said, 'The Herberts are good people. We're going to help him saw the timber for his house – he's bought fifty acres at Omata. He wants to move as soon as the baby comes.'

Rawinia glared at Arama, then at Jamie. 'Don't you have enough to eat? Why do you need to work for that Pakeha?'

Arama, as usual, left it to Jamie to do the explaining. 'I need money to buy equipment.'

Rawinia threw her arms in the air. 'Equipment! What

foolishness are you planning now?' She swung around to jab a finger in Arama's direction. 'Don't you remember what happened last time?'

Arama chuckled. 'I remember.'

So did I. There had been an explosion and the lead Jamie was heating flew out in molten droplets over the faces of both boys. Even when he was very young, Jamie's passion had been for inventions and science, but now he had a focus for his endeavours, for the businessmen of the town had clubbed together to offer a reward to the person who could make iron from the sand on the beach. Jamie knew the advertisement by heart and often I would hear him reciting it:

## ONE HUNDRED AND FIFTY POUNDS
to the person who can produce from the iron sand of this Province merchantable cast or wrought iron.

'You didn't learn from the burns all over your face?' Rawinia demanded.

Jamie engulfed her in a hug, lifting her off the floor. 'Rawinia, my new idea is brilliant! And if I win the money I'll buy you a library of books, a wardrobe full of dresses and a new pipe to smoke for each day of the week!'

Rawinia squealed and flapped her hands at him, grinning and laughing through it all. She wouldn't try to stop him, and as for Arama, he went where Jamie led in the Pakeha world.

The boys sat down at the table. The smell of the bacon

made my stomach rumble. How Papa could lie in bed half the day and not even think about food was beyond my understanding, but he never rose before ten o'clock.

We ate in silence, the way Rawinia preferred, only chatting over the cups of tea when we were done with the food.

'What are your plans for the day?' she asked the boys.

'We go to the blacksmith to learn more about iron,' Arama said.

I grinned at him and got a fleeting, flashing smile in return. He knew he just had to say *learn* and Rawinia would be happy.

I watched them run laughing out into the rain and a thought struck me – if Mama had lived, Arama would not have been born.

Mama, spoiled? It was Aunt Frances's jealousy that made her speak so, of that I was certain. People called her a handsome woman rather than a pretty one, for she had well-defined eyebrows that slashed two straight lines across her forehead above a nose slightly too large for beauty. I liked her face, for it was interesting, but Mama's beauty must have overshadowed hers. I lingered by the window, lost in a dream where one of Aunt Frances's suitors looked up from kissing her hand, saw my mama, fell in love with her instantly and abandoned his courtship of my aunt.

Rawinia's voice jerked me back to the present. 'Those dishes aren't going to wash themselves.'

No, they wouldn't. If only Papa didn't insist on us being so Pakeha we could have woven flax baskets to eat from

21

and thrown them away after the meal. I said as much to Rawinia.

She snorted. 'You'd soon complain about going out in the rain for the flax. You'd soon be moaning about how boring weaving is. You'd be asking for good Pakeha plates before the food had time to cool.'

I banged the dish bowl onto the table and poured water into it from the kettle, not caring that it splashed over the sides, and I washed the good Pakeha plates.

My life was changing. It seemed to me that I had become an adult with a woman's responsibilities, whereas Jamie and Arama were still free to go where they wished and do as they pleased. Only a year ago, they would never have gone anywhere without me.

My mind slipped into a familiar daydream where all three of us are running laughing along the black sand of the beach. None of us sees the wave that rears up to engulf Arama and me, sweeping us away in the turbulent foaming water. For a second, Jamie stands, aghast and staring. He can rescue one of us, and one only. Who will he choose? In my dreams, he never stops to think but acts from instinct. He plunges into the waves and swims to Arama, not to me.

Would I choose Jamie or Arama? Jamie was my twin, the other part of me. I would have to choose him, I *must*. But how could I leave Arama to drown?

My heart grew heavy. There was only one answer; we must all drown.

I washed the breakfast dishes and my tears fell into the water.

Rawinia heard my sniffs. 'What troubles your heart today, daughter?'

'It's nothing real,' I said. I pulled my hands from the water and wiped my eyes and nose on the backs of them.

'Those boys are becoming men,' she said. 'They look now to do men's work. It is fitting.'

I nodded, and knew the unspoken corollary; *and you must become a woman*. I glanced at her and pulled a face.

She chuckled. 'Ai! Don't you let Mrs Woodley catch you with your face looking like the backside of a pig. Come, we have work to do.' She piled plums into the jam pan.

I picked up the basin of dishwater just as a thundering knocking sounded at the kitchen door. 'Mrs Carstairs! Mrs Carstairs! Are you there?'

# 3

## Chapter Three

I dropped the basin back onto the bench, raced past Rawinia and threw the door open. 'Mr Herbert! What's wrong?' I seized his arm and pulled him out of the rain.

He spoke to Rawinia. 'Mrs Carstairs, ma'am, would you spare Hannah for a bit? The child's coming. I won't be long, but I don't like to leave the wife alone.'

I didn't wait for Rawinia's answer. 'Go at once!' I flung the door open again. 'I'll go this minute! I'll stay with her, I promise!'

Rawinia nodded at him and he went, running through the rain heavy-footed in his work boots. I snatched my sacking raincloak from the hook, hitched up my skirts, took off my shoes and stuffed them in the pocket of my apron. Rawinia handed me a basket. 'Bread and cold meat. Try to keep them dry.' She gave me last night's umbrella.

'Goodbye!' I was off, running fleeter and faster than Mr Herbert. I was halfway there before it occurred to me to think about where I was going and why. I gasped and choked on a dollop of rain blasting in under the umbrella. Mrs Herbert's baby was coming! What would I do if it came and I had to help her birth it?

*Oh, dear Lord save us all! I'll drop the baby, Mrs Herbert will die of a broken heart, and Mr Herbert will kill me.*

I kept an eye out for a woman as I ran. Any woman, but preferably one who had upwards of six children. The road was empty. But I'd arrived. Here I was at their gate. I was running up the path, jumping up the steps onto the verandah, knocking on the door. Good Lord save us all!

'Come in, Hannah dearie, and right glad I am to see you.'

Right glad I was that she could still talk. I'd thought she'd be moaning and screeching and wailing fit to raise the rafters. I slid past her, and walked down the short passage to the kitchen.

'Are you all right, Mrs Herbert? Do you want anything? Rawinia sent bread and meat.' I was gabbling but truly I couldn't help myself. I was terrified and I couldn't turn around to look at her. I wasn't even sure if she had followed me into the kitchen.

I heard her laugh, although she choked it off halfway through and it turned into more of a groan. I sneaked a glance and there she was, still in the passage, standing in the doorway of her bedroom, holding onto the woodwork like she'd crush it, half bent over and half straight, concentrating on whatever was happening within the huge lump of her stomach.

'Take your cloak off, child! You're wet to the skin. Put the basket on the bench. Tell Mrs Carstairs thank you.' She pointed to my feet. 'Get the towel from the kitchen door and see to your feet.'

I edged around her and ran into the kitchen to do as she bade me, trying all the while to get a hold on my fears. She was still alive. She wasn't lying down and screeching. Mr Herbert would be back soon. He could birth the child. He knew about cows and pigs.

To my horror, I heard the words burst out of my mouth: 'Mrs Herbert, is birthing a baby the same as a cow birthing a calf? Or a pig . . .' I recollected myself and slapped both hands over my mouth. 'Oh!' I stared at her and I knew my eyes were bulging. 'I'm sorry!'

But she was laughing. At least, I think she was. She let out a great hoot but then she was groaning again and holding her stomach. I ran to her. 'Mrs Herbert! Shall I help you to your bed?'

I hovered in front of her, dancing from one muddy foot to the other while she forgot I was there and thought only of the pain of her body.

'For the love of heaven, child, call me Polly. And no, I don't want my bed! When I want to lie down I'll do it. Don't keep on at me!'

'N-no, ma'am. I mean, Polly.' What was I meant to do with her? I looked around me. We were in the hallway, she half in and half out of her bedroom door, me in the doorway to the kitchen.

'I'll put the bread and meat in the larder,' I said.

She grunted, but didn't say yes or no. It took only seconds to put the food away. I leaned against the bench and looked at her clinging to the doorpost with her face all drawn and pale. 'Oh, you are so uncomfortable! Will you not come and sit down?' The cottage had no parlour, but there were two comfortable chairs in the big kitchen. I crossed the space between us. 'Lean on me, Mrs – Polly. I'm strong, don't be afraid. I won't let you fall.'

She didn't respond but I took her arm and put it over my shoulders, holding it there with one hand. My other arm I slid around her body, and I felt her stomach grow tight and hard. What had I done? Was I killing her? She bit down on her lip and the sweat stood out on her face. She groaned.

My legs trembled. Was she dying? I tried to remember if cows groaned when they birthed their calves, then I wished I hadn't, for the only time I'd heard one moan was when she was in trouble and we couldn't get the calf out.

I managed to support Polly's weight as she let go of the doorway and we tottered forward into the kitchen. Somehow I got her settled in the nearest chair. She leaned back for a second, her eyes closed.

'If Peter doesn't get back in time with the doctor, you'll have to help me,' she said, and she sounded as if that were an entirely reasonable and possible thing for me to do.

'They'll get back in time,' I said in a squeak of a voice. 'You'll see. Don't worry. You'll be fine and the babe will be bonny. Do you want a boy or a girl?'

I glanced at the door, longing with all my heart to run from that room and the groaning woman. 'I'll make you a cup of tea,' I babbled. If she didn't drink it, then I would.

I didn't wait for her to speak. I filled the kettle, put

more wood on the fire, collected cups and saucers, asked her if she took sugar, didn't get a reply. And all the time she kept her eyes shut and kept on with the gasping and groaning.

I brought the tea and set it down beside her.

'I'm never going through this again!' she said, spitting the words out. 'Never! I'll stitch the hems of my night-gowns together, so I will! Seems like it's me bears the pain and him the pleasure and so I'll tell him if he comes near . . .' She broke off, tensing her face against another wave of pain.

Where *was* Mr Herbert? It wasn't far to the doctor's house. What if he didn't come back?

I jumped up and ran through the house to peer out the front door through the rain. There was nobody in the road, nobody at all.

Oh! What to do? An idea, brilliant and obvious struck me. 'Polly! I'll run and fetch Rawinia. She'll know how to help you.'

Polly had her eyes screwed shut against the straining of her body but she heard me. 'Don't leave! Baby's just about here.'

I dithered in front of her, hopping from one grubby foot to the other. 'But you'll squash it! You have to lie down. You can't birth it sitting in that chair!'

'I'm not walking anywhere and don't you think I am!' she screamed. Her face was wild and contorted. I wanted to push her hair back, tidy it for her, but I was afraid to touch her, she was so angry.

28

It was too late to wish I'd got her to her bed earlier. The bed would have to come to her. There was a rug on the kitchen sofa. I hauled it off, doubled it over and threw it to the floor in front of her chair.

'Slide onto the floor, Polly!' I shouted the words at her. 'Come! How will the child be birthed if you're sitting on it?'

I seized her right arm, placed her left hand on the arm of the chair. 'Now! Before the pain comes again. You can do it! You have to lie down!'

Thank the good Lord, she obeyed me and I helped ease her onto the rug.

'Pillows.'

I scrambled to my feet, ran to the bedroom. Two pillows. Four cushions in the kitchen. Three spilled from my arms and I kicked them to where Polly lay groaning. She didn't seem any more comfortable once I'd propped her up on them.

'Lift my skirt,' she grunted. 'You'll have to catch the child.'

I couldn't! I simply couldn't lift her skirts and expose down there to my view and the view of anyone who came through the door. How I prayed that someone, anyone, would do exactly that.

'Do it!' she shouted, opening her eyes long enough to glare at me.

*Pretend she's a cow.* 'I'm never going to marry.'

She grunted but it was a laugh of sorts. Dear heaven, I'd said it aloud.

I shut my eyes and grabbed hold of her skirts, folding them up over the bulge.

'Is it coming?'

I managed a fleeting glance and saw nothing I could make sense of in my embarrassment.

'Aaagh!' Polly shouted, she moaned and her fists beat the floor.

I slapped my hands over my mouth to keep in what might want to escape and forced my eyes to look. Something bulged out from between her legs. It must be the child, I hoped it was the child. 'It's coming! It's got dark hair! It's nearly here!'

I think she heard, but another spasm of her belly made her shriek. Her whole body was one tight, hard mass – her belly, her face, her fists.

The bulge slid out further. I gulped. I was going to have to touch that slimy thing and I was only half convinced it was the child.

Polly let out another bellow, and there, sudden and shocking, was the child's head, poking out. 'The head! It's out! It's nearly birthed! You've almost done it, Polly!'

It was easier now I knew for certain it was a baby. I held my hands under it, ready to catch the rest of it. There was mud on my hands. It couldn't be helped now and the child was to live on a farm. There would be mud aplenty. It might as well get used to it early.

A shriek, a bellow and a groan and the child was there, slippery and crying in my hands.

'Polly, you've done it! The child is here and it's a boy!'

She sank back on the scattered pillows, gasping. 'Praise the Lord!' A moment later she opened her eyes. 'Let me see him, Hannah.'

I had nothing to wrap him in. I should have thought of that before. Next time, I would know.

Next time? Never, not again. Not ever.

I lay him on my lap, untied my apron, wrapped him and passed him to his mother. 'The cord, Polly. What should I do about it?'

But all her attention was for her son. 'He's so bonny! Ah, look at him then. What a noise, laddy!' she crooned and the smile on her face warmed my own heart. 'Isn't he wonderful?'

'He's lovely,' I said and it was as well for both of us she couldn't see him through my eyes, for what I saw was an unlovely squirming, bawling, red-faced object that had caused me to age a hundred years in less than an hour.

Where was his father? Where was the doctor?

'Bring a towel, Hannah, and some warm water. We must wash him.'

If she wasn't worried about the cord, then it must be nothing to worry about. I got to my feet but she looked up. 'Can you put my skirts down for me? It's right indecent I am!'

'But Polly, the afterbirth, it'll get all over your clothes.'

She didn't know about afterbirth. I explained as well as I could from what I had seen of the cows. I bit my tongue on telling her that dogs were particularly fond of eating it.

The afterbirth came away before I had time to bring

the water, but the baby was still attached. 'We must cut the cord,' I said.

We stared at it, snaking from the child's belly to the mess of the afterbirth lying in a splodge of blood on the newspaper I'd shoved under her to catch it. 'We might do it wrong,' Polly whispered. 'We might harm him.' Her arms curved protectively around the child who had caused her, only minutes ago, to shriek and writhe in pain.

In the end, I tidied her as best I could and she was sipping at a fresh cup of tea when Mr Herbert burst into the house, followed more sedately by the doctor.

I flopped onto one of the kitchen chairs and howled my eyes out. I did manage to see though, that Dr Feilding tied the cord in two places before he cut in between the ties and that he left around six inches of cord still attached to the child. I also noticed Mr Herbert's look of wonder as he gazed at his son. I heard him say to Polly that he was sorry he took so long but the doctor had been out on another call.

By the time Dr Feilding finished seeing to Polly and the child, my howls had become hiccupping sniffs. He rose to his feet and said, 'A fine child, Mrs Herbert. I congratulate you both.' He put a hand on my shoulder. 'You did well, Hannah Carstairs. Very well indeed.'

It made me cry again. 'I didn't know what to do. I didn't know how to do anything.'

Polly smiled at me and she was her normal cheerful self again. 'You were an angel, Hannah. I thank you from the bottom of my heart.'

'Aye, lass, you've been a right good neighbour in our hour of need,' Mr Herbert said. 'I thank you, indeed I do.'

The doctor took one of my bloodstained, muddy hands in his and helped me to my feet. 'I'll walk you home, young Hannah, and tell you a few helpful things, in case you're ever called upon again.'

'Never again!' I muttered, but I bent to kiss Polly, now lying on the sofa. 'I'll come back later and cook dinner for you.' I stood for a moment, staring at the child. 'He is lovely,' I said, and this time I meant it. There was a difference, I found, between a squalling unwashed newborn that I had to do things for, and a sleeping, clean child who was somebody else's responsibility. 'What will you name him?'

Mr Herbert spoke. 'He's to be Thomas David after both his grandfathers.'

For some reason that made Polly come over all emotional and tears ran down her face even as she smiled at her husband.

I left with the doctor.

# 4

## Chapter Four

Polly and Thomas David thrived. Polly, already on her feet, greeted me at the door when I went that evening to cook for her.

Aunt Frances, on the other hand, suffered as near to a spasm as I had ever seen. (Or what I imagined a spasm to be.) She came to visit the next day and Judith was not with her. 'What is this I hear?' she said, sipping the tea I made for her. 'It cannot be true, Hannah, surely? You were not present when Polly Herbert's child was born?'

By the tone of her voice, she was devoutly praying that it was not so.

'Yes, Aunt Frances,' I said, and hoped she would not ask for details.

She did ask, but while I was dithering and trying for the best way of putting it in a genteel manner, the boys came running in declaring their hunger.

Aunt Frances said, 'Good morning Jamie, Arama. Will you be kind enough to leave while I speak to your sister?'

Rawinia took a loaf of bread and began slicing it. She nodded her head at them and pointed to the door. But Jamie said, 'Aunt Frances, isn't it famous that Hannah birthed Polly Herbert's baby? I believe all the ladies will line up now and demand Hannah Carstairs instead of the doctor.'

Aunt Frances closed her eyes and her bosom heaved. We watched, fascinated as the colour ebbed and flowed in her face. 'It is something no respectable girl should even know about, let alone witness!' she said at last, clipping her words short. 'You will oblige me, all of you,' and here she glared at me, Jamie, Arama and Rawinia in turn, 'by endeavouring to forget this entire regrettable incident. You are never to speak of it again, do you understand?'

Rawinia rolled her eyes, Arama shrugged his shoulders, I hung my head, but Jamie said, 'Oh come now, Aunt Frances! I think Hannah's something of a heroine. When I spoke of it to Lavender Shapton she said she would have fainted and been no use whatsoever.'

Jamie's words might warm my heart, but they stoked the fires in Aunt Frances's breast. Scalding words poured over him and splashed onto me as well. It appeared that I was ruined socially and would never make a good marriage, for young ladies should not be privy to such knowledge or experience.

My own anger grew. 'Aunt Frances, please stop! What would you have had me do? Leave Polly alone? And you needn't worry about my marriage prospects for I never intend to marry. Especially not now I've seen what it does to a woman.' I glared at her. 'And I believe that is why nobody tells girls anything about babies, for if we knew then none of us would marry.'

Jamie shrieked with laughter and I heard muffled snorts from Rawinia and Arama. Aunt Frances got to her feet, her tea unfinished and when she spoke her voice trembled. 'I have done my best for both of you. Always. But I fear it hasn't been enough. I have sadly let down your mother and the promise I made her when you were born.'

Jamie and I stared at her, and then at each other. 'We're sorry,' I whispered. 'You are so good to us.'

'I apologise, Aunt Frances,' Jamie said, laying on the charm the way Papa so often did. 'We do not truly understand how to go on in polite society. If we had not had your example and your teaching we would indeed be lost. Please do not despair of us.' He smiled at her, his head on one side.

I wanted to shake him for such blatant cajolery, but at the same time, I hoped Aunt Frances would be comforted.

She sighed. 'We can only hope that the talk will have died down before the ball, otherwise I'm afraid you will have a difficult time of it, Hannah.'

Rawinia snorted, more audibly this time. 'The ball isn't for three weeks. Plenty of time for some folk to do stupid things and others to gloat about it.'

I wanted to know why I would have a hard time of it at the ball, but judged it would be an imprudent question to ask so I held my tongue.

Aunt Frances walked to the door but paused before she got to it. 'Hannah, I need not ask you, I'm sure, to say nothing of this to Judith?'

I hung my head. 'Of course, Aunt Frances.'

She swept out with her skirts all of a rustle.

Jamie pointed a finger at me. 'Of course, Aunt Frances,' he mimicked. 'You've already told her, haven't you?'

I hadn't, but if she asked me then I would. I could not see the sense of pretending childbirth didn't exist. Especially when the very people the pretence was practised upon were the ones who had to undergo the whole messy, painful and dangerous business themselves.

# 5

## Chapter Five

The three weeks until the ball passed quickly. I spent some time each day with Polly and Thomas David, who grew more attractive as the days passed until I became quite as enchanted with him as Polly was.

Jamie and Arama left each day at dawn, riding the horse Peter Herbert had borrowed for them to use. They worked till sunset, helping him saw boards for the house in the bush. However, Jamie made sure he was home each Tuesday in time to accompany me to dancing instruction at Mr Edmund's academy. I didn't flatter myself it was anything to do with me that made him so attentive, for Lavender Shapton was at the classes as well.

It appeared that Aunt Frances had forgiven me for she smiled quite as kindly as usual when I went to her house to try on my dress two weeks before the ball. I hadn't seen Judith since the birth, but I knew she would ask about it when the opportunity presented itself.

Her dress was new and the very latest fashion. 'Mama requested the pattern from Grandmother,' Judith said, her eyes sparkling as she twirled in the almost completed gown.

'You look beautiful,' I said. 'All the young men will

queue up to dance with you and the soldiers will pull out their swords and fight for the privilege.'

She and Aunt Frances laughed, but I suspected Aunt Frances was pleased for she loved her only daughter dearly, and truly Judith looked charming. The pale cream silk of her gown warmed her skin and the short sleeves concealed the muscles of her arms that Aunt Frances despaired over. Ladies, she said, should not look strong.

Aunt Frances held up my dress. 'Slip it on, Hannah. I think it should fit you now.'

I ran into Judith's bedroom, the dress of palest blue silk over my arm – my mama's very own ball dress. Darling Aunt Frances had kept it for me all these years. I put on the three petticoats that would hold out the skirt. Judith came in and closed the door behind her. 'Let me help you,' she said, picking up the dress, then glancing at the door, whispered, 'I want to know everything.'

'Polly Herbert and the baby?' I whispered back.

'Of course!'

We were both aware of my aunt just through the wall in the big kitchen, and so I smiled at her and nodded, but we talked of other things as she fastened the row of tiny buttons down the back of my dress.

'Done,' she said. 'I can quite see why fashionable ladies need a maid.'

We danced out to the kitchen, our arms entwined. Aunt Frances clasped her hands to her bosom and her eyes filled with tears. 'My darling girls. You look enchanting. Oh, you will take this town by storm.'

We pranced to the looking glass and posed before it, then burst into giggles. 'We look so different,' I said. 'I'm not accustomed to looking elegant.' Even the dress that I wore to church whenever Papa remembered to make us go was nothing like as elegant as the one I now wore.

Perhaps we might cause a sensation at the ball for we were such a contrast. Judith's hair was as fair as ripe wheat, her eyes grey and her face gentle and serious except when she smiled and her dimples peeped out. We were much of a height and both of us had neat waists with womanly curves although Judith's body curved more than mine did nowadays. I stared at our reflections. All my life I have been told how like my mama I am, and I know she was held to be beautiful. I can see that I am not ugly but my blue eyes and dark hair make me seem too bold when I compare myself with Judith.

Aunt Frances twitched at the skirt of my dress. 'I'm afraid it is sadly out of fashion, Hannah dearest.'

I beamed at her. 'But it still looks lovely, and it belonged to Mama so I don't care.' My dress was sleeveless and the skirt did not have as many widths as Judith's did, but it didn't look so very different.

'Nobody cares,' Judith said. 'There will be people who do not look half as elegant as Hannah.'

Aunt Frances shuddered. 'Indeed there will.' She made the last few adjustments and we changed back into our day dresses. 'Let's sit on the verandah,' Judith said. 'It's such a lovely day.'

We sat and stitched, Judith and Aunt Frances working

on the flounce around the hem of Judith's gown while I sewed back the pearl beads that had come loose on the bodice and skirt of mine.

Bees hummed in the roses around us. Today the sea, so close to us, sparkled blue and silver, and behind us the mountain rose out of its own sea of green bush. Further down Brougham Street, builders were working on the new house Dr Feilding was building for his bride and they'd cut down the huge rimu tree on the ridge of his land. 'I'm glad it's gone,' my aunt said, seeing where I looked. 'We have a wider view now.'

It was a view of the Sugar Loaves, standing up at the edge of the sea like teeth of a monster. A view of trees, and of the brighter green of the gardens and paddocks that surrounded white houses with smoke drifting sideways from their chimneys.

'I love this place,' I said, flinging out my arm to encompass the town. 'Can you imagine living anywhere else?'

Aunt Frances smiled. 'It is indeed beautiful, but we are so confined here.'

I supposed we were, but I liked the feeling of the bush around the town pressing up to its very outskirts.

'Does Rawinia think the natives will sell the Waitara?' Judith asked. The Waitara land lay to the east and much of it was fern land and easy to clear.

I shook my head. 'She says they are determined not to sell. She says there is much opposition.'

'I pray there'll be no trouble,' Aunt Frances said briskly

in the voice she used to indicate a topic was not to be discussed. 'But the soldiers are here if there is. Now, girls, are you certain you know the steps of the quadrille?'

We stitched and talked of nothing in particular until it was time to prepare the midday meal. I ran home to help Rawinia and left my aunt and Judith to prepare the meal for Mr Woodley and Judith's three brothers.

I looked for Papa to see if he was making his way home. There was no sign of him, but I wasn't worried for he never drank himself insensible these days.

I believe it was Rawinia who stopped his excesses, for when we were very young I remember her taking all three of us away and leaving Papa snoring on the floor. We children thought he was sleeping but I now believe he was unconscious from drink. She took us to her kin at the pa – it was a small village with a palisade of saplings around it and I remember how high they seemed to me.

Rawinia must have made it clear to Papa that she would not live with a man who drank to excess, for we stayed away several days. I remember vividly a girl older than me taking me by the hand and, speaking in Maori, leading me to a low, thatched house made from reeds. 'This is the whare where we sleep,' she said, bending to enter through the low doorway. Of course I looked for my bed, but she showed me a space on the floor covered in fern, and that is where I slept for those few days, on a bed of fern on a dirt floor. The girl slept on one side of me and Rawinia on the other. More families of Rawinia's kin shared the whare – I remember about fourteen people in total although Jamie says there were more.

We played inside the palisade all day, running about with other children, dogs and piglets, and nobody fussed about us. It was there that I learned to swim, for we went to the river each afternoon. We would have stayed longer had not Aunt Frances heard about it and come to take Jamie and me to her house.

Now I realise how horrified Aunt Frances must have been to find us living at the pa and turned quite native. I think, too, that it was brave of her to come for us, for she was never quite comfortable around Maori. They were too informal for her and she considered them disrespectful.

Such musings inevitably brought me back to my own mama. It had been my belief that Papa drank because he wished to dull the pain of Mama's death. But what if it were true and she had been spoiled? What if his drinking had nothing to do with Mama at all?

I shook my head. How could I even be thinking Mama might have been spoiled when I had shouted at poor Aunt Frances for uttering that dreadful word?

But alas, the crack in my certainties was widening and letting in ideas I did not wish to examine. Now, I wondered what Mama had done when Papa drank to excess. It made me angry to think he had been drinking to excess while she was alive, but the thought would no longer be denied. There was the story of our birth for one thing. Aunt Frances's words were engraved on my heart: *Your papa was so distraught when your mama died that he disappeared for a whole week and we had to have the funeral without him.*

Had he been distraught, or had he been insensible from drink?

I pressed my hands over my ears as if that would stop the thoughts flying into my mind. Papa might be unsteady and unreliable with money, but he was charming and much easier to love than Mr Woodley who never did anything wrong but never laughed either. Neither did he encourage Judith to express her ideas or to expand her mind.

Poor Judith to have such a papa. I would tell her every last detail of Polly birthing the baby and I would think not of how I was betraying Aunt Frances's trust in me, but of how angry her papa would be if he ever found out.

My papa was quite late for his dinner, and a little more affable than normal. I ran to him and wrapped my arms around him, embracing him.

He returned my hug, laughing and saying, 'What is this, my beauty? What mischief have you been up to that you must wheedle your old papa?'

'Nothing, Papa, I vow on my honour! It is just that I am so happy you are my papa and not Mr Woodley.'

He threw his hat at a chair but it missed. I danced over, picked it up and hung it on the nail on the wall. Rawinia chuckled and said, 'That one would crack his face if he smiled.' She strutted around the kitchen imitating Mr Woodley's prim manner of walking. We laughed until our sides hurt and after that we ate and we talked as we ate, and Papa was charming and funny and clever.

Then I asked, 'Do you remember the day we were born, Papa?'

He looked at me for a second, pushed himself away from the table and stood up. 'Of course I remember! It was the proudest as well as the saddest day of my life.' He stumbled and caught the back of a chair to steady himself. 'I also remember the day I met your mama. Best day of my life. Changed my luck with women.' He bowed dangerously in Rawinia's direction but righted himself before he reached the point of no return. 'Met her just four weeks before I was due to sail to this glorious outpost of the Empire.'

'Four weeks, Papa? Don't you mean four months?' For this was another story we had grown up on.

'Of course it was four months, child! That's what I said. Running away from a monster she was, on the very eve of her wedding. Rescued her. Found her a respectable hotel. Hid her. Married her myself two weeks later. Beautiful girl. Just like you.' He drew a hand down over his face as if wiping away memories. 'If you please, Hannah, we will not talk of it further.'

I began clearing the table. 'Of course, Papa. I'm sorry.'

There was no other way. When Jamie got home from sawing Mr Herbert's planks, I would have to talk to him. I would have to tell him Aunt Frances had said Mama was spoiled.

But there was no chance that day as it was a dancing class day, and the final one before the ball. Jamie ran home, leaped into the tub Rawinia and I had waiting for him, splashed water and soap suds all over the kitchen floor, got out and dripped more water into puddles.

'For goodness sake, Jamie! Think what you're about!' I scolded. 'Stay in one place and dry yourself.'

He grinned at me. 'You should take your maidenly eyes somewhere else. Aunt Frances would faint if she saw you.'

She probably would but Jamie was just Jamie in my eyes. Then I realised with a shock that I now never bathed in front of him and Arama.

Arama laughed as he stripped off his grubby work clothes and stepped into the tub Jamie had vacated. 'So much fuss about a dance! I'm glad they don't let Maori go.' He rolled his eyes. 'I might have to dance with Lizzie Bevan. I'd rather face a war party!'

Rawinia cuffed him. 'You'll have to if her father hears disrespectful talk like that.'

We laughed, for Lizzie Bevan was exceedingly proud and very conscious of the fact that she was related to a Sir in England.

I set a loaf of bread on the table, then crouched down to the same level as Arama's head and studied his face. 'You know, you're good looking. For a boy.' I tilted my head and frowned a little. 'Some might even consider you handsome. You'd better be careful – all the young ladies will be after you. When you grow up a little.'

I jumped up and skipped out of the way of the splash he aimed at me. But he was pleased; I saw his grin.

'That reminds me!' Jamie said, his head emerging from

the shirt I had ironed for him that afternoon. 'Have you heard about May Parsons?'

Rawinia snorted. 'That one! She won't be going to the ball.'

I grinned at Rawinia. 'You're just the same as Aunt Frances. She doesn't like May either. She says May does not bear a very good character.'

Jamie towelled his hair and said, 'Listen! It's famous! I heard it from Jimmy who had it from his sister who heard it from the dressmaker.'

'Heard what?' Rawinia asked. 'Tell us! You are like a stream that's in no hurry to get to the ocean.'

It was Arama, still soaking in the tub who answered. 'May Parsons has fallen in love with a Maori and asked him to marry her.'

Rawinia and I gasped. This was news indeed. White men married Maori women, Papa for example, but never had it happened the other way around.

I laughed at Arama. 'You're not safe after all. Take care! If May cannot marry her Maori she'll be after you next.'

Rawinia cut slices from a leg of cold pork, muttering all the while. 'She's no good, that one. The daughter of slaves and the heart of a slave.'

Jamie seized bread and meat and urged me to hurry. 'We'll be late. Are you ready?'

I was. I wore my blue cotton dress, carried my dancing shoes in a cloth bag and on my feet I wore my walking boots. Their soles were thin and my toes showed where I'd cut the leather to make room for them but they would keep my feet clean so long as the roads weren't muddy.

We bade Rawinia and Arama goodbye and ran from the house. I glanced at the mountain but it was covered in cloud.

'I hope it won't rain before the ball.'

'An entire week with no rain? Most unlikely,' Jamie said in his I-know-everything-I'm-a-man voice.

I jabbed his ribs. 'You don't look so superior when you are unclothed and dripping with water.'

He grinned but didn't respond. I wanted to discuss the subject of Mama with him, but his mind was clearly fixed upon the delight of whirling around the floor with Lavender clasped in his arms.

He escorted me to Brougham Street, where we collected Judith, and then he jogged away from us to join Hartley Pitts who stood at the corner and called to him.

'There is no young man who causes my heart to beat faster,' I declared to Judith as we watched them. 'Hartley is an admirable person and his character is sound, but . . .'

Judith giggled. 'Mama says not many young men would support their widowed mother and three little sisters but she would faint if I said I wished to wed him!'

I grinned. Hartley supported his family by taking labouring work. In Aunt Frances's eyes that did not add up to good marriage material.

Judith glanced around. 'Quickly! Tell me about the birthing.'

'Now?' I protested. The street wasn't the place I would have chosen to speak of such things.

48

'Yes,' she insisted. 'Who knows when we will next have an opportunity?'

So I told her, speaking quickly and in a whisper. When I had finished, I jabbed my elbow into her side. 'Watch out! Your eyes are near falling from your head.'

'But Hannah! Consider for a moment. If that's how a child comes out of the mother, pray tell me how it gets in.' She stopped in the middle of the roadway, her arms akimbo and glared at me as if the whole unsavoury business was my very own fault.

I took her arm. 'I don't know. For the love of heaven, Judith, keep walking.'

It wasn't true that I didn't know, for Rawinia and her sisters when they came to visit during the winter months sat smoking their pipes and talking of such matters, with much laughter and sly looks. But I judged it better to deny all knowledge to Judith. She was shocked enough for one day.

'Ask Rawinia,' she hissed at me, her eye on the approach of the Lang brothers, also heading for the dancing class.

'You ask her,' I hissed back. 'Come tomorrow, in the morning, before Papa is out of bed. Tell Aunt Frances you promised to lend me a book.'

But she didn't come the next day. I visited her on Thursday to see if she would walk with me for an hour on the beach.

Aunt Frances smiled and gave her permission. 'It's a beautiful day, it would be a shame not to make the most of it.'

49

Judith tied on her hat, took off her apron and we were off. I wanted to run, but Judith said we should walk. It wasn't ladylike to run. I rolled my eyes but stayed at her side. 'You didn't bring the book,' I said.

'I changed my mind.'

We walked down Brougham Street, crossed Devon Street which today was full of cattle being driven to the market further up the street. It was then only a matter of minutes before we reached the beach where I leaped onto the sand while Judith picked her way carefully.

I stopped and waited for her to catch up, and when she did, asked her, 'Why did you change your mind? You want to know, don't you?'

She didn't look at me. 'I believe Mama is right. A young woman shouldn't know about such things.'

I stared at her, baffled. 'But you want to get married. Isn't it better to understand what is expected of you?'

She tossed her head. 'Mama says my husband will teach me all I need to know.'

She turned towards the Sugar Loaves and began to walk. Our feet crunched the hard crust the sun had baked into the surface of the black sand. I wanted to slip off my shoes but if I did I would have to run, for the sand was too hot for bare feet to linger on, and Judith was determined to be genteel.

Could she truly believe her husband would teach her all she needed to know? I reviewed the young men who went to the dancing class. All were admirable and they worked hard with their big hands and solid bodies. It was on the tip of my tongue to ask her if she wanted her husband to teach her to chop down a tree, put up a fence or build a house for that is what they knew how to do. As for the business of being a husband, how would they know any more about it than we did of being a wife?

'Would you marry a soldier?' I asked instead.

She ducked her head and a blush rose in her face.

'Judith Woodley!' I cried. 'You are partial to a soldier! Who is he? What does my aunt think? Why haven't you told me?'

She lifted her head quickly. 'Hush! Nobody knows anything. Especially not him.'

Obligingly I whispered, 'What's his name?'

She sighed and her face was dreamy. 'He is Captain Miles Lindhurst. I saw him perform in the theatricals at the barracks on Saturday night. He is so handsome and charming. He spoke to us afterwards and his manners are everything one could desire.'

Her words shocked me and I could think of nothing to say.

She came out of her dream and demanded, 'What do you think? You're the only person who knows!'

'Oh, Judith! What do you know of him? Is he a good man? Will he be kind to you?'

It wasn't the response she wanted. She bent to pick up a piece of driftwood, then threw it away. 'You're such a child! What do you understand of the finer emotions?'

That was unfair. She was only eleven months older than I. 'I'm surprised, that's all. First Jamie, now you. Things are changing.'

She took my hands and squeezed them briefly. 'It will happen for you too and then you'll understand.' She walked over the hot black sand to the edge of the sea. 'I think of him constantly. I dream about him at night. I think I will fade and die if he doesn't notice me at the ball.'

'Is he going to be there?' It was all I could think of to ask, for I was deeply perturbed by the strength of her feelings, and on so slight an acquaintance.

She turned a radiant smile in my direction. 'Yes! He bowed over my hand and said he looked forward to dancing with me and . . .' she paused for effect, 'to furthering his acquaintance with me.'

I slipped off my shoes, held up my skirt and paddled in the water. 'Oh.' Not a satisfactory response. I tried harder. 'Judith, indeed I hope he is all you dream of. He will have to be special to deserve you.'

At last I had said the right thing, for her radiant smile broke out. 'Thank you Hannah. I couldn't bear it if you were not happy for me.'

We wandered on down the beach with me walking barefoot where the waves ran over my feet and Judith with her shoes on making sure she didn't get caught by the water. Never have I endured such an unsatisfying walk. She told me every small detail of the performance her captain had acted in. She described his face, his hair, his hands, his physique and all the time I listened and merely said *How charming, indeed, truly?* when what I wanted to scream at her was *But do you know what lies between his shapely legs? Do you know what he will want to do with it?*

I wanted to lie on the sand, beat my fists, kick my heels and weep. I was losing my friend. She was drawing away from me into the imaginary world of the young lady.

# 6

## Chapter Six

The weather indulged in one of its sudden changes and the heavens opened two days before the ball. I was rest less but I no longer wished to go and chat with Judith. I couldn't go and talk to Polly either, for she and Thomas David had left the cottage to live in the single room her husband had built with the help of Jamie and Arama.

'She wants you to go and stay with them when we've built another room,' Jamie told me. I was pleased, for it gave me something to look forward to after the ball. In the meantime I moped around the house, irritating Rawinia and not settling to anything. The day was long. Towards evening I prepared a stew for our meal and then there was nothing to do but mending and I wasn't in a mood to be patient over it.

'Do you think the weather will clear before the ball?' I asked.

Rawinia chuckled. 'The rain should stop tomorrow, but the mud will stay.' She pointed to her Bible. 'Read to me, Hana girl.'

I fetched it, opening it at The Book of Job which was her favourite.

She recited the words as I read them — a legacy of her mission school education. My thoughts wandered until she brought them back with a slap of her hand on the arm of her chair. 'You're no good for anything today, girl! Go out and milk those cows, that'll give you something different to do.'

I was glad to go. I took off my shoes, pulled on my sacking cloak and ran barefooted from the house. Rain dripped heavily from the trees in the orchard and the wind blew hard from a turbulent grey sea. Would Jamie and Arama have been able to do any work for the Herberts on such a day? My wish was that they would come home now, come into the cow paddock and that Jamie would listen to my story about Aunt Frances saying Mama was spoiled, whereupon he would laugh and say *nonsense*.

I'd almost finished milking Titania (Papa named both our cows after characters from Shakespeare) when the first part of my wish came true. Jamie hung over the gate and called, 'Hannah! Rawinia sent us to help you, but you don't need help. Bye!'

I lifted my head and shouted back, 'Jamie! Wait! There's something I particularly want to ask you.'

He grumbled to Arama who laughed, clapped him on the back and ran for the house. Jamie vaulted the gate, collected Hero and brought her up to the milking stall. He leaned on her, rubbing her neck and ears to keep her there while I finished with Titania. 'Sissy, you'll never believe it, but I think I've worked out how to make iron. All I need is . . .'

'Jamie! Listen to me! Please. This is important.' I took a deep breath and the words I had kept to myself for so long tumbled out. 'Aunt Frances said Mama was spoiled!'

There! I'd said it. I sagged with relief against the warmth of Titania's flank. All I needed now was to hear Jamie's scoffing and my world would be made whole again.

I glanced up at him. His head was on one side in a thinking pose. 'It's possible,' he said at last.

All the waters of the skies gathered themselves together and poured down on my head, drenching me, drowning me. I gasped for breath, for life. 'Jamie!'

For once he heard my distress. 'Come now, Sissy. Of course she could have been spoiled. Face the facts.'

I just sat dumb and shaking on the milking stool while Titania shifted her feet and gave a low bellow. Automatically, my hands took up the rhythm of the milking again. Jamie's voice hammered away at the certainties I'd lived my life by. 'She was an only child.'

I nodded.

'She was beautiful, even though she looked . . .'

Like me. I nodded again.

'She ran away. She didn't stay and face things out.'

I didn't nod. 'That was Grandfather's fault. What choice did she have? She was brave. She *was*.'

He shrugged his shoulders. Rain sheeted off the capes of the waterproof coat he wore. 'She probably was. But what about when she got here?'

I clung to my picture of our nineteen-year-old mother being carried through the waves by the surf-boat crew. I held fast to the image of her setting up home with our father, of her learning to cook, to clean, garden, make butter, sew clothes . . .

Jamie's voice cut through the pictures. 'Aunt Frances and Rawinia cared for her until we were born.'

He didn't say any more. He didn't add the part he should have added. It was left to me to do so. 'Because she was so ill. She was *ill*. Some women are when they're with child.'

Jamie said nothing, just shrugged his shoulders. 'Have you finished there? I'll milk Hero if you want.'

I stood up on shaking legs. 'Jamie?'

He reached out a hand to push at my sacking hood. 'What an urchin you are.'

I answered his smile with one of my own but it dissolved and ran with the rain down my face and into my clothes.

The mother who had lived in my mind all my life was dead.

I watched while Jamie milked Hero and I was aware of him talking about the method he would use to turn the iron sand into cast iron. He finished the milking, picked up the bucket of milk and tugged at my hand to get me walking. He glanced at my face and tried too late to comfort me. 'What does it matter? She met Papa. They came here. We were born. It's all history.'

But it did matter. I was adrift. My mother, whose image had sustained and nurtured me lay mortally wounded in the mud around me. The pain of it cut too deep for mourning.

*

The ball took my mind away from my worries for the time being. Wednesday dawned bright and sunny, but Rawinia was right about the mud.

'How shall I get there with my feet clean?' I wailed, poking my finger through the hole in the toes of my boots.

'Ask Papa to buy you new ones,' Jamie said. 'You'll be needing them when the cold weather comes.'

Arama said, 'There are none in the town. Peter tried to buy some for Polly.' He went to the door and picked up his own boots. 'You can wear these.'

I threw my arms around him. 'Oh Arama, thank you. I promise to clean them for you afterwards.'

I went to Aunt Frances's house after the midday meal to prepare for the ball. Judith was in a fine state of nerves. 'Is this neckline too low? Should I wear the silver locket or the pearl necklace?' She darted to the mirror a hundred times.

Even Aunt Frances lost her patience by the time we were attired in our gowns and she had done our hair for us. 'For goodness sake, Judith, I have never seen you in better looks. See for yourself.' She pushed a looking glass into Judith's hands.

As for me, I was enchanted with my reflection. 'Is it really me?' I asked as I twirled in front of the long glass in Aunt Frances's bedroom.

Her eyes misted. 'Dearest Hannah! You are the image of my lovely Angelina. How proud she would be at this moment.' She adjusted the curl that fell to my shoulder. 'Perhaps I shouldn't have dressed your hair like this, for it is exactly the same as she wore hers.'

I turned and embraced her. 'But I could not have any style I would like more, darling Aunt Frances. I am so grateful to you, for this, for my dress. For my life.'

Tears swam in her eyes, but she smiled and took my hands. 'Hannah, if anyone should be ill-mannered enough to mention the business of Polly Herbert's child, you will, with great dignity, say it was an emergency and you performed what was clearly your Christian duty.'

'Yes, Aunt Frances. I will remember.'

All was bustle and excitement as we left the house in our finery, carrying our dancing shoes with us. Mr Woodley escorted my aunt, Jamie took my arm but whispered that he had no intention of dancing with me other than for the obligatory first dance and I wasn't to expect it.

'I would decline,' I said, tossing my head so that the curl bounced on my shoulder.

Charlie took Judith's arm and said, 'I say, Judith, you make a fellow quite proud to be your brother.'

We walked down Brougham Street, keeping alert so as to avoid the worst of the mud. Devon Street was just as muddy but when we arrived at Mr Black's bakery where the ball was to be held, we found that the worst of the water had drained away from the lake that collected in front of when it rained and we were able to pick our way round what was left.

'Good evening!' we called to others shedding their walking boots.

We trooped up the bakery stairs to the long room. 'It's beautiful!' I gasped.

Aunt Frances smiled. 'Very pretty.'

I could tell she was comparing it with ballrooms she'd known in England, but to my eyes the candles, lamps and the green boughs decorated the room most elegantly.

We deposited our cloaks and collected our dance cards. Jamie, under Aunt Frances's eye, bowed in front of me and wrote his name opposite the first dance. 'But nothing else.' He caught sight of Lavender and hurried off to write in her card.

She gazed at him with plain and open adoration. 'He's much too young to marry. Don't fret,' my aunt whispered in my ear.

I smiled at her, then our eyes fixed on the uniformed officer strolling across the room. Judith dropped her head and the blush rose in her cheeks. This was her soldier? But he was so much older than she was; he must be all of six and twenty.

He bowed over Aunt Frances's hand, then over Judith's. 'Miss Woodley.'

Judith curtseyed and murmured shyly, 'How do you do, Captain Lindhurst.'

Aunt Frances had the air of one to whom the answer has been given to a particularly vexing puzzle. She smiled upon them both, then introduced me.

I murmured a greeting and withdrew my hand as speedily as good manners would allow. He was handsome enough, and polished with a certain charm, but I had seen his type before. He viewed everything before him with an amused air of superiority, as if we colonists were children aping their elders and betters.

He wrote his name in Judith's card, claiming her for the waltz and the gallop, then he bowed and asked if he might write in my card.

'I would be delighted,' I said, for I guessed he would dance admirably. He chose the polka. I smiled, he smiled and moved off.

'He is everything a gentleman should be!' Judith sighed in my ear. 'Do you not think so?'

'Indeed,' I said. 'And he is most handsome which is definitely an attribute a gentleman should possess.'

It was fortunate for me that Vernon Yates and Hartley Pitts came over to write their names in our cards for I was in no mind to listen to another cataloguing of the perfections of Captain Lindhurst.

Vernon grinned at me. 'I say Hannah, I scarcely recognised you. Are you too fine to dance with me?'

I laughed. 'You look very fine too.' And he did, although it was probably his father's suit he was wearing. 'And please, will you dance the waltz with me for otherwise I fear I must dance with Hartley and my toes are still aching from last Tuesday.'

Hartley grinned. 'I have made a solemn vow not to try the waltz again. Ever.'

From the corner of my eye, I caught Captain Lindhurst watching us, his eyebrows raised in slight amusement. I turned my back. Beside him, the others were mere boys, unworldly and out of place in such a setting. But so was I, and Judith too if she could but see it.

Moments later, Captain Lindhurst was bowing to me again and begging to introduce his fellow officer, Captain Sir Marshall Hendon. Captain Hendon was older than Judith's captain, but quite as debonair. He bowed over my hand and his smile was broader and friendlier than Captain Lindhurst's. 'Ma'am, your servant. I wonder if I might have the privilege of a dance?' He took my card. 'The second waltz, with your permission?'

'I would be delighted,' I replied. How differently I behaved to these men than I did towards the boys I had grown up with. I smiled upon Captain Hendon and prepared to like him, for he had an easier manner than did Judith's captain.

The dancing commenced and I enjoyed myself hugely. It was far different to be dancing at a real ball, dressed in a gown of silk, than it was attending dancing classes. I couldn't help too but be warmed by the admiration I saw in my partners' eyes.

All my dancing partners were the boys I knew, with the exception of Captains Lindhurst and Hendon. Captain Hendon did not dance every dance, for there were more men than ladies, but I observed that he performed with grace when he did take the floor. I looked forward to the waltz with him, which came after we had partaken of supper.

He offered his arm. 'Miss Carstairs. My dance I believe.'

We walked onto the floor and I ignored Judith whose

expression said plainly that she expected me to finish the dance quite as in love as she was.

The music began. At first, I did not try to make conversation for I needed to concentrate. How mortifying it would be if I stood on his foot.

He spoke first. 'You have lived in this delightful spot very long, Miss Carstairs?'

I smiled up at him. 'I was born here, sir. It is all I've known.'

He drew me closer to him, closer than I was comfortable with and closer than Mr Edmund had taught us was correct. I looked up. 'Sir? I ask you not to hold me so tight.'

The smile he gave me was quite different from his previous ones. It was more of a leer. 'But a girl like you would surely not object to a little, shall we say, dalliance?'

'A girl like me?' I repeated. The certainty that he spoke of Polly and the baby flashed into my mind, but I would make him say the words himself, for I was not ashamed of what I had done. 'Explain yourself, and kindly loose your grip while you do so!' I disengaged the hand he held, put both my palms flat on his chest and pushed sharply.

He merely laughed, grabbed my hand and pulled me closer still. 'Consider your mother,' he drawled. 'You hardly come from a respectable background and cannot expect the same treatment as, for instance, your pretty friend Miss Woodley.'

I stopped dancing, forcing us to a halt and tried to snatch my hand away. 'I have no idea what you're referring to! But I do know this – you are no gentleman.' I tried to wrench myself from his arms but he held me tight.

'Keep dancing, you little fool! Would you have us become a spectacle?'

If he thought that would intimidate me he had the wrong girl. 'Jamie!' I shouted. 'Help me!' I searched the crowd for someone who would aid me, anyone. 'Vernon! Mr Woodley! Help me!'

All around us, people stumbled to a halt, staring in disbelief while I struggled against the captain's embrace. It was only a second but it felt, oh, so long. Rescue came swiftly and from a quarter I had not considered. Captain Lindhurst pushed between Vernon and Mr Woodley whose faces were still frozen in disbelief. 'Miss Carstairs, may I escort you to your aunt?' He held out his hand and his eyes bore into those of my partner. 'I am afraid you have been severely discommoded.' Captain Sir Marshall Hendon's arms dropped from around me.

With more gratitude than I thought it possible for one heart to possess, I took Captain Lindhurst's hand. 'I thank you, sir.'

He tucked my hand through his arm. 'You will not be troubled again. I can promise you that.'

My entire body shook and I wanted desperately to burst into tears. 'I don't know why . . .' I stuttered.

'Perhaps we can discuss it tomorrow, when you have recovered from your distressing experience,' he said, passing me to Aunt Frances.

Jamie appeared. 'What happened? I'll kill him! What did he do to you?'

Captain Lindhurst drew him aside. I hoped he would calm him down. I was sure he would.

The music started up again and couples began to dance, but the buzz of speculation hummed around the room. I wanted to die. 'Aunt Frances, I am going home.'

'You are not!' she said sharply. 'Charlie, bring Hannah a cup of tea. You will drink it and calm yourself. Then you will lift your head and dance with your next partner. Who is it?'

I glanced at my programme. 'Hartley Pitts.'

'Excellent,' she said. 'A thoroughly reliable young man.'

While I was sipping the tea and trying to ignore the questioning and curious glances of the other guests, Captain Lindhurst came back, with Jamie still stormy-faced beside him. The captain bowed to Aunt Frances and said, 'I apologise on behalf of my fellow officer, ma'am. I am deeply mortified that he came here the worse for drink and subjected your niece to his most unwelcome attentions.'

Aunt Frances and Mr Woodley both nodded. 'It will do very well,' said Mr Woodley, 'and we'll hear the real story tomorrow.'

Jamie bent over me. 'Did he hurt you, Hana? I vow I'll kill him if he did.'

Aunt Frances drew in a breath. I hurried into speech before she could scold him. 'Dearest Jamie, of course he didn't hurt me! I'm just a little shocked.'

Mr Woodley touched Jamie on the shoulder and drew him away. I don't know what he said, but Jamie's face cleared and he shook Mr Woodley's hand.

65

It was thanks to Hartley that I got through the remainder of the evening as well as I did, for he made me laugh. He didn't mention my waltz with the captain. Instead, when he came to claim me for the gavotte, he said, 'Hannah, you must tell me when I go wrong, for I fear I am all feet in this dance, like a cow running off into the bush.'

Then, when the dance finished, Amy Bishop seized my arm. 'You're an inspiration to me, Hannah. I have wondered what I'd do if a gentleman the worse for drink made advances and now I know. I too will shout and it will be he who is shamed and not me.'

By the end of the evening I had almost completely regained my composure. Captain Lindhurst's story of Captain Hendon being the worse for drink sped around the room. People shook their heads. 'What a disgrace! I trust his commanding officer will discipline him.'

I began to relax. It was the captain who had been made a fool of and not me, thanks to Judith's captain.

I found time to murmur in her ear, 'You may marry him with all the good wishes of my heart. He is truly a gentleman.'

Her face glowed.

Jamie and I had been going to go straight home, but I said, 'Aunt Frances, may we come back to your house for a moment? I don't understand why . . .'

It was Mr Woodley who answered. 'Do you feel up to it, my dear? I would advise a good night's sleep.'

'But Papa, she won't sleep. Not for thinking about it,' Judith said.

We went home with them and I sat at the kitchen table with the men while Aunt Frances and Judith stirred up the fire and made tea.

'Now, tell us what happened,' my aunt said, when I had my hands wrapped around a tea cup.

I looked at their faces, these people who had known me forever and loved me forever, for after tonight how could I doubt that Mr Woodley did indeed care about me? I told them every detail of the dance.

My aunt and uncle stared at me, and then at each other, their faces blank. 'What could he be referring to?' asked my aunt.

'I'll kill him,' growled Jamie. 'I'll tell Papa and we'll demand satisfaction.'

I leaned my head on his shoulder. 'Dearest Jamie, I don't care about him. But why did he say that about Mama?'

Charlie leaned forward. 'Do you think he didn't mean your own mama? Do you think he perhaps doesn't approve of mixed marriages and referred to Rawinia?'

Jamie thumped the table. 'I will! I'll kill him! How dare he talk of Rawinia like that?'

'You'll do no such thing,' Mr Woodley said. 'Now I suggest you both go home and get some sleep.'

We bade them goodnight.

Jamie muttered all the way home. His anger burned hot on Rawinia's behalf but not Mama's.

I was almost too weary to put one foot in front of the other.

# 7

## Chapter Seven

I told Papa what had happened at the ball as soon as he had breakfasted. He thumped the table. "The cad! What's his name again? I'll talk to his commanding officer, not that I have any faith in the workings of British justice, particularly of military justice, but we can give the bounder a fright, just see if we can't!'

Rawinia asked the question burning in my mind. 'But what did he mean? Why does he say her background isn't respectable?'

'And why did he say *consider your mother*?' I asked, for I'd thought about it all morning and I couldn't believe he meant Rawinia.

'How can I know?' said Papa irritably, but he didn't quite meet my gaze. 'Possibly he knows the story about her running away. Thought she shouldn't.' He got up and reached for his hat. 'Don't fret about it, my dear. I'll talk to his commanding officer. I'll do it tomorrow.'

He left and Rawinia said, 'He knows more than he's saying.'

'And he'll never tell me.' Just like he wouldn't go and see the commanding officer, not that I cared for that.

Thanks to Judith's captain, I was a heroine and Captain Sir Marshall Hendon a drunken cad.

Jamie stormed in the door that evening demanding, 'What did Papa say?'

'Exactly what he always says,' I retorted. 'He knows more than he'll tell, and he said he'd go and see the cad's commanding officer, tomorrow.'

It took the efforts of both Rawinia and me to persuade the boys not to go and kill Captain Hendon right then and there. 'Why start a battle you can't win?' Rawinia asked. 'The whole town thinks he's a fool and a drunk. He'll have the minister calling on him; *come and join the temperance*, he'll say. That's worse punishment than killing him.'

They muttered but eventually agreed to leave well alone. Jamie remembered he had a message for me from Polly. 'She says you can go and stay if you don't mind that the room's not much. She'd love to see you and you can go home with them on Sunday when they come in to church.'

I didn't care if I had to sleep under the stars if it meant escaping from town for a week or two.

On Friday, Rawinia and I were surprised to receive a visit from Captain Lindhurst as we worked in the garden. 'Good afternoon, ma'am, Miss Carstairs. I'll not disturb you, I only wish to assure you there will be no repeat of the unfortunate incident at the ball.'

Rawinia got to her feet. 'He'd best keep away from her brothers or he'll be walking off without a heart in his body.'

He bowed in her direction, a fleeting smile of approval lighting his face. 'Just so, ma'am.'

I stood up, my mind racing. 'Thank you, Captain Lindhurst. And thank you for your intervention on the night.'

'It was my pleasure, Miss Carstairs.' His smile this time was for me, and I quite saw what it was that attracted Judith to him. 'I'll not interrupt you further.'

'Captain! Wait! Please tell me, why did he say those things to me? What does he know of my mother?'

He stepped over the pile of weeds on the path and took my grubby hand in his. 'Miss Carstairs, don't pay any heed to what he said. He was labouring under a misapprehension. That does not excuse him but it should reassure you.' He gave my hand a slight squeeze and let it go.

I clasped my hands in front of me, pressing them together until the dirt dug into the flesh. 'I see that you know,' I told him. 'But I see too that you do not want to distress me by telling me.' I gulped for air. 'I will not persist in my questioning for I am already most beholden to you.'

He looked at me strangely, a half smile on his lips. 'You are a most remarkable young lady, Miss Carstairs. I can tell you this: the man who wins you will be fortunate indeed.'

He replaced his hat and strode off down the path.

'Sweet on you or I miss my guess,' Rawinia said, staring after his shapely form.

I whirled round, looking at her in horror. 'No! Rawinia, you're imagining it. Judith loves him! She'll die if he doesn't love her back!'

Rawinia squatted and returned to the weeding. 'What we want and what we get don't always match up, and you'd do well to remember it.'

What with one thing and another, I was deeply pleased to escape to visit Polly.

It was a fine March day, hot and still, as I climbed with Polly and Peter onto the Walters' bullock cart to ride as far as Omata where the Walters would leave us. Mrs Walter and Polly chatted the whole way while Mr Walter harangued Peter. More than once he declared, 'The government needs to teach those Maoris a lesson. Only obey the law when it suits them. And what does the government do? Encourage them, that's what it does.'

I held my tongue.

We alighted at the corner of a rough road cut through the high denseness of the bush. 'Nearly there,' Polly said, tying Thomas David onto her back. Peter took her arm to steady her, for the road was full of stumps and branches.

It was cool in the shade of the trees. Polly talked as we walked. 'I'm that excited you've come, Hannah. You're our first guest and I hope you'll excuse the house.'

I assured her I wouldn't mind sleeping outside I was so pleased to see her, then added, 'So long as the weather holds, for I confess I can't abide thunder!'

Every now and again we passed tracks cut into the bush where other settlers were cutting out farms. Peter and Polly began to quicken their steps.

'We could have got our own land before this,' Polly

said, a little breathless now. 'There's cheaper blocks on the hill country. But Peter wouldn't hear of it. You get shut in up there in the winter. Roads are all mud.' She patted his arm fondly with her spare hand. 'Said it was too hard on a woman never to see anyone from one month's end to the next.'

'I would hate it,' I said, trying to imagine being shut in a house with only a crying child for company day in and day out. 'Peter is right, and very thoughtful.'

Polly beamed. Peter said nothing but a blush rose to his face.

Minutes later we turned into a track similar to the ones we'd passed.

'Here it is,' said Polly and the two of them stood and gazed at a tiny, rough cottage in a clearing, with the high bush looming up all around it. I glanced at them, then looked away hurriedly. Never had I seen such awe, such reverence.

'It's ours,' Peter said at last. 'All our own. Land.'

Polly shook herself. 'Take Tommy for me, Hannah, and I'll make afternoon tea. I declare I'm famished after that walk.'

I held the baby against my shoulder. 'You have flowers blooming already. You must work so hard.'

She grinned at me. 'We do, indeed we do. But Hannah, it's a wonderful thing to be working on your own land, to be making your very own home.'

She filled the kettle from a water barrel and hung it on one of the hooks suspended from a pole over the big, outside fireplace. 'Peter says we'll get the chimney built before winter,' she said.

Peter nodded and set about lighting a fire under the kettle.

Before night fell they showed me their property, the parts of it that were accessible. There was the clearing the house stood in, with the vegetable garden and orchard Polly cared for. Next, I followed them through a corridor cut through the trees. 'The home paddock,' Peter said, pride almost choking him. 'This is where your brothers are working. Good boys, they are.'

I gulped. 'You've all worked hard.' Felled trees lay half burned on the ground. Stumps stuck up raw from the rough earth. Ferns, mangled and broken showed through the churned up soil.

'This time next year we'll have cows grazing here,' Peter said. It was more a promise to himself than a remark to me.

The final part of our inspection was the river paddock. Here, grass grew and there were few stumps to mar it. 'Fern country,' Peter said. 'Much easier to bring in.'

Their three cows wandered over to investigate us. 'Bluebell, Daisy and Marigold,' said Polly.

The March days stayed fine and hot, passing most pleasantly and at night I slept on a mattress on the floor of what would become the kitchen once the house was bigger.

Every day we took a picnic lunch to Peter, Jamie and Arama as they laboured in the home paddock. Some days,

Polly tied Tommy on her back and we'd go exploring the lines cut in the bush between their block and the next farm.

It was pretty and I said as much to Polly, walking ahead of me on the narrow track. She laughed. 'It's normal to you, though, isn't it?'

'What do you mean?' I scrambled over a fallen log draped with fern and moss.

She stopped walking and extended her arms. 'All this! The trees so big towering up to the heavens. Those tree ferns, look at them. Isn't that moss on them the most beautiful sight you've seen in a month of Sundays?'

I agreed that it was, for it hung in festoons from trunks and stems.

'And the ferns!' She pointed at the ground. 'Some days I just sit and study them all. It's a fairer sight than a greenhouse in a castle so it is.'

Her raptures rather reminded me of Judith talking of her captain.

On another expedition we rested with our shoes off and our feet in a small stream. I breathed in the damp, earthy smell of the bush, glad to be here, away from the town and its difficulties. Around the banks of our stream grew rimu, kahikatea, ponga ferns and here and there a huge rata strangling its host tree as it reached upwards to the sun.

The water ran clear and cool. A busy little stream it was, narrow enough to cross in two strides and shallow enough to bath a baby in if you had a mind to.

Polly however, despite her raptures, wasn't content to sit in silent contemplation. 'You've not said aught about the ball. Tell me everything. That's the only thing wrong with being out here, a body does get starved of company.'

I splashed my feet and thought for a moment. 'Very well. I'll tell you everything, but Polly, please don't talk of it to anyone else. Except Peter, of course.' I knew he'd never pass on gossip.

Polly's eyes grew round. 'I promise! Goodness, Hannah, you're being very mysterious.'

I smiled and said, 'I have to start this story further back before the ball. But I'll get to it, I promise you.'

She settled herself, Tommy asleep on her lap. 'The longer the better for it's more to think about.'

She sat quite still while I told her of Mama, of Aunt Frances and the fateful word, of Papa and how he wouldn't tell us anything and then I told her of the ball and the cad of a captain.

'Eh, lass, what a tale,' she sighed as I finished. 'What a tale!'

She was quiet as we walked home and said little while we prepared the evening meal. When we settled ourselves on the cushions covering the rough chairs Peter and the boys had made she said, 'Hannah, I've been thinking. What of your grandparents? What do you know of them?'

I stared at her, struck dumb for a moment. 'Do you know, Aunt Frances has never told me about them, and it has never occurred to me to ask.' All my thirst for knowledge had been focused on Mama.

'What about your dad's family?' Peter asked.

I shook my head. 'He'll tell us nothing. They will only continue to send him money on the condition that there is no contact.'

He laughed. 'Must be a toff, then.'

Polly picked up a newspaper. 'Look at this.' She pointed to an advertisement on the front page. 'Why can't you do the same? Put an advertisement in one of those English papers and ask your grandparents to write to you?'

I took the paper Polly held out and read the advertisement aloud. 'James Smith, you are earnestly requested to communicate with your sister.' I lifted my head and stared at them. 'Do you think I could?'

'Of course you could,' Polly said, her eyes bright. 'What would you say?'

I gazed at nothing and thought for a time. 'The twin children of the late Angelina Carstairs (née Armitage) wish to communicate with their grandparents.'

'Wish most earnestly!' Polly said and we laughed.

My laughter died. 'Papa wouldn't like it.' Tears came to my eyes. 'But I so desperately want to know about Mama!'

'Best do it then,' said Peter.

I thought of another difficulty. 'It would cost money. I have none, and I couldn't ask Papa.' He wouldn't give it to me if I did.

'You know how to work,' Polly said. 'Look for employment.'

All in all, when the time came to go home I had much to think about.

# 8

## Chapter Eight

'I tell you what, Hannah,' said Jamie when I poured out my plans to him and Arama, 'you're making too much of all this.'

'It's her whakapapa – her ancestry. She should know it. Both of you should know it,' said Arama.

Jamie waved a hand. 'But it doesn't matter. It's not important. It's got nothing to do with now.'

We stared at each other, both of us baffled. I needed him to understand. At last I said, 'It's as important to me as the iron-sand experiment is to you.'

'Oh!' was all he said but he didn't try again to dissuade me.

'You have the aunt who knows the grandparents,' Arama said. 'Speak to her, then you do not need the money.'

Jamie and I burst out laughing. It was such an obvious step to take.

On Friday, clouds bunched in the sky and the mountain wore a white wind cap caught like a veil on its peak. I set out in the afternoon to visit Aunt Frances and Judith. They were baking. I breathed in the smells as I approached; the

Woodleys would eat meat pie for their evening meal, with fruit cake to follow. A bowl of bread dough sat rising on the window sill.

We talked of general matters, then I asked, 'Aunt Frances, I have been thinking, I would like to write to Mama's parents. Can you tell me their address?'

She was in the act of carrying the bread dough to the table and her hands clenched tight on the bowl as she set it down. Her movements became slow, deliberate. She folded the tea towel she'd covered the dough with, put it down square with the edge of the table, all without meeting my gaze.

'Mama?' Judith said.

Aunt Frances sighed. 'I have known this day would come, and I have dreaded it. But your uncle and I decided long ago that should either of you ask, then we would not hide the truth from you, no matter how painful.'

I stared at her, my heart beating hard.

'There is a letter. Wait one moment while I fetch it.' She left the room, returning moments later. She handed the letter to me and kissed my forehead. 'This is the reply, dearest child, that your grandfather sent in response to the note I scribbled telling them of Angelina's death and your births.' She moved back to the bread bowl. 'A ship was about to leave, I had only moments to write and your uncle ran with it. We thought, you see, that they would wish to know the fate of their daughter. We believed they would be comforted by the birth of their grandchildren.' She thumped a fist into the risen dough. The air hissed out as it collapsed around her clenched fingers. 'How mistaken we were!'

I couldn't move. I was cold. Hot. I didn't know what I was. 'Read it for me,' I whispered, moving the letter towards Judith.

She took it, opened it, scanned it. 'Hannah, it's dreadful.'

'Read it. Please.'

She took a breath but her voice trembled. I have read the letter since, of course, but even after hearing it once, phrases burned into my mind that I fear I shall never be able to forget.

*Mrs Woodley,*

*I am in receipt of your communication regarding the death of Angelina Carstairs, née Armitage. I wish to inform you that she was dead to me after she behaved in a manner which I will not sully this page in describing. As for her hell-born brats, I do not acknowledge them now and will not do so in the future.*

*Hugo Armitage*

The only sound in the room when she finished reading was the *thump*, *thump* as my aunt kneaded the dough.

At last I stood, leaving the poisonous letter open on the table. I went to my aunt and threw my arms around her. 'Dearest Aunt Frances, how much Jamie and I owe to you! You are more to us than they could ever be.'

She patted my hand. 'Oh dear, it still upsets me after all these years.'

'I'll make us a pot of tea, Mama,' Judith said.

I sat down again, trying to rearrange this new insight into my heritage. Always, in my mind, there had been the vague presence of distant and loving grandparents who might one day discover our existence and shower us with their affection. They would send us boxes of clothes, dress patterns, scientific journals for Jamie, boots.

I lifted my skirt in order to examine my tattered boots. Sitting there in my aunt's kitchen I finally faced reality. They would send us nothing, not even their love.

All the time we drank our tea I felt the concern of the dear friends who were not my kin by even the smallest drop of blood. I wished passionately that *aunt* was more than a courtesy title, that she really was my true aunt, or better still, my mother. She and Judith chatted of inconsequential matters, leaving me to my thoughts.

I finished my tea and placed the cup carefully on the saucer. 'Aunt Frances, I have been thinking. I intend to look for paid employment.'

Aunt Frances pressed her hands to her heart. 'Hannah, dearest!' she cried. 'Indeed you must not! Oh, I knew that letter would be a terrible shock! You will quite ruin all your chances of making a good marriage.'

To a man such as Captain Hendon perchance? But I did not say the words aloud. 'Darling Aunt Frances, it's not just the letter. I've been thinking of it for some time.' I showed her my boots. 'It will be so useful to me to have money.'

She shut her mouth on what I knew she wanted to say,

that if Papa refrained from drinking at the hotel every day we would live comfortably instead of scraping and making do. I wanted to defend him, to say that he never drank to excess these days, not like some, but the truth was that most of his money did go on drink.

I was grateful when Judith gave the subject a happier turn. With her face alight she said, 'You will be able to purchase a ticket to come to the performances at the Royal Military Theatre.'

That would not be high on my list of things to do with any money I earned, but I smiled at her and asked, 'Did you receive any callers after the ball?'

Her radiant face told its own story. 'Oh, yes! Many people came.'

She didn't elaborate and I laughed at her. She blushed and smiled.

'Captain Lindhurst called on me and Rawinia,' I said, my voice a study of innocence. 'He was so kind.'

Judith stared at me, her eyebrows raised in surprise. I was sorry for teasing her and dropped my play acting. 'Aunt Frances, he knows what Captain Hendon meant when he made those terrible insinuations about Mama, but he wouldn't tell me.'

Aunt Frances looked troubled. 'Hannah my dear, we have cudgelled our brains, your uncle and I, but we cannot understand what he meant.'

'Papa went to speak to the colonel,' Judith said. 'But he learned nothing, except that the colonel was most displeased with Captain Hendon.'

My face burned, for it should have been Papa who went and not my uncle. 'Please, will you thank him for me? It was most kind.'

Aunt Frances glanced at Judith who bit her lip and hung her head. She hadn't been meant to tell me, but I was glad I knew.

'Dearest Aunt, I am so grateful to you and I love you so much. I am truly sorry to be such a trouble to you.'

We parted on good terms, but I knew she would lie awake worrying over my plans to find work.

I walked home with the dirt of the road rubbing at my feet and the letter a weight in my pocket. I showed it to Jamie the moment he got home.

He threw it away from him. 'You were right, Hannah, she was brave to run away.'

How strange that now it was too late, he should say Mama was brave. We talked of it after our meal that evening.

'Did you know about the letter, Papa?' Jamie asked.

Papa stretched his feet out towards the fire. 'I believe I did, but it was of no consequence to me. I didn't know them and I didn't want to know them. I certainly didn't want them storming over here to snatch you away and take you home with them.'

'That's a most admirable sentiment, Papa,' I said. 'But why?'

He lifted his glass of port and sipped at it, staring into the fire. Jamie pulled a face. We weren't going to hear anything worth the listening to. But for once, Papa spoke without the theatricals he normally employed. 'They sold, tried to sell, I should say, their lovely daughter to the highest bidder. What mattered to them was class and position.' He shook a finger at me. 'If you'd been born in England, my child, you'd now be learning the useful arts of flirtation, man-trapping and fainting.'

Jamie looked up from the harness he and Arama were mending for Peter. 'I can see now that it would have been useless to appeal to her father. He's an ogre.' He grinned at me, a tacit apology for past opinions.

Arama nodded and Rawinia sighed, 'To die so far from your roots. Aue! It's a sad thing.'

Papa chuckled. 'Do you know what gives me great satisfaction when the matter happens to cross my mind?'

We couldn't begin to guess for the ways of Papa's mind were seldom straightforward.

He rubbed his hands gleefully. 'It's the thought of those two, sitting in their cold mansion not knowing that their grandchildren are mixing with labourers, peasants and natives.' He gave a great bellow of laughter.

'There's something else they might not like, Papa,' I said, for now seemed the ideal opportunity. 'I intend to look for paid employment.'

'You're right, my child, they'd hate it!' He chuckled and sipped more of his port.

Rawinia wasn't so complacent. 'It's not fitting, Hana, and so Mrs Woodley will tell you.'

'She already has,' I said. Poor Aunt Frances, it was small

wonder that she didn't see eye to eye with Papa, who was still chuckling.

As it turned out, I couldn't look for work immediately for Rawinia became poorly with a boil on her arm. It was too painful to use and I was needed at home.

'You must let me go for the doctor,' I begged on the third day she was unable to use it. 'Rawinia, please!'

She didn't respond, just sat in the easychair in the kitchen with her swollen arm propped on a cushion. She hadn't even been able to dress, so painful it was. 'I'll go and ask Papa for the money right this minute,' I said, untying my apron.

She lifted her head at that. 'No use. There's no more money till quarter day, and there'll be precious little then the way he's drinking on credit.'

I don't ever remember experiencing anger against Papa, but today it threatened to set fire to my blood. Rawinia, the dove of his heart, was in dreadful pain which he did nothing to alleviate when it was easily within his power to do so.

'I shall go for the doctor without the money then,' I said. I changed out of my work clothes, all the time expecting to hear Rawinia's protests, but she said nothing. It worried me more than anything else could have done. I prayed she wasn't mortally ill.

I ran all the way to Dr Feilding's consulting rooms and a cold wind from the mountain blew straight through the light shawl I clutched around my shoulders. My boots filled with mud before I'd gone half a dozen steps. As soon as Rawinia was well, I would find myself work of some sort. I ran through the streets, my mind on my problems or perhaps I would have noticed Captain Hendon before he accosted me.

'Pray don't be in such a hurry, Miss Carstairs,' he drawled, sweeping his hat off in an exaggerated bow. He stepped directly in front of me, a most unpleasant sneer on his face. 'You and I have a conversation to finish.'

I ran harder, only turning to dodge his outstretched hands at the last minute and I thanked the ancestors for all the times Jamie, Arama and I had played chasing when we were children. As it was, the captain caught hold of my shawl. I kept running, leaving him standing in the road holding it. I ran on, listening for the pounding of footsteps behind me but all I heard was the word *whore* carried on the wind. I was shaking and breathless by the time I reached the doctor's rooms.

Dr Feilding was in. 'Bless me, if it isn't my little midwife!' he said. 'And what can I do for you, Hannah Carstairs.'

I burst into tears. I seemed to do that whenever I saw him.

'Sit down, my dear, sit down. That's better. Now tell me your troubles.'

'It's not me, it's Rawinia.' I sobbed out the story of Papa and the money, and of Captain Hendon. 'He calls me dreadful names and I do not know why and now he's got my shawl too.' I desperately wished I had it still for

I needed something to wipe my eyes and nose with.

The doctor gave me a handkerchief, then, when I had tidied myself, he took my hand and pulled me to my feet. 'Your papa will deal with the captain, and let's not worry our heads about the money right now. Come, we'll go at once and visit your stepmother.' The black bag he'd carried into Polly's house was by the door. He picked it up and we left.

I was glad he would be walking back with me for I did not feel able to confront the captain again. I did not even want to think about him and so I said, 'I'm going to look for paid employment as soon as Rawinia's well again.'

'If I hear of anything, I'll let you know.' The doctor glanced down at me. 'If I may offer advice, my dear?'

'Of course. I'd be grateful.'

'Stay away from the hotels. They often need workers, but there's much drunkenness and men tend to forget themselves when they've drink inside them.'

I nodded. It was good advice.

The captain was not in sight, but we passed Ara, a kinswoman of Rawinia's, on her way back to the pa. She lifted her eyes, saw the doctor and hurried on. Tomorrow, Rawinia would receive a visit from her or one of the other old kuia. She'd smoke her pipe and stay till she discovered why the doctor was needed at our house.

Rawinia was exactly how I had left her. She looked up when we came in, but said nothing.

'Boil water, if you please, Hannah.'

I fetched the water, set the kettle on the stove and threw more wood on the fire.

The doctor looked at me. 'I'll be needing to lance this, make a cut to let the contagion out.' He smiled at Rawinia. 'Don't worry, it'll feel much easier and the pain will stop.' He spoke in Maori and she moved her lips in a slight smile.

Lancing the boil wasn't a procedure I relished seeing, but he required me to hold a clean rag under the infection while he cut it with the blade he'd first immersed in boiling water. He washed his own hands and made me wash mine as well.

The blade sliced into Rawinia's arm. She said nothing, just closed her eyes. Pus and blood spurted onto the rag I held. He made another cut. We waited while it drained. Then he sprinkled a powder on the wound and bandaged it. 'Burn those rags, then wash your hands again.' He soaped his own in the tin bowl I'd poured yet more water into. 'Be sure to wash your hands before and after you dress the wound.'

He asked Rawinia, 'How does it feel now?'

She drew in a deep breath. 'Much better. The taniwha has stopped gnawing my flesh.'

A vivid picture flashed through my mind of a monster gnawing Rawinia from the inside — she should have told me sooner how painful it was. Papa should have called the doctor much before this.

Dr Feilding laughed. 'Well, we should have tamed the taniwha now.' He glanced at us both. 'It should heal now, but you must come for me if there's any problem.'

I saw him to the door. 'Thank you, Dr Feilding. Thank you so much.'

He clapped his hat on his head and paused in the doorway. 'You know, young Hannah, you could do worse than become a nurse. Miss Nightingale is to establish a school for nurses in London, did you know?'

As it happened, I did know, for I'd read it in the paper. 'London is a little inconvenient to get to, Doctor.'

He laughed. 'I wouldn't put anything beyond your capabilities, Hannah Carstairs.'

Rawinia was on her feet when I turned back into the room. 'Help me dress, Hana. Ai, it's good to be free of that pain.'

She didn't ask about payment, instead she said, 'Hana, girl, it's no good trying to change your Papa and if you spit at him like I can tell you want to, then he'll just run off and drink more.'

I thumped and crashed the pots that day, but knew Rawinia was right.

Papa arrived home before Jamie and Arama, an hour earlier than usual. He threw his hat at a chair and tonight it stayed there. 'Hannah! I hear you fetched the doctor to my house today. Is anyone dying? Is there something I should know?'

Rawinia spoke before I could do so. 'It was my arm. The doctor fixed it.' She shook her head at me. 'Go and chop more wood for the fire, Hana.'

I ran out to the woodpile, seized the axe and crashed it down, splitting a log of matai. Gradually my anger changed focus from Rawinia to myself. *Your papa will deal with the captain.* Crash went my axe. *Thump.* I picked up the split wood and heaved it onto the pile of firewood. Might as well tell the wind as tell Papa. And I daren't tell Jamie and Arama for they would do something foolish and they were only boys. The captain would out-manoeuvre them, sneer at them and deny all.

My uncle? I shook my head. I could not bear to ask him to do what Papa ought to do. Judith's captain? Impossible.

I was still chopping when the boys arrived home. I ran to meet them and poured out the story of fetching Dr Feilding to Rawinia. 'I told him you'd pay,' I concluded.

'Give us food and we'll go immediately,' Jamie said. Arama disappeared out to the vegetable garden where they'd made a secret hidey-hole for their money so Papa couldn't find it.

'We'll speak to Papa,' Jamie said, looking at Arama who nodded.

'You mustn't. Rawinia doesn't want you to.' I repeated her lecture about not shaming Papa. Jamie snorted, Arama shrugged, but they agreed to say nothing.

It made me more determined than ever to find work. With a start, I realised I'd forgotten the original reason I'd wanted money. Somehow it didn't seem so important any longer. Perhaps Jamie was right and what mattered was now. Mama was in the past and we should leave her in peace.

Except that she wasn't. Captain Hendon had made that very clear.

# 9

## Chapter Nine

April came and with it our birthdays. Jamie and Arama gave me a copy of the scandalous book *Wuthering Heights*, while my present for Jamie was six handkerchiefs I had sewn for him from shirts too old to be mended. Papa smiled upon us benevolently and drank our health.

Two weeks later, at the beginning of May, when the winter wind and a sleety rain battered the town for the third day in a row, Dr Feilding came to find me. 'There's a month's work for you, Hannah Carstairs, if you want it.'

Mrs Walter whose bullock cart the Herberts and I had travelled in, had given birth to twins. 'She's already got three little ones and she's needing another pair of hands. They can't pay much, twelve shillings a week and your keep.'

'I'll do it!' The money was poor, Peter paid the boys seven shillings a day but that was for heavy labouring work, and a girl would never earn as much.

'Good girl,' he said. 'Can you be ready to go tomorrow?'

My family greeted the news predictably. Rawinia grumbled and Papa smiled. I borrowed Arama's boots and ran through the rain to tell Aunt Frances and Judith. Aunt Frances cried and Judith clasped my hands. 'You're so brave!'

The light was gone from her face these days. Her captain hadn't called again. There was nothing I could say to comfort her for I couldn't understand her anguish and truthfully, I was a little impatient of it.

The weather calmed overnight and I awoke to a day of light showers.

Dr Feilding came for me early, bringing a hired horse with him. 'I hope you can ride, Hannah Carstairs?'

'So do I,' I said. 'We rode when we were young, but I haven't sat on a horse for years.'

'I predict you'll be sore and stiff tomorrow in that case.'

I bade everyone goodbye and Papa threw me up into the saddle. Jamie handed me my bag and we were off, the wind and the rain blowing about us.

'Where do the Walters live?' I asked. All I knew was that they were at Omata but not in the direction of Peter and Polly.

'They're on the flat, about a mile out of the village. It's mostly fern country where they are. They've been able to clear much of the land already.' He grinned at me. 'How are you faring? Shall we go a little faster?'

For answer, I shook up my horse and drew ahead of him. I heard him laugh. We rode side by side out of the town until we reached the Omata settlement.

The village was small, with just a school, a brewery, an inn, a bakehouse and the general store where Polly and

Peter bought their supplies. However Polly would have nothing to do with the small wooden church. 'Primitive Methodist! It's the Church of England for me or nothing,' she declared. Peter hadn't expressed an opinion but he brought her into town to St Mary's when he could.

My thoughts turned to the task ahead of me. I'd not had much experience with babies and small children. 'I hope I can do this,' I said as much to myself as Dr Feilding.

'Of course you can,' he said. 'It's instinctive. It'll come to you quite naturally as it does to all women. You'll see.'

I trusted he was right.

After I'd been there three days, I knew that he wasn't right. The children cried, not just the new twins, but the older three as well. Mrs Walter cried. Mr Walter kept out of the house as much as he could. If it hadn't been a long walk home, and a wet one, I'd have left. But the rain fell, the wind blew and there would be a coating of fresh snow on the mountain under the clouds. Many a time as I hurried from one crisis to another, I glanced out the windows. It wasn't so far back to New Plymouth; I could easily walk it. A trip outside to fetch water from the well, or to chop more wood for the fire soon cured me. It was bitter cold and my boots were more holes than leather.

On the fourth day, in the midst of her tears, Mrs Walter said, 'Oh, Hannah! What a difference you've made! I feel so much better thanks to you.'

My knees went weak with astonishment. I held onto the bench where I stood preparing yet another meal for the family. 'I have? You do?' Surely I couldn't have heard her aright?

She sniffed and actually managed a smile. 'It's wonderful to know the meals are being prepared, and so capably. And you are so good with the children.'

'But ma'am, they cry whenever I come near them!' I worried that her brain was affected.

She gave a small chuckle. 'They're shy, that's all. Already Albert is getting less so.'

That was true. That very morning he'd hit my foot with a log of firewood.

She hadn't finished her catalogue of my virtues. 'You haven't once complained about all the washing.'

I was allowed to complain? I grinned at her. 'Be careful, Mrs Walter! You'll quite turn my head and I'll consider myself too important to do anything!'

She laughed, a full and proper laugh. 'And I do so enjoy having someone to talk to. It gets lonely here with just the children all day.'

I was more settled in my mind after that. I can't say the days went smoothly but they went. The weather improved too and we had days of sunshine with brilliant blue skies. On such days when I went out to draw water or fetch wood, I looked up to the mountain, remote and beautiful with a coat of snow covering the top half of its cone. It restored my soul.

By the end of three weeks I could see that Mrs Walter was stronger and heading once more to becoming the cheerful woman I remembered from the bullock ride.

I did not admire Mr Walter. He never spoke to his wife except to bark orders at her and he only ever grunted at me. Even on the coldest days when squally showers blew off the mountain he stayed outdoors sowing grass seed in the river paddock or anything else he could find to do.

The children caused me much thought. I asked Mrs Walter what their ages were.

Albert was just turned three. Sophia was a year and three days younger. George would be a year old in ten days' time, Gracie and Mary were now just over four weeks.

I mulled it all over, wanting to ask what I knew to be an indelicate question. In the end, it was she who made it possible for me to ask it.

'Hannah, I can't get more than a yes or a no out of you.' She hauled the drying rack full of newly washed nappies up to the ceiling. 'Have I offended you?'

I was horrified and didn't stop to think beyond the necessity of reassuring her. 'No! Of course not! There's something I want to know, but it's indelicate and I have no right to ask. I will not think of it again. I promise you!'

She looked at me, her hands on her hips and she was such a different woman from the weeping, pale creature of only three weeks ago. 'Let me guess.' She smiled at me, her head on one side. 'It would be to do with babies?'

I gasped and nodded.

'Let's have a cup of tea and you shall ask whatever is on your mind. I owe you that much and a whole lot more besides that I can never repay.' She put the kettle on as she spoke, allowing me to regain my composure.

We gave the three older children a baked crust each to keep them quiet.

'Let's have that question, then,' she said and by the tone of her voice, I realised suddenly that she was as embarrassed as Aunt Frances would be if she had to sit down and talk to me of babies.

I hurried into speech. 'It isn't how they are made or how they are birthed, those things I know.'

She was astonished, as well she might be. 'You're sure? How could you know?'

'Maori have different customs and different beliefs,' I said. 'We have always talked of such things at home ever since I was tiny.' Until Aunt Frances found out.

'What else can you wish to know?' she asked.

I took a deep breath. 'I want to know how long a baby takes to grow inside the mother.'

There! I'd done it, and she was smiling.

'Listen to the worst gossips in town and you'll soon have your answer. A girl gets married and then she has a child. The old women right away count the months between the wedding and the birth of the child.' She ticked numbers off on her fingers. 'It should be nine months, but it's purely amazing how many babes are said to come before their time.'

A curious hollowness sat below my heart. 'Nine months. Are you sure?'

She looked down at the three children on the floor and rose to pick up Mary who awoke with a cry. 'I'm fairly certain, Hannah,' she said dryly.

'I'm sorry! I didn't mean . . . it's just . . .' My words dribbled to a halt. I took a deep breath and strove to appear as usual. 'I'm surprised, that's all. I had thought it was a much shorter time.'

She put the child to her breast and settled back against the cushions of the sofa. 'A woman doesn't show much until she's about five months gone.'

I nodded. 'That would be why, then.'

As I had every other night of my time in that house, I fell exhausted onto my mattress on the kitchen floor. But I couldn't sleep. Around and around in my mind chased Papa's words the day he had come home a little more tipsy than normal.

*Met her just four weeks before I was due to sail to this glorious outpost of the Empire.*

Of course he had immediately corrected himself when I pointed out he'd said weeks when he should have said months. But suppose what he said in his tipsiness was right? Suppose he had met Mama only four weeks before they sailed for New Plymouth?

It had to mean . . . I turned my face into the mattress and beat my fists upon it. I wouldn't even think such a thing.

My mind wouldn't let me escape. A voice in my head recited the unforgivable words of Captain Hendon. *Consider your mother. You hardly come from a respectable background.*

He is wrong! It's a falsehood and a lie!

But there was the evidence too of Captain Lindhurst, who was a true gentleman and too kind to distress me by what he knew. I turned onto my back and stared upwards at the misty shapes of the washing on the rack above my head. I feared it all added up to one conclusion: Mama was with child before she met Papa.

I sat up and counted the months on my fingers, all the while trying to shut out the picture Mrs Walter had painted of gossiping women and their avid faces. The voyage out from England had taken three months. Jamie and I were born in April, two months after Mama and Papa arrived in New Plymouth. That was five months. Mrs Walter said it took nine months for a child to grow. That left four months, and Papa said he had married Mama two weeks after meeting her. He said they sailed for New Zealand four weeks after he met her.

I shivered and huddled the blankets around me, but I would never be warm again, not right down deep where my heart had turned to ice colder than the winds off the mountain.

I got up from my bed, opened the door of the stove and put more wood on the fire. I pulled my mattress close to the bright warmth and lay down, watching the flames.

Four months or four weeks?

A thought hit me with wounding force. If it were indeed four weeks, then Papa wasn't our father and Arama not our brother.

I curled up into the tightest ball I could, holding my arms around my knees and cried myself to sleep.

# 10

## Chapter Ten

There was one week left of the four I was to work, and in the end I was glad I couldn't go home immediately, for it gave me time to think and to grow accustomed to my thoughts about Mama.

I turned it over and over in my mind as I ran after the children, boiled the washing in the copper, hung it to dry, folded it, cooked, cleaned, chatted.

I would only tell Jamie. No, I would find Captain Lindhurst and ask if my horrid suspicions were true. No. I couldn't do that, not when he so clearly hadn't wanted me to know. I would tell Rawinia. But I couldn't, Papa was her husband, it wouldn't be fair. Aunt Frances? No, definitely not. Judith? No.

In the end, I decided to say nothing to anyone, not even Jamie. I pressed my hands over my heart. How quickly I had come to believe the worst about Mama. 'I am so sorry, Mama!' I whispered. I would visit her grave as soon as I reached home.

May drew to a close, and so did my employment with the Walters. On the last Sunday we rose before daylight, loaded the children onto the bullock cart and trundled into town.

Mr Walter paid me my money and by the look on his face it caused him much pain. Mrs Walter paid me many a compliment, and added her tears to those of the children. 'Hannah dearie, you saved my life and that's the truth of it.'

I bade them goodbye. Would there be another baby this time next year? I would have liked to tell Mrs Walter about Polly saying she'd sew together the hem of her nightgown, but I feared she would be shocked.

I turned my steps towards home, choosing to walk the length of Devon Street just for the pleasure of being among people again.

At the pa I stopped to pass the time of day with a group of kuia sitting in the shelter of a verandah smoking their pipes in the sun. The most wrinkled of the women took her pipe from her mouth and pointed the stem at me. 'Hana, that Rawinia needs to find you a good man. You tell her, girl.' She cackled with laughter but that was undoubtedly at the comments of her companions. I heard them and my face burned, even though I was accustomed to such talk when Rawinia's sisters came to visit.

They laughed harder at the redness of my face. 'Ai! She's a real Pakeha after all!'

I scuttled away, mightily discomforted. They were every bit as bad as Aunt Frances. *Why* must I marry?

The oldest kuia shouted after me, 'Ai, girl! A man can

buy you a cloak. Keep you warm when he's not around, eh?'

Their laughter followed me along the road.

It was a relief to reach home. Rawinia hugged me, and the boys ran in from the shed Jamie used for his experiments. 'Hello, Sissy,' Jamie said. 'You've got skinny.'

'Hana, you can come and help us,' Arama said. 'We need another pair of hands.'

Papa came out from his study. His steps were steady but I smelt the whisky as he kissed me, then swept a grand bow. 'Welcome home, daughter! It's too much to hope that your delightful presence sweetened the disposition of Harold Walter, therefore let us not speak of him.' He tucked my hand through his arm and led me into his study. 'Come and tell your papa all about it while Rawinia brews us a pot of tea.'

I went with him, this charming, feckless man who was my father and yet was not. And I kept the precious two pounds and eight shillings of my wages in my pocket.

The next day was the last day of May. 'It's good to have you home again,' Rawinia said as we prepared breakfast.

I wanted her to come into town with me to buy our boots but she wouldn't. 'Aue, that place gives me the shivers. Too many Pakeha. You go. Take a picture of my foot and buy a boot for that.'

She wouldn't change her mind. She put her left foot down on a page of the newspaper, drew around it and handed it to me to cut out. 'There! You buy a boot for that foot.'

I folded it and put it in my pocket with my money. Outside, the day was fine but cloudy and the roads tolerable.

Oh, it was good to be among people again, to be meeting them and talking with them. Ahead of me, three soldiers strolled, raising their hats to every lady they passed. They were not officers but I was sharply reminded that I must keep watch for Captain Hendon.

I saw Lizzie Bevan and Amy Bishop cross the road expressly to engage the men in conversation. Amy noticed me and waved. 'Hannah! I've not seen you since the ball! Is it true you've been working for the Walters?'

The soldiers raised their hats to me as I reached them. The handsome one with the elegant moustache bowed as well. Lizzie shook her shoulders and turned her back to me.

'It is indeed true that I have been employed by the Walters,' I said.

'Are you off to spend your money?' Amy asked.

In answer to Amy's question, I held out my foot to show my boot.

The handsome soldier whistled and said, 'It's a fine, neat ankle she has on her!'

Lizzie decided to join in at that point. She lifted the hem of her skirt, just a little higher than was necessary, to expose her own new boots. The soldier didn't notice, but Amy did and we tried not to laugh as our eyes met.

I couldn't wait any longer. I bade them farewell and walked to Mr Wood's establishment.

Mr Wood himself greeted me, and when I told him what I required, held up a pair of ladies' boots. 'The very latest fashion, young Hannah. Arrived a week back and unpacked this very day.'

'How much do they cost?' I asked. I wanted them so badly, with their shiny leather and the buttons climbing so neatly up the ankle. They would keep my feet warm and dry, and they were ten times nicer than Lizzie's.

'Sixteen shillings and a good bargain at that,' he said.

I could afford them. I felt such freedom, such power to be making this, the very first purchase of my life with my very own money. Mr Wood brought me water and a cloth to wash my feet so that I might try the boots for size. Then I handed him the drawing I had made around Rawinia's foot and he searched his stock until he found a pair that he declared would fit her to perfection.

My feet scarcely touched the dirt of the roads as I walked in my beautiful boots to visit Mama's grave. It lay in the churchyard of St Mary's in Vivian Street and was yet another testimony of how much Aunt Frances had loved her, for it was she and not Papa who had arranged for the headstone.

I picked a bunch of greenery, kissed it and placed it at the foot of the stone.

**Angelina Hannah Carstairs**
**1824—1843**
**Beloved wife of Ronald Carstairs**
**Loved daughter of Sir Hugo and Lady Armitage**
**Mother of James Cecil and Hannah Frances**

The headstone must have been carved before my uncle
and aunt received the letter from Sir Hugo. *Loved daughter.*
Poor Mama.

My heart overflowed. 'Goodbye, Mama,' I whispered
to the make-believe mother who had walked with me
through my childhood. 'Hello, Mama,' I said to the girl
who'd not had time to become my mother. I couldn't
know if she would have loved me as I wished her to. It
was past and time to bid it farewell.

'I'll not disturb you further,' I vowed. 'Keep your
secrets.'

I walked away.

My next call was to visit Aunt Frances and Judith. 'I am
so pleased to see you!' I cried. We embraced and retired
to the kitchen to drink tea and eat scones. They admired
my boots and all the time, I watched Judith closely. She
seemed animated and the colour was back in her cheeks.
I longed to ask about her captain but instead I said, 'Tell
me everything! I've been starved for news.'

Her two youngest brothers, drawn by the prospect of
food, appeared as I spoke. Stanley reached for a scone,
took a bite and said, 'Judith's got a beau. It's famous, he's
visited three times now. Once last week, then . . .'

'Stanley,' said my aunt, 'I suggest you leave the room until you mend your manners.'

He grinned and disappeared, Arnold following him.

I picked up my teacup and sipped decorously. 'The weather has been most unsettled, do you not think?'

Judith and Aunt Frances laughed. 'Very well, you shall know everything,' said my aunt. 'Captain Lindhurst has been most particular in his attentions.'

My cup clattered to the table. 'Judith! That's wonderful, I'm so happy for you. He is almost worthy of winning you and I would not have you marry a clod who will give you child after child and never speak to you from sun up to day's end.'

'Hannah!' gasped my aunt.

I covered my face with my hands. 'I'm sorry. Truly sorry. Forgive me. The past four weeks have been dreadful.' I raised my head. 'Aunt Frances, you would understand if you had been there. You smile when I say I will never marry, but I mean it with all the strength of my heart.'

Judith poured me another cup of tea. 'You'll feel differently when you fall in love. I know you will.'

Aunt Frances said, 'Dear child, I knew this scheme of yours could only end in disaster.'

I shook my head. 'It wasn't a disaster. It was dreadful and that is different from a disaster.' I looked at them, wanting them to understand. 'I learned many things and that cannot be bad.'

Aunt Frances smiled. 'But what you learned were

womanly arts which you will not need since you are determined not to marry.'

'Not those. I don't refer to those,' I said. I looked at Judith. 'I know you don't share my feelings about marriage, but truly I would do all in my power to stop you entering a marriage where you were a slave to your husband, where he demanded his . . .' I glanced at my aunt and spread my hands in frustration. 'Where he had no thought for your feelings. Where he didn't care if you were dead with exhaustion. Where he didn't let you use the brain in your head.'

My words left them pale with shock. At last Aunt Frances asked, with a tremble in her voice, 'Hannah, I must know, has your Papa ever given you the books of Mary Wollstonecraft to read? Has he ever spoken of her ideas?'

I was bewildered. This was a completely unexpected turn in the conversation. 'No, I don't recognise the name.'

'Who is she, Mama?' Judith asked.

Aunt Frances shuddered. 'A female who is a disgrace to our sex.' She shut her mouth tight.

'But why should you think Papa had given me her books?' A hope sprang into my head that perhaps another female thought as I did.

Aunt Frances put her hands flat on the table. 'I will only say this, Hannah. The wild sentiments you have just uttered bear such a similarity to her seditious volumes that I thought your Papa must have allowed, nay, encouraged you to read them.'

'No, Aunt Frances, I promise you, he has never mentioned her name.' But he would, for I intended to ask him about her that very evening.

'It's a fortunate thing she died young. She was a most immoral person.' She dropped her voice. 'She actually lived with a man without being married to him. I only tell you such an unsavoury tale to show you the sort of woman she was.'

'I see,' I said. 'Thank you. I understand.'

'Hannah! You've gone quite pale!' Judith jumped up and put an arm around my shoulders. 'Are you well?'

I reached up and clasped her hand. 'I think I'm a little weary. It has been a hard four weeks.'

Somehow, I extricated myself from their concern and walked home. I could never go to Aunt Frances with my suspicions about Mama. How could I say to her: *Aunt Frances, I believe Mama was with child before she met Papa. Do you know who our father could be?*

I scrubbed at my forehead. What was I thinking of? Had I not come that very afternoon from my mother's grave where I vowed to let the secrets of the past stay buried?

Captain Hendon's hateful words resounded in my head. *Consider your mother. You scarcely come from a respectable background.*

A wail of pain rose from deep inside me. It couldn't be true that Mama had behaved in such an immoral fashion. I stumbled down the road, the pleasure of my new boots quite dimmed. All I felt now was a terrible aching void and over it, thick and dark, was a stain reaching out from beyond my mother's grave to engulf me in its murk.

I think I spoke to people as I walked home. I have a vague memory of Polly's friend Freda Bell talking to me. I think she told me her sawyer husband had lost the top of yet another finger, but I can't be sure, for the turmoil in my head prevented me from listening properly.

Rawinia's joy in her new boots settled me somewhat. 'We won't put these where your papa will notice them,' she said. She opened the cupboard where we kept the linen. 'In here, right at the bottom.'

I spoke to Papa that evening about Mary Wollstonecraft. His reply was not what I had hoped for. 'I'm shocked, Hannah! Shocked that your aunt would sully your ears with that woman's name!'

'Papa, that's no answer. Where is the logic and reason in an answer such as that?' The prospect of a good argument restored my spirits.

He blinked at me while the others chuckled. 'Very well, very well.' He thought for a moment. 'She died around sixty years ago now. Her ideas haven't caught on, which should tell you something.'

'Papa! What ideas? Tell us!'

He grumbled but complied. 'Thought women should have the vote. Lot of nonsense.' He waved a hand at me. 'Don't shout at me again, child. Here's the nub of the matter that Frances spoke of. That woman, Mary Wollstonecraft, was against marriage. Said it kept women ignorant and made slaves out of 'em. Lot of nonsense.'

But it did! It was exactly as I'd seen in the Walters' house. 'Papa, she is right!' I outlined my arguments most convincingly.

He would not be convinced. 'I'm with Frances on this one, child, although I'd thank you not to tell her as much. Women are made different from men, for which we may offer thanks to whatever deity we happen to believe in. It's your nature to care, to bear children, to look after your husband. Can't escape it. Better accept it.'

Rawinia said, 'It's what men have to believe if they want a warm bed and a full belly.'

Jamie grinned at me. 'I'll take care not to wed a girl like you. I'd never have a moment's peace!'

I mulled it all over when I went to bed. Papa must have wed Mama and brought her over here away from her disgrace. Had she told him she was with child? Did my grandparents know and is that why they cast her out?

I tossed and turned in the bed, until at last I slept, waking in the morning none the wiser.

# 11

## Chapter Eleven

There was no more work for me and the days passed as winter days did, without much excitement or variety, although in July Aunt Frances bought Jamie and me tickets to a concert where Judith sang most charmingly.

Captain Lindhurst bowed over her hand afterwards and the words he uttered earned him a shy but dazzling smile. Captain Hendon lounged in a chair on the far side of the room and behaved with the utmost propriety except for sneering at me on the one occasion when he knew himself to be unobserved.

Hartley Pitts and Jimmy Lang called to take tea with us the evening after the concert. We played cards and neither Jamie nor I thought to mention to Rawinia that Aunt Frances would certainly not approve of us playing poker.

The following week, Jamie surprised me by purchasing a ball ticket for me paid for from his own money.

'Jamie! I am overcome! How kind of you!'

He grinned. 'A chap has to look to his sister, even one with such odd notions as those you keep in your noddle.'

Once again, I went to Aunt Frances's to get dressed in my finery. It was a day of scudding showers, I was glad of my boots as I walked the muddy roads to Brougham Street.

Judith's face glowed and she was so dreamy we could get no sense out of her. Aunt Frances put a hairbrush in her hand and pushed her down into the chair in front of her dressing table. 'Sit there and brush your hair, Judith. And do try to concentrate!' But she seemed to forget mid-stroke what she was doing. I don't think she noticed when we left the room.

I fastened the buttons down the back of Aunt Frances's smart gown of grey and white striped silk and said, 'Judith is very much in love.'

Aunt Frances smiled at me in the mirror. 'He is a most suitable man. I could not have wished for better. Thank you, Hannah dear; now let me fasten your dress.'

I turned so she could do up the buttons. How differently I felt now about wearing Mama's gown. Was this the dress she wore when she met the man with whom she had been so indiscreet? The man who had fathered Jamie and me?

Aunt Frances brought me back from my uncomfortable musings. 'All we need now, Hannah, is an equally suitable and charming young man for you.'

I laughed and shook my head. 'Aunt Frances, have you considered? If Judith weds the captain, she will have to live far away.'

She smiled. 'He has talked to your uncle of his hopes.

It is his earnest wish to leave the army in a year or two and settle in New Zealand. He declares he has quite fallen in love with the country.'

'Oh!' I said, frowning as I thought about it. 'But Judith would go away with him until he comes back?'

My aunt laughed at me. 'Heavens, child, it is much too soon to be making plans. It's true he pays attention to Judith, but I assure you it is nothing to give rise to gossip, despite what her brothers may say!'

It unsettled me to think that Judith might leave the country, that she might even go to England where she would enter the world of polite society. I pulled down my mouth and sighed. The captain would never have cause to blush over his wife's behaviour if he did marry her.

We had to swathe ourselves in cloaks and shelter under umbrellas in order to arrive at the ball with our clothing dry, for the showers turned to rain in the evening, becoming heavy a half hour after we arrived. This ball was held in the big corrugated iron building in Devon Street and the noise of the rain on the iron all but drowned out the music.

I looked around me, my heart lifting. How lovely it was to be with so many people. I thought of Polly and of Mrs Walter in their lonely houses.

'Hannah!'

I whirled around, not believing my ears. 'Polly? Can it be you? What are you doing here?' I embraced her, laughing with pleasure at seeing her.

'We thought we'd give ourselves a treat. Peter

borrowed the neighbour's bullock cart. We've left young Thomas with the Bells, and here we are!' She gestured at her dress. 'It's not exactly a ball dress, but Peter says I look lovely. But then, it's what he would say.'

Her dress was of fine wool, printed with a red and blue pattern. The sleeves were long and the neck high. An afternoon dress rather than an evening one, but not the only one in the room. 'You do look lovely,' I assured her.

'And look at yourself!' she said. 'The men will knock me down in the rush to write on your card.'

I grinned. 'You've been quite safe so far.'

But it wasn't long before I had several names on my card, including that of Captain Lindhurst. 'May I have the pleasure of a dance, Miss Carstairs?'

I curtseyed. 'Indeed you may, kind sir.'

He laughed and I didn't notice until he had moved on to chat with Judith that he had written his name opposite the second waltz. I glanced at him, wondering why he hadn't claimed Judith's hand for both the waltzes. Perhaps he didn't want to appear too particular in his attentions in public.

I had wondered if Captain Hendon would be there, but he didn't appear and I gave myself up to sheer enjoyment. Jamie, I saw with great interest, now hovered attentively around Amy Bishop. Lavender, meanwhile found much to laugh at in the company of Vernon Yates.

I danced the first waltz with a shy lieutenant who blushed whenever I spoke. It was a relief to dance with Hartley Pitts. He bowed and led me onto the floor for the polka. 'I say,

Hannah, if you ever want to wed, think of me will you?'

As a proposal of marriage it had charm and originality. 'Indeed I will, for you are the most kind-hearted person I know. But I must tell you that my mind is set against marriage.'

He pulled his mouth down and crossed his eyes at me. 'I feared it. There's something different about the way you look at a chap.'

I was vastly intrigued. 'Is there now? And what might that be?'

He grinned. 'Can't put it into words. There just is.'

I sat out two of the dances, for tonight there were more young ladies than men, but I chatted with Polly who declared she was getting too old for capering around the floor.

At supper, Judith handed me a plate with a cake on it. 'Hannah, is he not handsome?'

I teased her. 'Who, Judith? To whom do you refer?' Her face shone so brightly she nearly dimmed the candles. I leaned close and whispered, 'Has he spoken? Am I to congratulate you?'

She shook her head, her eyes fixed on her captain. 'No, he has said nothing. Not yet.'

It was plain she expected he would. I hoped she was right.

She smiled at us both when he bowed over my hand and led me onto the floor for the waltz.

The music started. I looked up at him after we had completed several steps. 'You dance divinely, Captain

Lindhurst. Is it a particularly military accomplishment? Do you undergo dancing drills?'

He laughed. 'It's a most useful activity for it brings us into charming company.'

I asked, 'Do you get weary of life in the barracks?'

We completed a particularly dashing turn before he replied. 'Sometimes, Miss Carstairs, I quite despair of such a life. It seems to me to serve no useful purpose.'

'May we execute another of those turns?' I begged. 'Then I promise you I will make some intelligent reply.'

He chuckled all the time he swirled me around and around in a double turn. 'There! I now await my payment.'

It was my turn to laugh. 'I fear it will be paltry. But I suggest it is your purpose to be trained and ready so that you may act when the need arises. Although . . .' I stopped, recollecting this was not Papa I was debating with.

'Although? Miss Carstairs, you cannot stop there. There will not be another turn if you do and we will collide with the wall!'

I smiled. 'Very well, you leave me no choice. I was going to say that your uniforms are most unsuitable.'

'A statement deserving of another turn.' We glided and laughed as we danced. 'Now give me your reasons.'

I spoke before I thought. 'The red coats in the green bush. What a target they would make. Far better to wear the traditional war dress of the Maori.' I gasped and sent him a glance. Did he know what the traditional war dress of the Maori was?

It would seem that he did, for he roared with laughter.

I could not help but smile too at the image of the British military naked except for the war belts that would hold their weapons. He chuckled for the duration of the dance. 'Oh, Miss Carstairs! How I would like to see you at work in an English drawing room!'

He led me back to where Judith waited beside my aunt. 'Miss Woodley, I return your friend to you.' He bowed to her. 'And now we have the two prettiest girls in the room sitting side by side.'

I was puzzled. Gone was the laughing man I had danced with and instead he had become just another army officer who mouthed meaningless compliments. Judith, however, smiled and glowed. She cast down her eyes and murmured that he was too good.

I thought about it in the days that followed and was conscious of a feeling of disappointment in the captain. It was obvious that he sought a wife who would not cause him to blush were she to be let loose in an English drawing room. Was he interested in Judith's opinions? He couldn't be, for in his presence she never articulated any.

I could see her in my mind saying, *Yes dear. No dear. Whatever you think best, dear.* She would chat with her friends and be one of those irritating women who said *my husband thinks* . . .

I vowed that somehow I would one day read the work of the scandalous Mary Wollstonecraft.

The spring winds of September blew rain through the cracks in the walls and shredded the petals on the cherry trees in the garden. I had no further work and we used the last of our flour to bake four loaves of bread on the first Tuesday of September.

Papa was unconcerned. 'The money will arrive any day now.' There were floods in the Waikato apparently, and the Maori runners could not get through from Auckland with the mail. 'Anyone will give you credit. They know my circumstances.'

The merchants knew only too well and probably compared how much he owed each of them for none would offer more credit.

'We'll buy the flour,' Arama said, and Jamie nodded without looking up from the drawing he was making of a machine for sawing logs.

'Good lads,' Papa said, clapping his hat on his head. 'I'll pay you back. Of course.'

'Of course, Papa,' Jamie said.

The boys had by now taken their money from the garden and deposited it in the Taranaki Savings Bank which opened for business every Friday evening between the hours of six and eight pm and so we had to wait for three days before they could get the money.

'It isn't right,' I raged to Rawinia. 'They shouldn't have to spend their own money to feed us.'

Rawinia shrugged. 'It's how things are. Other boys support their families.'

But boys like Hartley did so from necessity, not so their fathers could drink away an entire livelihood.

It then occurred to me that for all these years Papa

had supported Jamie and me, and we were not his own flesh and blood. I couldn't sort out my feelings. I took my usual remedy of going to the wood heap and chopping until I calmed myself.

'Jamie,' I said that evening, 'the axe is blunt.'

'And the woodpile is bigger than I've seen it for many a day,' he retorted, but he fetched the axe, the stone and the oil and sat sharpening it while Papa read to us. Tonight he chose the poems of Byron, for Rawinia was particularly fond of them.

But somehow during my chopping that afternoon, I had reached a decision. I would keep what I knew of our history to myself.

# 12

## Chapter Twelve

The next day Dr Feilding called on me again. 'Mrs Andrews is ill,' he said as he drank the tea Rawinia poured for him. 'She's got a child of fourteen months and another due before the month is out. Mr Andrews says he'll pay fifteen shillings a week and will you stay till the baby comes?'

I stayed in that house for two weeks and three days. But the baby didn't come. It died along with its mother. After the funeral I walked home with my money in my pocket and my bag in my hand. I had thought to call in at Brougham Street to visit Aunt Frances and Judith but instead I went home and burst into tears all over Rawinia, who scolded and told me it was foolishness to go out and work. 'No good will come of it, and so I tell you.' She made me tea and fussed over me until I was calmer.

It was good to be home.

We talked of the fabric we would buy with the money I'd earned. Rawinia wanted red, but I wanted a dress that held the blue of the summer skies, the green of the bush and the golden light of the sun. Rawinia turned her mouth down and shook her head. 'Ai! Where do you get such fancy ideas from, Hana girl?'

I was restless and I wanted things I couldn't have, things that would always be out of my reach. Things like the knowledge of who my father was, and of why Papa had married Mama.

So many questions but if I could choose to have the answer to just one, I would ask to know why Mama had behaved as she did. Why had she, my own dear mama, behaved in such an immoral fashion?

There. I had articulated it in my thoughts and there it would have to stay, for even thinking it left me cold and sullied in my heart.

'I can't stay inside today,' I said to Rawinia. 'I'll weed the vegetable garden.'

The warmth of the sun soothed me and I laughed at the fantails darting at insects I disturbed. It was good to laugh again.

The sun set and the air cooled. The boys would be home. I was in no hurry for their noisy company but the chill drove me indoors.

I flung open the kitchen door, the words of greeting dying on my lips. Jamie stood by the fire, drying his naked body while Arama was in the act of stepping into the tub Jamie had just vacated.

A million thoughts spun through my brain, settling into one, solid notion. Arama wasn't my brother and I should not look upon his unclad body. I cried out, turned and ran from the room back outside into the cold evening.

Through the open door, I heard Jamie's voice. 'Sissy? What's wrong? Come back!'

I kept running and seconds later found myself huddled in among Rawinia's flax plants in the hiding place we'd used as children.

They found me there, my brothers. They pulled at my arms, dragging me to my feet. 'Aue! I've grown ugly,' Arama mourned. 'So ugly that my own sister runs from me.' He shook his head. 'I'll never get to wed a nice Pakeha girl now.'

'I tell you what, Hannah,' Jamie said. 'You're turning into one of those squeamish girls. Screeching and running from your own brothers.'

I beat my fists on their shoulders. 'But that's just it! You're not my brothers. Oh, Jamie, you are, of course you are. But Arama . . .' I pulled myself away in order to stand back and face them, 'but Arama is not our brother. Jamie, we are not Papa's children and I hadn't meant to tell you, either of you. I'm sorry. I'm sorry.' I covered my face with hands still grubby from the garden. Great heaving sobs tore at my body. I tried to scrub away the tears.

Jamie took my hands and held them. 'Calm yourself, Sissy. You're hysterical.'

Arama said, 'Rawinia's right, going out to work's turned your brain.'

I sobbed harder.

Rawinia called from the house, 'Come inside! You'll catch your deaths out there.'

I turned to run in the other direction, but the boys

seized my arms and marched me back to the house.

Rawinia took one look at me, sat me down, picked up a damp towel and scrubbed my face clean, talking and scolding all the time. Jamie put a glass into my hand, 'Drink.'

I drank, but he hadn't warned me it was whisky and I nearly choked.

'Coughing is better than crying,' Arama observed.

Into this scene of domestic mayhem walked Papa. He stopped on the threshold, rocking slightly, his hat in his hand. 'What is going on here? Can't a man come home to an orderly household?' His eyes tracked over the tub still in front of the fire, the damp towels, the whisky glass beside me on the table.

'Hello, Papa,' I said, but my voice hiccupped on a sob.

The boys picked up the tub, walking around Papa to empty it outside. Rawinia took the cloth from the dresser and flicked it expertly across the table. 'Sit down. We'll eat.'

Papa threw his hat and sat down. 'We can't have you going out to work, Hannah, if you upset the entire household on your return. Not, of course, that I'm not delighted to see you. I've missed your cheery presence, your delightful face, your incisive arguments.' He tucked a table napkin under his chin. 'No doubt you have a compelling reason for the current upset?'

I was aware of the others watching me, their eyes wary.

I used my incisive brain to think up a plausible reason for my distress. 'Papa, it was Mrs Andrews. She died and left her little daughter motherless. My thoughts have been so much with her and with what happened to my own dear mama. I'm afraid I became overwrought with the relief of being home again.'

He patted my head. 'There, there. It's a sad thing for a child to lose a mother. I would give you a whisky to calm your nerves, child, except that I see someone has had the forethought to do so already.'

We ate our dinner with no further discussion of my behaviour. Papa spoke at length about the imminent arrival of the quarter day money. 'We'll celebrate,' he promised. 'Rawinia, dove of my heart, I'll buy you the best pair of boots to be had in the town.'

'When you've paid your creditors,' she said.

He pretended not to hear. Instead, he promised me a new cloak.

I excused myself as soon as Rawinia and I had finished the dishes for I was weary unto death. I slid into my bed and slept.

I awoke in the morning to a shining spring day. My spirits rose with the sun. I was home. I was away from that house of sorrow. I danced out to the kitchen. 'You're singing a different song this morning,' Rawinia said, giving me a beady-eyed look.

The boys merely grunted a greeting and applied them-selves to their food. The foolishness of their sister belonged to yesterday and they would not mention it again. I was grateful.

But I reckoned wrongly. They left the house at the same

time as usual, with the clock striking seven but returned half an hour later. Jamie ran in the door calling, 'You're coming with us today to visit Polly.'

Rawinia pushed my outdoor clothes into my hands. 'Hurry along now. You don't want to hold them up.'

They had arranged all this last night? To give me a treat, or to wring the truth out of me about my strange behaviour?

We went outside. Arama sat astride the horse he and Jamie always rode, and he held the reins of a second horse. 'Borrowed it,' he said, grinning at me.

Jamie tossed me up into the saddle and we were off. From time to time, I glanced at the boys. It didn't seem that they were curious. Perhaps I had wronged them, perhaps they really *did* only want to give me a treat.

I didn't believe it though, not in my heart, and my heart was right. When we were halfway along the beach between New Plymouth and Omata, they stopped and slid from the horse.

Jamie caught hold of my bridle. 'The horses need a break.'

I slid from my horse and handed the reins to Jamie. 'Must I tell you?'

That didn't even get me a reply, only a pair of incredulous looks. I gave in, and truth to tell, I wanted them to know. I hoped they would give me a different explanation from the only one I could think of. I prayed that they would laugh at my ideas, and scold me for my evil thoughts about Mama.

With my hands pressed tight against my heart, I poured out my sorry suspicions. 'My head is all tied up in knots with trying to make it untrue, but I cannot! I cannot!'

They said nothing for quite some moments. The waves thumped in beside us, birds screeched overhead. The world kept turning.

At last, Jamie whistled and shook his head as if to clear it. Arama kicked at the sand. 'It's true about babies? How long it takes? You're sure?'

I nodded. 'Quite sure.'

Jamie picked up a stick. I thought it was to do sums with on the sand, but he just scribbled with it, then jabbed it fiercely down. 'It would explain why Papa favours you,' he said, looking at Arama.

Arama shrugged. 'It could explain why I look like I'm his son and you don't.'

I put my hands over my ears. 'Don't! Don't look for reasons to support it! It's a preposterous idea! Tell me I'm wrong. Tell me I'm wicked for thinking such things.' I gasped in a sob. 'Tell me that Mama was not immoral!'

I had said it. I, her daughter had branded her with a vile name.

I think Jamie didn't even hear my pleas, for he continued with his train of thought. 'Her father must have known she was with child.' He tugged at his hair. 'And we are her hell-born brats. Bastards.' He spat out the last word.

We stared at him. I couldn't find the voice to ask him why he minded so much being illegitimate. How could it matter when nobody knew?

Arama punched his shoulder. 'She was your mother. Your ancestor. Show her respect.'

Jamie didn't answer. He kicked the stick out of the sand, then wheeled and ran, full speed off down the beach.

I looked at Arama. He shrugged. 'I don't know. He's never worried before about your mama.'

We found rocks to sit on and waited until Jamie returned. 'Let's go,' he said curtly. 'We're already late.'

Arama and I glanced at each other and stayed right where we were.

Jamie slammed his hat into his hand in exasperation, but then he sighed and shrugged. 'Very well. I suppose you've a right to know.' He threw himself down on the sand beside us. I bit my tongue on telling him his clothes would become damp. 'I want to go to England. I thought I could find Papa's family, or maybe even some of Mama's; uncles, that sort of thing. I need connections — somebody to introduce me to influential engineers. I want to build with iron. I want . . .' He stopped and when he spoke again his voice had lost its passion. 'It was a dream. And not the sort of dream a bastard child should have.'

My thoughts tumbled like the waves. I hadn't known he wanted to go to England. I hadn't known illegitimacy would matter. I wanted to protest, to say nobody would care. But I knew my words would be false.

Arama stood up. 'We must go. Peter will think we do not work today.' He stood over me. 'You are still my sister. You still do as I tell you.'

I struggled to my feet. 'Yes, brother. I hear you.' Tears stung my eyes.

Jamie climbed onto his horse, all the fierce energy of his being quenched.

I wished with all my heart that I'd said nothing, but it was done and there was no going back. The problem was, what to do now? 'We need to find out,' I said.

Jamie's sarcasm withered me. 'Exactly how do you propose to do that? Ask Aunt Frances for a list of the men Mama flirted with?'

I winced. He was trampling the torn remnants of my heart. When we arrived at the Herberts' my eyes were raw from crying, Jamie's face was stony and Arama kept shaking his head.

Polly greeted me with joy that turned to concern when she saw my tears.

'Tell her,' Jamie ordered, striding off towards the home paddock, Arama following him.

Polly clucked and fussed, just like Rawinia did. 'You'll tell me nothing until we're sitting down with a good cup of tea and a scone.'

I played with Thomas David as she made the tea and whipped cream for the scones. I let her chatter wash over me and soothe me.

'There now! Get that inside you!'

I couldn't, not until I'd told her the sorry tale of Mama. 'And I didn't even know Jamie wanted to go to England,' I sobbed. 'And he needs connections, people who will introduce him to engineers but now they won't because he's illegitimate and they'll be like Mama's father and refuse to recognise him.'

Polly took Tommy from me. 'Come on, Hannah. Drink up, and eat something too. I declare you're looking right peaky.'

I took a scone and spooned jam and cream onto it. I thought it would choke me, but I discovered I was hungry. 'Polly, what can we do?'

'We'll think about it,' she said. 'I confess that nothing comes into my mind immediately.'

We passed the morning pleasantly and I told her all the gossip of the town. All the time, though, I could tell her mind was busy with the problem of Jamie and me. My spirits rose. There must be something we could do, some way out of the coil of our parentage.

We took lunch to Peter and the boys. Jamie didn't come over immediately, but kept chopping at a tree trunk with furious energy. Peter pushed his hat back on his head. 'He's been like that all morning.'

I'd just finished telling him why when Jamie gave in and came over to throw himself down beside us.

'Has an idea flown into your head?' Arama asked Polly.

She shook her head. 'I can't think of anything useful at all, I'm afraid.'

Peter held out his plate for another slice of pigeon pie. 'Seems to me the only thing to do is write to the man your ma was supposed to marry. Can you find out who he was?'

I nodded. 'Aunt Frances would know.'

Polly clapped her hands. 'Peter! That is exactly what they should do! Oh, you are so clever!' She turned to us, eyes sparkling. 'This man will have no reason to think well of your mama, please excuse me for saying so. He might be very happy to tell you any gossip there was about her.'

The thought of action stimulated Jamie's appetite. He chewed on his piece of pie and stared at nothing. At last he said, 'Very well, we'll do it. If our father was a man of consequence he might feel guilty about what he did to Mama. He might just be prepared to help me.'

Arama brought him back to reality. 'He might be a slave. An ordinary person. Very handsome, of course, but not a high-born rangatira.'

'Thank you, brother,' Jamie said, but I was deeply relieved to see that the despair had vanished.

Polly and I worked on the letter during the afternoon. It wasn't easy to compose and we wrote many attempts along the margins of three newspaper pages before we were satisfied.

*Honoured Sir,*

*We send you this letter in the hope that you will be able to help us discover our father.*

*We are the twin children of Angelina Carstairs (née Armitage). Until very recently we believed our father was the man who raised us, namely Ronald Carstairs, but now we have reason to think this is not the case. We were born on April 18th in the year 1843. Our mother died the day we were born. We cannot apply to her family for information, for our grandfather, in response to a letter telling him of her death, stated he would have nothing to do with us.*

*With respectful thanks,*
*Hannah Carstairs.*

At the end of the day, Jamie read the letter, nodded once and signed it.

'Your name should come first,' Arama said. 'The man is more important.'

Jamie shrugged. 'He isn't going to worry about that.' He tapped the letter. 'How long must we wait before we can expect a reply?'

'Seven months by my reckoning,' Peter said.

Jamie counted on his fingers. 'April. It will be a fine birthday gift.'

'Jamie, he might not reply. He may regard us as hell-born brats as well.' His optimism worried me.

He grinned at me. 'And maybe he won't. Let's send this and see.'

'First we have to ask Aunt Frances for his name,' I said.

He tugged at the plait hanging down my back. 'You can do that. It would look odd if I suddenly showed an interest.'

I glared at him. I didn't want to raise the subject with Aunt Frances, yet I knew he was right.


I visited the Woodley house the next afternoon and found Judith and my aunt working among the vegetables in the garden.

My aunt straightened her back and smiled at me. 'Hannah! It is delightful to see you, for you give us an excuse to stop for a cup of tea.'

I held out my hand to help her up, then looked at Judith. 'Is there any news? Anything important that I may not have heard?'

She laughed and shook her head, but her eyes sparkled so I deduced that the captain continued to be attentive.

We walked into the house and my aunt said, 'It must have been difficult for you, Hannah, to be caring for little Maria Andrews. So tragic that her dear mother was taken. She was a charming young woman and very genteel. I always felt she married below her station, worthy though her husband is, of course.'

'Mama!' Judith protested. 'He loved her devotedly. What can it matter what his station was?'

My aunt was firm in opinion. 'It does matter, my dear, more than you can understand. If a man and wife come from similar backgrounds the chances of domestic harmony are almost assured.'

I wished desperately to defend Mr Andrews and tell my aunt of his love for his wife, but I saw a chance to divert the conversation towards the question Jamie and I needed answered. 'Aunt, I have often wondered but never thought to ask you, who was the man Mama was supposed to marry? Was he of her station?'

Aunt Frances began fussing with the teapot, then the sugar bowl. 'Goodness, child! Why do you ask?'

Judith's eyes were on me too, bright and questioning.

'Oh, it was something Papa said, the day I took the letter home, the one our grandfather sent you. Papa said they tried to sell her to the highest bidder. What did he mean? He will not tell us anything and it is most frustrating.' I screwed up my face and tried to look as if it were mere curiosity that prompted my question.

My aunt sighed. 'Your papa was right, in a way. But I think Angelina was happy to marry him. You must understand that her betrothal came after we had sailed to New Zealand and I never saw them together so cannot fairly judge.'

Judith leaned forward and asked, 'But who was he, Mama? Was he a man of consequence? Of wealth? Of position? Titled?'

'Oh yes, all of those,' my aunt said. 'And handsome too, if Angelina's letters were true.'

Judith and I stared at each other, then she giggled, 'Just think! You could have been the daughter of a – Mama, what was his title?'

Aunt Frances paused for a moment as if she were thinking whether or not to tell us, but then she sighed. 'It can't hurt for you to know. He was Lord Derringford. He was wealthy. He had large estates and he'd also invested in the railways. Your grandparents were delighted with the match, both for the money and the title.'

I was silent. Such a man could not have ravished a gently born girl and abandoned her, therefore we must be the children of . . . who? The butler, perhaps? A farm worker? An artist engaged to paint her likeness?

Judith asked, 'How is it that you never met him, Mama? Did he live far away?'

My aunt shook her head. 'His country estate was in Devon, but you must understand that while Angelina and I both went to the same school, we were not really in the same circles. My papa was a parson and there wasn't the money for me to be going to the fashionable balls and assemblies where I might have met Lord Derringford.'

I thanked my aunt, then turned the subject to a discussion of patterns for the dresses Rawinia and I would make. I managed to chat about sleeve widths and fabrics while my mind tussled with the question of Lord Derringford. I doubted it would be worth the cost of the postage to send the letter.

Jamie, when I told him, was of the same opinion. 'Our grandfather would have forced him to marry her. He cannot be our father and I doubt that he would know who was.'

I left the letter in the drawer of my dressing table to gather dust along with the horrid letter from my grandfather. That night, dreams haunted me and for much of the night I lay awake, my mind troubled. By the morning I reached a decision about the letter. I would post it. Jamie need not know. What harm could it do?

Accordingly, that very day, I carried the letter into town, walked to the post office, paid the money and sent the letter to Lord Derringford, County of Devon, England.

I had no idea if it would reach him, but I was pleased I had tried.

# 13

## Chapter Thirteen

The weather in the last week of October, apart from a day of heavy rain, was hot and sunny enough to remind me that summer was not far off and I would need my new dress.

Judith came with me to purchase the material. I bought a bright tartan with much red in the pattern for Rawinia. For myself I seized upon the prettiest of muslins printed with dainty pink and blue flowers. Judith applauded the choice for myself but could scarcely bring herself to look at the tartan.

I grinned at her. 'Rawinia will love it. That's all that matters.'

She shuddered but made no protest.

We left the shop and strolled along Devon Street in the bright sunshine. It was Saturday and the town was busy. We stepped aside to allow Mr Randell to drive his cows past us to the auction further down the street. He raised his hat to us. 'Good day, young ladies. Watch your step now.' He gestured at the ground where the cows had left evidence of their passing.

Many farmers were in town. I looked for Peter but did not see him.

Judith put her hand on my arm and whispered. 'Lizzie Bevan! She is all questions and sly hints. I cannot abide her.'

I had no time to reply for Lizzie, Caroline Spring in tow, bore down upon us. 'Good morning, Judith. Good morning, Hannah.'

Judith murmured a reply. I said, 'And a lovely morning it is.'

Lizzie wasted no time on idle chat. 'I hear a certain captain visited your house again last week, Judith. When may we expect an interesting announcement?'

Poor Judith's cheeks flushed, but my heart swelled with indignation. I hurried into speech. 'You mean Captain Lindhurst, Lizzie? May he not visit where he chooses? He visited my house last week too but I notice that you do not make your sly suggestions to me!' I leaned close and prodded her with my forefinger. 'Why not, may I ask? Do you think I am not sufficiently respectable? Do you think no man of honour could be serious about me?'

Lizzie tossed her head and stuck the thin, aristocratic nose she was so proud of in the air. 'Don't give yourself airs, Hannah Carstairs. I know what I know.'

She jerked at her skirts, pulling them away from my contaminating presence and walked off, Caroline trailing behind her.

Judith breathed a sigh of relief. 'Thank you, Hannah. I never know what to say to her.'

I shifted my parcel so that I could slide my arm through hers. 'You have to be firm with her. Attack is the best weapon with that one.'

'I'll remember,' she said, then she glanced at me. 'You did not tell me the captain had visited you.'

'For the very good reason that he did no such thing and I can think of no reason why he should.' I squeezed her arm. 'And you will notice, my dear friend, that I do not ask a single question of you and neither do I make the slightest of hints!'

I hoped she would tell me something, however small, but she merely said again, 'Thank you, Hannah.'

Her younger brothers, when I encountered them on my way home, were not nearly so reticent. I heard feet pounding along behind me as I approached the corner of Leach Street, and Stanley's voice calling to me, 'Hannah! We wish to talk to you! Wait!'

Obligingly, I stopped. There had to be some mischief behind this most flattering desire for my company, and so I told them.

Stanley grinned. 'No mischief, I promise you.'

Arnold, I noticed, didn't endorse Stanley's cheerful promise. I eyed him, my brows raised.

'It isn't mischief, truly it isn't,' he assured me.

'Out with it then,' I said, for truth to tell I was by now most curious.

A look passed between them. Arnold briefly inclined his head, a signal which launched his younger brother into speech. 'We want to know if Sister has told you whether the captain means to marry her.'

I put my hands on my hips. 'And what, pray tell, is your reason for wanting to know your sister's private business?'

Arnold dropped his eyes, but not so Stanley. 'You sound just like Mama, Hannah!' He looked at me reproachfully. 'We were sure you would help us.'

I regarded the scruffy pair of urchins in front of me. Stanley had ripped a button on his coat loose. I reached out and pulled it off. 'Put this in your pocket and don't forget to give it to my aunt. And now tell me exactly why it would help you to know about the captain and your sister?'

Arnold recovered his tongue. 'The thing is, Hannah, that old Mr Farnham has offered us odds that the captain won't pop the question until Easter. We stand to win a lot of money if we say he will do it by Christmas, but Christmas is only two months away and . . .'

He broke off at my shout of laughter. I was vastly entertained. My aunt would be shocked to her soul. 'Alas, I cannot help you,' I told them, 'for Judith tells me nothing.'

'Oh!' They were disappointed but cheerful. 'You won't tell Mama or Papa, will you?'

I should do so, there was no doubt in my mind, but I knew I would not and I gave them my promise. 'Do you like the captain?' I asked, curious to know how he would appear to boys of thirteen and eleven.

'Lord yes, he's a great gun. Talks to Stanley and me like we're real people and not just pesky nuisances.'

'That settles it,' I said, laughing. 'Any man who is pre-pared to spend time and effort with you two is definitely hoping to marry your sister. But as to when, only he can know.'

I went on my way chuckling. My laughter died. Was it real then? Was my friend about to become a married lady?

My spirits rose again with Rawinia's pleasure at my choice of material. That very evening we cut out our dresses using paper patterns my aunt had procured for us.

November came with a spell of fine, warm weather. We worked in the garden hoeing up the potatoes and keeping ahead of the weeds in the rest of the garden. In the evenings, Rawinia and I stitched our dresses while Papa read to us. I wanted to hear *Jane Eyre*, but he declared the Brontë sisters were a scandalous trio and refused to read it. Instead, he read us *David Copperfield* which the boys declared to be better than anything a woman could write.

I pondered and puzzled during the evenings it took to finish the book. Papa was so strict in his notions of propriety that I found it more and more difficult to believe he could have wed Mama when she was unmarried and with child by another man. I mentioned it to Jamie but he simply hunched a shoulder at me. 'Leave it, Hannah. We will never learn the truth, and I'm glad of it.'

I didn't bring the subject up again, and neither did I confess to him that I had sent the letter to Lord Derringford. It saddened me that once again, my beloved brother's ideas were so far away from my own. I would willingly risk being labelled a bastard if only I could discover the truth. But, unlike him, I had nothing to lose by such a discovery. Would I feel differently if, for example, the captain had chosen me instead of Judith? Would I be in agony wondering if I should tell him of the disgrace of my parentage?

I did not know, but such ideas allowed me to understand Jamie a little better. All in all, I was deeply relieved that marriage was not for me.

But if I was not to marry, then I must find some way of earning my living. I went to the merchants in town and asked each of them for work. There was nothing.

However, only a week later Papa came home with the news that Mrs Heskith had approached him. 'Said she's feeling her age. Wants a strong and willing girl to help her. Asked me to tell you.' He rocked on his heels and regarded me quizzically. 'Are you strong and willing, Hannah?'

I assured him that I was. I gave him back my own quizzical look. 'You stare at me so, Papa! Is it me you look at, or is it the granddaughter of Sir Hugo Armitage turned into a shop girl that you see?'

He roared with laughter. 'By gad, Hannah, you're sharp!' He threw his hat at the chair and sat himself down at the dinner table, still chuckling.

Jamie and Arama entertained themselves all evening by playing at being customers. Before I fell asleep that night I tried to imagine myself in England with Jamie. It disturbed me that I could picture Jamie there building bridges and railways, but I couldn't see myself there surrounded by servants, chandeliers, silks, satins and money.

I was to start at Mrs Heskith's shop on Monday. I put on my blue cotton dress and presented myself.

Mrs Heskith greeted me warmly. 'On time and tidy. A good beginning, Hannah Carstairs. We shall do very well together.'

And so we did. She threw instructions at me. 'Dust those shelves, Hannah dearie. And wipe the crockery. I declare the dirt that comes in from the road is enough to make a body weep.'

Late in the morning I served my first customer. It was Lizzie Bevan who, once she got over her surprise at seeing me, advanced with a look of glee on her face. 'Get me three yards of pink silk ribbon, Hannah and don't keep me waiting.' She slapped her gloves into her hand and tapped her foot.

I curtseyed to her. 'Yes miss. No miss.'

She shot me a look and decided to stop playing the grand lady. 'Hannah, have you heard? The younger Miss Waterford is to marry Mr Fulton.'

I gasped and chopped through the ribbon so pre-cipitately that Lizzie gained an extra two inches. 'Is it true?'

Mrs Heskith cackled and spluttered. 'It's the best tale I've heard all year and that's a fact!'

She repeated it to every customer thereafter so that by the end of the day I believed the truth of it and almost some of the embellishments she added as well.

At home, Rawinia snorted. 'Believe that and next you'll be saying cows give brandy.'

But Rawinia was wrong for on Wednesday, Miss Waterford came into the shop herself.

'I believe congratulations are in order,' Mrs Heskith said archly.

Miss Waterford nodded her head, causing the plume on her bonnet to sway and dip. 'Thank you, Mrs Heskith. Now, I want a charming shawl to wear for the wedding.'

Rawinia, when I told her of the purchase, shook her head and chuckled on and off all the rest of the evening.

She did not, however, find anything amusing about the next piece of news I brought home. 'The land at Waitara is to be sold. The governor told Teira that he is allowed to sell it and people say the first instalment of the money was paid today.'

She banged pots, rattled cutlery and slapped the cloth onto the table. 'No good will come of it, listen to my words! The land is not Teira's to sell. The governor knows this. He brings trouble to the land.'

Papa, slightly more unsteady on his feet than usual, swayed over to her. 'Rawinia, dove of my heart! It is for the best. The Maori race is dying. Soon none will be left. Accept the inevitable, my beloved.'

His words did not calm her. She twisted her body away from his embrace. 'It is not for the best. The land does not belong to Teira. It is wrong. I will never accept it. Never, never, never.'

Papa was startled. Jamie, Arama and I stared at her. She gestured for us to be seated. In silence we took our places. A pain knotted my stomach and I couldn't eat. Rawinia never argued with Papa. She never set her opinion against his. I stirred the food around and around on my plate. Papa ate calmly as if nothing extraordinary had occurred. Jamie glanced at me, pulled his mouth down but ate with an unimpaired appetite. Arama too, ate heartily but his eyes flickered between Rawinia and Papa.

We did not speak of it again, but the talk in town was all about the land sale. I listened to settlers and I listened to townsfolk as they gossiped in the shop. Every one of them rejoiced that the governor had allowed the sale. 'The Maoris don't even use it,' said Mrs Greenfell. 'My husband says they don't have a right to it anyway.'

Mrs Lynch pursed up her lips. 'Of course, dear Mrs Greenfell, *you* weren't here before that scoundrel of a so-called chief, William King brought his mob up from the south.' She looked down her nose and stretched her mouth a quarter of an inch in a smile. 'But we *early* pioneers remember it only too clearly. I said to my husband at the time, *they'll be trouble, mark my words.*'

It angered me that she called him *William King* instead of giving him his Maori name of *Wiremu Kingi Te Rangitake*. I glanced from her, so superior and condescending, to Mrs Greenfell, smarting at her remarks, and said, 'May I suggest the cream muslin for Maudie, Mrs Greenfell? She is fortunate enough to have inherited your pale complexion and the cream will look charming on her.'

The double compliment soothed her. Mrs Lynch took her own red complexion from the shop.

Mrs Heskith, when the shop emptied for a moment, scolded me for insulting Mrs Lynch.

*

It was the strangest of Decembers. Everything was as it always was on the surface; the sun shone hot and strong, making the road outside the shop dusty. The heat drew out the smell of dung from horses, bullocks and cattle. People shopped and worked and gossiped and I listened to them rejoicing that at last, there was land to buy; good land and New Plymouth could expand. *It is what we came here for*, they said. *We didn't come to be confined in a little town on the edge of the wilderness. The Maoris don't use it, and if Teira wants to sell it, then we're happy to buy it.*

I came almost to believe in the rightness and justice of it myself, except that always in my mind I heard Rawinia's voice. *It is wrong. I will never accept it. Never, never, never.*

A week passed, and the talk I heard grew louder and more confident. I repeated some of it to Rawinia one evening before the boys and Papa arrived home. 'Everyone is happy that the land is sold.'

Rawinia looked at me, her hands on her hips. 'Some Maori are happy. Some are not. It is the ones who are not who will be the mountain in the path of the Pakeha.'

I set the table in silence, for her words troubled me. I didn't want to ask the question in my mind for fear of what her answer might be, but I found the words escaping anyway. 'Rawinia, are you part of that mountain?' I kept my eyes down and wished I could close my mind and my ears as well.

Her answer, when it came, confirmed my fears. 'Hana,

my daughter, I am a rock in the mountain. To give up the land is to die. You heard your Papa. *The Maori race is dying*, he said.'

I was cold, my limbs shook and I had to struggle to speak. 'Wiremu Kingi Te Rangitake might yet agree that Teira can sell the land.'

She didn't need to answer me. We both knew that he would not, for the land was part of the ancestral home of the Te Atiawa people. I struggled to accept that for the first time in my life Rawinia had set her will against Papa's. I whispered, 'What will happen if . . .'

She shrugged. I wanted her to say she would stand by Papa no matter if she disagreed with his position. I wanted her to say . . . oh, what was the use of yearning?

'Rawinia, please excuse me. I'm not hungry. I think I will go to bed.'

She didn't say anything, just nodded. I went into my bedroom, closed the door and lay on my bed. It could not be so, it simply could not be that my family was about to split asunder with Papa on one side and Rawinia on the other. Which side was I on? And the boys? Such a struggle might force Jamie and Arama onto opposing sides. I could not think about it. I could not ignore it either, for it filled my heart and mind so that I was one huge pain.

If I had enough money I could go to England. Jamie and I could both go.

I sat up, took hold of my pillow and thumped it. Such thoughts availed me nothing. I could not go and I did not want to, but how could I stay here and watch my family and my country tear themselves apart? I wished with all my heart that I could not see both sides. How easy it would be to be Judith – in love with a British soldier and with parents who both said the land sale should go ahead, who both agreed that it was time that the Maori bent their knee to British rule.

In the days that followed I sought comfort in the thought that the governor might yet overturn the sale, but the more I listened to the settlers talk, the more I was convinced that the sale would stand.

We did not discuss the land sale at home. Papa read to us in the evenings while Rawinia and I sewed our dresses and the boys sharpened axes and knives.

Christmas offered a welcome distraction from the worry. Papa came home on Christmas Eve laden with gifts. 'Rejoice, my family! The quarter day money arrived this very day.' For once, the mail arrived early and Papa declared it was Heaven-sent and who was he to deny the workings of Higher Powers?

Rawinia shrugged her shoulders and tied the bonnet he had bought her onto her head.

'Thank you, Papa,' I said, putting my own new bonnet on and curtseying to him. How long would it be before he sold it again? But I would wear it with pleasure until that happened.

Arama stroked the rifle that was his gift. 'We'll try it out tomorrow, brother,' he promised Jamie, not taking his eyes off the polished metal and shining wood.

Jamie hefted his own gift, a knife, in his hand. 'Thank you, sir. This will be most useful. When Arama fires at a boar and misses, I will kill it with my knife.'

We laughed and toasted each other with champagne.

'There will be no money left for the rest of the quarter,' I said to Rawinia as we washed the dishes.

She shrugged. 'There is always the garden. We won't starve.'

Between us hung the unspoken thought that by next quarter day our lives could well have changed beyond recognition. But champagne bubbled in my blood and tonight the future appeared rosy and safe.

Rawinia and I dressed in our new dresses and bonnets for the New Year's Day picnic at the Waitara. We all went, Papa as well, although he refused to climb onto a bullock cart, preferring to hire a horse instead.

Rawinia and I walked down to Devon Street where we met the bullock carts which would take us to the picnic. Aunt Frances and Judith had saved us a place on the one they were riding in.

Captain Lindhurst with several fellow officers rode up in time to assist Rawinia into the cart.

I was about to climb in when Captain Lindhurst bowed and said, 'One moment, Miss Carstairs.'

I paused, regarding him with my eyebrows raised, as did Judith.

He frowned. 'It is probably best you know, Captain Hendon will attend the picnic today.'

'Oh! Thank you for warning me, Captain Lindhurst. It was most kind.'

He held out a hand to assist me into the cart. 'I am sure he will not trouble you.'

I smiled at him, hoping he could see the gratitude in my heart. 'I do indeed thank you, Captain.'

He bowed and remounted his horse.

I sat down beside Judith and squeezed her hand. 'He is truly a gentleman.'

She smiled at me and then upon her captain.

I resolved to put Captain Hendon out of my mind.

'Would it not be glorious to ride?' sighed Amy Bishop, watching the officers gallop away. She sat on a cushion and twirled a parasol. Already the sun was warm and the sky a clear, deep blue. The mountain, today a paler blue than the sky, rose to our right, snow shining near the peak.

'I would love to ride,' I said and even I heard the yearning in my voice.

Judith smiled in the manner that she seemed to be using more and more around me. It was a smile that told of her maturity and of my impulsive childishness. I did not find it endearing.

We stopped for more passengers, the elderly Miss Waterfords, Mrs Pitts and her daughters and, last of all, Mrs Greenfell who was at great pains to tell us that her daughters were riding out accompanied by their papa.

Amy and I rolled our eyes but said, 'How delightful.'

More riders passed us. Dr Feilding and his wife trotted

past, their horses kicking up little spurts of dust. They called a greeting and were soon out of sight. The virtues of Mrs Feilding, her beauty, her taste and her charm were discussed in every small detail.

I think it is akin to hell to be confined for the best part of a morning under a hot sun with people you have not chosen as companions.

The bullocks trod stolidly on, tails swishing away the insects. Their driver, Mr Jeffs called words of encouragement to them, especially on the hills. Some of his vocabulary drew gasps and blushes from his passengers. I shut my lips tightly and vowed I would not laugh. A quick glance at Amy told me she was similarly afflicted.

The elder Miss Waterford began a loud conversation when we came to the third hill. 'I declare, I cannot see what the fuss is over this land.' She waved a hand at it. 'Fern and more fern. Miles of it.'

Her voice didn't drown out Mr Jeffs' calls to his bullocks and she looked most discomposed. Aunt Frances ignored him and smiled at her. 'The land is fertile and easy to clear. And it does not have the deep river valleys that are so common in the rest of Taranaki.'

Mrs Bishop slipped her shawl off. 'It is so hot!' She stared ahead of us, and then back the way we had come. The road was little more than a track cut through the bracken fern which rose taller than a man on either side. 'One thing is certain – there can be no war, for how could anyone fight in such a dense tangle?'

Everyone murmured agreement, except Rawinia who

gazed ahead towards the north where the village of her people lay on the banks of the Waitara river. I had no doubt that she, as I did, thought of the battles they had fought on this very land, of how the Waikato tribes had invaded and Rawinia's people, Te Atiawa, had fled south leaving their land empty until they returned from their exile after the settlers had come to New Plymouth.

'There will be no war if the governor doesn't buy the land,' I said. I glanced at Rawinia but she sat stoical and still, enduring the day and the talk. For her sake, I tried to make those women – and Mr Jeffs – understand. 'This is the ancestral land of Te Atiawa. Teira does not have the authority to sell it. It belongs to the tribe. Wiremu Kingi Te Rangitake speaks for his people and their ancestors when he refuses to allow the sale.'

Mr Jeffs snorted. 'They don't do anything with it. Look at it! Don't deserve it, in my opinion.'

Aunt Frances, Mrs Greenfell – all of them, even Judith, frowned at me and began at once to discuss Captain Hendon. 'I warned my girls to stay well clear of him, you may be sure,' Mrs Pitts said.

Next they discussed babies, marriages, betrothals, oh, I forget! All I recall is that I wanted to scream with boredom. The only relief in the entire journey came when the younger Woodley boys rode past with their papa and Charlie. They greeted us with such cheerfulness that I wondered if perhaps they had made another wager and were hoping the captain would propose today.

I was not in the sunniest of moods by the time we

had joggled and shaken our way to Mr Babcock's field which served as the picnic ground.

I leaped from the cart and made to run off, but the combined voices of Rawinia and my aunt dragged me back. 'Take the picnic basket, Hannah.'

'Help Mrs Woodley, Hana.'

I helped settle our party under a tree for shade. We spread out our picnic which drew the gentlemen to us with spectacular promptness.

'New Year's Day, 1860,' Aunt Frances said, and she looked around at the colourful scene of cheerful picnickers dotted around the edge of the field wherever a tree offered shade. 'I wonder what the new decade will bring for us all.'

She didn't quite look at Judith as she spoke, but it wasn't difficult to guess what was in her mind. I still could not make up my mind about Captain Lindhurst. I seized the opportunity to observe him as carefully as I could without being so rude as to stare.

His manners were impeccable. He chatted to my aunt and the other ladies about news from England of the queen and the royal family. He drew Jamie into the conversation by asking him if he intended to go to the lecture on combustion at the Taranaki Institute. He talked to Arama about his gun.

He offered an opinion when, inevitably, the discussion turned to the land sales issue. 'No, Miss Waterford, it will not come to war. William King knows he cannot take on the might of the British army.'

Miss Waterford fluttered and gasped out how glad

she was to know the army was here to protect us. I cut across her twittering.

'Wiremu Kingi Te Rangitake,' I said, for it irritated me that he did not give the chief his Maori name, 'vows to keep his land. He has powerful allies.'

I collected pained looks from my aunt, my uncle, Judith and both Miss Waterfords. Rawinia's face was impassive.

Papa took no notice, or, more likely, he was quite unaware that I had committed a crime against young-lady-hood. 'Time for the government to take a stand,' he said. 'Put those rebels down once and for all. We need the land. How is New Plymouth to prosper if it cannot expand? I had hopes of this governor but I've been sadly disappointed.'

Mr Woodley placed his fingertips together, nodded and harrumphed, as if he couldn't bring himself to say aloud that he agreed with Papa.

Mr Bishop beat his hand on the ground in frustration. 'One man! I find it difficult to understand how one old man in a blanket can stop us settling on land already paid for.'

I felt my aunt's gaze drilling into my skull. I swallowed the words I wanted to speak. Instead, I contented myself with muttering in Maori to Rawinia, 'The mana of Wiremu Kingi Te Rangitake is not bound up in his appearance or his age.'

Judith's captain sent me a piercing look, but spoke before anyone could interrogate me as to the meaning of my words. 'William King is bluffing. It is my belief he will see he cannot take on the might of the British army, even with his land league behind him.'

'If he does try any nonsense,' Mr Woodley said, 'let us hope the army will be permitted to give him and his rebels a short, sharp lesson.'

My aunt said, 'I am sure the matter will soon be resolved, and in the meantime we have a picnic to enjoy. I suggest that you young people take yourselves off for a walk by the river.'

I leaped to my feet. Judith fussed with her skirts until Captain Lindhurst arrived at her side and offered his hand to help her up.

It was all I could do not to flounce. He was a dandy playing at soldiering while she, my erstwhile friend, played at being a young lady. A strong desire to push them both into the river surged in my blood.

Jamie slid his arm through mine. 'Hannah, I think you are right about the Maori situation. I think they will not sit back and wait for a short, sharp lesson.'

Arama took my other arm. 'Wiremu Kingi will not be trampled by the Pakeha.'

Did that mean Arama would support Wiremu Kingi if it came to war? I would not think of such things on so lovely a day.

The afternoon passed pleasantly. The boys and I wandered beside the river for as long as they could stand so passive an occupation. This river did not run skittering around boulders and then slowing into deeper, darker pools as did the rivers around New Plymouth. Here the water flowed lazily, uncluttered by boulders and it rose and fell with the tides.

Jamie dropped my arm. 'We'll be off now, Sissy. Take care to stay away from Hendon.'

I didn't ask where they were going – home I suspected. The men were gathering for a game of cricket, but Jamie would not play unless Arama played too, and he would not be asked.

From time to time I caught sight of Captain Hendon in the distance but he made no attempt to approach me.

I was delighted to find that Polly, Peter and Tommy had come in to attend the picnic. Polly whispered to me, 'There's to be a sister or brother for Tommy come the winter.'

I smiled at her, 'That is good news.' I leaned over and whispered back, 'Then you did not sew together the hems of your nightgowns?'

She looked at me, her mouth open, and I wondered if I had desperately overstepped some boundary. I took a breath to apologise before I ran away, but Polly crowed with laughter. 'I never said that! I never did?' But her voice rose in a question.

My knees sagged with relief. 'You did, Polly. I will always remember it.' I whispered again, 'I wanted so to tell Mrs Walter to sew up her gowns but I didn't dare.'

Polly wiped her streaming eyes. 'Oh, lordy lordy, Hannah Carstairs, you'll be the death of me, so you will.' She gasped for breath.

Judith, Amy and Lavender came to fetch me. Lavender curtseyed to Polly. 'Begging your pardon ma'am, but we have been instructed by the gentlemen to watch them play cricket.'

We joined another group of young ladies, among them Lizzie Bevan. We sat down under a tree and I soon grew restless. Judith applauded every move her captain made. Amy applauded any move any of the military men made. I was composing a graceful excuse to leave when I noticed something which entertained me far more than the cricket itself could do.

Lizzie Bevan, proud and haughty and so far above such common colonials as I was, watched and applauded another common colonial, one Frederick Jackson who worked for his father as a carter.

Lizzie and Frederick. How entertaining. Did he know of her interest? Did he reciprocate, and if he did not, would she allow him to escape her?

At the end of the day we packed up and climbed back into the bullock carts. Rawinia clucked at me. 'Goodness, Hana girl, look how burnt your skin is. You'll be as brown as I am if you're not careful.'

Mrs Bishop said, 'I fear we are all a little burnt.' She smiled at Rawinia. 'You have it all over us, dear Mrs Carstairs, for you do not need to worry.'

The officers did not accompany us home, but Amy made up for their absence by talking about them incessantly. Judith said little, her face dreamy.

We were halfway home when I could take no more of

it. 'Rawinia, Aunt Frances, please excuse me, but I am going to walk the rest of the way.'

They protested but I jumped down into the roadway, running to draw ahead of the plodding bullocks.

I ran as fast as I could where the road was smooth enough not to risk turning my ankle. I overtook two more bullock carts, one containing Mrs Lynch. I ran on, her words of outraged surprise beating at my ears.

Time passed and so did several horsemen who waved and called to me. Aunt Frances and Rawinia would both scold me and no doubt I deserved it, for I knew full well I should not be walking by myself in such circumstances. I did not care.

I did not look around as another horseman rode up. I moved to the side of the road to allow him to pass, but the horse slowed. My heart thumped. I had indeed been foolish. If this was Captain Hendon, then I was in trouble.

'Miss Carstairs, will you allow me to escort you home?' It was Captain Lindhurst.

I clasped my hands over my heart to still its pounding. 'Oh, Captain Lindhurst! You startled me!'

He slid down from his horse to walk beside me. 'Mrs Carstairs and your aunt are most concerned for your safety.'

I hung my head. 'I have just been thinking how foolish I am. I feared you were Captain Hendon. I am devoutly relieved that it is you and not he.'

To my astonishment, he threw back his head and laughed. 'Oh, Miss Carstairs! You are always unexpected.

I was about to utter a carefully phrased admonishment but you have entirely cut the ground from beneath my feet.'

'That is one scolding I have escaped,' I sighed. Then I told him of Captain Hendon's attempt to stop me in the street.

He frowned. 'The devil he did! Begging your pardon, Miss Carstairs. I will speak to him, I promise you.' By the look in the captain's eye, Captain Hendon would not enjoy the encounter.

We had been walking for some minutes when he observed, 'You appear to believe William King can defeat the British army, Miss Carstairs.'

All the indignation I had so resolutely repressed burst from me. 'I am happy my opinions amused you, Captain Lindhurst. I suppose I should be grateful you did not laugh aloud when I expressed them at them at the picnic.' I quickened my pace so that I might wipe my eyes without him seeing.

'Forgive me, Miss Carstairs. The truth of the matter is that I was picturing you in . . .'

'An English drawing room.' I stopped walking and rounded on him. 'Please do not do so, Captain. It is most unlikely that I shall ever travel to England and I am not an Englishwoman, I am a New Zealander.'

He gestured at the road ahead of us. 'Shall we continue? Or do you wish to discuss the qualities of roast pork, as I understand was the topic in the cart?'

He had made me smile again. 'It will by now be a discussion of who might marry whom.' Then I burst out, 'But

I am a fine one to talk!' I told him of Lizzie Bevan and Frederick Jackson, of how I had entertained myself for the duration of the cricket match by watching her.

He laughed the full-bodied roar I had never heard him employ around Judith, and we chatted of safe and unexceptionable topics until I reached home whereupon I expressed my gratitude for his escort.

'It was my pleasure, Miss Carstairs.' He mounted his horse and trotted away down the street.

I walked slowly into the house. I did not understand him. My opinions entertained him but he clearly thought that I was not a proper young lady. I tossed my head. I had no desire to be a proper young lady, especially one in an English drawing room. What would it be like to live in England? I would never know.

I prepared dinner in the hope of softening Rawinia's anger. It didn't work. She scolded me for walking alone. Jamie scolded me for walking alone.

I ignored Jamie, but apologised to Rawinia. 'I am sorry, Rawinia. It was foolish of me.'

She grunted and moved to the fire to bang pots around. 'You'll be the talk of the town, see if you're not.'

# 14

## Chapter Fourteen

It was fortunate for me that the town found a much tastier morsel to talk about than my behaviour. The week after the New Year's Day picnic, Lizzie Bevan and Frederick Jackson announced that they were to marry.

Papa rubbed his hands with glee when he heard of it. 'She's shrewd, that one. Knows where the money is and she's gone for it.' He shook a finger at me. 'You could do worse than follow her example, child. Find a man who can earn good money and reel him in.'

Rawinia made no comment then, but when Papa left for the hotel, she said, 'It's a good thing to have a man who will work hard for you, and don't you forget it.'

But people did not talk of Lizzie and Frederick for long. The land purchase at the Waitara consumed us all.

'Everyone says there will be war.' Jamie attacked his food, stabbing potatoes and meat to emphasise his words. 'The settlers are all saying we need to have it out with the Maoris and settle Wiremu Kingi and his rebels once and for all.'

Papa said, 'We must be ready if it comes to war. The

army cannot lose with the Carstairs men fighting along-side it.'

I stared at him. I had not thought he would fight. I had not allowed myself to believe that Jamie would, or Arama. 'Arama is too young,' I said.

'Nonsense,' said Papa.

'Nobody will care,' said Jamie.

Arama said nothing, but as he ate, his eyes strayed time and again to his rifle hanging proudly on the wall.

War. The talk of it seethed around me all day as I worked. I hurried home in the evening and burst through the door. 'Rawinia?' I called, running through the house to find her. She came in from the back garden, a load of washing in her arms.

'There is war?' she asked.

I slumped into a chair. 'You would think so to listen to the talk.' I straightened my back and wailed, 'They want it. They all want it. They rub their hands and laugh.' I flung out an arm, pointing in the general direction of the town. 'It is like a huge happy picnic out there.'

She just shrugged and set a basin of water and the potatoes for dinner in front of me. I fetched the paring knife and my apron. 'Have you ever seen a war party?'

'A taua?' She shook her head. 'Not many people have now. Only a few of the chiefs. Wiremu Kingi Te Rangitake – he has.'

I picked up the knife but my mind wasn't on my task. Instead of a basin of muddy water and potatoes, I saw red-coated soldiers marching on a pa built high on a hill.

Behind the palisades, crouching deep in the gun pits I saw the Maori defenders. I could hear their voices united in defiance, thundering out the words of a haka. I heard the ferocious rhythm of their war dance, beaten with hands on naked skin and by bare feet on the soil they fought for; all of it perfect, chilling and disciplined.

'It won't come to war. Will it?' I whispered.

She didn't answer. I peeled the potatoes.

For the first time in my life I wished I lived far away in England.

I was glad of the distraction of work and also of an invitation from the Woodleys. Judith, accompanied by Charlie, came to deliver it in person.

'Mama and Papa are to have a dinner party,' Judith said. She smiled at me and her eyes sparkled, but not as much as I thought they should do if the captain had, to use Arnold and Stanley's words, popped the question. 'It is to celebrate their wedding anniversary. Please, will you and Jamie come?'

I took the liberty of answering for Jamie although I suspected he would not be as delighted by the prospect of a dinner party as I was. 'Of course we will come. When is it to be?'

'In two weeks,' Charlie said, 'on Sunday, February the twelfth.' He dropped the formality. 'I say, Hannah, isn't it exciting! Is Jamie to join the volunteers? Papa is going to Auckland tomorrow and he's promised to buy me a rifle of my own.'

I made some reply, I scarcely knew what. To Judith,

I said, 'Tell my aunt that I will be pleased to help with the preparations.'

Rawinia added her voice to mine. 'Tell her we can cook the ham or roast the fowls. Whatever she wants.'

They thanked us and left. I could not bear to talk of war, or of Jamie, Arama and Papa fighting in it. Instead, I asked, 'Rawinia, do you think Judith hopes the captain will propose to her in time for it to be announced at the party?'

'He's a handsome man,' Rawinia said, for he had made a great impression on her. 'Who knows what a handsome man will do?'


For the next two weeks I tried to keep my mind on the party and on the interesting question of Judith's possible betrothal. Amy and Lavender came into the shop to buy lace for their dresses, for they were invited as well. 'We think the party is really for Judith, and her captain,' Amy said with a giggle.

Lavender nodded and sighed, 'He is so handsome. And his uniform! A man in uniform is so attractive.'

I had no time for more talk and as it was, Mrs Heskith cleared her throat meaningfully. I cut the lace to the required length. 'It is beautiful. You will both look most charming.'

On the Sunday before the party I walked home from church with the Woodleys. After we had dined, the men vanished and left my aunt, Judith and me in possession of the kitchen table. Aunt Frances put paper and a pencil in front of me. 'Will you write the lists, Hannah? We need three . . .'

Judith interrupted her, 'Things to buy, things to borrow and things to do. And Hannah, there is to be dancing after dinner.'

I picked up the pencil, glancing at her as I did so. I could not understand it. She was excited but she did not have the look of a girl whose lover had proposed to her, but neither did she look despairing. I asked, 'Shall I write on the list of things to borrow: one handsome soldier who will dance elegantly with Miss Hannah Carstairs?'

I hoped she might say something about her captain, but she merely laughed and turned the topic to her papa's visit to Auckland. 'The shops are much more numerous there. He bought us all manner of delightful things.'

My aunt frowned at her for she was always careful not to emphasise the difference in wealth between her family and mine.

I put down the pencil and leaned my arms on the table. 'Judith, are you to have a new dress for the party?'

She glanced at her mama, but I said, 'Oh, do pray tell me! I do not yearn for a new dress, truly I do not.' That was not entirely true, I discovered as I gazed at the charming dress Mr Woodley had purchased in Auckland. 'It is beautiful. All the gentlemen will clamour to dance with you.' I touched the white tulle overskirt with its silver stars and ran my fingers over the flowers embroidered in lilac that decorated the hem. 'Your papa has excellent taste.'

Judith smiled and my aunt embraced me warmly as I left.

I took with me the table napkins to starch and iron. Rawinia and I would also roast the five fowls promised to my aunt by Mr Woodley's business partner.

I was happy to have the party to look forward to, for that week was a strange one in the town. The governor ordered the land at Waitara to be surveyed, and all around me people acted as if he had said that war, and not a survey of land, would begin on February the twentieth. People and rumours streamed into the town.

'Nothing will happen,' Mrs Walter said to me when she came into the shop. 'It's just for safety. My Harold says the Taranaki niggers are marching to support William King.' She clapped a hand to her mouth when she saw the shock on my face. 'Oh, Hannah, I'm that sorry! I don't mean to insult your family, indeed I don't.'

I managed to smile at her, then bent my head to wrap her purchases. Far better to die an old maid than marry a man like Harold Walter.

There were so many rumours. I grew to dread the words *people say,* and *have you heard?*

*People say* HMS Niger *is coming to anchor off New Plymouth.*

*Have you heard? There are five hundred Taranakis marching up from the south!*

*Have you heard? We'll all starve because the farmers won't be able to harvest the wheat before the war begins.*

*What war?* I wanted to shout. *Nobody has declared war.*

The sun shone hot. The sky spread above us, blue and brilliant. The mountain, the constant backdrop of our lives, appeared far away, coloured in its summer hue of pale blue. On my way to and from the shop, I raised my eyes to it. It had overlooked centuries of battles. *This too will pass*, it seemed to say.

'So it will,' I muttered, 'but I am not made of volcanic stone that will survive the centuries.' My thoughts turned again to escape. To England. But only if I could take Jamie and Arama with me. Useless.

'Hannah Carstairs, watch where you're stepping!' Maggie Barrow, one of Polly's friends, bent and picked up a bundle of clothes I'd trodden on.

I helped her gather the things she'd dropped. 'Can I help you carry them, Mrs Barrow? Have you come into town?'

She straightened and clasped the clothes to her chest along with her child. 'My husband said I had to. Take the children, he said, or we'll all be murdered in our beds.' She burst into tears and I walked with her to the house where they were to stay. We had to walk around to the gateway left in the fortification ditch men were digging to defend the town.

Maggie gestured at it. 'I hope they'll finish it soon. We'll all feel a lot safer when it's done.'

'My brothers are helping dig it,' I told her. I didn't tell her they helped too, to break the bottles to throw in the bottom of it for I could not bear to think of it. Maori invaders would come bare-footed. Pakeha defenders wore boots.

'Your house is outside the ditch,' she said. 'Will you move?'

I didn't know.

I felt removed from all around me in the town where excitement floated in the air as if for a holiday, like the picnic at the Waitara. No one said it was wrong to survey land you did not legally own. With shame in my heart, I did not say it either.

Rawinia no longer sang as she worked. I wanted to speak words of comfort, but they would be false. There was no comfort.

Two evenings before the Woodley's party, Jamie and Arama stood in the kitchen getting in the way as usual. Jamie said through a mouthful of stolen potato, 'We joined the militia today.'

Rawinia turned from the stove. She set down the roast of pork she held. 'You will fight.' It was a statement, not a question.

I was not so calm. I shouted at Jamie, 'It's wrong! You should have refused to take the oath, you should refuse to fight!'

He rounded on me. 'What do you say when you hear talk in the town? Do you say the war is wrong? Do you?' He thumped the table.

I slumped into a chair and burst into tears. 'No! I'm a coward. I want to be strong but it's dreadful. Have you heard what they say about Mr Gilbert and his son?'

They had, for it would be impossible not to. Mr Gilbert and his eldest son refused to join the volunteers when they were called up. 'The people say they are cowards,' Arama said. 'They say Mr Gilbert is weak and mean spirited.'

I lifted my head although the tears still fell. 'Arama, you're too young. You don't have to fight.'

Rawinia became still as if she gathered strength for her own battle. Arama answered me, but his eyes were on his mother. 'I will fight. I will fight for what is right.'

I left the table, stumbled out the kitchen door and was sick. I leaned against the wall of the house. The wood was warm from the sun. My brothers. They would go to war. Perhaps one on one side and the other opposing him. How could I bear it?

Jamie came to fetch me. He put his arm around me and led me back into the house. 'I want to make things from iron. I don't want to fight. Peter doesn't want to fight.' He shrugged. 'Nobody wants to, but if they say it is war then we must fight.'

I knew he was right. We were Pakeha and we must cast our lot with the English, for if we did not, it would be impossible to live in Taranaki.

'Jamie,' I whispered. 'Let's go to England. All of us — you, me and Arama.'

He didn't answer me.

The next day, Papa came home early from the hotel so angry he could barely speak. 'That coward Gilbert! He's smuggled that spineless son of his out of the settlement. Left on the steamer last night.'

I picked up Papa's hat and hung it up. 'I'm glad he escaped, for he is brave, not weak.'

Papa's face turned purple. I shivered and sickness roiled in my stomach. I yearned to take back my words but it was too late. 'Traitor! Infidel!' He smote the table with the flat of his hand and shouted into my face, 'All these years I have nourished a viper in my bosom. How sharper than a serpent's tooth it is to have a thankless child.'

The air around us quivered. Thoughts tumbled and spun through my mind and the one that came to the surface was that I wasn't his child. I opened my mouth, stuttered out, 'I'm not . . .'

Jamie's voice, sharp and urgent, cut across mine. 'Hannah! Show respect!'

I breathed out, then in. The words dissolved, unspoken. I bowed my head. 'I'm sorry, Papa.' Sorry that our world was tearing itself apart. Sorry that Jamie, Arama and I could not escape what was to come.

That night, we ate a silent dinner.

It was a relief to attend the Woodley's dinner party, despite Jamie's reluctance to go. But when he emerged from his bedroom clad in Papa's best suit, I clasped my hands to my chest in admiration. 'Jamie, you have grown so tall! And you are so handsome these days. Be careful! Some girl will ensnare you!'

He chuckled. 'I have only to think of the awful fate of Frederick Jackson to make me as wary as you could wish.'

Belatedly, he recalled that he should compliment me too. 'You look delightful, Sissy.' And that despite my hair draggling around my face waiting for Judith's skilful attention.

I laughed at him. The others bade us farewell and we

walked to the Woodley house. I tucked my arm through his and said, 'Do you think we will have an announcement tonight?'

'What about?' he asked. Boys! I could not believe he knew nothing of the captain's interest, but it was so.

I told him about it, and also of the wager Arnold and Stanley had made. He was still chuckling by the time we arrived.

I saw at once that Judith glowed with happiness. She was beautiful in her new dress but it was more than that. She whisked me off to her bedroom, sat me in front of her mirror and attended to my hair. I reached up to press her hand. 'He is lucky to win you.'

Her eyes met mine in the mirror. 'Is it so obvious?'

I turned to her. 'Do not try and hide it! It gladdens my heart to see you so happy.'

She bent and dropped a kiss on my forehead. 'Thank you, Hannah, my dearest friend.'

'When are you to marry?' I asked.

Her smile dimmed. 'We are undecided. It is because of this dreadful war. It is so difficult to make plans.'

I refrained from pointing out that there was no war, and indeed as the evening progressed, it seemed that everyone considered we were at war.

Lavender and Amy came in with their parents, took one look at Judith and as soon as they politely could, came to find me. 'He's asked her, hasn't he?' Amy demanded.

Lavender didn't wait for my reply, but whispered, 'When are they to marry? It's so romantic, is it not? To marry a soldier and wave him goodbye as he marches off to war.'

'Would you like to marry a soldier?' I asked, hoping to turn the conversation from questions I didn't feel it was my place to answer.

Amy giggled. 'Haven't you heard? They say we are to get hundreds more soldiers to protect us. Some of them must be handsome.'

'And rich,' said Lavender, and they laughed.

I smiled. 'Excuse me, I must go and help my aunt.'

Hundreds more soldiers could only mean that the Government did mean to go to war. I comforted myself that it probably wasn't true, that it was just another rumour.

I hurried to the kitchen to help my aunt, Mrs Bishop and two more of my aunt's friends serve the food. 'Bless you, Hannah,' Aunt Frances said handing me one of her enveloping aprons.

I think I will never forget that meal. We were so happy, even Jamie who seemed to have reignited his interest in Lavender. The women wore their jewels and the soft lamplight hid the wear in the dresses of those of us who did not have new ones. My uncle even smiled when Arnold and Stanley managed to fill their water glasses with wine. 'You may share one between you,' he said, holding out his hand for the return of one of the glasses.

When we sat, replete, with the dishes cleared away, my uncle rose to his feet, and the chatter of the twenty guests hushed to a murmur then ceased.

'Ladies and gentlemen,' he began. He spoke fluently and

well of the happy marriage he and his wife had enjoyed for nineteen years. He said how blessed they were in their children. He spoke of their love and affection for them, particularly of their daughter Judith.

She blushed and dropped her head. Her mama took her hand.

'And now,' Mr Woodley said portentously, 'it gives me the greatest pleasure to announce that our beloved daughter is to become the wife of Captain Miles Lindhurst. I ask you to charge your glasses and drink to their health.'

We stood, lifted our glasses and chorused, 'Miss Woodley, Captain Lindhurst.'

I watched Judith as she stood with her captain to receive the congratulations of their friends, and my conclusions were that she was a graceful and gracious lady. I sighed and wished that I could be the same.

The guests crowded around, offering their congratulations. Jamie came up to do what was proper. He bowed and said, 'Captain, I felicitate you. Judith is as charming as she is beautiful. You are a lucky man.'

I wondered if perhaps Jamie was Papa's son after all. He had certainly acquired Papa's gift of the smooth compliment.

Arnold pushed his way through the throng, seized the captain's hand and pumped it. 'Well done, Captain. We're pleased, Stanley and me. Capital!'

I turned away to hide my laughter. What new wager had they made?

My aunt announced that the dancing was about to begin,

but first would the men please carry the tables out of the drawing room?

My opinion of Judith's suitability as a wife was confirmed as the evening progressed. When she wasn't dancing she made sure she chatted with her guests. Miss Waterford — oh dear, I must try to remember to call her by her married name, beamed as she talked to her. The wife of her papa's business partner smiled as she sat down beside her. She helped my aunt ensure each young lady had a partner if she cared to dance.

The captain was a lucky man. I had just reached this conclusion when he bowed and requested my hand for the next dance. But he was so correct in his conversation that I wondered if I had offended him and was pleased when the dance finished.

Judith was to become a wife. Good heavens, it did not seem possible. Amy and Lavender too, were momentarily overcome. 'Who will be next?' Lavender asked. 'First Lizzie, now Judith.'

'It will have to be one of you,' I said. 'For I am determined not to marry.'

They laughed at me, but I was glad I would not have to worry about a husband if it came to war. Two brothers and a father were more than enough to worry about.

At the end of the evening, as Jamie and I walked home he tucked my arm through his. 'Do you wish it was you, Sissy? I thought you liked him.'

I rubbed my head against his shoulder. 'I have no wish to marry. You know that.'

He laughed at me. 'That doesn't answer my question. But I won't pry. A woman needs her secrets.'

That was what Papa said whenever we asked about Mama. I made up my mind right then to have no more secrets from Jamie. 'Jamie, I want to tell you something. I did send that letter to Lord Derringford.'

His shoulders rose in a shrug. 'It'll do no good. And what, pray, does that have to do with the topic in hand?'

'Papa and secrets. I don't want to have secrets from you.'

'Tell me about your feelings for the captain then,' Jamie said, unimpressed by the workings of my mind.

I shivered in the night air. 'I do like him, but he puzzles me. He can be so kind, then the next time I meet him he is perfectly correct and formal. Cold almost. He appears to enjoy my company but makes it clear that I am not a suitable candidate for the wife of a man with aspirations.'

Jamie laughed. 'He is right about that, but I shouldn't worry. Judith's caught him because she's turned herself into a ninny without an idea in her noddle. Can't have a proper conversation with her these days.'

'If I want to marry it will have to be Hartley Pitts,' I declared. 'He does not mind my opinions at all.'

The next week had a feeling of unreality. Everyone talked of the imminent survey of the land at the Waitara, Judith's betrothal was barely mentioned, not that she cared about that. She cared for nothing except her captain, and she worried that war would carry him away from her, perhaps forever. The prospect of war worried others too. Every day, more and more settlers from the outlying farms came into town with their cattle and their chattels. I kept watching out for Polly and Peter, but they did not come.

I visited Judith and my aunt at the end of the week.

Judith glowed with happiness and my heart rejoiced for her while at the same time I had to repress the selfish thought that she was truly moving away from me into a world I had no wish to enter.

I walked home in a thoughtful mood. Why had Jamie thought I liked the captain in that way? I did like him, of course I did. But I did not want to be his wife and it was fortunate for me that I did not.

*How I would like to see you at work in an English drawing room.*

I indulged myself in a daydream of my letter bringing a wonderful reply. Lord Derringford, in my dream, begged us to come to him without delay. He sent money so that we might travel cabin class on the first ship suitable for the children of his dear Angelina whom he had lost in mysterious circumstances.

I reached our house and shrugged my fantasies away. We were hell-born brats and I had best remember it.

I think Monday, February the twentieth, the day the surveyors went to the Waitara, will live forever in my memory, for that day destroyed my stubborn hope that we would not be plunged into war.

Almost as soon as the surveyors left, the rumours started.

*The surveyors have all been slaughtered.*

*The surveyors have killed a hundred Maoris.*

*The Niger has arrived off the coast and fired rockets at the Maoris.*

I smiled at each customer, listened to each new rumour and hid my breaking heart.

When the surveyors returned we learned the truth. They hammered in the pegs. The Maori women and their children followed them and pulled the pegs out again.

At home we smiled, but not when Papa would see us. People in the town weren't amused.

'This means war! By gad, let me at them!' said Lizzie Bevan's future father-in-law when he came into the shop. His views harmonised completely with the views of the townspeople and settlers.

'The government will have to act now.'

'The niggers have flouted British law for the last time.'

'Let's fight and be done with it. I have wheat to harvest.'

Two days later, Colonel Murray declared martial law.

I walked home in the evening through the busy streets with tears in my heart, for I feared to show my feelings freely amid the rejoicing. Papa came home late and in a most jovial mood. He rubbed his hands. 'This is our hour! We'll show them what it means to defy England. One good encounter with the British army and they'll be singing a different tune. William King will come begging for mercy, his tail between his legs.' He sat down rather abruptly for his own legs were not quite steady.

Arama picked up Papa's hat. He threw it at the nail and it hung there. 'Wiremu Kingi will fight, Papa. He is a warrior.'

Papa tilted his chair. We watched it, poised to leap and save him if he teetered too far. 'He cannot beat the might of the British, my son. It's as well for you that you'll be fighting on the winning side. One good scrap and it'll all be over.'

Rawinia served the food and said nothing. Jamie wouldn't look at me. He concentrated on his meal and didn't talk. Papa talked enough for all of us.

The next night he came home early. He shouted, threw his hat at the wall and then his stick.

'Papa! What is the matter? What has happened?'

'A private!' he roared. 'They've made me a private! Me! This is Cecil Woodley's influence, damned if it's not. Scoundrels, the lot of them!'

Jamie too was given the rank of private. He was in the town militia and Arama in the native contingent. They reported for drill and guard duty, all as Jamie said, for the princely sum of one shilling a day.

I met Vernon Yates and Harry Arkwright as I walked to work. They called each other Private Yates and Private Arkwright. I wished them good day and walked on.

How could it be a war when not a shot had been fired? I felt as if I were in the sea being carried away by a current too strong for me.

I kept watching for Peter and Polly as outlying families straggled into town with their livestock and all the goods they could cram into carts. By the end of the weekend, the town bulged at the seams, but Peter and Polly did not come.

Jamie refused to discuss anything to do with the war. Arama grew silent and did not smile. Papa rubbed his hands and repeated every rumour he heard. The Carstairs men, he said, would march gloriously into battle, rout the rebels and return triumphant to be promoted to the rank — depending on how much drink he had taken — of captain or colonel.

He did not see our pain.

# 15

## Chapter Fifteen

At the beginning of the last week of February, Judith sent Arnold and Stanley to give me a note. I took it from them, remarking as I did so, 'You two are looking especially pleased with yourselves. It wouldn't have anything to do with a certain wager, would it?'

Stanley couldn't hold his excitement in. He pushed the note into my hands. 'Read it! Judith is to marry the captain tomorrow!'

The note fluttered from my grasp and fell to the floor. 'Tomorrow? Are you sure?'

Arnold laughed out loud, picked up the letter and tossed it into the air. 'We're sure. And we wagered two pounds that she would marry before Easter.'

I smiled, but there was no laughter in my heart. I opened the letter.

*My dearest Hannah,*
*Captain Lindhurst and I have decided to marry at once, for we do not know what the future may hold. We do not want to become a spectacle for the town and so the vicar is to marry us tomorrow morning in St Mary's at half past the hour of eight.*

*Please, my dearest Hannah, will you stand with me as my attendant?*

*Your loving friend,*

*Judith.*

I couldn't speak. I handed the letter to Rawinia. She nodded to the boys. 'Tell your sister Hannah will be there.'

'Yes,' I whispered. 'I will be there. Of course I will be there.'

Judith was to be married. She would be a wife, and in nine months a mother.

What did she know of being a wife? I hoped the captain would be gentle with her for she would be shocked to her bones. But perhaps my aunt would tell her what to expect. Yes, of course she would.

I found it difficult to sleep that night. My thoughts chased themselves around and around in my mind. The captain and Judith. Judith and the captain. He was to marry my dearest friend. I was happy for them. They deserved to be happy. I loved them both.

I sat up and punched my pillow. No, I did not love the captain, but I did hold him in high esteem.

I rose early in the morning, washed myself in a tub of water that was only just warm, for I was too impatient to heat enough to make it hot. I put my hair up as well as I could, pulled on my best dress of pale yellow satin and ran back to the kitchen, bonnet in hand, where Rawinia fastened my buttons.

'Off you go,' she said. 'And smile. It's a wedding you're

going to.' The look she gave me suggested she'd be only too happy to say more. I ran from the house.

Charlie answered my knock on the door. 'I say, Hannah, you look fine! Mama says for you to go straight to Judith's room.'

I hurried down the passage, tapped on her door and stopped on the threshold. 'Oh! You look so pretty!' She wore the beautiful dress she had worn the night of her betrothal, and her mama was pinning a veil of finest gauzy lace onto her head.

'It was Mama's. Hannah, am I not lucky!' She smiled at me and I had not known anyone could shine so with happiness.

My aunt cast a swift look over my dress and bonnet. 'You look lovely too, Hannah, my dear. Let me just fix your hair. Ah, that is better. Now, shall we go?' She handed Judith a bunch of white roses that lay waiting on the bed. There was another smaller bunch for me. She called my uncle. Judith stood up as he entered the room. He stopped, took a deep breath and said in a gruff voice, 'My dear daughter!'

She stepped forward, took his arm and he led her from the house she had lived in all of her life.

She paused on the verandah and stared into the road. 'Papa! Is that carriage for me?'

He beamed at her. 'Indeed it is, my dear. Can't have you walking to your own wedding you know.'

She stood on tiptoe to kiss his cheek.

He handed us into the carriage. It was the first time

I had ridden in a real carriage and only the second time Judith had.

Arnold and Stanley waved us farewell. 'Goodbye, Miss Woodley. We'll see you in church, Miss Woodley!'

'Oh dear,' said my aunt. 'I suppose when we leave the church they will be calling out, *Hello, Mrs Lindhurst!*'

Judith smiled. 'How wonderful it sounds! I shall not mind their teasing, Mama.'

They scampered the short distance to the church, determined to reach it before the carriage, or their father and Charlie did.

'Judith,' I said as they vanished from our sight, 'I cannot believe it! You are to be married! But where will you live? The town is so crowded there cannot be a house left to rent.'

'It is all settled. My dear Miles has arranged everything.' Her face was alight with love for her captain. 'He has secured Mr Bradshaw's cottage for us. And Hannah, it is so charming! There are roses and clematis climbing the verandah posts.'

We arrived at the church before I could respond. I knew the cottage she meant. It was tiny and I suspected was not at all the sort of house my aunt and uncle would want for their daughter in normal times. But the times were not normal. Judith's wedding was not normal.

My uncle opened the door of the carriage and helped my aunt out. I arranged Judith's veil so that it fell over her face then took the hand Mr Woodley held out to assist me from the carriage. We watched Judith emerge, a butterfly from the chrysalis ... I was becoming fanciful. This would never do.

She walked into the church on her father's arm, I followed them. Charlie accompanied my aunt, while the boys came behind.

For a second, I wondered if the captain would be there. I glanced up, caught a fleeting, blurred glimpse of two scarlet coats. I gripped my roses and wished my aunt had left at least one thorn to pierce my flesh. What ailed me? Why did I even think of so terrible a thing happening to my beloved Judith?

I raised my eyes, determined to do my best for my friend. I discovered that the second scarlet coat belonged to Captain Liverton. I saw Captain Lindhurst's smile for Judith as she walked towards him. There was a moment when she looked down to move her skirts out of the way of a pew. In that second, he glanced up, his eyes met mine, he frowned and turned his attention back to Judith.

What had I done to incur his displeasure?

I would not cry. I would not appear unhappy. This was Judith's day and no one, especially not me, would spoil it for her.

I need not have worried. The vicar intoned the words of the service and got no further than *Dearly beloved, we are gathered here*, before my aunt whipped out her handkerchief and dabbed her eyes. I relaxed. Women cried at weddings. I could cry if I wanted, and of course, knowing that I could raised my spirits so that I no longer desired to.

'I now pronounce you man and wife.'

My aunt gave a small sob. My uncle cleared his throat. The captain lifted Judith's veil and kissed her cheek. 'My very dear Mrs Lindhurst,' he murmured.

She blushed and smiled.

They signed the register, Captain Liverton and I signed as witnesses and it was over. My friend was a married woman.

We were to go back to the Woodley house to eat breakfast. 'I fear I cannot stay,' I said. 'As it is, I am late and Mrs Heskith deplores unpunctuality.'

Mr Woodley patted my hand. 'I will write her a note and Arnold shall run with it. She will forgive you if she is the first to hear the news of the wedding. You must stay. I have arranged a surprise!'

He would not tell us what it was. I swathed myself in one of my aunt's aprons and helped her prepare breakfast. We could hear the piano in the drawing room and Judith's voice mingling with that of her new husband's.

Husband. Wife. Married. I could not grow accustomed to the idea. 'Do you know what the surprise is?' I asked my aunt to distract my mind.

She shook her head. 'I cannot begin to guess. It is all most mysterious.'

We set the table with the white damask cloth we had used for the dinner party. I ran into the garden to pick a bunch of late roses for the table. The day shone fair and fine, a truly auspicious day on which to begin a lifetime partnership and so I told my aunt when I returned.

'Thank you, Hannah, that is a beautiful thought.' She

lifted a tray of scones from the oven. 'There now. I believe we are ready. Would you be so kind as to tell them to come, my dear?'

I trod down the passage and waited in the doorway of the drawing room until Judith finished her song. 'Breakfast is served, Mrs Lindhurst.' I dropped her a curtsey and then spoiled it by laughing at her blushes.

The captain offered her his arm and I stood back to allow them to walk past me. Captain Liverton bowed to me, held out his arm and escorted me to the kitchen.

My aunt and I served dishes of ham, fried potatoes and tomatoes. We set out whipped cream and peach jam for the scones. Stanley dropped cream and jam all down his suit. He and Arnold offered Judith food, salt, tea. 'Mrs Lindhurst, would you like the butter? Mrs Lindhurst, can I pass you another scone?'

The captain ate well, but managed to be quietly atten- tive to Judith who ate little but glowed with an inner joy quite unruffled by her brothers' teasing.

Thanks to Mr Woodley's surprise, nobody talked of war.

'I think it must be a horse,' Arnold said. 'Papa must have bought one in Auckland.'

Stanley treated the suggestion with scorn. 'He brought it home in his pocket, I suppose. No, it has to be somebody to entertain us.'

A look of horror crossed Charlie's face. 'Papa, if it's that horrid screeching woman we had to listen to last October then I'm off!'

Mr Woodley merely laughed and gave away no clues, not even when we heard the front door open and close. All he said was, 'Ah, that will be the surprise arriving.' He chuckled at his sons' impatience. They looked hopeful when he stood up, but their faces fell when he began to speak. 'It is with great pleasure, Captain, that I welcome you into our family.' Mercifully, he kept it brief for had he not, I believe Arnold and Stanley would have expired.

The captain rose in his turn. His only response to two loud sighs was the pronounced twinkle in his eyes. He thanked my uncle and aunt for the gift of their daughter. 'I promise to take care of her and do my utmost to ensure her happiness.' He bent down and reached for Judith's hand and spoke directly to her. 'My very dear wife, I know my family will love you. I long to make you known to them.'

Very pretty. We applauded, and Arnold said, 'Now can we see what the surprise is?'

Truth to tell, I was as curious as they were by the time we trooped back to the drawing room.

Judith paused in the doorway, oblivious of her brothers jumping up and down behind her. 'Papa! A photographer!' She looked at her captain. 'We will have a record of this happy day! Oh, it is splendid.'

My uncle beamed with pleasure at her delight.

'You must stay quite still,' Mr Gill instructed us. 'Do not try to smile for if your mouth moves it will spoil the image.'

He sat Judith in a chair and placed the captain behind

her. 'Put your hand on your wife's shoulder, sir. Now, Miss Carstairs, if you would be so kind as to sit here, and Captain Liverton, you stand behind her if you please.'

Wife. My dearest friend was now a wife.

# 16

## Chapter Sixteen

Captain Liverton escorted me home, although I protested there was no need. 'Do not deny me the pleasure, Miss Carstairs,' he said, laughing.

What engaging manners the military men had. I kissed Judith farewell. 'I will visit when you have settled in, if I may?'

She pressed my hand. 'Of course you must visit us.' She sent a shy smile to her husband.

He bowed to me. 'Please do, Miss Carstairs. These are uncertain times and I may not be able to be home as much as I would wish to be.'

Captain Liverton offered me his arm and we left the house. 'Tell me,' he said, 'what do you think of your friend marrying so suddenly?'

'I hope and pray it is unnecessary for them to marry so soon,' I said, tightness clamping down in my chest at the thought of war. 'But I can understand. She loves him dearly.'

He patted my hand where it lay in the crook of his arm. 'Come now. Miss Carstairs, you need not be concerned for your friend's happiness. There'll be a bit of a scrap with the natives. Nothing serious, you know. It'll all be over before it starts. No cause for alarm.'

I withdrew my hand and it was all I could do not to wipe it where he had patted it. 'I think it is alarming that we are considering war. It is wrong.' I dropped him a curtsey. 'I am nearly home. Thank you for your escort. Good day to you, Captain.' I left him with a swish of my yellow skirt. I did not like him. I did not like any of the military, Captain Lindhurst included.

Rawinia took one look at my face. 'You enjoyed the wedding, I see.'

I stamped my foot. 'War! Captain Liverton saw me home. Rawinia, he is so arrogant!'

She turned me around to unbutton my dress. 'He's a man. He's English. He's a soldier.'

I stepped out of my dress and kicked it. 'And that is too tight and too old-fashioned!' I reached out and threw my arms around her. 'Rawinia! Judith is married! My friend is not my friend any longer.'

If I had hoped she would deny it and comfort me I should have known better. 'Life is a river. You can't stop it.'

I laughed. At least she didn't change.

As it happened, I saw Judith on the beach before I was able to visit her in her new home. On the first day of March, Governor Gore Browne arrived by ship bringing with him a colonel by the name of Gold who had in his charge hundreds more troops. I hurried to the beach to watch the landings and I was probably the only person there who hoped the surf-boat crews would today not have skill enough to land the men and their equipment safely. I wove my way through groups of people all laughing and chattering until I reached a spot where I could see the surf-boats rowing out to the ship.

Judith saw me and hurried across the black sand. 'Hannah! Wait for me!' She laughed as the breeze caught her bonnet.

My heart rejoiced to see her for she was happy, there was no doubt about it. She pulled me by the hand. 'Come where we can see. My husband is in the welcoming party. And Hannah! It is so exciting! We are to dine with the governor tonight!'

I said all that was proper as we pushed our way through the people, and I admired Captain Lindhurst standing straight and tall on the beach.

'Miles says the governor will force the survey,' she told me. She pulled her cloak around her shoulders and kept her gaze on her husband. 'He says William King will see it is hopeless to resist. He says there will be no war.'

She had never called the old chief by his English name before she married. 'I hope he is right,' I said. I hoped it with all my heart, but I knew he was wrong.

'Judith, Hannah!' It was Amy and Lavender. We made room for them beside us.

Lavender burst out, 'Isn't it exciting! They say there will be more than four hundred troops in the town when these are landed.'

'You may be sure neither of us will have a secret

wedding if we find a handsome soldier,' Amy said, shaking her head at Judith.

Judith just smiled.

But Lavender was right – it was exciting. The surf-crews fought the waves and just when we expected a boat would be swamped and go down along with its cargo, the skill and strength of the crews would prevail. All the people cheered and I hurrahed along with them. The tide of the day caught me up and swept me with it. There was no time for thinking, for reflection or sorrow. Men in uniform jumped from the surf-boats. Then came boatload after boatload of their horses, carts, huge guns, tents – all manner of equipment.

Judith's face glowed with pride. Her husband was part of this army, the best in the world. Amy and Lavender glanced at each boat as it was unloaded onto the sand, but their eyes never strayed far from the soldiers.

As for me – I gasped when it seemed certain a boat was doomed. I cheered and clapped when the crew brought it safely to shore. My heart swelled with pride at their skill. Nowhere in the world could there be men with such strength and courage, of that I was sure.

Then for a moment my mind would slip sideways so that I saw the piles of gear on the beach for what they were – instruments of war – and pain clutched at my heart.

Only days after the landings, I was sweeping out the shop in preparation for closing when I looked up to find Polly at the door.

'Polly! Is everything all right? Is Tommy well? Where is

Peter?' I ran to her, concerned at the worry on her face.

She straightened her back and put on a smile. 'We're all fine, Hannah. It's just this dreadful talk of war. I know it's a good thing, but it scares me.'

I asked her to wait while I collected my bonnet. 'Have you come into town to stay?'

She nodded. 'We've buried the china and we've brought our bedding and clothes with us, along with the cows.' A shadow crossed her face. 'We had to leave the cat and the lamb. Hannah, it near broke my heart, the cat cried and the lamb ran after us all the way to the road.'

I took her arm and led her out into the street where Peter held Tommy who sat on Daisy. Marigold carried a load of blankets and baggage. 'Where's Bluebell?' I asked.

'Ran off into the bush, along with our floor rug,' said Peter.

I took Tommy and dropped a kiss on his hair. 'You must stay with us.'

He nodded. 'Thank you Hannah but it will be Polly and the lad, if your folks agree. I'll go back and help build the stockade.'

I assured them that of course Rawinia and Papa would agree. Papa was so caught up in the war talk that he was prepared to make any sacrifice, even the peace and routine of his house. And Rawinia? I frowned. 'There is just one thing. It will distress Rawinia if you talk of the war being a good thing.'

Peter nodded his head. 'Aye, we thought she'd likely have a different opinion.'

'I'll be careful, I promise you,' Polly said.

I smiled at her. 'I'm so happy it is you who are to stay with us for I could not have been polite to Mr Walter.'

They laughed and we walked to our house in perfect accord.


'I am so comforted by the volunteers,' Polly said as we prepared dinner on the second day of their stay. 'We can come to no harm in the town with them to protect us, I pray that Peter is as safe.'

I murmured something soothing about Peter.

She glanced at Rawinia. 'Begging your pardon, Mrs Carstairs, but everyone's that fired up. It's hard to be downhearted, indeed it is.' She pulled at her apron. 'I don't feel scared now — except when I think of Peter out there away from the town.'

My own emotions rose and fell like a surf-boat in a rolling sea. One moment I hated all the talk of war but in the very next second my heart would swell with pride when Jamie and Arama shouldered their arms and went out on duty to guard the town.

Perhaps the town would need guarding, for the governor ordered the survey to proceed. Colonel Gold and his troops were to ensure that it did so.

Papa was full of delighted anticipation. 'Now we'll see some action. The troops will occupy the land. Wiremu Kingi will bow to a superior force and New Plymouth can expand.' He leaned backwards in his chair. 'It's time. Time for the Maoris to accept the inevitable. And we, my sons, are helping change the course of history.' He brought all four legs of his chair back into contact with the floor. 'It's heady stuff, my family.' He rose from the table and left the five of us sitting there, silent.

Polly got to her feet. 'All I can say is I'm that glad Tommy's too young to be mixed up in all this. It's bad enough that his father is out there and who knows what's happening.' She snatched up cutlery and clattered it.

The next day the troops prepared to leave for the Waitara. It was as Papa had said – they were to occupy the land so that the surveyors could do their work.

Rawinia came with Polly and me to watch them go. We joined Judith and the rest of the Woodley family. Judith said, 'My dear Miles says William King isn't stupid. He'll soon see that he cannot oppose the might of the British forces.'

I did not want to argue with her, so I said nothing. My eyes followed the soldiers, marching off down the road. They had so much to fight with, all loaded on carts. I looked at the guns – two 24-pounders and a 12-pounder – and imagined what they would do to the palisades of a pa, and to the flesh of those holding it. Except that there were no fighting pa at the Waitara, only unfortified villages like the one we had stayed at when we were very young.

'Rawinia, I'm frightened. What will happen?'

She shrugged. 'We wait and see.'

Polly gave me a quick hug. 'The town will be safe with the volunteers to guard it.'

Jamie, Arama and Papa were all required to do picket duty guarding the approaches to the town. I did not think that Papa would manage to stay awake all night but I could not worry about it.

My dreams at night were of blood and bullets as we waited out the following days. Papa, after his first attempt at night guard-duty, pleaded illness and did not present himself for duty again. The boys came and went, irritated at having to attend the daily parade at nine every morning. 'What is the point of it?' Jamie demanded. 'If we've been on duty all night we're half asleep anyway.'

But Colonel Gold demanded it and they had to do it.

In the middle of the month news came that shots had been fired. We were at war.

It was the boys who came home with the news.

'Wiremu Kingi's men built a fighting pa in the night,' said Arama.

My heart chilled for I saw the hero-worship in his eyes.

'On the flat land they built it. Double stockades.'

Jamie gave a snort of derision. 'Colonel Gold breached it with his guns this morning but of course they'd all escaped in the night.' He shook his head. 'That man is so ignorant! Didn't even understand that the galleries inside were gunpits, which he should do because they fired through the palisades all day and killed nobody.'

Polly shook her head and her eyes turned towards Omata. She jumped to her feet and bustled around preparing to wash the dishes. Tommy sat in his chair and chortled at Jamie and Arama.

I went to work to find Mrs Heskith fuming. 'That Gold! Calls himself a colonel. I could have done better myself and now those heathens have got away with it, who knows what they'll try next.'

She didn't seem to expect me to reply. I did the dusting and kept my opinions to myself. All day, people rushed into the shop with another story about Colonel Gold's incompetence or yet another rumour that we were about to be attacked by those rebel niggers. Not one person apologised to me for using such a term in my hearing.

I went home and burst into tears at the sight of Jamie and Arama readying themselves for night guard-duty. 'Where is Papa?' I sobbed. 'He thinks the war is wonderful. Why isn't he doing his duty too?'

None of them answered me, but I knew. Papa was too inebriated to do anything except stay in the hotel and take more drink.

Rawinia picked up Tommy and gave him to me. 'He took his first steps today.'

I hugged him and watched Polly's proud face through my tears. Peter should have been able to see his son take his first steps too. It wasn't fair. Nothing was fair.

In the morning, Mrs Heskith greeted me with my wages and a sorrowful look. 'I'm that sorry, Hannah, but I'm going to have to let you go.'

I stared at her, shocked.

She hastened to reassure me. 'Oh, don't look like that, dearie! It's nothing you've done or haven't done. It's the customers. They come in but all they give us is rumours, and that won't feed the chooks nor fatten the child, now will it?'

I nodded. I should have realised. I took the money she held out to me.

'The moment things pick up, I'll have you back if you'll come.'

I managed to smile at her. 'Of course, Mrs Heskith. I'll be glad to.'

I wandered home. I had no occupation. Now I was just another woman at the mercy of the rumours.

# 17

## Chapter Seventeen

I didn't know what to do with myself. Between them, Polly and Rawinia kept the house immaculate, the garden tidy and the boys and Papa fed — whenever he came home.

Rawinia said, 'Go and help Mrs Woodley, Hana girl. She'll be glad of an extra pair of hands.'

She was right. Aunt Frances almost cried when I arrived. She pulled me into the house quickly in case I vanished. 'Hannah dearest, you can have no notion how welcome you are. Judith does her best to help, of course, but she has her own house now.'

I changed into my house dress and tied an apron around my waist. 'Shall I do the washing, Aunt? I think the rain will hold off long enough to dry things.'

Judith joined us when we ate our midday meal and my aunt did not reprimand Arnold and Stanley when they recounted the latest rumour in the town. She merely asked Judith, 'Miles has no news?'

Judith shook her head. 'It is all waiting and wondering with the military as well.'

Later in the afternoon when my aunt and I were alone

again, I said, 'Judith is so happy. I'm glad they married when they did.'

Aunt Frances took out her handkerchief and gave her eyes a quick wipe. 'It does my heart good every time I see her. But, oh Hannah, I worry so. What will she do if . . .' She could not continue.

'Nothing has happened,' I said. 'Perhaps all will yet be well.'

'Perhaps.'

Only two more days passed before we discovered what a false and foolish hope it was that nothing would happen. Judith ran to find us. We heard her calling our names before we saw her.

'Judith! What is it? What has happened?' We ran to meet her.

'Miles has heard . . . Mama, it is dreadful. Some men – settlers at Omata – they've been killed. Massacred in cold blood.' Tears spilled from her eyes but I had no time to comfort her.

'Who? Judith, who? Peter Herbert? Is he . . . ?'

She shook her head. 'Miles didn't know names. Or how many, only that it is true.'

'I must go to Polly.' I dragged off my apron and sped from the house, only to meet Polly running into town.

'Those murdering devils!' she shouted as soon as she caught sight of me.

I ran with her into the town. All around us, people

eddied and whirled. *Who? How many?* Questions poured over us, but nobody knew anything for sure.

'Peter?' Polly ran through the crowds, but her voice mixed with other voices calling other names.

A hand grabbed my arm. 'Hannah! Come over here. The volunteers are going to Omata.' It was Amy. She tugged me with her to where Lavender and Lizzie waved to us.

Lizzie, her eyes fever-bright, hastened over to us. 'They're going to bring in the families still out there. Frederick is going. Isn't it exciting!'

I scanned the lines of volunteers. Jamie and Arama were among them.

'Rawinia. I have to tell her.' I dodged through the press of people and ran home.

Rawinia's mouth set in a thin line but she said nothing, just went to the cupboard for her boots, pulled them on and together we hurried back into the town.

'They'll be safe,' Lavender said. 'The troops are going too.'

The people cheered as the troops and volunteers marched off to Omata and then there was nothing for us to do but return to our houses and wait.

In the afternoon, when Judith arrived, I said, 'Aunt Frances, if you don't mind I will go home. Polly and Rawinia will both be anxious.'

Polly was cleaning when I arrived. She paused to snap out, 'Is there any news?' When I shook my head she went back to her furious scrubbing of the floor.

I helped Rawinia care for Tommy and we stayed out of her way.

Late in the afternoon a booming sounded out over the town.

'What's that?' I lifted my head. It couldn't be thunder. A second boom rattled the crockery.

'The alarm guns!' Polly shouted. 'Those murdering devils! They're attacking!' She dropped her cleaning cloth, grabbed Tommy up into her arms and sped from the house without a bonnet or shawl.

I ran after her and together we made for the barracks on Marsland Hill. Other women ran too, streaming from every house. Many were like us, bare headed and clutching children. I ran to catch up to Lavender's sister, struggling with a child under each arm. I took the toddler from her. The child added her wails to the mayhem.

'What is happening?'

'Can you see them? We'll be murdered where we stand!'

All around us questions mixed with cries, but no answers came.

I set the child down. Women still trudged up the steep pathway. I saw a woman from an outlying farm, a child under each arm and two small ones clinging howling to her skirts. I ran back down the path to help and my heart bled for her. I think she scarcely knew where she was or what she should do. 'We had to leave everything. We had to move to town. And now this!' She wept tracks into the dust on her face.

I was relieved that Polly took her in hand when we reached the barracks.

But after all, it was nothing. Nobody attacked us, we saw no warriors. Nothing.

Slowly, we dribbled in ones and twos back down the path we had scrambled up so urgently.

Rawinia said nothing when we came in, just made us tea and gave us food.

Polly kept glancing at the sky. 'It'll be dark soon. They'll be back by nightfall. I'm going into the town to wait.'

We all went. Aunt Frances and Judith found us. 'They'll be back soon,' Judith said. 'Miles told me they wouldn't leave the town undefended at night.'

I hoped she was right.

'Here they come!' The shout came from a boy racing down the road towards us.

I breathed a prayer of thanks but did not say anything aloud for Polly looked strained to breaking point. 'Peter?' she whimpered.

A silence fell upon us, broken by a ragged cheer when the line of marching soldiers appeared.

Beside me, Judith drew in a deep breath. 'There's Miles. Mama — he's safe!' She burst into tears. Aunt Frances patted her shoulder but looked beyond the soldiers for the volunteers. 'My husband? Charlie? Where are they?'

I whispered, 'Aunt Frances, they haven't come back.' I saw my own cold fear reflected in her eyes.

'They've left them behind!' Lizzie Bevan shrieked.

'Why?' She ran shouting to the line of troops but no one answered her. My eyes flew to Captain Lindhurst. His face was grim but he was marching off to the barracks and nobody would tell us anything.

Rumours flew. I knew better than to believe them all, but I believed enough to make me cold with fear for the safety of my brothers.

All we could do was wait. We stood with other women who held babies, who had toddlers clinging, crying, to their skirts and we waited for news of our men. We grew cold and hungry. Tommy struggled in Polly's arms, crying for food, but Polly didn't seem to notice. I took him from her, carried him home, fed him then ran back with him sleeping on my shoulder. Still they didn't return. Tears dripped down Polly's face but she didn't notice them either. I stood beside Rawinia who didn't speak but her lips moved and I knew she recited karakia praying for the safety of the boys.

It was after midnight when somebody shouted out, 'Hush! Listen!'

We stopped talking – stopped breathing. Was it the volunteers returning, or was it the rebels come to attack us?

'Rule Britannia! Britannia rules the waves!'

Aunt Frances gasped out, 'Praise the Lord! They've returned.'

'It's the volunteers! They're back!'

They came marching down the road in the darkness shouting out the song. I had never heard so sweet a sound.

Several women fell to their knees exhausted from the strain of the vigil.

Polly didn't move except that her hand clutched my arm with strength enough to leave bruises. I searched for my brothers. I saw Mr Woodley, Charlie, Frederick Jackson. Just as my heart was about to fail me, Rawinia said, 'There! Both of them.'

I stood on tiptoe and shrieked, 'Jamie! What of Peter?'

Jamie waved. 'He's fine!'

Polly burst into tears and didn't stop until we all crowded into the kitchen. Then she bustled about helping Rawinia make food, for the boys were starving.

'It was a botch-up from start to finish,' Jamie said.

Arama ate and didn't talk.

Neither of them could understand why Colonel Murray had withdrawn his men. 'Colonel Gold's orders apparently. But Murray shouldn't have left us there. If it hadn't been for the sailors from the *Niger* creating a diversion then we'd be dead.'

We were so grateful to the men of the *Niger*. I could not look at my brothers without sending a prayer of thanks to those gallant men.

March faded into April and I no longer complained to Rawinia that it was like a party in the town. People walked with heavy steps and grim faces. There were no more massacres, but Colonel Gold had no tactics to stop Wiremu Kingi Te Rangitake and his men. They torched farms and houses then vanished into the bush.

Polly went about her work with a set face. I was happy to escape to the Woodley household where there was as much work as I could wish to keep my mind from brooding. I could not bear to think of Polly and Peter's house burning and with it the garden, the flowers, the young fruit trees and their hopes. I shook my head. I would not think of it. Instead, I would dream of a letter and money arriving from Lord Derringford. *Come and speak to me of Angelina,* he would say. But it was a dream I could not sustain.

There was no hiding from what was happening. Every day, smoke thickened the sky and the sunsets ran red.

Jamie came home one morning from guard-duty and he was alone.

Papa sat at the breakfast table, but even so Rawinia spoke in Maori, her voice sharp. 'Hemi, where is your brother?'

'He has joined Wiremu Kingi's men.' He too spoke in Maori and it was left to me to translate the words to Papa.

Papa lurched to his feet. He stumbled from the room, came back for his hat and his stick and left us without a word.

Jamie sat at the table and refused to talk about it. He wore a tight, contained expression that made me ache to see. I felt as if I had been struck in the chest and all the air knocked from my body.

'He did not say goodbye,' I whispered.

The next day, after the evening meal, Rawinia went into her bedroom.

'It's not like her to disappear like that,' Polly remarked.

Fear gripped me. I dropped the dishcloth and ran to the bedroom. 'Rawinia, what is happening? What are you doing?' I flung the door open. She raised her eyes from the petticoat she was folding. 'Where are you going?' I could scarce say the words for the constriction in my throat.

She came to me, put her hands on my shoulders and pressed her nose to mine in a hongi of farewell. 'I go to my people, my daughter.'

She bade Jamie farewell and left.

I couldn't cry. I was frozen. Jamie too. His face looked carved from wood. If Polly hadn't been with us, neither of us would have eaten until we dropped down faint from hunger.

With all the strength of my being I wished I too had kin to go to. Kin a long way from Taranaki and kin who had no interest in the war or what side to fight on.

There had been no reply from Lord Derringford.

The order came from Colonel Gold: all families outside the defendable zone of the town must move to within it. We were outside the defence ditch which surrounded such a small area of the town.

'You will come to us, of course,' Aunt Frances said.

I couldn't speak. I hugged her and hurried home to help Polly gather her things together. It did not take Jamie and me long to pack our belongings. What Papa would do we didn't know for these days he didn't come home.

We paused on the verandah as Jamie shut the door behind us.

'Where will it all end?' Polly muttered.

Jamie shrugged and set off down the path between the tidy flowerbeds. I wanted to weep. Polly had lost her house but I had lost Arama, Rawinia and Jamie, for he shut me out and stayed locked in a bleak world where he would admit no one.

It was a relief to stay with the Woodleys. Among the rush of people and the hurly burly of comings and goings I could hide a little from Jamie's pain and drown my own in work.

We saw much of Judith and although she too worried for her menfolk, the quiet aura of joy stayed with her. Her happiness encouraged me and gave me hope in the darkness of our troubles. I saw little of Captain Lindhurst and when I did, he was formal and distant. I did not have thoughts to spare for him.

Some days after we had moved into the Woodleys' house, Judith arrived as usual after luncheon and she was hurrying.

'Judith!' my aunt exclaimed. 'Is all well?'

She nodded but looked at me. 'Hannah – did you know? Jamie is waiting on the beach. He has a bundle with him and there are so many ships anchored in the roadstead – some of them sailing today.'

All my blood, all my emotions fled from my body. I was numb. I just gaped at her. She seized my hand and pulled me towards the room Jamie shared with the Woodley boys.

'He's left you a note.' She snatched it up and pressed it into my hands. 'Read it, Hannah. Hurry!' She took my shoulders and gave me a shake. It woke me up. I tore the note open.

*Dearest Sissy,*

*Please forgive me for abandoning you but I cannot stay here. The thought that I might kill Arama never leaves me. I am going to England to try my luck.*

*Your loving brother,*

*Jamie.*

I pushed it into Judith's hands. 'Show my aunt.' I whirled and ran to my own room, snatched up my hairbrush from the dresser where it lay beside Polly's and then seized a blanket from my bed and tumbled onto it the dress I had made, the gold dress I had worn to the wedding, my blue cotton dress, my nightgown, my two extra petti-coats, the hairbrush, boots and the small amount of money I possessed.

'Hannah!' Judith cried. 'What are you doing?'

Aunt Frances and Polly crowded into the room, staring at my frenzied packing. 'Hannah!' gasped my aunt. 'Think what you are about, child!'

I shouldered the bundle and kissed all three of them. 'He will not go without me!'

My aunt's face was pale and tears wet her cheeks. She hurried from the room and I thought I had wounded her to the heart, but in a moment she returned and flung her warm woollen cloak around my shoulders. 'Take this, my child, with my love.'

I kissed her cheek, I could not speak. Oh, I would miss her sorely, but my determination did not waver.

'Hannah!' Judith wailed. 'You cannot do this!'

But I could. I sped from the house, Judith running after me. People stared but I had no thought for them. I felt every knobble in the road through the soles of the light slippers I wore, but I could not take the time to change into my boots.

I reached the beach in time to see Jamie stepping into the surf-boat. 'Wait!' I shouted.

He didn't hear. The men settled to their oars, they dipped them into the water. I raced down the sand. 'Wait!' Still they didn't hear me. I called again as I splashed through the waves. 'Jamie! Wait for me!'

They stopped the boat. Jamie threw his hands in the air, but his face wore the first grin I'd seen on it since Arama left. He pulled me in. 'You're wet.'

'And you're horrid!' I burst into tears. 'How could you go without me?'

Through my tears, I saw Judith waving from the beach. Beside her stood my aunt and Polly. I waved back. Would I ever see them again?

Neither of us spoke for our hearts were full.

I could not bear to watch the figures of our dear friends grow smaller and further away and so I stared around me at the ships – not one of them bound for England. 'Jamie?'

He turned to look at me, his brows raised.

'How are we to get to England?'

He threw back his head and roared with laughter so that

I smiled too. 'This is a fine time to be asking,' he said. He pointed to the ship we were approaching. 'That brig is bound for Sydney. We'll get a ship from there.'

'But I have no money to buy a passage,' I said, clutching his arm. 'Promise me you won't leave me behind. *Promise me.*'

'I promise.' He patted my hand. 'Truth to tell, Sissy, I'm pleased you're with me. Don't worry. We'll look for a family who have ten small children and require a nursemaid.'

We climbed up onto the deck of the brig where we waved and waved to our friends on the beach. Behind them smoke from burning farms clouded the sky.

# 18

## Chapter Eighteen

The brig sailed beyond sight of our friends on the beach. I turned to Jamie. 'We have left our home.' My chest squeezed tight and I pressed my hands over my heart.

Jamie said nothing. He stared at the land sliding away from us until all we could see was the peak of the mountain. Then he sighed, shook his shoulders and bade me follow him. 'We must speak to the captain. You will need a bed.'

He didn't mention money and the tightness in my chest eased a little. However, I said, 'Jamie – I have some money.' I scrabbled in my bundle.

He just grinned at me. 'We're in this together, Sissy. Don't fuss.'

There was no problem about accommodation for me. 'You're the only female on board, Miss Carstairs,' said the captain and he called a sailor to show me the women's quarters.

Jamie and I followed the man down the steep ladder below decks. At the doorway to my quarters, Jamie put his hand on my arm. 'I'll be just across the corridor, Hannah. Shout if you want anything.' He looked hard at the sailor as he spoke.

I smiled at him. 'Of course. And don't worry, I can shout very loudly.'

The sailor sniffed and stomped away.

Jamie came in with me and looked around. 'We should have brought blankets.'

He was right. The beds were bare wood and offered no comfort. 'It is too late now for such thoughts,' I said. 'I have my aunt's cloak.' I unwrapped my belongings and handed him the blanket. 'You take this.'

We survived the week it took to sail to Sydney, but I think I have never been so uncomfortable in my life. Seasickness kept me in my bed and Jamie was no better. We lay on the hard bunks and expected that every hour would be our last but it was not and the day before we reached Sydney we were well enough to get up, wash in saltwater and eat a little food.

Jamie screwed his face up. 'I hope the ship that takes us to England has better fare than this.'

I sighed and pushed the dry biscuit and salt pork around on the plate loaned to me by the cook. 'I would like a new potato from the garden.'

Jamie didn't answer. His face was tight and I guessed he thought about Arama and Rawinia. Where were they? Were they well? I did not wonder if they were happy, for how could they be, living as they must in the turmoil we had fled from?

'We will look for a ship in Sydney,' he said.

I kept my eyes on my food. What if we couldn't find a family who needed a nursemaid? Would Jamie leave me there alone? I did not think it, but then, I was no longer sure I knew him as well as when we were younger.

We went up on the deck to be in the fresh air.

The next day we sailed into Sydney town and I saw for myself how glorious a harbour could be. Blue water and green hills; the coastline dived in and out of numerous bays and inlets. 'Jamie — we could stay here. There must be people here who work with iron and machines.' I glanced at him and my words died. He wore his stubborn look and nothing would change his mind. I resigned myself to the long journey north.

'We will need provisions,' was all he said. 'Warm clothes, bedding, plates and cups.'

I knew it, but I whispered, 'Jamie, we cannot afford it. How will you pay for your passage if we use all our money on supplies?'

His eyes sparkled. 'We will contrive. We'll get there, Hannah. Somehow.'

I laughed suddenly for this was the old Jamie speaking. The Jamie who went off on outrageous adventures with Arama. He grinned at me and we ate our last sad meal on the brig in perfect harmony.

The ship berthed at Circular Quay. We stood at the rails amid the noise and bustle, our belongings at our feet, for it was our intention to quit the brig as soon as we could.

'Sydney is so large,' I said. Even from the boat we could see that it spread much further and wider than New Plymouth did. The port seethed and clamoured around us, men shouted and I was glad Aunt Frances was not here to hear them. Horses – more than I had ever seen in my life – pulled loads to and from the ships. Sailors, soldiers, labourers . . . my head pounded at all the noise and excitement.

Jamie picked up his bag. 'Let's go, Sissy.'

I swung my bundle across my shoulder, followed him down the gangway and stepped onto the soil of another country. I paused to savour the moment but Jamie turned around to look at me. 'Keep up, Hana. If we get parted I'll never find you.'

He did not need to remind me again.

'Do you have a plan?' I asked. I had to run to keep pace with him and I hoped to slow him down by making him talk to me.

For answer, he accosted a man driving a loaded dray. 'Where are the ships bound for England?'

The man spoke around the pipe in his mouth. 'Down yonder.'

I scampered down yonder after Jamie. I supposed it was as good a plan as any to go to where the England-bound ships were berthed.

It took us some time to get there for there was so much to look at. 'A ship must be sailing soon,' Jamie said. Ahead of us we could see carriages laden with people and luggage making their cumbersome way further down the docks. 'Let's hurry.'

I wanted to protest that there was no need, that no ship could be loaded swiftly enough to enable it to leave before we could reach it, but I saved my breath for hurrying.

The ship, when we found it, was a clipper. 'It's nearly loaded,' Jamie said, and I thought he was probably right for there was little cargo left on the dock and the carriage passengers tumbled out as if they were in a hurry. 'Look, Hannah – there's a family with children. Go and speak to them.'

I resisted the pressure of his hand on my shoulder. 'And do you notice that they are farewelling that young man?'

He laughed and his eyes flitted over the people milling on the docks, as did mine. 'I think it is mostly older people and men travelling alone,' I said.

'Wait here,' Jamie said. 'I will speak to that sailor.'

I stared after him. Would he come back for me? I shook my head – how could I have so little faith in him? Of course he would not abandon me here in this strange land. He spoke to the man. I saw him grin then he beckoned for me to come. I picked up our luggage and threaded my way through the tearful farewells taking place around me.

'Hannah, this gentleman,' he nodded towards the sailor, 'says to go and see the captain. He says I might work my passage if I'm handy enough.'

He bounded up the gangway before I could ask what he meant. A sailor? Could he be thinking of signing on as a sailor? And him so ill on the voyage from New Plymouth?

But that is exactly what he meant.

We made our way to the bridge. The captain, his eyes not straying from the loading of his ship, listened to Jamie's request. When Jamie finished speaking, he subjected him to a swift scrutiny. 'Very well, lad. You look fit and strong. I'll take you on, and it'll be sixteen guineas for your sister's passage.'

'Thank you, sir.' Jamie grinned at me, elated and no doubt seeing in his mind structures of iron blossoming all over England.

I said, 'Sir — we have no provisions for a long voyage.' I gestured to the luggage we held. 'This is all we possess in the world.' I did not know how much money Jamie had, but I guessed it would not be enough to equip us for the voyage, pay for my passage and leave us enough for travel and what accommodation we might need in England.

The captain kept his eyes on his work and said briskly, 'Well, lad — you work for no pay and I'll provide you both with what you'll need for the voyage. It stays on the ship when you leave. Fair enough?'

Before Jamie could speak, I said, 'Thank you, sir — we agree, but the cost of my passage in that case will be ten pounds.' I put a hand on Jamie's arm and squeezed tight to warn him not to speak. The captain would be getting the best of the bargain, for Jamie was a good worker.

The captain looked at me, taking notice of me for the first time. He frowned but I did not drop my head. His eyes flicked away from me, and he spoke to Jamie, 'What do you say?'

Jamie put his free hand over mine where I clutched his arm. 'I say that is a fair bargain, sir, for I'm guessing I'll be working hard and long.'

The captain stared out over his ship and didn't speak

for some moments. Finally he nodded. 'Very well. Go to the purser and tell him to equip you.' He gave me a swift glance through narrowed eyes. 'Both of you.'

I smiled at him, for there was a twinkle in his eyes.

The purser was Mr Watkins, a man of about Mr Woodley's age, but there was no other similarity between them. Mr Watkins was thickset, tanned to a rich walnut colour and the tattoo of a mermaid on his forearm arm moved her tail when he flexed his muscles. I had to drag my eyes away from it in order to pay attention once Jamie had told him the captain's orders.

Mr Watkins chuckled and rubbed his hands. 'Good for you, young miss. Good for you. It's not many as wrings a bargain out of our captain. A good man – you'd never find a better, but he keeps a tight ship and drives a hard bargain.'

He motioned for us to follow him, and led us to a store cupboard, opened it and began piling a treasure trove of clothing and equipment into our arms. For Jamie there were oilskin trousers, coat and hat, then more trousers and shirts. For me a warm dress of coarse material. 'You'll be glad of it, miss, once we get down among the icebergs.'

I glanced at Jamie. 'We will see icebergs!'

Mr Watkins harrumphed. 'They're not so exciting when you're trying to dodge the dratted things.' He tugged out blankets for me. 'Follow me. We'll get you established and then we'll see if the cook can spare a plate and mug.'

The only other woman in steerage was a young mother with a baby, a toddler and a child of about three. She started up when we came in, snatching her children to her. She watched us with wide, wary eyes and didn't return my smile.

Mr Watkins slapped the blankets onto one of the beds. 'There we are, lassie. Now for the galley.'

I put down my bundle, smiled at the young woman and followed Mr Watkins to the galley where the cook grumbled, but found utensils for me. I bobbed a curtsey and smiled as I thanked him.

We were to sail on the tide — an hour hence according to Mr Watkins, who carried Jamie away to begin his duties. I took the things the cook gave me down to my accommodation. Again, the young woman jumped as I came in and didn't return my greeting.

I chose a bed in the bottom row and placed my belongings on the one to my right. It was separated from mine by a plank of wood not high enough to afford privacy. My bed was luxuriously wide for one person, but how had Polly and Peter survived when they had made the journey? And Lavender's parents who had to fit their four children into the space as well?

I stared around the cabin. I had not imagined so many beds could fit in so small a space although Polly had told me about it many times. 'Side by side we slept,' she said. 'The next couple so close you could poke them if they snored.' How lucky I was not to have to share with a full complement of passengers. It should be pleasant enough down here with just the young woman, her children and me.

I left her alone with her children.

I stayed on the deck watching the bustle and hurry and I thought about home. What madness had possessed me? Would I have accompanied Jamie if I'd had time to consider? All in all, I was glad it had happened as it did for I would have worried about leaving Aunt Frances, Judith and Polly. I would have worried about money and insisted on waiting until we could afford to go – or said we should wait another month in case Lord Derringford replied.

The sun shone bright in the blue sky – a happy day to begin a journey. I felt myself relaxing, for there were three months in front of me where Jamie and I would have food and a place to sleep – and with every day we would leave the war further behind us.

It must have been mere minutes before we were due to sail that a man came running and shouting along the docks. He pushed past the sailor positioned at the gang- way, but the sailor pursued him and dragged him to a halt. The man cursed and swung a fist but the sailor ducked and hollered for help. Several of his shipmates ran to his aid. I edged closer wanting to hear everything. Aunt Frances said curiosity was vulgar, but I gave into it with scarcely a pang and offered her a silent apology.

But in truth, I think the whole world would have heard him, so loud were his demands and his cursing. 'Just wait till I get my hands on her! I'll teach her to run away.' He tried to jerk himself free of the sailors' grip. 'I demand to search the ship!'

Mr Watkins hurried past me to where the men

struggled on the gangway. 'You're looking for a woman with three young children?' he asked and my heart sank. The wife he sought had to be the frightened woman in the steerage accommodation. Oh, he would beat her senseless and maybe the children as well.

The man bellowed, 'That's her! The whore! The lying, cheating whore!'

I whirled around to run to her. I had a wild notion I could help her hide although in my heart I knew it could only make matters worse, but Mr Watkins's words carrying clearly on the hot air stopped me. 'Turned her away, I did. *Don't want the likes of you*, I told her. *Run a tight ship, we do and your sort aren't welcome*, I said.' He pointed down the docks. 'Headed off in that direction. Suggest you try the *Nightingale*. Not fussy about who they take on board.' He gestured to the sailors. 'Let him loose, men.'

The man shook himself and ran down the docks in search of the *Nightingale*. Mr Watkins walked past me and I heard him mutter, 'I'd as soon give a kitten to a tiger as tell him where she is.'

And so it was that Aggie Billings and her three children were my sole companions in the steerage accommodation. She recovered her spirits once she heard the story of how her husband had been sent on his way.

'He's not my husband,' she said. 'Wouldn't marry the likes of me. Didn't mind getting a child on me every year and beating me black and blue when he felt like it – but as for marriage! Not him.'

She stayed below decks as we sailed out of the beautiful harbour and when I at last went below, it was to discover that all four of them were suffering from seasickness. But I — and Jamie too — had gained my sea legs on the voyage to Sydney. I cared for the children and Aggie until they recovered and then we fell into a routine as we sailed through the southern ocean. Together we played with the children and kept them entertained and out of the way of the sailors. Shipboard life lacked excitement. 'Nothing wrong with a bit of boredom,' Aggie said. 'Beats a hammering any day of the week.'

But slowly, we became useful to the crew and some of the passengers who employed us to do mending. I tried to give the money I earned to Aggie, but she pushed it back to me. 'You've a good heart, Hannah and I thanks you, truly I do.' She lowered her voice and glanced around. 'You heard my man when he came looking for me?' I nodded and she dropped her voice to a whisper. 'He was in such a rage because of his gold. I took it, you see.'

I shouted with laughter. Tatty, battered Aggie who wasn't much older than I was, was a wealthy woman and who would suspect it? She grinned at me. 'I'm going home to me mam and we'll buy a house. I'm going to be a widow woman all sad and grieving for her man.' She grew solemn and when she spoke it was as if she was making a vow. 'And I'll tell you this, Hannah, I'll never take up with another man in all the days of my life.'

In my turn, I told her our story. She listened, wide-eyed.

'What a tale, Hannah! What a tale.' She leaned forward to settle baby Molly on the deck at our feet. 'It's my belief you'll turn out to be quality. And an heiress, and all the young bucks will fight with pistols to win you.'

I laughed and told her of my determination never to marry. 'Then you must come and live with me,' she said and we laughed.

The days passed and always the thing on everyone's minds was how far we had come each day. There were storms but not bad ones. There were icebergs but we didn't get trapped among them.

There were dolphins and sharks and the huge seabird with wingspans wider than a man is high.

I cut up my flannel petticoat to make gloves for Jamie to wear inside the ones Mr Watkins had issued him. He cut his knee during a storm and I ripped up one of my cotton petticoats to bind it with. Mr Watkins told me the next day when the storm abated that the ship had bandages and it looked after its crew. But he smiled at me and said, 'Your medical skills could be useful Miss Hannah. We should have a doctor on board, but he jumped ship in Australia to try his luck in the goldfields.'

Then there was the heat of the tropics and the ceremony of crossing the line. Jamie got his head dunked in evil looking water because it was his first time. They made me do a forfeit so I chose to sing a song. Aggie held the baby and laughed. With every passing day she grew more carefree. It was good to see.

After the tropics we met rain again which lasted for days. Aggie ran out of nappies for the baby. I tore up my last petticoat and we used that.

I saw a little of Jamie, but mostly he was busy or he preferred to relax with his messmates. 'Do you like being a sailor?' I asked.

He grinned. 'It serves the purpose, but no, I won't be signing on again.'

Mr Watkins called on my medical skills twice more. Once because a cabin boy had boils, and once because one of the cabin passengers fell and sprained her wrist. I did the best I could but the strange thing was, everyone believed I knew what I was doing and thanked me most sincerely.

Aggie laughed when I told her. 'It's like me pretending to be married,' she said. 'Everyone treated me like I was and when I gets home, they'll treat me like a widow. You just got to believe it yourself.' How true — for had we not believed Papa to be our father for all the years of our lives?

On the occasions I did see Jamie, we discussed what we would do when we got to England. I wanted to visit our grandmother. Jamie didn't. 'She'd have written to us if she wanted to know us,' he said.

'I want to go anyway,' I answered.

But we did agree that we would go straight to Devon, find Lord Derringford and listen to what he could tell us. What we would do then, we didn't know. 'I'll find work,' I said, 'and you'll be able to. We won't starve.' Brave words, but sometimes in the nights when the ship rocked and creaked I stared into the future and shivered.

Aggie said, 'You come to me if you gets stuck. There's always a place for you in my house.'

I hugged her. I loved the way she said *my house*. She mixed pride and wonder and determination into those two words.

The ship drew nearer our destination. I cleaned the woollen dress Mr Watkins had issued me with and returned it to him.

We sailed into the Thames and up the river into London town on a day where the rain fell lightly, but even so Aggie and I huddled together at the rail, clutching the children. 'London,' I whispered. 'I can't believe it.'

Aggie shook her head. 'I can't wait to leave it. I'll be on a train for Liverpool before you can blink, just see if I'm not.'

When the ship docked, I helped her with her luggage and handed the children to her after she climbed into a cab. She leaned out and hugged me. 'Mind, you come to me if you needs to, Hannah. You hear me?'

I kissed her cheek. 'I do indeed. Thank you, Aggie, with all my heart.' Then she was gone.

I went back to the ship to wait for Jamie and I was glad to be back on board, away from the chaos and noise pressing at me from all sides. I looked around, wishing he would come.

I was hungry by the time he was free to go. 'Let's find something to eat,' I said as we stepped once more onto a surface that didn't buck and roll beneath our feet – except that it felt as if it were doing so.

Something like guilt flashed across Jamie's face. 'We'd better find lodging first, and buy our tickets for Devon. Then we can see if we've got money for food.'

I stared at him. 'Jamie – how much money do you have?'

He grinned at me. 'Not a lot. I gave most of it to Rawinia when Arama left. I thought they would need it.'

I hugged him. 'Oh Jamie, I'm so glad. And I have the money I earned on board as well as what I brought from home. Let's get a cab to the hotel. Let's have a wonderful meal with fresh vegetables!'

He laughed and I could see that the idea of squandering the little money we did have appealed to him immensely. Perhaps, after all, we were Papa's children.

# Chapter Nineteen

Jamie hailed us a cab. 'I say, Sissy – this is different from New Plymouth.'

I did not have time to reply, for the cab driver called down from his perch, 'Where to, young 'uns?'

Jamie grinned at him. 'We want a good but cheap hotel near Paddington Station.'

The cabbie tipped back his cap and gave us a considering look. 'You'd be best off taking an omnibus.' He settled the cap back on his head. 'Unless you've got more money than it looks like?'

We took his advice and an uncomfortable and odorous ride it was, although with so much to see the time we spent jammed in a crush of other vehicles passed well enough. Jamie craned to see bridges, towers and buildings. I watched the people, the rich and the poor – poorer than the most indigent beggar at home. All around me were people, carriages, more omnibuses, buildings whose pictures I had seen in the *Illustrated London News*. It was too much after the monotony of the voyage and my head throbbed. I closed my eyes and thought of Aggie and was comforted to have one friend in the mayhem of this land.

The afternoon was old by the time we found a hotel respectable enough and cheap enough for our means. The landlady showed me to my room. 'Take the bed over there.' She pointed to one of the ten in the room. 'And watch your belongings. You can never be too careful.'

Jamie knocked on the door. 'I'll buy our tickets, Sissy. Do you want to come?'

I smiled at him and shook my head. He would not want me hanging onto his shirt-tails when there was a station full of engines to explore. 'Come back in time for dinner, or I'll eat without you,' I said.

However I did not have to face the dining room un-accompanied, for Jamie's stomach ensured he returned on time, but he was no company — his eyes shone with dreams made of iron.

I ate a meal of roast beef and turned my mind to the next day and Lord Derringford. Perhaps he knew nothing of our parentage, and if that should prove to be so, then I was determined to visit my grandmother — with or without Jamie.

In the morning we ate an early breakfast then stepped out into the street. I felt a little more accustomed to the bustle and noise and was tempted to linger but Jamie took my arm and hustled me forward.

He propelled me into Paddington Station and I thought he had led me to hell. I shrank back and back until I could retreat no further as monsters roared and bellowed around us. All was steam and noise and shouting. I thought of Rawinia and of legends of terrible taniwha. Jamie did not notice and I was only able to follow him because I feared he would lose me in the inferno.

He dodged and twisted his way through people and luggage, with me close behind and shading my face from the monstrous engines. I half hoped he would not be able to find the correct platform for I knew I would never be able to bring myself to climb into a carriage. I trembled and held my hands over my ears. Jamie though, danced on the very edge of the platform, paying no heed to my calls of distress.

'This is it, Hana! This is our train!' He ran up and down, desperate to drink in every feature of the great brown engine called the Iron Duke.

We nearly missed catching the train, for he was engrossed in the engine and I was too terrified to move. At the last second, he came running, grabbed my hand and hauled me into our second-class carriage.

The kindness of our fellow travellers helped settle my nerves. I would not be so afraid again, but the journey was not a comfortable one, crammed as we were with ten other passengers in a tiny compartment, sitting bolt upright on hard wooden seats. I was happy to alight in Plymouth, a vastly different place from its namesake half a world away.

Jamie walked backwards as we left the station, his eyes feasting upon buildings, engines and rails. I put a hand on his arm. 'Jamie, we do not have any money left.'

That caught his attention. 'Are you sure. Sissy?'

I nodded and he rubbed a hand over his hair. 'What will

we do now?' He grinned at me. 'My mind has been rather occupied.'

I shouldered my bundle. 'We will walk,' I said, 'but we had best find out which direction to go.'

Jamie dragged his mind from his beloved engines and asked directions of the stationmaster, who pointed the way for us. He gave us the sort of look that suggested he wanted to question us, but he didn't.

We began walking. Jamie didn't talk and my thoughts flitted from Aggie, to Rawinia, Arama and the Woodleys. I would write to my aunt as soon as I could.

I tried not to think of Papa or of Lord Derringford.

A cart rumbled past us and jerked me from my reveries. It was empty. I ran after it, calling, 'Oh, sir! Wait! Might we ride with you?' I looked up at the driver, bobbed him a curtsey and smiled. 'That is, if we are going in the same direction. But I should tell you that we have no money to pay you.'

He took the pipe from his mouth and considered the pair of us. Then he nodded. 'Aye. The cost will be a story or two, and a song if you can sing but not if you can't.'

We jumped up into the cart. I smiled at the man. 'Are you a farmer, sir?'

'Aye, lassie, that I am. Now, I'm guessing you don't come from these parts or my name's not John Lugg.'

So between us, Jamie and I entertained him with stories of our journey, our homeland and our childhood and we were all well pleased with the bargain we'd made.

Darkness was falling by the time John Lugg stopped his

wagon. 'There you are, young 'uns. Follow that road to top of hill, and there you'll see Derringford Park.'

We jumped down. Jamie shook his hand and I smiled and dropped him a curtsey. 'Thank you kindly, sir, for we'd not have arrived before dark if you hadn't taken pity on us!'

'You're welcome, missy. A pretty face always sweetens a journey.' But it was Jamie's face he looked at, not mine.

We followed the road he pointed to and began walking up a gentle slope. Where the gradient flattened we found ourselves looking down at a beautiful prospect. 'Jamie – do you think that is the house? It looks like a palace.' We put down our bundles and stared at our first view of an English country house.

'It is bigger than the hotel in London,' Jamie said. 'All this – for just one family.'

We were silent. My thoughts turned to London. Perhaps Jamie's did too, but it was more likely that he was wondering if the owner of the house would be able to introduce him to the engineer who built the iron bridge over the river Tamar that he was determined to see before we left Devon. I think we were both too keyed up to think about the question the owner of this imposing house might be able to answer for us. The question as to who our father was.

'Come on,' Jamie said. 'Let's go and knock on the front door.'

'They'll throw us out,' I said. I rubbed at a mark on the skirt of my blue dress. The train journey followed by the ride on the cart had left their traces. Jamie didn't look much tidier, but he squared his shoulders and began to walk.

I hurried to catch him up. We had come too far and too much depended on this meeting to lose heart now. Trees spread leafy shade above us, their branches meeting so that we walked in a tunnel of dappled light. 'Do you think they are oaks?' I asked, for I had seen a similar tree in Mr Cook's garden in New Plymouth. 'They are so different from the bush at home.'

Jamie shrugged and I chuckled. 'You would know what they were called if they were railway engines. You would tell me: *yes, Hannah, that is an entire row of Iron Dukes and they will pull you all the way from London to Plymouth via Bristol.*'

He grinned. 'Wasn't it something? Hannah, I want to travel on every line and see every engine in England and Scotland!'

# 20

## Chapter Twenty

We fell silent as we drew nearer. The late afternoon sun warmed the stone walls of the house so that it appeared mellow and welcoming. I prayed its owner would indeed welcome us. Our futures depended so much upon what he could tell us.

'If he cannot tell us who our father is,' I said, 'then I think we should visit Mama's parents.'

Jamie answered as he always did when I brought the subject up. 'It would be a waste of time. And anyway, do you want to visit the man who was so cruel to Mama?'

'It cannot make things any worse and perhaps Grandmother is still alive.' It was what I always said.

It was comforting, going over familiar arguments, for I think we were both a little overawed by the immensity and grandeur in front of us.

'It is all so tidy,' I said. We paused, looking around us at the stone fences, the little stream that ran between neat edges down to a lake. Beyond the park, cattle grazed on smooth green pastures without a blackened tree stump in sight. 'Do you think Polly and Peter will be all right?'

Jamie didn't reply – maybe he too thought of the smoke

billowing and blowing in the sky as Omata and the surrounding farms burned on the day we left. Polly and Peter would go back when they could and start again. Jamie wouldn't be there to help and Arama wouldn't be welcome if he wanted to. I would never again sit with Polly, our feet in a bush stream.

I quickened my steps to catch up to Jamie. 'I wish . . .' I stopped. What did I wish for? I'd been about to say I wished I was back home, but for all we knew, New Plymouth had burned to the ground as well. I shivered and uttered a quick prayer for the safety of our friends and family.

We reached the house. Wide steps invited the visitor up to a set of double doors, all carved and curlicued.

Jamie grinned at me. 'Here we are, Sissy. Are you ready?'

I nodded and a reckless excitement filled me. We had nothing to lose. It was a heady feeling. We trod up the broad stone steps and Jamie sounded a loud tattoo upon the knocker.

'Who do you think has the job of sweeping these steps?' I asked.

He pulled a face at me.

The door opened to reveal a smart young man in uniform whose lip curled as soon as he saw us. 'We wish to see Lord Derringford, if you please,' Jamie said.

Surely the young man couldn't be a servant? He looked every bit as fine as the captains in their scarlet coats and white trousers. He, however, did not have the charm of the military captains. He looked us up and down, arranged his face into a sneer then uttered the chilling words: 'Lord Derringford is not at home.'

Jamie's face fell and he stepped back. I jumped forward, crashing the door open into the young man's face. 'I am so sorry! Have I hurt you?' I didn't give him the chance to reply but turned to Jamie. 'He means the lord is at home but that we aren't the sort of people he would want to see.'

Jamie stared at the young man, then at me. 'How do you know that?'

I shook his arm. 'Jamie! If ever you'd taken the trouble to listen to Aunt Frances's stories!' I pushed past the young man, cast my eyes around an entrance hall larger than the whole of our house and walked to a chair set beside a wall. 'We will wait here until he can see us.'

The young man dithered, muttered, glared and finally took himself off, marching stiff legged but with his dignity dented by the blood that dribbled from his nose. 'Oh dear,' I said. 'I didn't mean to hurt him!'

Jamie sat down beside me. 'Serves him right. Shouldn't lie, it's wrong.' He wriggled on the chair. 'I say, Sissy – these chairs are more uncomfortable than the train.'

'They are for decoration, not for use, that is why,' said a voice.

Jamie jumped to his feet and bowed. 'I beg your pardon, sir. We didn't hear you approach.'

I, too, stood up. The man was perhaps of Papa's age but the lines carved deep around the sides of his mouth spoke of disappointment with the world rather than of Papa's exuberant enjoyment of it. He stared from Jamie to me, back to Jamie then back to me. 'Well, I'll be damned!' He recollected himself and bowed to me. 'Pray forgive me, Miss Carstairs but – well, I'll be damned!'

Jamie frowned. 'How do you know my sister's name?'

The man ignored the question, but it did seem to settle him somewhat. 'Allow me to introduce myself – Anthony Chapman, secretary to Lord Derringford, at your service Mr Carstairs, Miss Carstairs.'

'How . . .' we both began, but he cut across our question.

'If you would care to follow me, I will take you to the housekeeper and you can tidy yourselves – and, if it is not too forward a suggestion – change your clothing.'

I picked up my blanket-wrapped bundle. 'Thank you, Mr Chapman. But we are wearing our best clothing.'

He seemed to notice our bundles for the first time. 'Put those down, sir, miss. A servant will carry them for you. Now – where is the rest of your luggage?'

Jamie grinned. 'No need to trouble a servant, Mr Chapman. We can manage fine for this is all we have.'

We watched him in fascination. He shuddered, but then a look of unholy glee came upon his face. 'Life is about to get most entertaining,' he murmured. He walked towards the stairs and spoke to us without turning his head. 'Leave your bundles and follow me. Frant! Carry the young people's – er – baggage to the housekeeper's room.'

232

Frant turned out to be the superior young man upon whose face I had slammed the door. He took the bundles from us and walked away, holding them out from his sides as if he feared they would contaminate him. We hurried to catch up with the secretary ahead of us on the curving staircase.

Mr Chapman led us along a passageway wide enough to take a bullock cart. Paintings lined the walls. We slowed our steps for we had never seen such magnificence. Mr Chapman didn't hurry us, but stood a little way off watching. When we reached him, he pointed to the portrait on the wall beside him. 'This is the present lord painted when he was twenty years of age.'

I glanced at the portrait, gasped and clutched Jamie's arm. 'It is you!' It wasn't quite, but the resemblance was unmistakable for there was the determined chin, the narrow nose, the brown eyes and the same fair hair, even though it was tidier than Jamie's.

I held onto Jamie for my thoughts whirled in my head and I feared I would fall down from dizziness. He glared at Mr Chapman and snapped out, 'Fetch Lord Derringford. Now!'

Mr Chapman smiled and nodded as if Jamie had just confirmed something for him. 'All in good time, young sir. Shall we give you something to eat first?'

'Oh, yes please!' I said. 'We have not eaten since this morning.'

He led us to the end of the gallery, up some stairs and back along another passageway. 'You took us past that painting deliberately,' Jamie said. I sighed and hoped that food would cool his temper.

Mr Chapman paused to usher us into a room. 'But, dear boy, the temptation was irresistible!'

I feared Jamie would punch him and I stepped between them saying with all the dignity I could command, 'It is a game to you, Mr Chapman, but to us it is our lives. And now, will you please take us to the housekeeper?'

He gestured to us to enter the room and bade us make ourselves comfortable, promising the housekeeper would be with us shortly. He left, but we heard him mutter, *very entertaining indeed.*

We stood in a room crowded with tables, rugs, chairs and ornaments. The housekeeper had a taste for china dogs, shepherdesses and strange jugs. I pulled my skirts in around me and edged towards a chair. Jamie negotiated a track through to the window where he leaned against the wall.

We heard the housekeeper before we saw her. Her petticoats must have been starched as stiff as cardboard to rattle the way they did. She bustled in, talking as she came. 'Now then, young lady, young sir – food is on its way.' She looked at our faces and her welcoming smile vanished. 'Lawks a mercy me!' she shrieked. 'Oh dearie me! I never thought I'd see the day, I swear I never did!' She collapsed onto a handy footstool, her skirts filling with air and ballooning around her.

Jamie and I stood, dumbstruck, watching her weep and wail and bless her soul.

Mr Chapman waited in the doorway. I dragged my eyes from the housekeeper. 'We appear to have an unsettling effect upon this household, Mr Chapman.'

He allowed a small smile to lift the lines in his face. 'Oh, I think the unsettling has only just begun, my dear Miss Carstairs.'

So. It must be true. Lord Derringford, the owner of all this wealth and magnificence, must be our father. My heart squeezed tight in my chest. Poor Mama — how could he have treated her so ill?

A maid knocked on the door. Mr Chapman moved aside. We watched her, wondering if she too would have hysterics, but she put down a tray laden with food and turned to leave the room.

'One moment,' I said, glad to turn my thoughts to something practical. She paused, her face blank. 'This lady might be better if she could rest on her bed. Would you be so good as to help her?'

Mr Chapman nodded approvingly. 'An excellent suggestion, Miss Carstairs. Jenkins — you heard the young lady.'

Jenkins looked at the pair of us and if she wondered why a ragged urchin such as myself should issue orders she must obey, she kept her thoughts to herself and helped the housekeeper from the room.

Mr Chapman favoured us with his small smile. 'Ring that bell by the chimney when you have eaten. A maid will come and you may tell her to fetch me. We will then decide when to introduce you to his lordship.' He left the room.

Oh, but I was hungry. We rushed to the table and lifted the lid on the dishes – cold meat, bread, cheese and pickles. We didn't talk as we ate. My thoughts skipped and skidded around and around the portrait and what it might mean. I couldn't think. I didn't want to think. Jamie's face frightened me. It was fierce, a warrior before battle – a warrior facing death, but for Jamie it was the death of his hopes. *We were bastards.*

I poured the tea. We drank it without speaking. When we had drained the pot, I said, 'Mr Chapman doesn't intend for us to meet Lord Derringford tonight.'

'But we're going to,' Jamie replied.

I nodded. 'Yes. I rather thought we were.' I got to my feet. 'I wish I had another dress to put on. It would help if I could just tidy my hair and wash my face.' The muslin dress I had made had not survived the rigours of three months at sea.

Jamie strode to the door. 'What does it matter? We are the bastard children. He's not about to fall on us with open arms.'

I ran after him to take his arm. 'Wait for me! Don't run ahead. We are here together.'

We found the stairs and walked down them. Jamie's face wore the same look as it had when Arama left. What had he hoped for? We knew we must be bastards, we'd discussed it thoroughly and I believed he had grown accustomed.

He answered my thoughts. 'I find it is quite different, Sissy, to come face to face with the rich and powerful man who abandoned Mama and her unborn children.'

He was right. Mama should have been mistress of all this. I imagined her floating down this very staircase, and it would be her portrait in the gold frame on the wall to our left.

We paused at the bottom. Which way to go now? We heard a door open; laughter and talk floated out before it closed again. We took the right-hand passageway and followed the sound. 'They are at dinner,' I said. I wanted to say that we should talk to his lordship alone – that Mr Chapman was right and we should wait. But I knew Jamie wouldn't wait, and in my heart I didn't want to either. I burned to confront the man who had so callously cast off our mama.

Ahead of us, a door opened and a servant backed out pulling a dinner wagon after her. 'Jamie – it's a dinner party! They must have guests.' We couldn't go in, not now.

He paid me no heed. I took hold of my courage and his arm. Together we opened the door and stood silent looking about us.

I looked at a world so different from mine that I lost all my nervousness. A dozen diners sat at a long, polished table but these people were not real to me – the men with their sober, immaculate suits of black and the shirts so snowy white. And the women, all delicate hothouse flowers with bare shoulders, sparkling jewels around their throats, in their ears, and on the hands they raised to their mouths at the sight of us.

It was seconds before anyone reacted, and when they did, my first thought was that Mr Chapman would be disappointed to have missed it.

Three people spoke almost simultaneously. They were the man at the head of the table, an elderly woman wearing a sort of jewelled turban on her head who sat facing us halfway down and a clerical gentleman diagonally opposite her who might have been her husband and who swivelled around in his chair to see what the others stared at.

'Good God!'

'Bless my soul, are my eyes deceiving me?'

'I never thought I'd see the day. I declare I'm ready to faint!'

A girl a little younger than us cried out, 'Papa? What is happening? They are beggars! Why are they here?'

I became aware of a bell ringing and ringing, of people running down the passageway at our backs. Jamie stepped forward, pulling me with him. He slammed the door shut behind us. The bell ceased, but its clamour was replaced by the shrieking of the woman at the end of the table. 'Edward! Do something! That boy! Look at him! Oh, it is too bad, it is too bad!'

The girl looked from one end of the table to the other. 'Papa? Mama? What does this mean? Why does the beggar boy look just like William?'

A tall, lanky boy who must be the girl's brother fixed his gaze on Jamie and curled his lip just as the young man-servant had done.

The woman in the turban recovered her breath. 'The

girl! Look at the girl! Angelina. I declare she is Angelina to the very life.'

I stepped forward. 'Dear ma'am – did you know our mother?'

But she seemed to have used up for the moment all her powers of speech for she just looked at me and fanned herself with a fan whose handle glinted with jewels. The eyes of the other six guests darted from Jamie, to me, and back to the man the girl had called Papa. They drank in the drama, storing it up, soaking in every tiny detail.

Jamie's voice, heavy with threat, cut the air behind me. 'And you, sir. Did you know our mother?'

The man – our father – crashed both hands onto the table making the cutlery rattle and the other diners jump in fright. He pushed himself upright, filled his lungs with air and shouted, 'Don't be impertinent, you young jackanapes! Of course I knew your wretched mother, God damn her soul to hell!'

Jamie took a step towards him, fists bunched, arms swinging.

I cried out in Maori, 'Do not fight a battle you cannot win! Live to fight another day.'

It halted him, but did not diminish the ferocity of his voice. 'Answer me this. Why did you not marry her? Why did you abandon her – and us, your unborn children?' They glared at each other, their stances exactly the same, from the set of the shoulders to the tilt of the head.

'Good God!' breathed the gentleman next to the daughter.

Our father threw up his hands and barked out a crack of laughter. 'Marry her? Why didn't I marry her? You impudent young cub! How dare you accuse me of . . .'

'Edward!' That was from the woman with the bell. His wife, I supposed.

The clerical gentleman fluttered narrow pale hands in our direction. 'Dear boy, he *did* marry your lovely mother. I should know. I officiated. Remember it well. Beautiful gal, she was. Lovely Angelina they all called her.'

Our father's voice choked him off. 'Your precious mother ruined my life! Scandal, running off in the middle of the night. And now this!'

He had married Mama? It could not be. But the clerical gentleman said it was so. I looked from him to the furious man who so much resembled Jamie. I could not take in the information. It was too sudden. Too different from what we had believed to be true. I breathed a prayer to Mama, pleading for forgiveness for my thoughts about her.

My heart began to beat again. I stepped forward to stand beside Jamie. There were questions I wanted answers to. 'Why did she run away? Why did she need to leave all this?' I lifted my arm and swept it around, indicating the silver on the table, the velvet curtains at the windows, the paintings on the silk-covered walls – and more, so much more.

Silence fell upon the room, a sizzling silence. Our father wiped a hand over his face. Every eye in the room stayed on him as he sat down, easing himself into his chair by gripping the arms as an old man would. He glanced around the table and shrugged. 'It is old history now.' But by tomorrow it would be the talk of the county and he knew it full well. He picked up his wine glass and drained it. The guests sighed. The end of tonight's drama.

Not quite. Jamie, his jaw set with the determination I knew so well, said, 'It is our history and we have travelled half the world to hear it. You will tell it now, if you please.'

Our father glared at him. 'I do not please! Now take yourselves off!'

His wife looked to be holding onto her command of her senses by a very slim string. In a high, strident voice she said, 'Your precious mother ran off in the middle of the night and threw herself into the river. That's what happened.' She nodded vigorously as if repeating it would make it so. 'It was a scandal. In all the papers.'

I said slowly, 'But she didn't, so why did you think she had?'

The clerical gentleman glanced at his host, but our father stared into his empty wine glass. 'As I remember it,' the clerical gentleman said, 'Lady Angelina's father found items of her clothing beside the river. The river, of course, was searched but nothing was found.' He coughed discreetly and murmured, 'The papers made much of the case. There had been a quarrel you see. The servants . . . no loyalty these days.'

Beside me, Jamie let out a deep sigh. He spoke in Maori. 'Shall we ask him why they quarrelled?'

I murmured, 'How fast can you run?'

The turbanned woman leaned forward, her eyes gleaming like her jewels. 'Tell me, dear children, where is your lovely mother now?'

The silence of delicious anticipation fell on the older guests. His lordship's wife flushed an even brighter pink. The eyes of every person in the room were on us – except for those of our father and his wife. 'Shall we tell them?' I asked Jamie, in Maori.

He swept a glance around the guests as if he saw them for the first time. He shrugged and spoke in English to the entire room. 'Our mother died when we were born.'

William and his sister kept glancing at their father, then back to their mother. It was plain that they knew nothing of us, or of the letter we had sent, but the older diners shifted in their seats as if waiting for the crux of the matter.

The turbanned woman flicked her tongue along her top lip and asked the question whose answer they were all so avid to hear. 'And exactly when were you born, my dears?'

'April the eighteenth, 1843,' I said. The story would be out soon enough anyway.

'A pity.' Someone murmured the words but it was only what the others were thinking.

William and his sister didn't understand. Their mother glared at them, daring them to ask.

We had the bones of our story and we would get no more of it tonight. Our father sat leaning back in his chair with his head bowed. He had the air of a man who had used all his strength in running a race that was yet unfinished.

He stirred and straightened. 'There is much to be settled in this whole deplorable business. You'll have to stay, God damn it.'

I heard Jamie's breath hiss out, and I wasn't best pleased myself at being described as a deplorable business. 'Thank you so much for your welcome, sir. We are overcome by the warmth of your greeting.'

The man beside the daughter gave a bark of laughter, but our father frowned. 'Be careful, young lady. I may yet throw you out without a penny.'

I was tired. My mind skittered around all we had learned in the past few minutes. I did not care for the man in front of me. 'You may do so with our good will, sir. We came with nothing, we hoped for nothing but knowledge. That we now have, and you cannot take it away.'

Our father snapped, 'Hoity toity! Take yourselves off, the pair of you. Mildred, ring that damned bell.'

We didn't wait for the damned bell, but turned and left the room. The door closed behind us on a wail from our stepmama, more cursing from our father and a hum of chatter from the guests. Our sister's voice rose above the rest, 'Papa, where have they come from? They are so dirty!'

In the passageway, Jamie wrapped his arms around me. 'Sissy! We're not bastards! I can become an engineer!'

He was so elated, so lit up with relief and joy and happiness that I could not bring myself to tell him of the pain eating at my heart. It was the pain of knowing Mama had run from her marriage, run off with a man she had met by chance and lived with him as his wife when all the time she had a husband here in this palatial house. I could understand neither her nor Papa for aiding her flight.

A servant came and we followed her upstairs. The housekeeper, a handkerchief clutched in her hand, greeted us tearfully. 'I'm that sorry, miss, sir. It's the likeness to Lady Angelina – it gave me such a turn.'

She showed us to the rooms prepared for us. There was a bathroom just down the hall with running water and a device for heating it. We both bathed and I nearly fell asleep in the luxury of the hot water.

In the morning, I vowed to ask our father exactly what the quarrel had been about that made Mama run away.

# 21

## Chapter Twenty-One

I awoke early as usual but lay idle in the luxurious bed with its frills and curtains, staring around me at the beautiful room. Even in the gloom of the early morning I could make out the pattern of the plaster ceiling and the roses on the wallpaper. There was a dressing table such as the one Judith had, with a mirror and a tapestry-covered stool in front of it. A tapestry screen stood in front of a fireplace. I sat up, pondering the strange change in our circumstances that had brought me to a bedroom with a fireplace and blue satin curtains at the window.

I regarded the curtains. They were the only items in the room that did not please me. If it were up to me, I would have pink to match the roses. I laughed and jumped from the bed and ran to the window to draw back the curtains I objected to.

We were legitimate. We weren't bastards. But Mama . . . Mama had lived with Papa without being married to him.

My thoughts cut me to my heart and activity was my only solace. I dressed, then knocked on Jamie's door. He too was awake and dressed.

'I'm hungry enough to eat three horses,' he said. 'Let's find food.'

The dining room, the scene of last night's drama, was deserted. We wandered through the ground floor of the house, opening doors and peering into each elegant room as we passed.

'Do you wish you'd been born here?' Jamie asked suddenly. 'I've been thinking about it all night, but try as I might, I can't see myself belonging.'

I shook my head. 'It is strange. I can picture Mama here so very clearly, but not me. It doesn't feel at all like a home.'

He tucked his hand in my arm. 'I don't think Lord Derringford wants it to become our home either. It's lucky we don't yearn to be taken in and fawned upon.'

In the end, we found our way to the kitchen. The cook flapped her apron. 'Oh dearie me, but you can't come in here, young miss, master. It isn't fitting.'

Jamie turned on his charm. 'My dear lady — look at us! We aren't in the least bit fine or important — but we are very hungry.' He smiled at her and we watched her melt.

'Jenkins — take miss and the young master to the dining room.'

It was my turn to display some charm. 'Oh please, Mrs . . .'

'Farley,' she said.

'Mrs Farley, may we not eat here? It is so much more homely and friendly.' I crossed the floor to the stove as

I spoke. 'What a wonderful thing this is! I have never seen anything like it. Does it cook well?'

She scarcely noticed when I picked up a knife to slice the bacon, she was so busy praising her stove. But Jenkins noticed. 'Miss! You must stop! It isn't fitting!'

Jamie laughed. 'Do let her. She always cooks and she'll be fretting for lack of employment if you stop her.'

By the time we sat down to eat at the scrubbed kitchen table, we had an audience of three maids, Frant who still looked down his damaged nose at us, the housekeeper Mrs Smith, Mrs Farley the cook and the elderly butler called Sykes who had missed all the fun of last night because he had been poorly.

Lord Derringford, however, when we met with him in the study at eleven by the kitchen clock, was not nearly so appreciative.

He stared first at Jamie, then at me. Neither of us pleased him. 'Is this display of poverty meant to impress me? It doesn't. Go and change into decent clothing, if you please.'

Mr Chapman, seated in the shadows, coughed.

Jamie rubbed his hands down his trousers. 'What's wrong with our clothes?'

I knew only too well what was wrong and his lordship's total ignorance of us and our situation infuriated me. 'I am wearing the best clothes I possess. Other than this I have a house dress. It has patches under the arms and the skirt is darned in three places. I also have the dress I wear to church. It is of gold satin and might please you more, but it is too tight and too short. My cloak was given to me by a friend, because Papa sold mine to buy drink, but to be fair, he gave me a bonnet last time the quarter day money arrived.' I held out my foot to show him my boot. 'This is all the footwear I have and I bought them myself with money I earned myself.' I lifted my head the better to stare at him. 'I can earn my own living. I've done it before and I can do it again. So can Jamie.'

Beside me, Jamie chuckled. 'That's telling him, Sissy.'

Lord Derringford thumped his desk. He started to say something and changed his mind. He stood up and his chair tipped over but he left it lying on the floor. 'What the devil do you want? Why did you come? Why the hell couldn't you have stayed in that God-forsaken country Angelina took herself off to?'

Jamie said shortly, 'There's a war. We ran away.'

'I might have known it!' Lord Derringford said. 'Angelina's son – a coward.' His mouth curved down and if he could have crushed Jamie under his boot he would have done it with pleasure.

Jamie shrugged but made no effort to defend himself.

I had no such inhibitions. 'You, sir, are a most unpleasant and ignorant man! You know nothing yet you assume everything.' I gathered arguments to fling in his stunned face. 'Jamie found he couldn't face the thought that he might kill his own brother. Is that the action of a coward?'

My speech didn't have quite the effect I had anticipated. His lordship snapped out, 'Brother? You have a brother?'

'Yes,' I said. 'His name is Arama.'

'What sort of a heathen name is that?' demanded Lord Derringford. 'Oh good God, don't tell me you're mixed up with the natives!'

'Arama means Adam,' Jamie said, and in a spirit of pure mischief he added, 'Papa's wife, the woman who was our mother, was called Rawinia. It's Maori for Lavinia, you know.'

His lordship groaned and sank down onto the padded seat under the window. 'You had better tell me everything. I might as well know the worst.'

Between us, we told him the story of our lives. When we finished, he got up and stood staring out the window. 'And so you have come to claim your birthright. By God, it's too much!'

I slapped my hand flat onto his desk. 'You really are the most infuriating man! Didn't you hear a word we said? Jamie wants to work with iron and all I want is to know about my mama.'

He roared at me, 'Don't be impertinent, girl! Can't you get it into your skull that your precious brother is my heir? He inherits all this.' He swept both arms around him. 'He gets the land, the money, the houses – everything.' To himself he muttered, 'A brat brought up by a native and that drunkard. I can't believe it.'

In his dark corner, Mr Chapman coughed again.

A look of horror settled on Jamie's face. 'Your heir? No thank you! I don't mean any offence, sir, but I have no wish to be burdened with all this.'

An interesting series of expressions played over our

father's face. There was fury, incredulity and finally hope. 'You don't want it? You don't? You're mad!'

It did not take him many minutes, however, to accept that Jamie was in earnest. 'I'll call in my solicitor. Have him draw up the papers.' He chuckled and rubbed his hands. 'Well, well – things may not turn out so badly after all.' He smiled on the pair of us. 'I'll talk to Mildred – my wife – good God, I suppose she's your stepmother! She'll take you shopping. Get you clothes and that sort of thing. But first, I'll send for old Branscombe. My goodness, he will be surprised. Pleasantly, I think.'

'Is Branscombe your solicitor, sir?' I asked and I could almost hear Mr Woodley's voice in my mind: *Always have your own solicitor. Never trust anyone.*

Lord Derringford rubbed his hands. 'Yes. Old now, but a good man. Been my solicitor for I don't know how long.'

I smiled at him. 'Will you send for our solicitor as well?' I knew our uncle had a brother in Plymouth who practised law and I thought he would act for us.

My words stunned our father, but not for long. 'You young jezebel! Just like your mother, I'll be bound. Coming in here and demanding your own solicitor! For God's sake, don't you trust me?'

Jamie said, 'Do not swear at my sister, sir. And as to trusting you – you have given us no reason to do so.'

His lordship glared and dismissed us. Mr Chapman, the victim of yet another coughing fit, bowed us out.

'What do we do now?' I asked.

Jamie sidled towards the door. 'I'm going to the stables. There should be something to ride.'

'You're going to look at the iron bridge, aren't you?' I asked. I didn't want to be left alone, but better that than a fretting brother. I bade him goodbye and tried to think what I should do.

I wandered outside into a sunny afternoon where Jenkins found me after I had examined the rose garden, the herb garden and a scented garden. 'Oh, miss – the mistress is wanting you and the young master. We didn't know where you'd got to and she's waiting luncheon for you.'

My stepmother was not pleased when I presented myself in her parlour. 'Have you no consideration? And where is your brother?'

While I explained, I studied the others in the room. There were the girl and William from the dinner party last night, and three younger children, two boys and a girl.

My stepmother made no effort to introduce me so I smiled at them and said, 'Hello. I am Hannah, your sister come from across the ocean.'

Lady Derringford sighed and performed the introductions. 'Adelaide. William, whose inheritance your brother has stolen. Stephen. Louisa. Grantley.'

William turned his back on me. Adelaide flounced and the other three stared, all of them hostile. How typical of his lordship not to inform his family at once of Jamie's decision. It was not my place to do so, and they deserved to suffer for their bad manners. Aunt Frances would be shocked.

'We will wait while you change your dress,' Lady Derringford said, shuddering and shading her eyes from the sight of my offending garment.

I produced a smile of blinding sweetness. 'Which one do you suggest I wear, ma'am? The one of gold satin that is too tight and too short, or my patched and darned house dress?'

She gaped at me, flummoxed. Perhaps she had never met a person before with so limited a wardrobe. 'Gold digger!' she snapped.

William turned himself around in order to cast me a furious look, grumbled of hunger and we trailed into the dining room.

I ate a cold luncheon of pie, jellied eel, cucumber and tomatoes and not one of my relatives spoke to me. They talked to each other of local people and happenings I could know nothing about. I ate and I fumed. When I had finished I placed my cutlery on the plate with enough of a clatter to gain their attention. 'You enjoy gossip, ma'am. It must please you greatly to know that all your neighbours will be gossiping about you and your newly acquired stepchildren.'

Aunt Frances would not be proud of me. I did not care. They were hateful and they were rude.

Aunt Frances. I must write to her for she would be so worried about us. I found Jenkins and asked for writing materials . . .

Dearest Aunt

I stopped. The news about Mama would shock her to

her soul. I sighed and picked up the pen again. It had to be told. I completed the letter and hurried with it to Sykes, in case my courage failed me and I screwed it up. Then I returned and wrote to Aggie. It cheered me to imagine her glee when she read that I was the daughter of a lord, just the way she had predicted.

I passed the remainder of the afternoon by exploring the house, in the course of which I happened upon Mr Chapman on his way from Lord Derringford's study.

He nodded his head in its general direction. 'Is Mr Jamie back yet, Miss Hannah? He's to sign away his inheritance and my lord is most anxious in case he changes his mind.'

I frowned. 'No, he's still out, but tell me, Mr Chapman – are the solicitors here already?'

'Only one, my dear young lady. Old Mr Branscombe, sound and solid is our Mr Branscombe.' He moved away from me and spoke without turning his head as he'd done last night. 'Tell your dear brother to hurry when you see him.'

Interesting. Well, my precious father, you will find that we did not grow up around a solicitor for nothing.

I went to the stables and waited to be sure that I would not miss Jamie. Joe, the groom, gave me a low stool to sit on. I placed it against a stone wall warming my back where the sun had baked heat into the stones.

Jamie and his lordship arrived together albeit from different directions. Jamie appeared to be in his very own heaven; our father, on the other hand, was shouting. 'How dare you vanish – on one of my horses – with never a word to anyone?'

Jamie dismounted. 'I beg your pardon, sir. Were you worried about your horse? There was no need, I promise you.'

Lord Derringford controlled his anger and attempted a mild reply. 'Well, well, no harm done I suppose. Let's go to the study, dear boy. The papers are all ready for you to sign.'

I stood up but he flapped at me with a hand. 'No need to trouble your sister. This isn't female business.'

I spoke in Maori. 'He means to cheat you. There is only his man here with his papers.'

Jamie shrugged. 'I don't think so, Sissy.' I knew in that moment that he would sign anything put in front of him. He just wanted to get the formalities over so that he could get on with the business of becoming an engineer.

'Don't sign anything if I am not with you,' I begged in Maori. 'Promise me, Jamie.'

He laughed but said, 'I promise.'

Our father said, 'Never use that heathen language again, do you hear me?'

I smiled. 'May your eyes be pecked by the birds and your entrails become food for worms,' I said very politely in Maori.

I feared we would never like each other.

Lord Derringford barred the study door with his arm. 'Off you go, girl.'

My heart warmed, for Jamie said, 'Come, Hannah,

we'll both go.' We moved away from the door towards the stairs. His lordship ground his teeth behind us.

'Very well! She can come in — but don't blame me when it curdles her brain and she lies screeching on the floor!'

Mr Chapman sat in the study in a chair by the empty fireplace. He steepled his hands but I think it was to prevent himself from rubbing them together with glee at the prospect of the coming spectacle. Beside him in a more comfortable chair sat an elderly man who regarded us both in silence, then blessed his soul and said, 'No doubt about it at all, my lord, I'm sorry to say.'

'I'm not blind,' snapped his lordship. 'Now get on with it, man.'

Jamie stepped over to the elderly man. 'I am Jamie Carstairs, sir, and this is my sister Hannah.'

'How do you do, Mr Branscombe,' I said, curtseying.

'Charming. Most charming,' he muttered. Our father was not in the least charmed, and Mr Chapman had another of his small coughing fits.

Mr Branscombe put a paper on the table at his side. 'If you would just sign here, dear boy.'

Jamie scanned the paper and a smile lit his face. He grinned at me. 'Sissy, this is jolly decent. I'm to become apprenticed,' he glanced down at the paper, 'to an engineer of repute. And as well as that I'm to have fifty pounds a year for the next five years.'

Jamie seized the pen, but before he could sign, I picked up the paper. He shrugged, put down the pen and sat himself down on the window seat. Our father snapped at me.

'Stop your meddling, girl! Give him the paper. Sign it, get it over and done with.'

I kept reading. Jamie kept an eye on our father.

When I reached the end I said nothing for a moment. I must be wrong. Lord Derringford – our father – could not be so duplicitous. I turned to Mr Branscombe and spoke slowly, trying to make sense of what I had read in the document. 'There are two parts to this . . .'

Our father shouted, 'This is not the business of women. Be gone, girl!'

Jamie turned his back on him. 'What is it, Hannah?' He came over to me and together we studied the paper.

'See here,' I said, pointing to the first paragraph, 'you agree *today* that you are no longer the son of Lord Derringford and have no claim whatsoever on him or his property.'

Jamie nodded, intent on the words in front of us. Our father crashed and ranted behind us.

'But in this second part, which takes effect tomorrow, it says that Lord Derringford will apprentice his *eldest* son – he does not name that son – and pay him an annuity.'

Understanding dawned in Jamie's eyes. He straightened, took the paper in his hands and spoke directly to the solicitor. 'If I sign this, will it mean that by tomorrow, I will legally not be the eldest son? That I will therefore have no claim at all on what is, at this moment, legally mine? That in effect, the agreement to apprentice and sponsor the eldest son will apply to William and not to me?'

He did not raise his voice, but had I been in our father's shoes I would have been trembling.

Mr Branscombe sighed. 'That is correct.'

Jamie tore the paper into shreds.

'Jezebel!' bellowed our loving father, striding towards me with his fists clenched.

Jamie leaped into his path. 'You will apologise to my sister, sir – or I sign nothing. Never! And may you rot in hell for a liar and a cheat.'

For answer our father slammed from the room and the very air vibrated behind him as he went.

Mr Chapman didn't bother to turn his laughter into a coughing fit, but I was shaking.

Jamie hugged an arm around my shoulders. To the solicitor he said, 'You may tell his lordship that I have changed my mind. I shall take the inheritance and before his body is cold I'll sell the lot to the highest bidder.'

Mr Branscombe pushed himself upright. 'Miss Hannah, Master Jamie – to tell you the truth I am very glad you tore up the agreement. It was infamous and so I told his lordship.' He shook his head. 'Headstrong, he is. Won't be told.'

We were not invited to dine with the family; in fact they made no arrangements for our comfort. Jenkins came to find us. 'Cook says to tell you, master, miss – she'll send food to your rooms.'

So ended our second day in the home of our ancestors.

# 22

## Chapter Twenty-Two

Had it not been for the servants being so kind to us, we may well have starved in those first days. Cook made sure we had good food and plenty of it, while Jenkins and Mrs Smith the housekeeper, cleaned our clothes and pressed them for us.

I was determined to visit our grandmother. Jamie protested but gave way. I believe he looked forward with relish to a battle with our grandfather. I did not. Battling with our father had left me no taste for it.

We went to the stables after we had breakfasted. Jamie chose the black gelding he'd taken yesterday, while Joe, muttering that the master would have his head, saddled a docile old plodder for me. 'I'm that sorry, miss, but it's more than my life's worth to give you one of the ladies' horses.'

I did not care, so long as it got me there.

We followed the directions old Sykes the butler had given us through Derringate village, over the Derring stream then out onto a high road. It was market day, judging by the amount of traffic we passed heading in the same direction as we were.

'I feel as if I'm living in a story book,' I told Jamie. He raised his eyebrows and laughed at me, but Judith would have known what I meant. The landscape appeared to me as if somebody had arranged every piece of it, placing each part with care to make sure it was in harmony with each other part. Everywhere I looked, was orderly neatness.

'I keep looking for the mountain,' Jamie said suddenly. 'And the hills. I think I might come to miss the hills.'

How very odd it all was. At home in June the mountain gleamed white with snow, or it hid under clouds while the winds raged and rain slashed the land. In June we stayed indoors as much as we could, sheltering from the cold and avoiding the mud. June here smiled upon us and warmed us under gentle blue skies.

Our grandparents lived just outside what Sykes had described as a small market town, although to our eyes it appeared large and very busy. It was much larger than New Plymouth.

We found Norwood Manor without difficulty.

'They are not as wealthy as Lord Derringford,' I said. The house, which only a few days ago, I would have looked upon as grand, was much smaller than our father's. The grounds we rode through showed signs of neglect. It was little wonder my grandfather had been delighted with Mama's match with Lord Derringford. 'Jamie, I'm scared!'

He didn't reply, but the grin he sent in my direction showed very clearly that he was not.

A stable boy ran up and took charge of our horses. He showed no surprise when he looked at our faces, but he was too young to have known Mama. So too, I was relieved to see, was the little maid who answered the door.

'Mr and Miss Carstairs to see Lady Armitage,' Jamie said.

The maid twittered. 'Oh sir, she's still abed. She never rises before midday.'

'How well she would get on with Papa,' Jamie muttered.

I frowned. What to do now? The maid was no help. She stood waiting patiently until we should take it into our heads to leave. 'Please tell her ladyship that we are here,' I said. It suddenly occurred to me that we might be a shock to our grandmother if she truly believed Mama had died that night in the river. 'Please tell her we are the children of Miss Angelina.'

The maid's eyes near dropped from her face. She curtseyed. 'Yes, miss. At once, miss.' She showed us into a small parlour. 'Please to wait here, miss, sir.'

But it was not our grandmother who charged, roaring through the door some minutes later, but her husband, our dearly beloved grandfather. 'Get out! Out of my house! How dare you! I'll have you whipped, see if I don't!'

Jamie and I stood, staring at him, this elderly, bent man who whirled his arms and berated us.

'How fortunate we are in our male relatives,' I said, speaking clearly, for I hoped he would hear me. My fear had left me. I felt nothing but contempt for him and pity for my mama.

'Leave this house at once! Benson! Craik! Where the devil are they?' He yanked on a tasselled cord near the fireplace and shook a fist at us. 'Leave of your own free will or I'll have you thrown out, by God I will!'

I sat down. Jamie remained on his feet. Both of us stared at our grandfather. He opened the door and bellowed down the hallway. 'Benson! Craik!'

A skinny lad of around twenty came running. 'Benson! Throw them out!'

He skidded to a stop. 'Sir?'

'You heard me. Get rid of the pair of them.' He moved from the doorway to allow Benson room for the throwing of us.

Jamie rocked on his toes, he flexed his shoulders and put up his fists. 'Try if you want to,' he invited Benson.

I jumped up. 'Jamie, it's not fair! You're twice his size.' It was true – poor Benson was weedy and pale. Probably my grandfather didn't feed his servants well. I went to my grandfather, put my hands on his shoulders and moved him in the direction of the nearest chair. 'Sit there, sir. We intend to visit our grandmother whether you give permission or not.'

Jamie, in the meantime, picked Benson up with one hand on the back of his jacket and the other hooked into his trousers. He deposited him beside Grandfather who screeched and bellowed and flailed his arms at both of us. Into this mayhem tottered our grandmother, clad in a nightcap and robe. 'Oh, it cannot be true! Oh my dears!' Tears drenched her face but she didn't appear to notice she was crying. 'Angelina! Oh, it is too much, I cannot take it in. And a son too. It is a miracle.'

She fluttered to me, embraced me and then did the same to Jamie.

'They are not staying, woman. They are nothing!'

We watched, fascinated, for she rounded on him – no doubt it was the first time in all their years together that she had done so. 'I *will* see them. I *will*. You may throw me out of the house to beg for my bread. What do I care if I cannot see Angelina's children?'

The effort cost her dearly for she stumbled. Jamie and I leaped to her aid and helped her to the sofa. 'Benson,' she whispered, 'get Bessie for me, if you would be so good.'

I kissed her forehead. 'Dear Grandmama, we will leave you now. Will you write and tell us when we may come again?'

She pressed my hand. 'I promise.'

Jamie said, 'Grandmama – may I help you to your room? We would like to see that you are comfortable before we leave.'

She managed a smile at both of us. 'Oh, I am comfortable, so comfortable. It is the first time I have felt so since my Angelina was taken from me.'

Between us we supported her to her bedroom. Our grandfather sat glowering but silent in the chair where I had put him.

Bessie, who turned out to be the maid who had answered the door, fussed around our grandmother, tucking her into bed.

We left without saying goodbye to our grandfather.

\*

We rode for some while, each busy with our own thoughts. Jamie broke the silence. 'You know, I think I am glad we had Papa for our father. He is altogether more charming than either of this precious pair.'

I agreed wholeheartedly and resolved to write to Papa that very day telling him how much I loved him. Suddenly I laughed. 'Papa only ever sold the clothes off our backs — he never tried to cheat us of our inheritance.'

Then I thought about it some more. 'Well, actually, I suppose that is exactly what he did do.'

We rode more slowly the closer we got to Derringford Park. 'Jamie — let's not stay here. Let's go and, I don't know — find a position somewhere. Just go away.'

Jamie wore his stubborn look. 'Sissy — I want to be an engineer. I want it so badly! I can take a few knocks. He won't harm you — I promise you.'

It wasn't that. I didn't like the tantrums but they did not upset me the way Papa upset me whenever he was the slightest bit angry with me. It must be because I had no affection and certainly no respect for Lord Derringford.

Jamie grinned at me. 'Cheer up, Sissy. It has occurred to me that we hold all the cards in this little game.' He bowed in my direction. 'Thanks, I'll admit, to you.'

'You would have fifty pounds in your pocket,' I reminded him. It was such a lot of money but all the same, even I could see that it did not begin to match the fortune possessed by our father.

We returned our horses to the stables and went into

the house. Nobody lay in wait for us. 'The kitchen,' Jamie said. 'I'm famished.'

We hurried along the hallways, half expecting to be accosted by Frant or Mr Chapman who would order us to attend our father – at once. But we arrived unscathed.

Cook served us stewed rabbit and thick slices of newly made bread then, while we ate, a girl called Mary who was one of the housemaids, told us the news of the day.

'The master's been shouting all morning,' she said. She was cheerful so I guessed she had managed to avoid him. 'Upset my lady. She cried, he shouted then she shouted. Then Mr William shouted and Miss Adelaide had hysterics.' She grinned at us. 'Been quiet since luncheon though.'

Sykes came in as she spoke. 'His lordship has just thrown a paperweight at the study door.'

After we had eaten, Jamie muttered about a forge that looked worth a visit. I asked Mary if there were any books I could read. 'Lawks, miss – there's a whole library of them.'

She showed me where it was, but out of all the treasures around me, I chose *Jane Eyre*. I wanted the familiar, I wanted comfort. I, like Jane, knew now what it was to be unwanted and unwelcome. I thought again about leaving, but I would not do so without Jamie and it was plain that he would not leave until our father arranged for him to work with an engineer.

The day ended without Lord Derringford or his wife attempting to talk to us. Mary came in to turn my bed down, although I told her there was no need. 'It's my pleasure, miss,' she said firmly. 'And miss — such goings-on there've been! The mistress got an invitation today. It's from Mrs Clement Delaney — she's so rich and well connected the mistress fair swoons when she says her name. But the jest of it is — the invite says to bring you and Mr Jamie! Dear Angelina's children, she called you.'

Mary didn't know what we were invited to, or when. Jamie, when I told him in the morning, laughed and declared he would go even if he had to listen to some screeching singer, and what's more, he would wear the clothes he'd worn ever since we arrived.

I sighed and wished I could enjoy the situation the way he appeared to be doing, but I couldn't. I was used to being around people who loved me and were kind. I thought of visiting my grandmother, but she had sent no message. If I didn't hear anything from her soon, then I would visit her anyway.

The day, however, brought about a change. Jenkins came to where we sat in the enclosed garden arguing over how to spend the day — or rather, I was arguing while Jamie sat and looked stubborn.

'Master wants you both in the small parlour,' she told us.

Jamie jumped to his feet. 'The small parlour! Is the dragon-lady to be present as well?'

Jenkins giggled. 'Oh, Master Jamie!'

We followed her indoors to the small parlour, a room as big as half our house in Lemon Street. There waiting for us was the entire family – stepmother, father, Adelaide, William, Stephen, Louisa and Grantley.

They must have practised the routine they now performed.

Father spoke first, his voice and smile hearty. 'Ah, there you are. Good. Sit down. That's better. Now, first, I'd like to apologise.' He beamed at us and I had the feeling he expected us to get down on our knees and sing his praises.

I nodded my head and said, 'Thank you.'

Jamie just frowned and stroked his face.

Apparently, this wasn't the response they'd planned.

He hurried on. 'The thing is, you caught us by surprise. No idea you existed. Total surprise. Appearing out of the blue like that. Thought your mother died, you see.'

Jamie narrowed his eyes. 'Mr Chapman knew our names. The only way he could have known is from the letter we sent. Are you saying he neglected to show it to you?'

Lord Derringford exploded from his chair. 'Damn you! You insolent . . .'

'Edward! Sit down,' his wife said. She didn't wait to see if he would do so, but took up her thread of the story. 'It was a shock. You see, we had decided if we didn't reply then that would be that. We never imagined you would come here.'

Had it not been for the war we would not have come and were it not for the war I would have returned that very minute – with or without Jamie.

'Go on,' Jamie said.

She cast him a look of intense dislike. 'We have come to realise we must make the best of things.' She took a deep breath. 'My husband informs me that you do not want to inherit the estate.'

Jamie let a silence grow before he said, 'That is correct, I didn't. Not until he tried to cheat me, that is.'

She shuddered. William muttered something about killing. Adelaide pouted and told nobody in particular that it was so unfair. The three younger children wriggled on their chairs and looked as if they wanted to be elsewhere.

Lord Derringford took hold of matters again. 'Look here – to speak plainly – I wish to heaven you didn't exist. But you do. So here's what I propose. We draw up another settlement. I'll set you up with an engineer I know. Capital chap. You sign the settlement.'

Jamie swung a foot and pretended to consider it. I looked down at my lap, trying to hide my smiles.

'Here's what I'll agree to,' he said, and our father and his wife blenched. 'In one year, I will sign an agreement drawn up by a solicitor I choose – if I am satisfied with the training your engineer is giving me.' He paused and smiled at the entire family. 'And what about Hannah? She's your daughter. What do you propose to do for her?'

I was quite overcome. I had not thought of becoming part of his bargain. It seemed though, that we were back with the script they had prepared, for our stepmother said through gritted teeth, 'We will treat her as our own.' She stood up. 'Please stay in after luncheon. You are to be measured for new clothes. Both of you. We are invited to a picnic next Wednesday and you simply cannot go in those dreadful clothes.'

The family trailed from the room behind her.

I seized Jamie's arm. 'I do not want to stay here. Let me come with you! I can keep house for you. Please, Jamie.'

He patted my hand. 'You must know that you cannot. Not yet, anyway.' He frowned and thought for a moment. 'Do you wish to go home? Back to New Plymouth?'

Oh, how much I wished it, but I shook my head. 'No, not with the war raging. And I could not bear the thought that I might never see you again.'

'Come now, Sissy — no waterworks, if you please.' He gave me a bracing hug. 'Let's go and get this wretched clothes business over with.'

I cheered up. I was to have new clothes. Perhaps living here for a time would have its compensations.

# 2 3

# Chapter Twenty-Three

And so began my life as a young lady.

Jamie got the clothes business done with as quickly as he could. I, on the other hand, trod up the stairs to the room where the dressmaker waited, full of excited anticipation.

Lady Derringford performed the introductions. 'Miss Everton, this is the girl. Kindly make her a dress suitable for a picnic. It must be ready by Tuesday morning.'

'Certainly, my lady,' Miss Everton bobbed a curtsey.

Her ladyship snapped the door shut behind her and left us alone. The dressmaker was a tall woman of around Aunt Frances's age. She kept much of her sewing equipment about her person – a tape measure hung around her neck, the bodice of her dress featured a neat row of pins and a shorter one of needles, and the cap she wore over her greying hair jiggled with lengths of lace and ribbon.

She measured me quickly, then showed me the fabrics she'd brought with her. They were charming but I had no trouble choosing. 'It has to be this one.' I put my hand on a bolt of the finest pale blue cotton printed with a darker pattern of butterflies. My eyes stung, for I saw not the blue of the fabric, but the blue of the mountain in summer when it seemed to float pale and distant against the sky. 'This one,' I repeated.

I chose the pattern next. After that, there was nothing for me to do except wait until dinner. I watched Miss Everton busy with her pins and her scissors. 'Miss Everton, may I help you sew my dress?'

She was shocked. 'Oh no, miss. It wouldn't be fitting. Her ladyship would be most displeased.'

Yes, I supposed she would be.

The day passed.

The next day was Thursday. Jamie stayed with me in the morning, partly because of the rain that drizzled softly down, but mainly because today he was to meet the engineer. Our father introduced us both to Mr Winterton who appeared promptly at three in the afternoon. An hour later, all was arranged. Jamie was to leave with him on Tuesday. He would work and study with Mr Winterton for one year at which time Jamie, Mr Winterton and our father would meet and, as our father delicately put it, clear up all the pesky loose ends.

I felt happy for Jamie. Mr Winterton's eyes held the same spark of excitement as Jamie's did when he talked of engineering and his work. Jamie's dream was coming true.

'You will not be able to attend the picnic with me,' I said that evening before we went to bed.

He grinned. 'My heart is broken, I assure you.'

But my heart was too full for me to smile. 'I will miss you.'

He hugged me. 'I will speak to our father – tell him I'll only sign away all this if you are happy. Don't worry, Sissy. You'll soon settle in.'

I didn't speak to him again of how much I dreaded the thought of being here without him. All I could see for the future was a series of empty days, whereas his would be full of interest and activity.

However, the next day brought some interest and activity to me. The first thing that happened was Sykes bringing a letter addressed to Jamie and me. It was from Grandmama asking us to visit the next afternoon.

Lady Derringford frowned. 'You cannot possibly go. You have nothing to wear.'

'Our grandmother wishes to see us, not our clothes,' I said.

Adelaide tittered.

I carried the letter with me all of the morning and read it many times even though I already knew every word of it.

*My dearest grandchildren,*

*I must tell you how very much you gladden my heart, for it is as if my beloved Angelina has reached out to me from heaven with this miraculous gift.*

*I have not been well these past few days, but am stronger now and impatient for you to visit me. Tomorrow, after luncheon would be convenient if your family allows it.*

*Your loving grandmother,*
*Rosa Armitage*

\*

271

We concluded that our grandfather would be absent on Saturday afternoon.

After luncheon, Jamie and I went to the library. He wanted to search for anything scientific of which, rather to my surprise, there was plenty.

'You shouldn't be surprised, Sissy. After all, I had to get my interest in engineering from somewhere.'

That was true, and when I thought about it, there was plenty of evidence of Lord Derringford's interest in things mechanical – from the plumbing to the stove Cook loved so dearly.

Jamie sat down, buried his nose in a book and thereafter forgot about me. I wandered around the room, picking a book here, looking at another there but not settling to anything. I envied Jamie, not for being able to live the dream he had held so long, but for having a dream at all, for knowing what he wanted to do with his life.

I stood at the window and looked down upon the park and on up to the rise where we had first sighted the house. 'There is no place for me here,' I said.

'Hmm,' Jamie replied.

'I am not useful here. I don't like not being useful.'

'Is that so?'

I gave up. I could have said I was the Empress of India and he would have responded no differently. I didn't bother to report on the interesting fact that two carriages had crested the rise and were at this moment approaching the house.

The window gave me an excellent vantage point from

which I was able to see who alighted. From the first carriage stepped none other than the turbanned woman from the dinner party. She brought with her a younger woman of great animation – her daughter I guessed. The second carriage held a young woman of about Polly's age who wore a most elegant bonnet and shawl. She alighted, followed by her maid.

They trod up the steps where Sykes admitted them.

A very short time later, Jenkins came running to find me. 'Oh miss! The mistress wants you in her sitting room.'

I laughed. 'Jenkins, I'm sure you are mistaken! Did you not know? Visitors have just arrived.'

Jenkins hopped from one foot to the other. 'Yes, miss – it's her ladyship's At Home day and the ladies have asked to see you.'

The disturbance pulled Jamie from his book. 'Off you go, Sissy. You can be useful entertaining the dragon-lady's guests.'

So he *had* heard me.

I followed Jenkins from the room. 'Jenkins – her lady-ship isn't going to be pleased with my appearance.'

Jenkins stopped, glanced around her then whispered fiercely, 'It's her own fault. She could have found you something pretty to wear, but did she try?' She shook her head. 'Not her!'

We reached Lady Derringford's sitting room. Jenkins opened the door and announced, 'Miss Carstairs, my lady.'

My lady stretched a pained smile across her face. 'Ah, there you are. Come in and sit down.' She introduced me to the turbanned lady who today wore a blue and white arrangement. 'Mrs Poulter, may I present Miss Carstairs.' Her daughter was called Mrs Lyden, and the woman of Polly's age was Lady Featherstone.

'How do you do?' I curtseyed and sat down on a sofa next to Adelaide who inched herself away from me, a movement not lost upon the turbanned Mrs Poulter.

'Now, my dear — do tell us. How are you settling in here? It must be very different from what you are accustomed to.'

Lady Featherstone leaned forward. 'New Zealand! How terribly romantic!'

Mrs Lyden who had the same snapping dark eyes as Mrs Poulter smiled at me. 'Do forgive my impertinence, my dear Miss Carstairs, but you do not wear the crinoline. Are the ladies in New Zealand not interested in fashion?'

They looked at me, all three of them like a menagerie of birds waiting for food. Mrs Lyden waited with lively curiosity, her head on one side in the manner of a fantail. Her mother nodded her turbanned head and smiled — a vulture viewing its prey. Lady Featherstone reminded me of a kereru; plump, pretty and perhaps not as stupid as she appeared.

Lady Derringford closed her eyes, as if in prayer. Adelaide moved away another inch.

I smiled at the visitors. 'Oh yes, I assure you we are. But I have never owned a crinoline petticoat, for they are costly, you understand.'

Their eyes glistened as they drank in my words. 'But

ordinary petticoats?' enquired Lady Featherstone. 'Why do you not wear those to hold out your skirt?'

I laughed. 'Oh, I had three when I began my journey here. But one I tore up for a bandage when Jamie cut his knee, I made gloves for him with the flannel one and the other I used for the baby I helped care for during the voyage. There was a storm you see, and we couldn't get things dry.'

Mrs Lyden seized my words and it was as if she held them delicately for examination. 'You were employed as a nursemaid? My dear child, how did you know what to do?'

I smiled at her, striving to appear at ease with her probing questions. 'I was not employed – the baby's mother was the only other person in steerage. I helped her with the children. It was not difficult. I did not have to learn anything new. I had done those tasks at home often enough.'

Adelaide sighed and said in a bored tone, 'One does not do tasks oneself. One has servants to do them.'

'Servants are difficult to come by in New Zealand.' I smiled at her to soften my words, for I did not like to contradict her, but she hunched a shoulder and turned from me.

Mrs Poulter, her eyes missing none of the by-play, asked, 'But dear child – you must have had help in the house of some description?'

Lady Derringford made no attempt to come to my aid or to change the conversation to a topic more suited to her taste. I could see no choice but to answer Mrs Poulter's question. 'Ma'am, I can cook, clean, milk a cow, make butter and cheese, tend the garden, sew my own clothes and those of my brothers.'

Adelaide tucked herself right into the very corner of the sofa. 'Those are things peasants do.'

I turned so that I faced her. 'They are things everyone does in that country if they wish to stay alive.'

My aunt should have stepped in at that point. She should have chided Adelaide for her bad manners. She could have smiled at me and said how she looked forward to seeing me in a pretty dress and she would make sure it had the best petticoat available. But she stayed silent and thus allowed Mrs Poulter, with her vulture expression, to ask the next question. 'You said *brothers* my dear Miss Carstairs. You have other family besides the delightful young man who looks so like Lord Derringford and William?'

All I could think of was Arama riding away from us. Arama slipping through the bush. Arama with his rifle over his shoulder. 'Yes,' I whispered. 'But he is fighting in the war. I do not know if he is safe.'

At last Lady Derringford bestirred herself, but it would have been far better had she not done so. 'Well, after all, he is not your brother so you may be easy.'

Her words stung me and I dropped my head.

Lady Featherstone probed gently. 'How very interesting. Do tell us about him. What is his name?'

But I had had enough of their avid eyes and their unfeeling questions. I stood up. 'Pray excuse me, Lady Derringford. It distresses me greatly to speak of my brother and the war.' I put my hands over my face and left the room.

I ran back to the library and to the comfort of Jamie's presence. 'Don't worry your head about them. Lot of old cats,' he said and went back to his book.

Lady Derringford sent for me even before their carriages vanished over the rise at the top of the oak avenue. Adelaide still sat on her sofa. I chose a chair as far away from her as I could get.

Lady Derringford began infelicitously. 'How dare you run out like that! Adelaide is right — you are a peasant! Isn't it bad enough that you appeared wearing that garment you are so proud of!'

'Forgive me, ma'am,' I said swiftly and it felt to me like sparks flew from my eyes. Certainly my temper burned hot enough to ignite the very air around me. 'I left the room so as to avoid telling your *friends* that my brother is Maori. I did it from the mistaken idea that you would not wish me to mention it.' I stood up. 'But I will know better in future. Thank you for teaching me how to behave in an English drawing room.' I had reached the door before I remembered her other complaint. 'And as to my dress, madam, you know full well it is all I have.'

I left the room but she didn't let the matter drop.

At dinner, Lord Derringford received the full litany of her complaints. I was rude, I was mannerless and why dear Mrs Poulter, sweet Mrs Lyden and the delightful Lady Featherstone had left invitations for me was exactly what she could not understand. She glared at me. 'You will write and refuse, of course, for you simply cannot go.'

Adelaide smirked and rattled off the longest speech she had yet made in my presence. 'I shall be going – Lady Featherstone is to give a ball. Mrs Poulter is getting up an expedition to view the priory ruins which are most picturesque and Mrs Lyden particularly asked Mama and me to come to her At Home next week.'

I looked at them both, then at our father who ate his beef and ignored his wife and daughter. 'But I would like to go.'

Lady Derringford sighed. 'You cannot go. You do not have suitable clothes.' She spoke slowly and clearly as if I had as few brains as she and her daughter between them.

I blushed – that was a most uncharitable thought. Aunt Frances would not be proud of me.

Her ladyship didn't notice. She gave a satisfied smile. Apparently my blue dress for the picnic was as far as her generosity would stretch.

Jamie waited until he was certain she had finished, then he spoke directly to me. 'Hannah, will you write to me when I'm away? I shall want to know that you are happy.'

That was all he said, but our father paused between one forkful of food and the next. He sent a frowning look at his wife but made no comment.

It was with relief that I rode out with Jamie the next afternoon to visit our grandmother. She lay on a day bed in her room but her face glowed with joy as we kissed her. There was no sign of our grandfather. 'He knows you are here,' she told us, 'but he will not see you. Let us not waste our precious moments by talking of it.'

She asked us about our lives, starting with what we knew of Mama's life since she ran away, and of her death. When we had told her all we could, I asked, 'Grand-mama – please tell us, why did she run away? Do you know?'

She wiped her eyes with a lace-edged handkerchief. 'My poor Angelina! She had such delicate sensibilities and she was not used to being crossed.' I glanced at Jamie and he nodded. Aunt Frances was right – Mama had indeed been spoiled. Grandmama sighed and went on, 'She came here in the middle of the night vowing she would never go back to her husband for he had a mistress and refused to give her up.'

So that was it. Our grandfather had told her not to be missish, that all men took mistresses and that she had better go home and start getting used to the idea. But instead she had vanished leaving only a cloak and shoes at the river's edge.

'But Grandmama,' I said, thinking it through, 'she arrived in New Zealand with clothes she had worn here. She had jewels.'

'Which Papa sold,' Jamie said.

Grandmother fluttered her hands. 'I do not know the answers, dear children. She may have brought things with her when she arrived here, for your grandfather did not let her in the house. She didn't have a servant with her.'

'What? Grandmama, did she drive the coach herself?' Jamie asked, prepared at last to admit Mama was brave and adventurous, but Grandmama shook her head.

'No, not a coach. It was a gig your father had made for her. He was totally in love with her, you know.'

'What happened to the gig?' Jamie asked.

Grandmama shook her head. 'I believe the horse was found later along with the gig. I do not recall exactly.'

She did not want to talk of that terrible night. We told her instead of Aunt Frances, of Rawinia and Papa and our lives. We did not stay long, for she tired easily. 'Come next Saturday, dear child,' she said to me, and I promised her that I would.

We discussed it as we rode home. 'She must have met Papa on the road,' Jamie said.

We would never know.


The next day was Sunday. We went to church with the family. 'Of course you must go,' Lady Derringford exclaimed.

Lord Derringford, for once, agreed with her. 'Sunday. We go to church.'

We went. Everyone stared at us. Lady Derringford was struck by a violent headache which made it essential for her to climb into her carriage and carry us away from neighbours who clamoured for an introduction to us.

Tuesday came, the day Jamie was to leave me. It was only his excitement that stopped me weeping on his chest and begging him not to go. His new clothes arrived before

Mr Winterton did. Jamie threw the parcel of them into his bag without opening it. 'Jamie! You must wear them,' I scolded him.

He shook his head and grinned at me. 'Women concern themselves with clothes, not men.'

I said slowly, 'I think you must look like a gentleman. I think people will not listen to you if they think you are not a person of standing in the world.'

He frowned and thought for a moment. 'Perhaps you are right, Sissy. Very well, I will play their game.' He ripped open the parcel and changed into the new clothes.

My heart was full. I threw my arms around him and sobbed, 'You look so handsome! Rawinia would be so proud of you.'

He patted my shoulder. 'Don't turn on the waterworks, Sissy! By the time I see you again you'll be so fine yourself that you'll hold up your nose at me.' A thought occurred to him. He grabbed my shoulders and held me from him in order to glare at me. 'Just promise me one thing, Hannah Carstairs.'

I sniffed and nodded. I would promise him anything.

'Don't turn yourself into a ninny like Judith did.' His glare changed to a grin. 'I shall come back for your wedding, I promise you.'

I could not even manage a protest. I held in my tears and waved goodbye. He leaned from the carriage and shouted, 'Remember, Sissy! Write to me!'

I watched until the carriage vanished over the rise, then I ran and cast myself on my bed and sobbed my heart out.

Mary brought me luncheon on a tray. 'There, there, Miss Hannah. Don't fret now. Here, I'll pour you a cup of tea. You sit up now and sip it, there's a good girl.'

I sat up, and thanked her through my tears.

She handed me the tea, then placed a wafer-thin slice of bread and butter on a dainty plate. 'Eat this, Miss. Cook says to tell you she cut it special.'

I ate and drank to please her, but I felt better for it. 'Thank you,' I said again.

She smiled. 'That's better, miss. And Jenkins says to tell you that your new dress has arrived.'

I could not but help be cheered by the dress. It was so pretty. Life, it seemed, would go on whether Jamie was with me or not.

In the morning, I jumped from my bed and ran to the window. The day shone bright and fresh. I opened the casement and leaned out. I would not think of the pain of Jamie's absence. I would look forward instead to wearing my new dress and going to a picnic.

Mary helped me into my dress. She arranged my hair for me too, parting it in the middle and looping it up at the sides of my head.

I pulled on my boots, for Lady Derringford had forgotten about footwear. She screeched when she saw me. 'You cannot wear those! Mellet! Find something for Miss Hannah to wear. Hurry, woman.'

Mellet was her ladyship's maid and a most superior creature according to Mary and Jenkins who did not like her. However, she found a pair of blue slippers for me. They were a little tight but not too uncomfortable. I tied my bonnet on my head and I was ready.

'For the love of heaven, girl,' said Lady Derringford, 'do try to mind your tongue today.'

'Perhaps you will have the goodness to turn the conversation if your friends ply me with questions,' I retorted.

'Mother!' Adelaide wailed. 'Let us set out or we will never get there.'

I looked forward to travelling in the carriage that awaited us at the front of the house. How smart it looked. The paint shone and the gold and red on the coat of arms gleamed in the sun. The coats of the horses, though, almost rivalled the coachwork.

I waited while Frant handed my stepmother and sister into the coach and I waited while they fussed with their skirts.

'Hurry up, Hannah,' called my stepmother. 'Must we wait all day for you?'

I smiled at Frant, stepped up into the carriage and arranged my own skirts over the seat. 'It is so exciting! Do you know, this is only the second time in my life I have ridden in a coach?'

Adelaide tossed her head. 'How very provincial you are! I suppose you will be sick since you have your back to the horses.'

'I will tell you if I feel unwell,' I promised. 'Then we may swap places.'

She glared. 'No, we may not.'

It was not a promising beginning, but I persevered, for I sorely missed Judith and longed for a friend again. 'How charming you look,' I said, smiling at her. She would be a pretty girl if only she would smile.

She tipped her head a little but didn't answer me.

I tried again. 'Tell me, Adelaide – have you been often to Mrs Delaney's?'

'No,' she said.

Lady Derringford said nothing. I did not try again and after a mile or two they began to speak to each other as if I did not exist. My stomach did not protest at the jolting of the carriage, but perhaps it was anger and hurt that kept sickness at bay. It was only the thought of my grandmother and how she looked forward to my next visit which cheered me.

Mrs Delaney lived not far from Plymouth. Lady Derringford appeared most anxious that Adelaide understood the honour of the picnic invitation. Mrs Delaney, it appeared, was rich, well connected and exceedingly influential. 'It is most flattering that she has invited us,' she said. 'Of course, I have been expecting it all this summer.' She cast a look in my direction. 'It is such a pity she waited until now, but we must make the best of things. Be sure and smile at her, Adelaide. A little animation is a good thing, you know, and I know *you* would never go beyond the line of what is pleasing.'

I decided I would dislike Mrs Delaney excessively.

We arrived at her house which was similar to Derringford Park in size and grandeur. A servant led us along a path bordered with lavender to a large lawn enclosed with sculptured hedges. I looked around, enchanted. The lawn dipped down to a stream in a series of terraces. Flowers bloomed in beds planted in front of the hedges and here and there, big trees offered shade.

Mrs Delaney proved much younger than I had thought she would be, somewhere between thirty and thirty-five I guessed. Her hair was as fair as Judith's, and she shaded her delicate skin from the sun with a cream parasol painted with parrots.

'Oh, how charming your parasol is,' I said when Lady Derringford murmured my name to her.

Lady Derringford looked pained, but Mrs Delaney laughed. 'I am so glad you like it. I painted it myself, you know. My husband quite despairs of me – he says if I must paint why don't I paint flowers or something sensible!'

I smiled back at her. 'There is altogether too much in the world that is sensible.'

She looked much struck by the notion. 'How right you are. Lady Derringford – allow me to congratulate you on your two delightful daughters.' She smiled at us all and excused herself. 'The problem with hosting a party is that one never gets time to talk properly to the people one is most interested in.' She flitted off.

Lady Derringford walked on air all the rest of the afternoon. She remained gracious even when guests approached her with the sole intention of meeting her strange new daughter. Until, that is, we sat down at white-clothed tables set under the shadiest tree to drink tea and eat cakes.

The trouble came from an elderly gentleman called Major Bedlington. He sat at the next table to ours but his voice was loud and he spoke as if he were on a parade ground. 'So you are the young lady from New Zealand, what?'

I agreed that I was.

'Nice little war you've got there at the moment. A good scrap – won't amount to much though. The army will mop up the rebels in no time.' He looked at me and tapped a finger on the table. 'Who's in charge? Can't remember names these days.'

'Colonel Gold,' I said.

'Ah, Gold. Of course. Fine man, Gold. Excellent soldier.' He did not seem happy that I made no reply. 'Well, girl?'

I put down my cup and clasped my hands together on my lap. 'No sir, he is not a good soldier. And it is not a good scrap, as you put it. It is a most unjust war.'

Around us, the chatter stopped dead. The major spluttered and gasped before he managed to get enough breath to shout at me. 'How dare you, missy! How dare you!'

Mr Delaney rose unhurriedly from his chair, moved to the major and put a hand on his shoulder. 'The young lady has the advantage of you, Major, for she has first-hand knowledge of the situation. But the day is too fine to quarrel.' He summoned a servant with a flick of his hand. 'Bates, would you be kind enough to bring whisky for the major?' He stayed chatting to the major about the war in India until the whisky arrived.

Lady Derringford's graciousness evaporated. I did not look forward to the journey home, particularly as at least three groups of people turned their backs as I wandered through the grounds behind her and Adelaide.

Lady Derringford turned to me after the third instance and snapped, 'I hope you are happy! You have quite ruined all Adelaide's chances and made me the laughing stock. I have a headache. We will go home immediately.'

Adelaide, showing more animation that I had yet seen, spat at me, 'I hate you! Never call yourself my sister again.'

I felt battered by their hatred. All the joy of the day was gone.

Mrs Delaney and her husband bade us farewell. 'Dear Lady Derringford – how sorry I am you are feeling poorly,' said Mrs Delaney and she sounded sincere, although she must have known why Lady Derringford was escaping.

Mr Delaney smiled at her. 'Your daughters are most charming, ma'am. Quite the prettiest girls present. Will you bring them to visit again? We are to have a dinner and dancing next week and we are in need of beautiful girls.'

Lady Derringford's graciousness bounced back. 'Of course. I will be delighted.'

He handed us into the carriage. 'Thank you,' I murmured when he took my hand.

Both he and his wife smiled and their eyes twinkled. 'We look forward to furthering our acquaintance with you and your sister.'

Lady Derringford didn't know whether to scold me on the way home, or to crow about the dinner invitation. In the end she did some of each. I turned my head and stared out at the countryside. Adelaide muttered every now and again, uttering the word *she* whom I supposed was me.

The upshot of the day though, was unexpected. Lady Derringford almost fell from the carriage in her haste to pour her complaints into her husband's ears.

That evening when Mary came to turn my bed down, she could scarcely talk for laughing. 'Sykes heard the master shouting at the mistress, Miss Hannah. *Get the girl fixed for clothes and don't spare the expense*, he said. She screeched. He shouted. But, miss — you are to have a proper wardrobe!'

In the morning, her ladyship sent for me. She had decided, she told me in voice cold enough to freeze water, that I absolutely must have clothing suitable to my station in life. I refrained from asking what that station might be. What it meant though, was a trip to Plymouth to a dress-making establishment where I was briskly measured and where Lady Derringford, with a look of pain on her face at the money she was being forced to spend, ordered an immense amount of clothing for me.

I enjoyed every second. I relished too, being away from the rest of the family who all ignored me when they could and treated me with disdain when they couldn't.

I looked forward to visiting Grandmama on Saturday afternoon. I put on my new riding dress and danced out to the stables.

Joe, however, when I went to get my dear old plodding horse, refused to let me go alone. He whistled up the youngest groom, a lad called Bobby and bade him accompany me.

I considered Joe for a moment, debating whether to argue with him but the light in his eye and the determined way he stood solid in the stable door suggested it would be futile. I gave in. 'Thank you, Joe. I appreciate your care for me.'

He gave a gruff growl. 'Aye, lass, well somebody's got to look out for you, for them's as should be doing it ain't, to my way of thinking – and I'm not alone in my opinion neither.'

He threw me up into the saddle. I leaned down to grasp his shoulder. 'Thank you!'

Bobby rode behind me despite my efforts to engage him in chat and get him to ride alongside. After a mile or two, I stopped trying and instead applied myself to enjoying the sunshine, the freedom from disapproval and the prospect of visiting my grandmother.

We had gone through the town and were plodding our way along the final leg of our journey when I heard hoofbeats behind us. My first thought was to be glad Joe had insisted on Bobby accompanying me.

I guided my horse to the side of the road, but the rider slowed and drew alongside me. 'Good afternoon to you, miss.' He swept off his hat and made me a laughing bow as much as he could from the back of a horse. 'May I be so bold as to ask if you are making your way to Norwood Manor as well?'

It was so pleasant to be smiled at. 'Indeed, I am, sir.' He

reminded me of the military officers at home with his polished manner.

His eyes crinkled with pleasure. 'Why, that is wonderful! So am I — allow me introduce myself, my dear young lady — Charles Rathbone at your service.'

I told him my name and he gave a shout of delight. 'You are the young New Zealander who has set the county talking! How delightful to meet you, Miss Carstairs.'

He told me he had business with my grandfather but was not at all downcast when I said I doubted he would be at home. 'In fact, it is a lucky stroke for now I will join you and your grandmother if I may?'

And that was how I met him. He charmed my grandmother. He laughed when I described my contretemps with the major at the picnic. 'Damned old fool — please excuse my language, ma'am.' He bowed towards my grandmother. I could not but feel that Captain Lindhurst, for example, would never have used such language around an elderly lady but his charm was such that my grandmother merely smiled upon him.

He asked me why I believed the war to be unjust, listened carefully and said he had often felt the Empire trod over the rights of the peoples it conquered. I quite forgave him his intemperate language.

He insisted on pouring the tea for us. 'I am never allowed to do so, you know,' he said, pulling a comical face. 'It is most unfair that it is only ladies who are permitted to perform the one interesting task at a tea party!'

'It is not at all unfair,' I retorted. 'Would you enjoy

a life where pouring the tea was the highlight of your days?'

He looked much struck by that and soon I found myself telling him of my resolve never to marry. He threw back his head and laughed. 'What a refreshing young lady you are, Miss Carstairs. But you haven't a hope of escaping marriage, you know.'

'I have managed thus far very well,' I replied.

He shook a finger at me and his grey eyes twinkled with mischief. 'Do but consider, Miss Carstairs! Until now you have just been beautiful and charming. Now you are beautiful, charming and a young lady of fortune as well.'

There was the slightest of questions in his tone as he made the statement and I hastened to disabuse him of any notion that I might be an heiress. 'Indeed, sir, you are mistaken. I am entirely dependent on the charity of my father. I have no expectation of fortune from him.'

He regarded me in silence for a moment and I wondered if suddenly he did not find me so charming, but then he said, 'Upon reflection, Miss Carstairs, I do not think it will make the slightest bit of difference. Your own charms will carry the day.'

I laughed with pleasure that he did not mind my lack of fortune.

My grandmother smiled upon us both but did not speak, indeed I do not think she took in one word of the conversation. She seemed content just to lie and look upon me as if I were her own beloved daughter returned to her.

I begged Mr Rathbone to tell me something of his life.

He spread his hands. 'I fear my story is plain and simple compared with yours, my dear Miss Carstairs.'

I assured him I would not find it so. 'For I know nothing of plain and simple English lives.'

He pulled his mouth down in a grimace. 'Oh, my story is common enough. I am the younger son. My papa is not quite respectable because he acquired his money in trade. Mama, however, is most respectable for she is the daughter of an earl – an extremely poor one, but an earl nevertheless.' He pulled another face and said in a lugubrious tone, 'I am giving myself this one last summer before I give in to my papa's demands and go to work for him.'

I laughed at the way he mocked himself. 'Truly, you are fortunate to be able to work.'

I told him of my wish to be useful in the world. 'But I cannot quite see how I may achieve my desire,' I added.

Whereupon he leaned back in his chair and chuckled. 'I return to my prediction that you will marry a man of birth and fortune, my dear Miss Carstairs. Then you will be useful to your family.'

'You are wrong, sir! Such women are of no use as far as I can tell. They do nothing all day but gossip.' I shook my head. 'No, if I must marry, it will have to be to a man without a fortune.'

My notions amused him. We argued back and forth until the clock struck four times. It was so late. I jumped to my feet. 'I must go! Grandmama, I am so sorry. I hope I have not wearied you.'

'Never, dear child.' She squeezed my hand, but she

looked tired. I vowed to be more thoughtful next Saturday.

Mr Rathbone accompanied me down the stairs. 'I must thank you for a delightful afternoon, Miss Carstairs,' he said as he bowed over my hand. 'I can safely say that never before have I so enjoyed the company of a young lady.'

I smiled upon him. 'Thank you for the compliment sir, but you are so easy to converse with that I fear my tongue ran away with me.'

He kept holding my hand, and asked, 'Might I come next Saturday when you visit your grandmother?' He tilted his head to one side and begged most charmingly, 'Do say I may!'

I retrieved my hand. 'That would be delightful. I will look forward to it.'

He stepped back and let me go, lifting a hand in farewell as I rode away.

I spent the ride home reliving the entire afternoon over in my head. I recalled what he had said, how he had looked. I relived the charming things he had said to me. I basked in the admiration I had seen in his eyes. My hand glowed warm where he had held it.

If only Judith were here we could discuss his perfections together.

Oh! I pulled my horse to a stop. Bobby, patient as ever behind me, stopped as well.

Could this be love? Had I fallen in love with Mr Charles Rathbone? I kicked my heels into my horse and set him moving again. Surely I could not have done so. But the more I thought about it, the more I had to conclude that if I had not yet fallen in love then I was well on the way to doing so.

I frowned, thinking it over. What did I know of him? I had chatted so freely all afternoon that he by now knew a good deal about me, but had told me almost nothing of himself. I shook up my horse. That could easily be remedied when next I saw him.

I could not wait until next Saturday to see him. Seven whole days! Surely my impatience to meet him again meant that I loved him.

Judith would have been able to tell me. Finally, I began to understand her passion for Captain Lindhurst. I sighed. If only she were here I could pour out to her how perfect Mr Rathbone's person was, how delightfully his sandy hair curled, how charmingly his grey eyes twinkled and what a fine, upright figure he had.

I contented myself when I reached the house I could never think of as home, with writing her a long letter instead. Then I wrote to Aggie. She would clap her hands to hear that the grandson of an earl – even an impoverished one – wished to meet me again.

# 24

## Chapter Twenty-Four

Being in love, if that is what it was, cushioned me against the barbs of my family. I needed such cushioning for Lord Derringford departed noisily for London the Monday following my momentous visit to my grandmother and left me alone with his family.

The departure was noisy because Lady Derringford ran out of the dining room after him, wailing, 'You cannot go! You cannot leave me alone with that girl!'

'Madam,' he snapped, 'you are hardly alone! You have a parcel of servants to help you. Now, let go of my sleeve if you please. I must go and that's an end to it.'

His lady threw up her hands. 'It is too bad! You are her father, yet I am the one who must bear the burden of her. I insist upon your staying, sir!'

He shook her off and headed for the stairs. 'Find her a husband. That'll get rid of her.'

I slipped outside and ran down to the beautiful spot where the stream fed into the lake. It was not pleasant to be regarded as a burden. Jamie was so lucky. How I longed for my own place in the world, a place where I would be loved, or if not that, then where I would be useful.

Dr Feilding's words came back to me. *You could become a nurse, young Hannah.*

Perhaps I could.

But what of Mr Rathbone? I shook my head. Such was the stuff dreams were made of. I had spent a pleasant afternoon with a charming and handsome young man; that was all. He probably wouldn't be there when I visited again.

What I had not imagined, however, was that he would be at the social events I went to. He bowed over my hand on Tuesday at Mrs Lyden's house. He danced with me after dinner. He danced as beautifully as Judith's captain did.

He sat beside me a musical soiree at Lady Featherstone's. He muttered wry comments under his breath on the efforts of each performer.

I laughed but scolded him. 'You are too harsh, sir. I enjoyed that song immensely. Pray do not spoil it for me!'

He immediately apologised and promised to mend his ways. He eyed the next performer – a young man who pushed at a lock of artfully tousled hair. 'I am prepared to admire his playing,' Mr Rathbone whispered. 'He has the appearance of an artist. He will perform admirably.'

The young man began. I was not accustomed to violin music but I did know it ought not to sound like a saw being drawn slowly along an iron roof. The audience endured it, and in the polite applause, Mr Rathbone whispered, 'What talent! What a performer. He is truly remarkable!'

I found I greatly enjoyed the company of a man who could make me laugh.

He was not the only young man who sought my

company. Lady Derringford was forced to present me to half a dozen during that week who begged her for an introduction. I found that Mr Rathbone had become the standard by which I judged them all.

On Friday, after a dance at their parents' house, Mr Wally Sanford and his younger brother Percy came riding along the oak avenue to Derringford Park. Frant came to summon me from my retreat by the stream. 'Miss Hannah, the mistress wants you.'

I put down my book and smiled at him. 'I am quite sure she does not, Frant!'

He grinned, for by now he had quite forgiven me for the bloody nose I had inflicted upon him when I first arrived. 'There's two young gents, miss. They've come to call and the mistress was all puffed up and smiling because she thought it was Miss Adelaide they were after, but then they up and asks where you are, miss.' He chuckled and helped me up from my perch on a rock. 'Sykes says it was all she could do to speak civil. And as for that Miss Adelaide — I pity the man as weds her.'

I did too. Adelaide continued to rebuff any attempt I made at friendliness. I had quite given up on William and the younger children but I still cherished the hope that Adelaide might become the sister I craved.

Today's visit widened the gulf between us. When I entered the room, she was speaking. I waited until she had finished her story about how Mrs Delaney had smiled at her and invited her to dinner.

Wally Sanford said, 'Capital, Miss Adelaide. We will see you there.'

Percy nodded his head. 'First rate, Miss Adelaide. It will be a pleasure.'

But then they turned their attention to me. 'Delighted to see you again, Miss Carstairs,' Wally said.

Percy was not so formal. 'I say, Miss Carstairs — you dance splendidly. Will you come to Mrs Delaney's too?'

I glanced at Lady Derringford, but she did not assist me so I said, 'She invited both of us. Are you to go as well?'

Percy grinned at me. 'I'll go if you promise to be there. The Delaneys terrify me — they talk in riddles. A fellow gets quite befuddled trying to keep up with them.'

I laughed and turned to Adelaide. 'They were perfectly charming to us, were they not, Adelaide?'

She shrugged and fiddled with her fan.

The young men, too did their best to include her, but it is difficult to make conversation with a girl who sulks, tosses her head and gives but one word answers. They soon gave up and I confess I so much enjoyed the nonsensical fun of their observations on the world that I too ceased to try and involve her. Lady Derringford did nothing to help her daughter — or me either had I needed it. But I was quite at ease with the two young men who reminded me of Hartley, Vernon and the Lang brothers with their light-hearted nonsense.

I reaped the whirlwind of the joint venom of Lady Derringford and Adelaide at dinner. The younger children stared, their eyes wide. They looked from their mother, to Adelaide, and then to me.

'Have you no gratitude?' demanded Lady Derringford. 'I have beggared myself to provide you with the very clothes on your back and this is the thanks I get! Making a spectacle of yourself with every young man for miles around.'

I put my hands in my lap for I feared to hold onto my cutlery, so strong was my urge to skewer her with my fork. 'Forgive me, ma'am. I will return the clothes this very day. I still have the dress I arrived in. I shall wear that.'

William, perhaps with the memory of Jamie's statement that he would only sign away his inheritance if I were happy, said, 'This is a fuss about nothing. I say let every man in England beat a path to our door, for the sooner she marries the better for us.'

I refrained from saying I did not intend to marry. We ate the rest of the meal in silence.

I did not accompany them to the drawing room after dinner, instead I walked in the gardens in the cool of the evening where the scent of roses and lavender soothed me.

Was it true that I no longer wished to marry? Mr Charles Rathbone made my heart beat faster, his very existence caused my whole being to suffuse with happiness, but I could not imagine myself as his wife. The trouble was, I decided, that I was fast arriving at the place where I could not imagine my life without him,

He too was invited to the Delaneys'. 'Ah, I see you have met Mr Rathbone,' said Mrs Delaney. 'Well, he is a charming rogue, to be sure.' She rapped his knuckles with her fan and shook her head. She gave me a considering look and I felt she wished to say something but, in the end, she smiled and moved away.

I was vastly relieved that the loud-voiced major was not a guest, but even so the military again caused me problems. The young man sitting on my right at dinner told me he was about to join the army. His mama spoke across the table, smiling at him with fond pride. 'I cannot wait to see you in your uniform, my dear George.' To me, she said, 'There is something so romantic about a scarlet uniform, Miss Carstairs, I'm sure you agree!'

I thought of the scarlet coats, vivid against the green as the regiment marched to the Waitara. Would Arama, shooting at a scarlet jacket, kill Captain Lindhurst? I shook my head. 'I'm afraid I cannot think anything to do with war romantic, ma'am.' I smiled at the young man beside me and added too late, 'But I am sure Mr Curran will be a fine soldier.'

Mr Rathbone, sitting next to Mrs Curran, soothed her motherly pride by asking what regiment he would be joining. 'You must be so proud of him, Mrs Curran. Britain is most fortunate in her fighting men.'

I smiled at him, gratitude in my heart for rescuing me from an awkward situation, especially when I knew what his true sentiments were concerning the army.

There was dancing after dinner. Mr Rathbone claimed my hand for one of the country dances and I was able to thank him for his timely intervention.

'It is my pleasure to serve you, fair one,' he declaimed, and I laughed.

Mr Delaney asked me for the next dance, then smiled and said, 'Would you mind very much, Miss Carstairs, sitting this one out and talking to me instead? I want to ask you about the war in New Zealand, if I may?'

He laughed at my expression. 'Please feel free to tell me what you know. I am most interested in the colonies, you see.'

I dropped a curtsey and said it would be my pleasure.

He conducted me to a pair of chairs set near the open doors where the fresh breeze wafted in from the gardens. 'Now then, my dear, tell me if you please why you told the major the war was unjust.'

Two dances were not long enough to finish our conversation. He listened and asked intelligent questions so that I lost all my shyness. After the second dance, his wife came over to, as she put it, rescue me. 'For he is quite fanatical about the colonies, you know.' She smiled at him fondly. 'He would sail there tomorrow if he could.'

His conversation with me did not go unnoticed by my relatives.

All the way home, either Adelaide complained to her mother about how I had monopolised Mr Delaney all evening, or her mother complained to me that I should have known better than to make such a spectacle of myself by laughing with a married man in such a hoydenish fashion.

I stared out the window at the dark landscape and

relived the evening in my head, especially the parts that contained the smiling face of Mr Rathbone.

We met on many occasions as July slipped into August. Always, he came to Norwood Manor when I visited my grandmother and he fell into the habit of riding home with me afterwards. Lady Derringford even went so far as to welcome him and bid him call whenever he wished.

I wrote to Jamie that our stepmother had softened towards me. I suspected she saw my partiality for Mr Rathbone and was determined to get me married to him and off her hands before Christmas. I wished I could make a wager with her, for she would lose. I wrote too to Judith, and counted the days until I could expect a reply from her.

Oh, it was wonderful when I was in his company. I loved it when he talked to me at a party or dance and kept a distance between us in order to shield me from gossip and speculation. I melted when we chatted alone, chaperoned by my grandmother who lay dozing on her daybed.

My heart swelled with pride when I heard gentlemen describe him as a capital shot and a bruising rider.

Hostesses called on him to make up numbers at a dinner party, or they would whisper to him to ask a shy girl to dance. I could not help but hear too, that mothers warned their daughters not to lose their hearts to him. I thought it was because his father had made his fortune from trade and was not considered to be a gentleman. I despised them for their prejudices.

He discovered I did not know the names of English wild flowers. He took to picking them for me and presenting them to me with elegantly written notes. *This, my very dear Miss Hannah,* went one, *is the marsh marigold. I chose it in the hope that the shape of its leaves might remind you of the kidney fern you told me of that grows in the bush (what a strange name to call your woodland!) of your home.*

He reminded me sometimes of Papa — it was particularly so when he was being irreverent or scathing about a person he considered stupid. I laughed at his castigations even if sometimes I felt a little uncomfortable about doing so. But he was everywhere received in drawing rooms and ballrooms so I concluded that I was wrong in my feelings.

It soothed my heart to think of him. On many occasions when we rode home in the carriage and Lady Derringford and Adelaide ignored me, or worse, talked about me as if I were not present, I brought to my mind Mr Rathbone's smile, the warmth in his eyes when he bowed to me, the way he pressed my hand when he danced with me.

Lord Derringford came home for a brief visit at the start of September. He brought with him a letter for me from Jamie. I seized it with joy and ran outside to the peace of the garden to read it.

*Dearest Sissy,*

*Are they being kind to you? You must tell me if they are not, for I mean what I say about the inheritance they all care about so much. Enough of that.*

*Sissy, I am learning so much, you can have no idea. It is*

*all wonderful and I have even met a man who worked with the great Isambard Kingdom Brunel.*

*I read in the papers that the war in Taranaki drags on. You had better say a prayer for Arama and Rawinia when you go to church. I wonder how Papa is doing.*

*Your loving brother,*

*Jamie.*

I wiped the moisture from my eyes and sniffed. Darling Jamie – I was so glad he was happy. I wandered beside the lake to the charming little building Lady Derringford called a folly. I think that was its proper name, rather than a comment from her upon its foolish uselessness. I sat on the bench inside it and thought about the men in my life – Jamie, Papa, Arama, Mr Woodley and now here in England there were Lord Derringford, William and – becoming increasingly important to me – Mr Rathbone.

I closed my eyes and conjured up his face. He reminded me a little of Papa in his looks as well as his manner, with his grey eyes and sandy hair. His charm too, was very like Papa's. Was that why I liked him so much?

Somebody approached the folly, whistling to warn me. It was Frant. 'Miss, I've been sent to fetch you.' His face was worried.

'Frant – is anything wrong? Is it Jamie?' I clasped my hands over my heart. What had happened?

Frant shook his head. 'Nothing like that, miss. It's the master. He's thrown his teacup at the mistress and he's shouting the place down.'

'But Frant!' I wailed. 'I cannot think of anything I have done to displease him!' I had to run to match Frant's hurried stride.

'Well, miss — it seems he's taken against one of the young men what comes calling on you.' He stopped to let me catch up.

'Who?' I asked, completely bewildered. 'Who can he possibly object to?'

It was, of course, Mr Rathbone. I reflected that it would have to be the one man who meant something to me that my father forbade me from seeing ever again as long as I lived, which would not be long if I defied him.

I sat in the chair Mr Chapman held out for me in my father's study. 'But sir, I don't understand! Lady Derringford has made no objection. Mr Rathbone attends every party we go to. Everybody approves of him. Why do . . .'

He cut me off with a crash of his hand on his desk. 'It is your duty to obey, not to question, girl! And you will not see him again! Is that clear?'

I glanced at Mr Chapman but, as usual, he was too busy appreciating the drama of the situation to assist me even had he wished to. 'Explain to me, please, how I am to do that? Are you ordering me to stay at home? Is that what I am to do from now on?'

It silenced him but only for a second. 'Just stay away from him — that should be simple enough, even for you. And if he tries to come here again he'll be thrown out. Do you understand?'

'Oh, yes sir. Even my inferior brain can comprehend

that!' In his corner, Mr Chapman had one of his coughing fits. 'Please tell me why I am not to see Mr Rathbone, sir,' I asked again.

'Because I say so,' he bellowed. 'That is reason enough.'

I forgot which of my fathers I was arguing with for I said, 'But that is no reason at all, sir. Where is the logic? On what do you base your orders?'

Unlike Papa, this father was unable to relish the cut and thrust of a reasoned debate. His method was noise and plenty of it. I stood up and walked to the door.

'Where do you think you're going?' he roared.

'Calm yourself, sir. I am not running off to meet Mr Rathbone,' I said and was not surprised to hear yet more coughing from Mr Chapman.

It was such a pity Mr Chapman did not dine with the family for he would have derived no end of enjoyment from it. I did not.

Lady Derringford played the injured party and blamed me for the upset. Adelaide dropped acid whenever she got the chance. 'Papa, she flirts dreadfully with all the young men. I am so ashamed of her.'

I stared at her. Is that how it seemed? Was I considered a flirt?

'Lady Derringford,' I asked, turning to her. 'I must know. Please tell me – is my behaviour unbecoming?'

She glanced at her husband, caught between a desire to denounce me and the knowledge that if she did, he would blame her for not guiding me better. I cared not for her dilemma, for she had brought it on herself. 'Please tell me, ma'am.'

'Well, ma'am – you heard her. Answer the girl.'

She shook her head petulantly. 'Adelaide makes too much of it.'

The exchange did nothing to endear me to Adelaide.

Lady Derringford told me I need not come to the drawing room after dinner that night. 'I know you prefer to read in your bedroom,' she said. I did not argue. There was much to think about.

What was Lord Derringford's objection to Mr Rathbone? I could not begin to imagine. I had thought he would be delighted that a young man was showing so decided an interest in me.

Was I distressed at the thought of not seeing him again? I wandered to the window and opened it, climbed onto the sill and sat with my legs dangling.

I thought of never laughing with Mr Rathbone ever again. I thought of the discussions we had as we rode back from Norwood Manor. He told me gossip about Lady Derringford and how she had set out to capture my father. It was quite scandalous and he must have seen the shock in my face for he said, 'Believe me, my dear Hannah, I would not repeat it to anyone but you.'

I was his dear Hannah.

I had come to rely on his sympathy for my peculiar situation. Nothing seemed so unbearable when I knew I might share it with him, for I knew we would laugh about it together.

I drummed my heels against the wall. I loved him and it was time to face it.

My shoe fell off. I laughed and ran downstairs to retrieve it.

My mind was made up. I would not give up Mr Rathbone. There was no reason to do so and he alone – apart from my grandmother – was the only person in this hostile world who cared for me now that Jamie was far away.

I sat down at the little table in my room and poured my heart out in another letter to Judith.

# 25

## Chapter Twenty-Five

It was fortunate that Mr Rathbone did not call on me before I met him on Saturday, for at Norwood Manor I was able to tell him of Lord Derringford's orders. I concluded by saying, 'I do not understand it at all, do you?'

He rose to his feet and walked to the window. He balled his left fist and thumped it into his right hand. 'I cannot begin to imagine! Oh, Hannah! My sweet girl, I am so sorry to have been the cause of distress for you!'

It was worth every ounce of my father's rage to hear Mr Rathbone call me his sweet girl.

My grandmother said, 'He was always given to shouting. My beloved Angelina was forced to flee from him. He is a monster.'

Mr Rathbone strode from the window and came to where I sat. He knelt at my side and took my hands. 'Hannah, dearest girl – you shall not suffer one moment of pain on my account, I promise you. I will be careful, but I will not give you up. I will keep my distance when I see you in company. But here we may speak the truth in our hearts. What do you say?'

I pressed the hands that held mine. I gazed into his dear grey eyes. I owed my father nothing. 'I say thank you sir, from my heart.'

My grandmother wiped tears from her eyes.

That day set the pattern for subsequent Saturdays. Mr Rathbone waited for me on the highroad outside Derringate village and we rode slowly to Norwood Manor, our pace dictated by our hearts rather than by my plodding horse. We trod up the stairs to my grandmother's room where he poured the tea and my grandmother lay and smiled upon both of us. The ride home necessitated many breaks, for he liked to lift me down from my horse to show me a plant or an especially pretty aspect.

I knew myself to be deep in love and he loved me, I was in no doubt of it. It was a relief to me that he did not mention marriage for I did not know what I would say. I wanted to be with him for the rest of my life, but what sort of life would it be? It would most certainly mean children and I did not want to die, not yet when the world was so beautiful.

Autumn stole over the land, enchanting me with its colours. Mr Rathbone laughed at my delight. 'But Hannah, dear girl – trees always turn red in autumn. It is what trees do, you know!'

It was my turn to laugh at him. 'You must come to New Zealand, dear sir, where the trees stay green all the year round.'

He pretended not to believe me, then he sprang from his horse to gather me a bouquet of the glorious leaves. He kissed my hand as he gave them to me. I would keep them until they withered and crumbled.

We rode on and he asked me to describe the New Zealand bush. I did so, telling him of the majestic trees, the tall, straight trunks, the vines, the ferns and the cool damp smell. I spoke of the birds and I heard in my voice my longing for home. I saw in my mind Arama moving through the density of the greenness, silent and stealthy.

'You miss it, don't you?' he asked, his voice full of gentle concern.

I could only nod. I missed it more than I could say. More than I had let myself believe.

I awoke every Saturday, terrified that it would be raining, but it never was.

It rained on a picnic Adelaide particularly wanted to attend. She sulked and shouted at me that it was all my fault.

It rained one evening as we returned from a dance at Mrs Lyden's house. Thunder crashed and the rain fell hard. I pressed my hands together, determined I would not show my fear. I hoped Adelaide would shriek and wail when she heard the thunder but the wretched girl enjoyed it. I distracted my mind by recalling the evening and how Mr Rathbone bowed to all three of us. He was formal as he always was now in public. He paid attention to a lovely young woman with a very rich papa.

Lady Derringford, had she but known it, helped me endure the storm for she spent much effort in making sure I knew Mr Rathbone was not pining for me.

I met him again at a soirée given by the Delaneys. The November evening was cold, with the dark falling early. I pulled my warm cloak around me, glad of its protection. I still could not take my beautiful clothes for granted and Mary, when she helped me dress was apt to laugh at me.

I stepped into the carriage behind Adelaide to find that somebody had put warm bricks to keep our feet from freezing in the light shoes we wore. I leaned forward, lowered the window and called to Frant, 'Thank you for the bricks!'

Adelaide and Lady Derringford both sniffed at me. 'You are so utterly provincial!' Adelaide sighed. 'And kindly put up the window. We are late enough as it is because of you.'

I grinned at her which did nothing to change her opinion of me. I didn't care any longer that she blamed me for everything. We were late it was true, but our lateness was due to her changing her mind four times about what she should wear. I turned my thoughts to the evening ahead. Mr Rathbone would be at the soirée and, he had told me, he hoped to sit next to me if he could do so without arousing suspicion.

The Delaneys greeted us all warmly. 'Do come in, Lady Derringford. Thank you so much for venturing from home on such a cold evening.'

Lady Derringford nodded graciously. Adelaide smiled and murmured, 'Delighted.' I dropped a curtsey.

Mrs Delaney ushered us into the large drawing room crowded with guests who chatted and laughed. They reminded me of the gaily painted parrots on her summer parasol.

'Dear Lady Derringford, Miss Derringford – I think you will find these chairs comfortable.' Mrs Delaney waited until they sat before turning to me with a smile. 'Now, Miss Carstairs, we have a surprise for you! Do come with me.'

She threaded her way through her guests, pausing for a word here and there. She paused to speak to Mr Rathbone. He seized the chance to bow over my hand and press it. I murmured that I was charmed to see him. We moved on.

Mrs Delaney led me to a chair set in the corner near the fire. An elderly lady with sharp blue eyes sat upon it, fanning herself and chatting with Mr Delaney. He rose to his feet when he saw me. 'Ah! At last, Miss Carstairs. Allow me to present you to Mrs Lindhurst.'

The three of them laughed delightedly at my start of surprise. 'Ma'am – I am acquainted with a Captain Lindhurst. Are you, perhaps, a relative of his?'

She snapped her fan shut. 'Miss Carstairs, I am his grandmother. And you, I see, are the pretty little girl in the wedding photograph.'

I seated myself on the chair Mr Delaney found for me. 'Oh, ma'am – I have never seen that photograph for I left before it was finished.'

'Well, well, is it not fortunate that I brought it with me?' She pointed her fan at Mr Delaney. 'Bertie, dear boy, find one of your servants and desire her to bring the photograph from my room. My maid knows which one it is.'

Mrs Delaney chuckled and explained for my benefit. 'Mrs Lindhurst never travels without the complete photographic history of her family.'

We laughed and while we waited she fired comments in my direction. 'Tell me about the war my grandson is fighting, Miss Carstairs, but do not tell me too much, for I have no wish to imagine him in danger.'

I was fortunate that the servant appeared at that moment with the photograph. Mrs Lindhurst handed it to me saying, 'There you are, my dear. Must say your taste in gowns has improved.'

I stared at the photograph in my hands. There was Judith, beautiful and dear to me. Even though we had been forbidden to smile, her joy shone plain to see. I was unsurprised by Mrs Lindhurst's strictures on my gown. It was terrible.

'Pretty little thing,' Mrs Lindhurst said. 'Can quite see why Miles wed her. Shocking misalliance, of course. His parents were distraught.' I looked up, startled. Mr Delaney went to say something, but Mrs Lindhurst had not finished. 'Well, no harm done to be sure. Gal's dead, poor little creature, and that's an end to it.'

I think my heart stopped beating. 'Mrs Lindhurst, she is not dead. She is not!'

She realised my distress. 'Dear gal, did you not know? She died of the typhus. Wouldn't be evacuated. Must have loved him.' She tapped the photograph. 'To be sure you can see she did, poor child.'

I stumbled to my feet, I had to escape, I had to leave.

Judith. My dearest friend was dead of the typhus these many months and I had not known. 'When did she die?' I whispered.

Mrs Delaney stood by my elbow, her arm around me.

Judith had died in June. She had been going to leave on the next ship to Nelson, Mrs Lindhurst told me, for she was with child and had at last agreed to go.

I felt myself swaying. Hands guided me to a seat. Somebody handed me a glass. I drank. It was whisky and I coughed. I thought of Mr Chapman and I began to laugh and to cry and I did not know what I did.

Somebody slapped me. Lady Derringford's voice hissed. 'Control yourself! How dare you make a spectacle of yourself here!'

Mr Rathbone spoke. 'Lady Derringford, Mrs Delaney — with your permission I will take Miss Carstairs home. She has had a severe shock.'

Mrs Delaney protested but Lady Derringford brushed aside her concern, so anxious was she to get my embarrassing presence out of that august house.

People fell silent, watching as I was helped from the room. Some of the faces were avid, but some showed real concern. I could not think about them. Judith was dead.

Mr Rathbone helped me into his carriage. When we moved off, he shifted to sit beside me. He put his arms around me and cradled my head on his shoulder. 'My dearest Hannah! I am so sorry!'

He gave me his handkerchief and held me while I sobbed.

It seemed no time before the carriage stopped but when it did, my sobs had eased and I simply felt ill and numb. Tenderly, he handed me out into the cold night. He held an umbrella over me although the night was only damp and hurried me into the house. I had sunk onto a sofa and an unfamiliar servant was stirring up the fire when I realised I was not at Derringford Park.

'I thought it best to bring you here, dearest,' he said. He sat beside me and held my hand. 'Once you feel calmer I will escort you home.'

I nodded. I could not think. Judith — my mind could not accept it. She was dead.

The servant brought tea. Mr Rathbone coaxed until I managed to drink half a cup. Then he took me in his arms and kissed me. 'Dearest Hannah, how I long to have the right to comfort you, to protect you!'

He should not be kissing me, alone in that room in his own house, but I could not think of that. All I knew was the comfort of his arms, the balm of his love for me. I did not resist. His kisses grew more frenzied, more intense. I let them carry me away from knowledge of death, carry me away from my unloving family. I gave up all struggle to think of my future and let his kisses and caresses carry me forward where they would.

He tumbled me onto the floor and his hands lifted my skirts. It was as if I stood outside myself and let him do what he pleased. I felt my body lift to meet his. My lips sought his with a fervour to match his own. The final act was done quickly. I felt some pain. He cried out, then he collapsed upon me crushing my petticoat. Firelight chased shadows through the room.

He lifted himself off me, turning his back to arrange his clothing. I pulled my skirts down and thought of Polly giving birth. Perhaps I was now with child. I shrugged. What did it matter? Death could come in other ways besides childbirth.

I turned my head to look at him, this dear man who had just made himself my lover. He watched me. His face was impassive where I had expected tenderness and love. I pushed myself to sit up. He did not come to assist me, not even when I struggled with my skirts in order to sit upon the sofa.

'Charles?' I had never used his name before. It was sweet upon my lips. Warmth flowed into my heart, for I saw that he was distraught at what he had done to me. I leaned back against the sofa, bone weary. I stretched a hand towards him but lacked the energy to hold it out. It fell to the empty cushions beside me.

He moved at last. 'Get up. I will send you home in my carriage.'

Slowly, so very slowly, I straightened my back. 'Charles? Why do you speak so?'

I looked at him, standing there beside the fire and I asked, 'But you will come home with me? You will speak to my father?' He said nothing. I managed to get to my feet. 'You will tell him we are to be married?'

He strolled towards me with the strangest of smiles

on his lips. 'Oh, I will certainly speak to your father. I look forward to it.'

I could not understand it. The numbness I had felt when I first learned Judith was dead fell upon me again. He rang for a servant. It was he, not my lover, who put my cloak around my shoulders and handed me my bonnet. It was he who saw me from the house and assisted me into the carriage.

Why? What did it mean? The carriage jolted over the roads and *why, why, why* beat in my brain.

Lights still shone from Derringford Park when I arrived. I was surprised, for it seemed to me that a lifetime had passed since I left it. I walked up the broad stone steps that I now knew were swept by Linnie, the youngest of the housemaids. I lifted the knocker once. Sykes opened the door. I stumbled and fell to my knees where I stayed wailing and crooning as Rawinia's people did to mourn a death.

I was lucky that Lord Derringford did not appear. Instead, Frant, Jenkins and Mary half carried me to my room. Mary clucked and scolded, Jenkins muttered that somebody would answer for this just see if they wouldn't. Frant said nothing, but his strong arm supported me.

I stayed in my bed for the next two days. Mostly I slept and when I awoke I cried for Judith. Always there on the edge of my mind I felt the shadow of Mr Rathbone.

Mary carried bouquets of flowers to my room. I snatched the notes that came with them, reading them with hope flaring. The first was from Mrs Lindhurst. It was prettily phrased and she begged my forgiveness and hoped I would consent to see her again.

Mr and Mrs Delaney sent flowers too and expressed their sympathy for my loss. Wally and Percy Sanford left flowers and notes. Kind notes came from people I had not thought cared enough about me to make the effort to write.

I was relieved that my stepmother did not come near me.

I could not fall asleep on the night of my second day in bed. Judith was dead. At last I allowed myself to believe it. I wept again for her. I got out of bed, wrapped a shawl around my shoulders and wrote to my aunt and uncle. Perhaps my uncle would still be in New Plymouth although Aunt Frances would almost certainly have gone to Nelson with Stanley and Arnold by now. I wrote the New Plymouth address.

It was as if writing the letter released the barrier in my mind that held back the agony of Mr Rathbone. The memories propelled me to my feet. I paced the room.

I must be mistaken. He could not have done what he did, then cast me off. I crouched beside the fire. An ember glowed. I blew at it and fed it with coal until flames glowed bright and strong.

Mary crept in, a candle in her hand. 'Oh, miss! You're out of your bed! Oh, miss – we've been that worried about you!'

I looked up from my perch by the fire and smiled at her. 'Dear Mary, you are all so kind.'

She came over to me, set the candlestick on the floor to the side of the fire and sat beside me on the floor. 'Miss — I don't want to upset you further, indeed I don't.'

She stopped. I held out my hands to the flames. I didn't look at her as I said, 'Tell me what it is, Mary. I do not believe I could be any more upset than I am now.'

Her words came in a rush. 'Miss, I know what happened. It was that Mr Rathbone, wasn't it?'

I did look at her then. 'How did you know?'

'Oh, Miss! You were that upset, and your dress. It was . . .'

I wrapped my arms around my body. 'Yes. It was him. Oh, Mary! Why? He doesn't love me. He . . .' I couldn't go on.

'There now, miss. You have a good cry and you'll feel better.' She put her arms around me and rocked me the way Rawinia would have done.

The flames had burned low again by the time she helped me to my feet and tucked me into my bed. 'Darling Mary. What would I do without you?' She shook her head at me and bade me sleep.

I think I slept before she left the room because I did not hear her open the door.

It was early next morning when I awoke. My first thought was of Judith and the pain my aunt and uncle would be feeling.

Mr Rathbone. I wanted to understand why he had done to me what he had. For a moment I indulged in a dream where he came to me and begged my forgiveness. He explained why he had behaved so strangely. He carried me off and married me vowing to love me for all the rest of our days.

The trouble with such a dream, I discovered, was that I could think of no explanation for his behaviour.

I took a bath. Blood had dried on my thighs. I scrubbed my body clean. I would miss the plumbing when I returned home. Home. I sat up in the warm water and thought about it. I would go home. I would say I was widowed in case Mr Rathbone had got me with child.

What would I tell Jamie? The truth? I couldn't think.

The water cooled and I got out. I dressed then waited until Mary came to fasten my dress for me. I would go home and make myself a thousand dresses that all buttoned at the front.

I stayed in my room for I did not have the strength of mind to face my stepmother and Adelaide. Mary fussed around me, bringing me food Cook had prepared especially. I ate to please them, but I felt better.

It was in the afternoon just as the light was fading from the day when a horseman came riding down the oak avenue under the bare trees. Even before he was close enough to identify I knew it was Mr Rathbone. I backed away from the window.

He had come as he had said he would. A wild hope sprang into my heart. He had come to tell my father we were to be married.

I sank into the chair by the fire. No, I could not indulge

in such foolish dreams. I remembered too well how he had not lifted a finger to help me that fatal night. He had ravished me then sent me away as if I were no more to him than a cow he was sending to market.

I heard the knocker sound on the front door.

Sykes would show him to my father's study and then the shouting would begin. I waited and sure enough, on the floor below a door crashed shut. I crouched by the fire, cowering as if I too were in the line of fire.

How many more disasters could befall me? How much worse could my life get? Between them, the two men downstairs were deciding my fate – one of them had given me to believe he loved me, the other ought to have loved me for myself but hated me for being my mother's daughter.

Before I thought what I was doing I sprang to my feet and ran from the room. I would be there too. I would hear what Mr Rathbone wished to say to my father. If it were not to ask for my hand then I must know what it was for therein would be the answer I sought.

The door to my father's study was no match for his voice. I did not pause for if I had my courage would have vanished. Sykes appeared. 'Are you sure, Miss Hannah?'

I nodded and he opened the door.

My father was looming over Mr Rathbone who lounged quite at his ease in the most comfortable chair. Mr Chapman, as ever, hovered in the shadows.

I could not have planned a more dramatic entrance if I had tried. My father choked off his tirade in mid sentence.

Mr Rathbone shot bolt upright in his chair, his mouth agape. Mr Chapman, of course, indulged in a coughing fit.

'Hussy! Brass-faced jezebel!' It did not take my father long to recover his voice.

I walked to the window seat but didn't sit down.

My father shouted, 'How dare you show your face! You whore!'

I spoke to Mr Chapman. 'Sir, perhaps you would be good enough to tell me what Mr Rathbone's business is with my father?'

'Tell her!' shouted my father. 'Spell it out for the jade. Let her see how she's ruined me.' He threw himself into his chair. It creaked but held him.

Mr Chapman explained concisely. 'Mr Rathbone is the nephew of Ronald Carstairs.' He paused for me to take in what he had said.

'Of Papa?'

He nodded his head. 'Precisely. Mr Rathbone's mother is the sister of Mr Ronald Carstairs, who ran off with Lady Angelina.' Lord Derringford growled in his throat but other than that, kept silent.

I stared at Mr Rathbone. 'You are Papa's nephew? Oh, why did you not tell me?'

Mr Rathbone examined his fingernails. He did not speak.

Mr Chapman coughed and this time it was to gain my attention. 'Perhaps you would care to hear why he has come today?'

It was too much for my father. 'You're an old woman,

Chapman!' He pointed a finger at me and roared. 'He's come to extort money from me, girl, that's why he's come! All because you're a slut like your damned mother before you.'

I did sit down then. 'I don't understand.'

Mr Chapman forestalled another tirade from my father. He spoke succinctly. 'Mr Ronald Carstairs as a young man wished to marry his lordship's sister. His suit was refused.'

'The man was a blackguard and a drunk,' growled my father, glaring at me as if I too was both of those.

'We heard he had emigrated to New Zealand but we did not connect him with Lady Angelina,' Mr Chapman concluded.

I still failed to understand what this had to do with Mr Rathbone and myself, for it had all happened before I was born and when he was a child. 'You think Papa ran away with my mother because he was not allowed to marry your sister?' I asked Lord Derringford.

'That is exactly what I think,' snarled his lordship. 'Revenge! And if I know him, he spent the rest of his life laughing about it.'

I stared at him. How well he must have known Papa.

Mr Rathbone moved in his chair. 'This is ancient history. Let us come to the matter in hand, if you please.' He didn't speak to me. I might as well have been a coal in the scuttle for all the attention he paid me.

In essence it came to this: my grandfather had for all the years of Jamie's and my lives nursed a burning hatred of Lord Derringford. He blamed him for the shame of my mother's flight and supposed death. I appeared and he saw, not his granddaughter, but a weapon with which to punish Lord Derringford.

'He told that blackguard to smile at you,' he spluttered, 'and you, you stupid girl fell right into bed with him – and now look where that's got us!'

His eyes on his nails, Mr Rathbone said, 'This is all conjecture, my lord. Let us get down to business, if you please. For the sum of ten thousand pounds I will agree to keep silent about the fact that even now, your daughter may be carrying my child.'

The room darkened and swirled around me. From a long way off, my father's voice bellowed to the world that he'd be damned if he'd give Mr Rathbone a farthing. I leaned my head upon my hands, breathed in, breathed out and gradually the room came into focus. I lifted my head to find Mr Rathbone watching me, a faint smile on the lips that had kissed mine with such passion.

He would not get away with this. If it killed me, I would thwart him. 'How much is my grandfather paying you?' My voice was not steady, but he heard the words for he jumped as they hit home.

'Well?' demanded my father with a swift look at me that bordered on respect. 'Answer her, damn you!'

'That,' he said, 'is none of your business.'

He had courted me and ruined me all for money.

'Are you so desperate?' I didn't want to ask but the words came anyway. 'Your father is wealthy. Why?'

My father snorted. 'Wealth he's got the sense to keep from this bounder. You're an idiot, girl. Every Tom, Dick and Harry knows he won't get a groat.'

'Enough,' snapped Mr Rathbone. 'Lord Derringford, I feel we shall do much better without the girl.'

The girl. It was that casual dismissal of me that fired my anger. 'Father, do not pay him anything. Not a thing.'

My words failed to calm him. 'You're an imbecile, girl! It'll ruin the whole family if this gets around. First your damned mother and now you.'

I saw his point. Adelaide and her mama would never be able to ride the wave of gossip with dignity. They would sink with shame and Adelaide would be forever doomed to spinsterhood.

I smoothed my hands down my dress, my mind working fast. What I was about to say was a gamble, but then the game Mr Rathbone played was a gamble too and only one of us could win. We would see who was the better player, him or me. I looked at Lord Derringford and played my first cards. 'Father, he did nothing to me. I cannot think why he says I may be carrying his child.' I stared wide-eyed from one to the other. 'Does a gentleman give a lady a baby when he lends her his handkerchief? Surely that cannot be so!' I shuddered, and let my gaze drift from my father to the man who would ruin me and my family. 'I know I cried a lot that night and he did put one arm around me in the carriage. Was that wrong, Father?'

'Come come, that won't wash,' drawled Mr Rathbone.

My father spoke at normal volume and for the first time

in our acquaintance he looked into my face. 'What's this? What are you saying, girl?'

I looked back at him. 'Father, I have a confession to make. I have met Mr Rathbone every week when I visited my grandmother. We visited her and talked together.'

'Is this true?' He bent a piercing glare upon me but he did not bellow.

Mr Rathbone snapped, 'Quite true but not relevant.'

'Oh, it is relevant,' I said. 'Father, he wrote me notes. He held my hand. He gave me to believe he loved me.' I sighed, kept my eyes on my father's face and took the biggest risk of all. 'He asked me to run away with him. He said we would be married.'

Mr Rathbone gasped with outrage. 'Lies!'

But I found I could lie very well, for had he not taught me? 'Father, I could not do it. I knew there would be gossip and people would remember my mama. I refused and we parted. He was angry, and now I see why.' I wiped at my dry eyes and managed a sniff to rival Mr Chapman's coughs. 'I thought he was angry because he loved me.' I swivelled in my chair to look full at Mr Rathbone. 'How you must have rejoiced at the Delaneys when I collapsed from grief.' I spoke slowly now for the pain beat again in my heart. 'You looked upon a girl you had sworn you loved. You saw in my distress a way to be revenged on me for my refusal of your hand. You saw a way to make my father pay.' I laughed at him. 'Do you worst, sir, for I shall tell the world how I refused you.'

The room rang with silence. Mr Chapman didn't cough,

my father didn't shout. It was left to Mr Rathbone to say in tones of loathing, 'You forget, madam, that my servant saw you.'

I shrugged. 'I hope you will pay her well to say so.' The servant had been a man.

But I'd had enough of the pack of them. I rose to my feet. 'Father, if I were you I'd throw him out. But you may please yourself for I truly do not care.' I blocked the view Mr Rathbone had of my father. 'I will talk with Jamie. Probably I will keep house for him.' I had the satisfaction of seeing my father frown at the reminder of Jamie.

I opened the door and left the room. In the passage, Frant grinned at me, Sykes wiped his eyes, Mary and Jenkins ran to me and I threw my arms around them.

'Good for you, miss!'

'That'll spike his guns!'

They led me to the kitchen and plied me with tea and cakes which I couldn't eat. Cook tutted over my lack of appetite. 'Take her upstairs, Mary. She's exhausted and no wonder. That monster! I hope his horse throws him and rolls on him, not that I wish him any harm for it's a Christian body I am.'

I laughed and followed Mary up the stairs. 'Mary,' I said when we reached my room, 'how will I know if I am with child?' It was one piece of information missing from my otherwise broad education in such matters.

'Lawks, miss – it's easy to tell. If you don't bleed, then you start worrying.'

'Oh! I see. I'll soon know, then, won't I?'

She hustled me to the chair by the fire. 'Don't you worry your head about it, miss.'

I sat and watched the flames and found I didn't have the energy to worry about anything.

I heard hoof beats on the driveway. Good, he was gone. I pressed my hands over my aching heart. I had not thought one body could contain so much pain.

Mary came back. 'The master wants you in his study, Miss Hannah.'

I shook my head.

She tiptoed out and the next thing I was aware of was my father standing beside me – not shouting. He saw I was awake and looked around for another chair. There wasn't one. 'God damn it! Why hasn't Mildred fixed a proper room for you?'

I attempted a smile. 'It's a grand room. I like it.'

He tugged the bell-pull, ordered a chair from Mary, then sat down upon it when she brought one. But he didn't speak.

To break the silence I asked, 'Did you pay him?'

'No. Threw him out with a flea in his ear.' Now that he had the chair he didn't use it but got up and stalked around the room. 'Girl – you'd better tell me what happened. I don't trust him and that's a fact.'

I sat up and glared at him. How odd it was that rage was so energising. 'I will tell you nothing! Why should I? You could have saved me heartbreak had you told me everything instead of shouting at me. Well, sir – shout all you like for I am done with you and your family.' The burst of energy lasted for one more shot. 'And I have a name which you have never once used.'

He stared at me, opened his mouth several times, took a deep breath, closed his mouth and finally got to his feet. 'I'll send Mildred to talk to you.'

'If you do that,' I said through set teeth, 'then I will tell the world exactly what has happened to me and believe me, sir, your wife would not show up well in the telling. No more would you.'

He went out and I noted that he didn't slam the door behind him. If I had an atom of love for him I could be sorry for him. What I would tell Jamie about this business must weigh upon his mind – as it did on mine.

I took off my hooped petticoat and crawled, fully dressed apart from that, onto my bed. I slept until morning when I awoke to find that Mary had covered me with a quilt. I also awoke to the knowledge that I was not with child. I cried yet more tears, but whether they were of relief or pain or loneliness I didn't know.

# 26

## Chapter Twenty-Six

Two days later I was tired of my own company and tired of my room. I woke early, put on my clothes, flung a shawl over my unbuttoned dress and went in search of Mary or Jenkins to ask them to fasten it for me.

Mary met me on the stairs. She shook her head over me. 'Oh Miss Hannah! When will you learn to ring the bell? It isn't fitting for you to go traipsing all over the house, indeed it isn't!' Her fingers made short work of the buttons as she scolded.

I laughed. 'Mary, I am going home where I'll not have even one servant.'

I made my way down to the kitchen. Fancy that — I was going home, and I hadn't even been aware of making the decision. I'd write to Jamie today and tell him. He might miss me a little, but not very much, for his new life fitted him like a second skin whereas mine did not.

Cook piled a plate high with enough food to keep an army and I ate at least half of it. I went then to the library and wrote Jamie a letter. It caused me as much difficulty as had the letter Polly and I had composed to send to Lord Derringford a lifetime ago, but in the end it was done.

*My dearest brother,*

*Much has happened to me that I will not write about.*

*Oh Jamie, it is dreadful and my heart is broken, for I discovered quite by chance that Judith is dead. She died of typhus fever in June. I have written to our aunt and uncle but I cry whenever I think of their pain. I have heard no news of the war and wonder if you know anything.*

*I have decided to return home. Will you come here for Christmas? I cannot go without seeing you one more time.*

*Your loving sister,*

*Hannah.*

I waited for Mr Chapman to appear then gave him the letter. 'Will you post it for me, sir?'

He promised he would and actually rubbed his hands together, anticipating more ructions when Jamie arrived I suspected. I shrugged. I mightn't like him, but he would certainly post the letter if it meant the possibility of more dramas.

Then there was nothing to do and the day lay ahead, empty of occupation. I changed into outdoor clothes and walked in the cold air until I grew hungry. I returned to the house, ate in the kitchen then walked again until darkness fell. Walking made me tired. When my thoughts dwelt on Mr Rathbone my feet thumped the ground, I swung my arms and shouted at the bare dead trees. 'I hate you!' I screamed, shaking my fists. I shouted out in Maori all the curses of the ancestors that I had ever heard. And sometimes I crouched at the base of a tree and wept from the depths of my aching heart.

On other days, I thought of Judith and I walked slowly. I spoke to her in my mind and often I felt that she walked beside me and shared my sorrows.

One day, as Mary fastened my dress for me, she said, 'Today is my lady's At Home day.'

I had not seen Lady Derringford since that awful night and I didn't want to see her now. I shrugged. 'I've given up trying to be a young lady, Mary.' I left the house and walked again under bare trees and between brown hedgerows. If Jamie didn't come for Christmas, I would go to him and then I would sail home. I didn't think there would be any difficulty in getting the money for my passage from my father.

I thought a lot about Mama in those days of walking in the cold December weather. I no longer thought her immoral and how could I, who had committed an act every bit as immoral? Things happened and we could not undo them however much we might wish. I knew that now.

Perhaps she had wished she hadn't run away that night. Perhaps she wished she hadn't met Papa as she drove home. There must have been many times she wished she hadn't allowed him to persuade her to sail to New Zealand, for I was now sure that that was what had happened.

Papa, Lord Derringford, Mr Rathbone and my grandfather. Between them they had done their best to ruin my life.

I picked up my skirts and ran down a gentle slope. They wouldn't succeed. I could make a life for myself in New Zealand. What it might be I didn't know but it would be a useful one, of that I would make sure.

I stood on a rise and held my arms out to the wind. 'Judith! I am coming home!'

Beyond the trees, in the open land a horseman galloped. I watched him and thought of Mr Rathbone. This horseman wasn't Mr Rathbone, it was Joe come to find me. 'Miss Hannah! The mistress wants you at once. Mrs Delaney is asking for you. Frant says to tell you Mrs Lindhurst is there too and they're both that concerned about you.'

I would have to go. 'Very well, Joe. I'll come.'

He slid off the horse. 'Take The Prince, miss. He's good tempered, You'll manage him fine.'

He tossed me up into the saddle. I kicked my heels into The Prince's sides and we were off.

I walked around to the front door from the stables. Sykes was watching out for me. 'Her ladyship's in a temper,' he warned me as he took my cloak and bonnet.

I grinned at him. 'Dear Sykes, do you know? I don't care!'

He walked with me to the drawing room, opened the door and announced me. 'Miss Carstairs, my lady.'

I walked in. Adelaide as always was on her sofa. Her mother sat enthroned in her chair beside the tea table.

Mrs Delaney rose as I came in. 'Dear child! We have been so concerned for you. I am vastly relieved you are well enough to be out walking.'

Mrs Lindhurst too, stood up. 'Adelaide, dear gal — change seats with me if you please. I must apologise to your sister and I cannot do it satisfactorily across the room.' She walked to the sofa as she spoke. Adelaide had no choice but to obey.

We all sat down. Mrs Lindhurst took my hand and turned in order to look into my face. 'I cannot forgive myself for my shocking manners, dear child. Do tell me you are better!'

I smiled at her. 'I am much better, ma'am. Thank you.'

Mrs Delaney said, 'Excellent! We have come to beg you to spend Christmas and January with us, my dear. And your brother if he should like it. Do say you will.' She smiled at me.

Lady Derringford gasped and Adelaide hissed. I didn't even glance at them. 'Thank you. I would love more than anything to come.'

I quit that house the following week, and the people I sorrowed to leave were Mary, Jenkins, Sykes, Cook, Frant and Joe who had all been so good to me. I asked my father for money to give them vails as I understood was the custom. He made no comment but gave the order to Mr Chapman who seemed disappointed at the lack of shouting.

Mrs Delaney sent her carriage for me, with a maid to accompany me. I waved goodbye to my own dear friends.

Lord Derringford forced his family to come and bid me farewell. It was a strange leave-taking, for they didn't want me to go but were pleased to be rid of me, although when my father handed me into the carriage he muttered, 'If things had been different . . .' He shook his head as if to clear it. 'Well well, it's water under the bridge now. But you've a good head on you, Hannah. I'll say that much for you.'

I pondered on his words for all of the journey. Could we have come to like each other after all?

The Delaneys and Mrs Lindhurst couldn't have been kinder or more welcoming. The five Delaney children crowded around me and demanded to be told stories of my life in New Zealand. Their mother smiled and promised them I should do so later if they were good. They left with their governess and nanny, running back several times to exact the same promise from me.

Mrs Delaney shepherded me upstairs to show me my bedroom – a small room with rich and luxurious furnishings all in shades of pink. I loved it instantly.

I was to go with them to parties if I felt like it, she told me, and not if I didn't.

To please them, I decided to go to the first party and none thereafter. I didn't have a black dress to wear to mourn Judith, but I sewed black ribbons on my bonnet. On the day following my arrival we climbed into the carriage and Mrs Delaney insisted I sit facing the horses.

They chatted as we bowled through the dark country-side. 'Tell us about Christmas in New Zealand,' Mr Delaney said.

'But make it sound unattractive,' laughed his wife, 'or else he will drag us there next Christmas.'

I told them of sunshine and strawberries, of digging the potatoes and picking the peas, of how we walked to church if Papa remembered to make us go. I spoke of the terrible state of the roads and how I had only once ridden in a carriage and that was to Judith's wedding.

Mrs Lindhurst took my hand and clasped it. 'Dear gal, you are homesick! Tell me about my grandson, if you can bear to.'

I smiled in the darkness. 'Indeed I can bear to, ma'am, for he was most kind to me and rescued me from difficulty on several occasions.' I recounted the story of the ball and Captain Hendon.

The women gasped and exclaimed in horror, but Mr Delaney said, 'I congratulate you, Miss Hannah. You are a most redoubtable young lady.'

I needed to be that evening. The occasion was one of the soirées the Delaneys so enjoyed. A poetess was to read her verses, a husband and wife were to sing a series of duets and there was also to be a lecture given by a gentleman recently returned from Turkey.

The first person I saw across the room after we had been greeted by our hosts, was Mr Rathbone. A hush fell upon the crowd as we entered, people glanced from me to him then back again as if their heads were on swivels.

So – the game was not yet played out. My mind raced in that second of time. I recalled Aunt Frances and how she bade me hold my head high at the ball. I turned to Mr and

Mrs Delaney and spoke quietly, but because of the silence my words were clearly audible to most of the room. 'Will you excuse me one moment, ma'am, sir? I must speak to Mr Rathbone.'

I trod across the room on legs that shook. I curtseyed to the man who had so cruelly betrayed me. 'Mr Rathbone, I wish to thank you so much for conducting me back to Derringford Park that terrible night.' I put a hand to my brow. 'The shock of hearing of my friend's death . . .' I shivered and groped in my reticule for a handkerchief. Mrs Delaney appeared at my side and pushed one into my hand. I held it to my face, leaving it there while I gathered my strength. I lowered my hand, and the grim set of his mouth heartened me. I managed what I trusted would be interpreted as a brief, tragic smile. 'Pray forgive me if I neglected to thank you at the time, but I do so now – with all my heart.'

Mrs Delaney put her arm around me. 'Dear child, you are so brave. Do come and sit down.' She conducted me to a chair beside Mrs Lindhurst, who leaned towards me and whispered under the safety of the sudden flurry of conversation, 'Bravo my dear. What a general you would make!'

So they knew, or had guessed – but still they accepted me.

I heard snatches of conversation during the evening.

*It cannot be true, she is so calm.*

*Rathbone isn't a man I'd leave alone with a daughter of mine.*

*So tragic. The shock of hearing like that.*

I didn't care what any of them thought. Soon I would be half the world away and living a life none of them could imagine.

The invitations continued to flow into the Delaneys' home, with my name added to them. I went with them, partly because they were so kind and partly because I would not allow Mr Rathbone the pleasure of my absence.

Gradually he began to be asked to fewer occasions. The talk was that he was in debt. Hostesses decided his charm had become beyond the line of being pleasing. He was dropped.

Jamie wrote that he would be with me for Christmas. Mrs Lindhurst too received a letter. We sat at breakfast and when the butler brought in the mail, she glanced at her letter, but left it lying beside her plate. 'It is from my daughter-in-law — Captain Lindhurst's mother you know. Begging me to come home again, no doubt.'

I put down Jamie's letter. 'Mrs Lindhurst, would you mind terribly reading it? I would dearly like to know if she has news of Captain Lindhurst.'

She gave me a considering glance, but obligingly opened the letter. 'Oh my goodness! Yes, dear gal she has news. Oh, my dear! He has been wounded.' Her eyes scanned down the lines while I waited, my breathing suspended. 'Ah! Here's the nub of it. He has come home!' She looked at me, her eyes bright with happiness. 'D'you hear that, Hannah Carstairs? He is home with only a wounded shoulder.' She read some more and some of her joy faded. 'His mother writes that he has been ill – terrible epidemics in that God-forsaken place she says. He's thin and she worries that his spirits are affected.'

I couldn't take it in, except for the one fact that he was here in the same country that I was in – for the time being anyway. 'I would dearly like to see him before I return.' He would know what was happening with the war. He might have news of Rawinia, of Arama, Papa and most certainly of the Woodleys.

'I will make sure you see him,' Mrs Lindhurst promised.

I asked if I might have his address and after breakfast I hurried to the library to write to him, telling him of my sorrow at Judith's untimely death and offering him my deepest sympathy. I read the letter over. I could not begin to express how I felt or tell him how my heart bled for him and my aunt and uncle. In the end, I sealed it. It would have to do.

The children came running to find me and I was glad to be distracted from my sorrow.

Jamie arrived three days before Christmas. Mr Delaney ordered the carriage so that I might go to the station to meet him. The Iron Duke roared in, but I danced on the edge of the platform, craning my neck to get a glimpse of my brother.

'Jamie! Jamie!' I ran, skirts, cloak, bonnet strings all flying – and cast myself into his arms. Of course, I burst into tears. 'You are taller! Oh, Jamie!'

He endured my embrace for a moment, then took hold

of my shoulders and looked into my face. 'I think, Sissy, that you had best tell me everything.'

So I did just that as we rode back to the Delaneys.

He vowed to kill Mr Rathbone, then our father, step-mother and the entire parcel of them. I let him rant for it did my heart good to hear him. However, in the end I persuaded him that I had dealt with Mr Rathbone myself, and as for our family, 'Let us be done with them.'

He threw himself back against the cushioned seat. 'To tell the truth, Sissy – I don't need him any longer.' He grinned at me with pride. 'I am doing very well and con-stantly meet men who can help me far more than he can.'

I leaned my head on his shoulder. 'I am so glad. But how I will miss you when I go home!'

We enjoyed Christmas in the Delaney household, but the important thing for us was that Mr Delaney took Jamie off to the library on a drear day between Christmas Day and the New Year and spoke to him about the inheritance. The upshot was that Mr Drury, Mr Delaney's solicitor visited us and drew up an agreement that gave Jamie a yearly income large enough to support him even if he never received payment for his work.

I was pleased, and unkind enough to be delighted that our father would be furious at an agreement so advan-tageous to Jamie. Then Mr Drury picked up a second sheet of paper. 'And this is what I am proposing for you, Miss Carstairs.'

He read what he had written and my mouth dropped open. 'Sir! Surely, you are jesting?'

But he was not, and a week later he returned with both agreements signed. Jamie had given up his right to inherit in return for an income for life. Part of the agreement, was an income for me for as long as I should live of three hundred pounds per year.

Mr Drury said in a dry tone. 'His lordship was not pleased to sign it, but I prevailed, for you see, my dear young lady, the other agreement was not valid unless he agreed to yours.'

I couldn't take it in, but then I laughed. 'Mr Drury, I would be willing to wager you a considerable sum that our father shouted and threw any object close to hand. And also, I would wager that Mr Chapman stood in the shadows and coughed.'

He smiled. 'You would win both wagers, Miss Carstairs.'

I was a young lady of independent means.

# 27

## Chapter Twenty-Seven

Our days passed happily with much to occupy my mind. The Delaneys enjoyed debate and conversation, as did Mrs Lindhurst. They were delighted to find that Jamie and I were happy to join in their talk. We talked of Jamie's work and his excitement over the newest engine design. We often talked of home and made them laugh and exclaim as they grew to understand what our lives had been.

'And this Rawinia?' Mrs Lindhurst asked. 'Will you live with her when you return?'

I shook my head. 'I do not know, for I don't know where she is. She has probably stayed with her kin, but if she is in the town, then, yes – I will ask her if she would wish to live with me.'

Jamie asked, 'But Sissy – will you go back to New Plymouth? The fighting still goes on, I believe. It will be such a sad place.'

I looked into the fire. 'I will go if I can. I miss the mountain and the sea. Do you remember how the crust on black sand breaks under your feet? And the wild winds, Jamie – I long for wild winds and slashing rain. I miss Polly, and Amy and Lavender. I'd even be delighted to see

Lizzie. I miss Dr Feilding striding up the path and shouting, *I have work for you, Hannah Carstairs.*'

'What of Papa?'

I said nothing for a moment. 'Perhaps. Oh, I don't know. I feel he has played with our lives – laughed at us. He has known who we were and I believe he should have told us, especially he should have told us about how he ran off with Mama.'

Mr Delaney asked Jamie if he too, would return one day. I listened, hope in my heart, but he grinned at me and said, 'Maybe one day, but there's much I want to do here first.'

Jamie left us two weeks after Christmas. He hugged me and promised to visit before I left. 'And when will that be, Sissy?'

'I think after the summer. I would like to see the summer.' I didn't tell him, but I was developing a plan to go to London and enroll in Miss Nightingale's School of Nursing, and if I did that I would be staying for much longer. There were other things I wished to do too, such as read the works of Mary Wollstonecraft. I was beginning to realise that as well as independent means, I had independence and could please myself.

The Delaneys and Mrs Lindhurst, when they heard my plans were horrified, but I smiled and said I planned to be useful and I had no intention of marrying. 'Nursing is useful but I should like to be trained and then I would feel competent.' I regarded them and an imp of mischief sat on my shoulder. I said with as straight a face as I could manage, 'I should like to have some training behind me next time I birth a baby.'

For a moment they did not comprehend, then Mrs Lindhurst said faintly, '*Next* time, dear child?'

I nodded.

'Er, that suggests there has been a first time?' enquired Mrs Delaney, a half smile on her face.

I laughed aloud and told them the story of Polly. I told them everything including her determination to sew up her nightdresses. When I was done, they looked at me in amazement. Then Mr Delaney chuckled. 'Indeed, Hannah Carstairs, you are a most redoubtable girl.'

My amusement faded. 'But not a respectable one, I fear.'

'Pshaw!' snorted Mrs Lindhurst. 'That sister of yours is as respectable as one could wish, but may the good Lord preserve me from ever having to spend another five minutes in her company.'

'Hear, hear!' said Mr Delaney.


Ten days had passed since I had written to Captain Lindhurst. Every day I hoped for a reply, but there was nothing. A cold, hard winter clamped down upon the land. I took to running outside with the children after the midday meal. We played chasing around the trees and hide-and-seek near the stream which ran beside the ruins of an old abbey. When I ran with the children, or talked with my kind hosts the shadow of Mr Rathbone faded, only to appear again raw and ugly when I was alone.

Mrs Lindhurst watched me narrowly. 'It will go, dear gal. Time heals. You will survive.'

I was grateful to her for her understanding. As the end of January drew nearer, I dreaded more and more having to return to my father's house, and then it occurred to me that I did not need to. I had money enough to live where I pleased. I broached the subject with the Delaneys and Mrs Lindhurst for I could not begin to decide where I should live until the time came for me to return home to New Zealand.

Mrs Lindhurst snapped her fan shut. 'That is easily answered, Hannah my child. You will come to me.' She held up a hand. 'You will be doing me a favour. My family keep nagging that I need a companion. You shall be it. Can't abide the notion of some fawning ninnyhammer without a notion in her head.'

I rose and kissed her cheek. 'Thank you ma'am. I should like that above everything.'

In the morning, I awoke early and as soon as it was light, dressed and walked outside. Such a lot had happened to me in so short a time, but I could not repine – I was alive and my beloved Judith was not.

Today I walked along the driveway, the ground underfoot being wet. I reached the road and paused. Should I turn back? It couldn't be very late yet and I would dearly love to walk further. The matter was decided for me when I heard the clopping of a horse on the road. I turned back.

Mr Rathbone had made me wary of being alone in the company of a man, if man this was.

It was a man, and the coachman turned the carriage into the driveway I walked upon. I moved to the side but it drew up just beyond me. The door opened – I waited. I would shout and run if I had to. But all such thoughts fled when I saw who it was.

'Captain Lindhurst! Oh, Captain, how pleased I am to see you!'

I ran towards him, my hands stretched out in welcome. He grasped them. 'Miss Carstairs!'

My eyes were wet, but his were no better. 'Please tell me everything, sir. I still cannot believe it.'

His face was set in sterner lines than I remembered. He seemed older, much older than the ten months that had passed since we last met. 'She should not have died,' he said. 'Hannah, I find it difficult to forgive myself. I should never have married her with war so imminent.'

We began to walk, and he motioned to the driver to take the carriage up to the house. I gathered my thoughts, for I did not want to offer him mere soothing platitudes. 'It was what Judith wanted, you know. I have never seen in another human being such happiness as you gave her.' I turned to him and said urgently, 'You cannot regret it, you cannot! Who can say which is better – a few sweet weeks of pure joy or a lifetime with all the sorrows that time must bring?' I dashed tears from my face. 'I miss her, Captain Lindhurst, I miss her so sorely that I ache – but do you know? I envy her too. She was so certain in her love for you and so happy.' I could not continue. We walked in silence for some little way.

Beside me, I heard him draw in a ragged breath. 'Thank you, Hannah Carstairs.'

After a moment, I asked, 'Can you bear to tell me about it?'

She had become ill, he told me, at the beginning of June. The town was crowded and unsanitary, food was scarce. She became ill and died two days before the battle of Puketaukaere in which he was wounded and many of his comrades killed.

She had died the month we arrived in England and all the long summer I had not known she was no longer alive.

Belatedly, I thought to ask him how his shoulder fared.

He shrugged it. 'Well enough.'

'You will return then?'

He shook his head. 'No, I have given up the army. I am now plain Mr Lindhurst and very good it sounds too.'

I smiled at him, 'Well, plain Mr Lindhurst, pray tell me why you have given up the army.'

He did not smile back. 'It is a bad war we are waging. I want no part of it.'

I struggled with myself, but managed not to say *I told you so*.

We reached the house and he was lost to me in the flurry of greetings. He was evidently no stranger to the Delaneys, and their children flocked to him, calling him Uncle Miles and asking for stories of far-off places.

His grandmother glared at him and snapped, 'You look old and ill, dear boy. It will not do!'

Over the days that followed he told us of the war. I saw it all as he described the pa the Maori threw up in a night, how they defended them, then slipped away in the dawn leaving an empty victory for the troops. I felt the cold and the dragging mud, the hunger as New Plymouth became a town under siege. People died, men were killed.

'Arama?' I whispered. 'Papa?'

He knew nothing of Arama, and Papa continued to drink himself insensible.

'Will you still go back?' he asked me.

I nodded. 'It is my home. I will go back.'

He gazed at me for a long moment, then shook himself as if coming back from a long way off. 'Sing for us, Hannah. Sing something you used to sing with Rawinia.'

I asked Mrs Delaney to play for me. 'You know the tune of Greensleeves, ma'am?'

She played and I sang to its tune the love song Rawinia and I often sang when we worked outside, for it was a song that belonged out of doors. Inside, it had a haunting, yearning quality that disturbed me with its sorrow.


Every morning for the remainder of my stay, I walked as soon as it was light. Plain Mr Miles Lindhurst met me as he too, walked in the dawn with his sorrows.

We didn't speak much, but wandered in companionable silence. On the second day, he said to me, 'I think, Hannah, that you have been wounded too.'

And so I told him the story of my life at Derringford Park, and of the love which had betrayed me. 'I was so distraught to know that Judith was dead,' I said, 'that I didn't care what happened to me.'

'He had best pray that I never meet him,' he said in a low voice that trembled with passion, 'for if I do, he is a dead man.'

He did not seem much soothed when I told him I had suffered no lasting harm.

'You should not have had to suffer any harm at all,' he snapped.

I thought it best to turn the subject and asked what he intended to do now that he had left the army. That made him laugh and I was glad, although it was me he was laughing at. 'Hannah, how like you! You ask the question all my friends and family are too afraid to ask me outright.'

'But that is no answer,' I objected. 'You have told me nothing.'

He shrugged. 'That is because I don't know. I will soon grow tired of idleness, that I do know.'

Mrs Lindhurst and I left for London at the end of January. I bade farewell to my kind hosts and hugged each of the children.

Mr Lindhurst, as I was learning to call him, accompanied us to London and saw us settled in his grandmother's house in Russell Square. I asked him if he would come with me the following day when I went to visit Miss Nightingale's

School of Nursing. I wanted information but the thought of finding my way around London by myself daunted me.

I was doubly glad he was with me, for the reception I got was most disappointing. I was told briskly that I was much too young and they preferred their ladies to be at least twenty-five before they accepted them for training.

Mr Lindhurst visited me the next day with a gift. I opened it and gave a cry of pleasure. He had bought me Miss Nightingale's *Notes on Nursing*.

We met when he visited his grandmother which he did often as they loved each other dearly. I could not help but compare the visits with those to my own grandmother. How different these were. Mrs Lindhurst never dozed. She was often acerbic. She was always energetic. She demanded that he take us to see the sights. 'Hannah simply cannot return to that rural backwater without seeing the British Museum.' Or it might be that I had to walk in Hyde Park and view the spring flowers. Another day she insisted we all attend a service in St Paul's.

He made no protest, and I enjoyed his company. He showed me London and we walked miles through streets and parks in the afternoons when his grandmother visited her friends. 'It is so different from New Plymouth,' I would say.

'But how glad I am that you were not born here,' he replied, 'for you would have held up your nose at the notion of walking with a mere Mr such as I.'

I laughed at the mere Mr by my side and tucked my hand through his arm. We were so easy together and I counted his friendship as more valuable than my annuity. It gladdened my heart too, to see the pain of guilt fade from his face as we talked of Judith. In its place was the same sorrow that I felt over her loss.

When the season began and people flocked to town in order to marry off their daughters, Mrs Lindhurst took me in hand. 'You will have a proper ball dress, my child and that's an end to it.' It was to be her gift to me and I wasn't to argue.

I gave in. 'To be truthful, dear ma'am, I have the liveliest curiosity to attend such a ball.' My only sadness was that Mr Lindhurst would not be going, for his year of mourning for Judith was not up.

He insisted though, that I parade before him in my dress. I trod down the stairs, the fan he had presented me with fluttering in my hand. He stood with Mrs Lindhurst at the foot of the stairs as I made my grand entry. I reached the floor and swept them both a laughing curtsey. 'Do I pass? Am I sufficiently elegant to grace an English drawing room?' I sent him a teasing glance.

'You are beautiful,' he said, taking my hand and bowing over it. 'But were you dressed in rags you would still grace any drawing room.'

'Why, thank you kindly, sir.' I turned to his grandmother and told of his habit of laughing at me in New Zealand.

He ignored her admonishment but said, urgency in his voice, 'Grandmama, play a waltz for us. I must have one dance before the world claims her.'

Mrs Lindhurst nodded as if something gave her immense satisfaction, and led the way into the music room. She sat at the piano and began to play.

Miles led me onto the floor and we danced. He didn't speak. I looked up at him from time to time, but stayed silent. He was gone from me again in the way he had often done so puzzlingly at home in New Plymouth. The music stopped. He released me, stepped back, bowed and thanked me most formally.

'Thank you, Grandmama. Pray excuse me. I must leave.' He walked swiftly from the room, leaving me staring after him wondering again what I had done.

Mrs Lindhurst said nothing except to tell me it was time we left. I caught her chuckling to herself as we rode to the ball in her carriage, but she made no attempt to tell me what amused her and my heart was too sore to ask.

The ball lacked spice. The young women smiled so anxiously and the young men paraded so arrogantly. How lucky I was that I did not wish to marry. I danced every dance and my partners for the waltz were graceful and correct but they did not throw back their heads and laugh as Captain Lindhurst had done in New Plymouth. They did not threaten to refuse to make a turn unless I spoke what was on my mind.

I wished with all my heart that he had danced and laughed like that tonight.

'Did you enjoy yourself?' Mrs Lindhurst asked as we travelled home in her carriage.

I sighed. 'I did – but ma'am, I fear I am getting old. Everyone seemed so dull and proper!'

She chuckled all the rest of the way home and I could not think what was amusing her.

I prepared for bed, thinking of things I would tell Miles, such as the lady with the brooch in the shape of a crocodile and how it had caught her lace in its mouth and torn a great rent in it. And I must remember to tell him of the young man who said he believed New Zealand was full of men whose faces were in their stomachs.

I stopped dead in the act of plaiting my hair. I plumped down onto my bed and groaned. Drat the man! I had fallen in love with him. Why was my wretched heart not content to enjoy his very dear friendship?

I rose to my feet and walked to the mirror to stare at my face. It looked the same, with no trace upon it of the emotions rocking my world.

I sat down at my dressing table. Thoughts tumbled and chased through my head about what I should do, but it was useless. There was only one course of action open to me. I would have to go away. I could not face seeing him every day, loving him and having him treat me with nothing more than friendship.

I cried myself to sleep.

Accordingly, the next morning I said to Mrs Lindhurst. 'Ma'am, I must talk to you.'

She put down the letter she was reading with her breakfast. 'You sound serious, my dear. Please do not keep me in suspense.'

I sighed. 'I am serious. It breaks my heart, dear Mrs Lindhurst, but I am going to go away. I think I will go home as soon as I can arrange it.'

She didn't look as distressed as I had expected. I was hurt, for I thought she liked me enough to miss me. 'And why this sudden decision?'

I decided to tell her the truth. She knew so much about me anyway, what did one more thing matter? 'I find I have fallen in love with your grandson. It is most inconvenient and I wish it was not so.'

'Inconvenient?' She seemed much struck by the word.

I snapped at her. 'Of course it is inconvenient! How can I remain his friend now? And he is so dear to me that I do not know how I shall exist without him,' I wailed and burst into tears.

She patted my shoulder. 'There, there, child. Let us not be hasty. Things may not be as bad as you expect.'

I got up. 'You are kind to say so, but I cannot face meeting him today. Can you please make some excuse when he calls?'

She agreed most cheerfully to do so. I took myself off to the library with the *Notes on Nursing* he had given me. Miss Nightingale had omitted to write a chapter upon the treatment of broken hearts.

I heard him enter the house and it was all I could do not to run to him and throw myself into his arms. Instead, I threw myself into the late Mr Lindhurst's large leather armchair. What would Judith think of me? 'Dear friend,' I whispered. 'You were right, he is wonderful!'

But not for me.

The door opened. He hadn't stayed long. I went to get up and face my hostess, but his voice said, 'Hannah?'

I stood. 'Miles — what are you doing here? I didn't want to see you today.'

He came towards me. 'No? What about every day for the rest of our lives? Could you stand that, my very dear love?'

I'm afraid I gaped at him. My knees buckled and I collapsed back into the chair. His very dear love? Could it be so? He leaned forward, put a hand under my chin to tilt my head up. I stared at him — at his tender, loving smile. I could not speak.

His hand moved to caress my cheek. 'Hannah,' he said and my name was music on his lips. 'You have brought the light back into my life.'

Still I could not speak. My hand crept up to touch his.

He pulled me to my feet and took me in his arms. 'I love you, my wild girl. Ah, how I love you!' He kissed me gently, firmly — I do not know, all I know is he told me again and again that he loved me.

I managed at last to find my voice. 'Miles. My love.' I touched his dear face. 'Is this true? Am I dreaming?'

For answer he tightened his arms around me and held me close for a moment. Then he took me by my shoulders so that he might look into my face and his eyes glinted with mischief. 'I do not intend proposing marriage to you, Hannah Carstairs.'

'No, sir?' I answered his smile with one of my own.

'I am profoundly shocked!' And truth to tell I was a little surprised, for I knew he would not live with me unless he became my husband.

He laughed with joy that gladdened my heart. 'No, I am *telling* you that you will marry me. I do not ask you if you will be my wife, for I know your opinion of marriage and I will not risk a refusal.'

'Very well, sir,' I said with a womanly meekness that lasted only until he kissed me again.

He led me to the window seat, sat down next to me and put his arms around me. 'Dearest Hannah,' he murmured. 'Do you think you can be happy as a married woman?'

'Only if I am married to you.' Then I drew back a little and said, 'Judith is so much in my thoughts.'

He held me to him, both arms tight around me. 'I can never forget her. I do not wish to forget one second of our life together. It's not a year since she died, but it seems like another life. So long ago, so far away.' He stopped and rested his cheek against my hair. 'It is the war, I think. It breaks the rules of everyday life.'

I turned in his arms. 'Life is so fragile, so fleeting. I know that now. I hope – I think – she would wish us to be happy.'

We kissed and only broke apart at the sound of the door opening. His grandmother came in. She took one look at us, crowed with delight and rubbed her hands with glee as she hurried over to embrace us.

It was all her doing, of course. She was a wily old bird, she informed us with most unbecoming smugness. 'I saw at once you were miserable apart and delightful together.

357

Miles, your parents say to tell you they are delighted but hope you will persuade Hannah to stay in this country.'

But I wanted to go home. Miles too, wished very much to return. 'I will find something to do,' he said. 'Something where I can build rather than destroy.'

He took me to meet his parents. I was nervous, remembering Mrs Lindhurst's comment that his marriage to Judith was a shocking misalliance. 'Of course they will love you,' he said, but I knew now how different I was from somebody like Adelaide, or like Judith herself who would have fitted here perfectly.

But they welcomed me. I think it helped them to see Miles happy again, and in my more cynical moments I thought it possibly didn't hurt that I was the daughter of a lord and could call myself the Honourable Miss Derringford had I a mind to do so. They asked him what gift he had given me to mark our betrothal, but we explained that nothing was to be announced as it was not yet a year since Judith's death. 'Although it feels like a hundred years,' he said.

When we returned to London, he did give me a betrothal gift, but it was not one we would tell anyone else about – not even his grandmother, for as he said, there might be limits even to her broadmindedness and he had no desire to test them to find out. His gift to me was to find out about methods to stop me from bearing a child. 'It is called contraception,' he told me. 'I have lost one wife and I have no desire to lose another.'

It was the most loving thing he could have done. I now

looked forward without fear to the day when we would marry.

We talked often of Judith. He told me of his attraction to her, of how he admired her quiet dignity and her graciousness. Then he utterly dumbfounded me for he told me how I had upset all his plans every time he met me. 'I knew Judith was the perfect wife for me,' he said. 'I loved her and honoured her. And then I would meet you with your wild ways and your fierce independence. I would want to take you in my arms and dance with you to the ends of the earth. You were unsuitable, your ideas were enough to terrify a braver man than I – but you were as honourable as you were vulnerable. I told myself you were a child, and I married your friend.' He was quiet and we strolled together in the early summer sunshine under new green leaves. 'I never regretted marrying Judith and I loved her deeply – but I was glad when you left New Plymouth.'

I wrote to my grandmother Armitage telling her I was to marry, I sent a brief note to my father and a longer one to Aggie. I had written to Aunt Frances and I worried that she would be distressed, but could not expect a reply before the wedding. I was astonished to receive a reply from my father congratulating me and wishing me well. Along with the letter he sent a delicate necklace of diamonds that had belonged to my mother.

Miles and I decided not to return to New Zealand until the following year. We would travel a little first and see something of the world.

We married in a quiet ceremony at the end of July. Jamie gave me away. He kissed my cheek and shook hands with Miles. 'Welcome to the family, brother.'

For our honeymoon, Miles took me to the Lake District where he had spent holidays as a child. I looked up one evening as he came through the door into our bedroom and smiled at him. 'What now?' he demanded. 'I know that look!'

'I was merely reflecting that home for me now is wherever you are,' I said demurely.

'And? I don't believe that was all you were thinking. Not with that look on your beautiful face, my love!' He sat down beside me and made threats of an interesting nature if I refused to tell him my thoughts.

I laughed with delight. 'It occurs to me that if I can think of such a sweetly sentimental notion, then why don't I write lurid romances? I could dedicate them to you, my beloved.'

He didn't play fair, for he carried out his threats even though I had told him my thoughts.

I thoroughly enjoyed my honeymoon.

We travelled back to London on the train, my hand resting in my husband's. I watched the landscape, so different from the one waiting for us on the other side of the world, and I thought about the years to come. Perhaps one day, far off in the future, we *would* have a child, one who would run barefoot on the black sands of Taranaki. I hoped for a girl, a daughter we could call Judith.